W9-AST-264

Praise for Brenda Minton and her novels

"Minton's characters are well crafted."
—*RT Book Reviews*

"This wonderful romance has good characters and a great story."
—*RT Book Reviews* on
The Cowboy Next Door

"[A] heartwarming story."
—*RT Book Reviews* on
Jenna's Cowboy Hero

"This easy, sensitive story…is quite touching. Don't miss [it]."
—*RT Book Reviews* on
His Little Cowgirl

"A lovely story of faith, trust and taking one day at a time."
—*RT Book Reviews* on
A Cowboy's Heart

Brenda Minton

THE COWBOY NEXT DOOR

and

JENNA'S COWBOY HERO

◆HARLEQUIN® LOVE INSPIRED®CLASSICS

Recycling programs
for this product may
not exist in your area.

ISBN-13: 978-0-373-60115-8

The Cowboy Next Door and Jenna's Cowboy Hero

Copyright © 2015 by Harlequin Books S.A.

The publisher acknowledges the copyright holder
of the individual works as follows:

The Cowboy Next Door
Copyright © 2009 by Brenda Minton

Jenna's Cowboy Hero
Copyright © 2009 by Brenda Minton

HARLEQUIN®

www.Harlequin.com

Printed in U.S.A.

CONTENTS

Brenda Minton lives in the Ozarks with her husband, children, cats, dogs and strays. She is a pastor's wife, Sunday-school teacher, coffee addict and sleep deprived. Not in that order. Her dream to be an author for Harlequin started somewhere in the pages of a romance novel about a young American woman stranded in a Spanish castle. Her dreams came true, and twenty-something books later, she is an author hoping to inspire young girls to dream.

Books by Brenda Minton

Love Inspired

Visit the Author Profile page
at Harlequin.com for more titles.

THE COWBOY NEXT DOOR

Truly my soul silently waits for God;
From Him comes my salvation.
—*Psalms* 62:1

This book is dedicated to my mom,
Rosetta (Kasiah) Cousins
(May 1937–November 1980).
She taught me to dream and she encouraged
me to use my imagination. She put up with baby
birds and mice in the house, numerous wild
kittens, possums, ponies, goats and puppies.
And to my dad, Don Cousins, who is still
excited by every accomplishment. You taught
me the value of hard work, even when I didn't
appreciate it. I love you. And to the memory of
Patsy Grayson, encourager, friend, blessing.

Chapter One

◦━◦

"Lacey, when are you going to go out with me?" Bobby Fynn hollered from across the dining room of the Hash-It-Out Diner.

"Maybe next week," Lacey called back as she refilled an empty coffee cup, smiling at her customer, an older woman with curly black hair and a sweet smile.

"Come on, Lacey, you can't keep turning me down."

Lacey smiled and shook her head, because Bobby wasn't serious, and she wasn't interested.

"Ignore him," Marci, the hostess, whispered as Lacey walked past.

Lacey shot her friend a smile. "He doesn't bother me. I'll be back in a minute. I need to get a pitcher of water."

She hurried to the waitress station, set the glass coffeepot on the warming tray, and grabbed the pitcher of ice water. The cowbell over the door clanged, announcing the arrival of another customer. She hustled around the corner, pretending her feet weren't blistered and her back wasn't aching from the double shifts she'd worked for the last week.

If it wasn't for the perfect piece of land she wanted to buy…

Two strong hands grabbed her arms, stopping her mid-stride and preventing a near collision. The pitcher of ice water she'd carried out of the waitress station sloshed, soaking her shirt. She looked up, muttering about clumsiness and met the dark gaze of Officer Jay Blackhorse.

Gorgeous, he was definitely gorgeous. Tall with black hair and brown eyes. All cowboy. All rugged and sure of himself. But not her type. He'd been back in Gibson, Missouri, for a month now, and she already had him figured out. He was too serious, not the kind of customer who chatted with a waitress, and she was fine with the knowledge that they weren't going to be best friends.

Several men called out, offering him a chair at their table, as Lacey moved out of his grasp. Not only was he the law, his family also raised cattle and horses. He hadn't lived in Gibson for the last seven or eight years, but he still fit in on so many levels that Lacey didn't know how he could do it all.

She was still trying to find something other than round holes for her square-peg self.

She was the girl from St. Louis who had showed up six years ago with a broken-down car, one hundred dollars and the dream of finding a new life.

Jay waved at the men who called out to him, but he didn't take them up on their offers to sit. Instead, he took hold of Lacey's arm and moved her toward the door.

"Lacey, I need to talk to you outside."

"Sure." Of course, not a problem.

She set the pitcher of ice water on a table and followed him to the door, trying hard not to remember her other life, the life that had included more than one trip in the back of a police car.

It would have been a waste of breath to tell Jay she wasn't that person any more. He didn't know her.

He didn't know what it had been like to grow up in her home, with a family that had fallen apart before she could walk. Jay had a mom who baked cookies and played the piano at church. Lacey's mom had brought home boyfriends for herself and her daughters.

Instead of protesting, Lacey shot Jay a disgusted look—as if it didn't matter—and exited the diner at his side. When they were both outside, she turned on him, pushing down her pain and reaching for the old Lacey, the one who knew how to handle these situations.

"What's this all about, Blackhorse? Is it 'humiliate the waitress day' and someone nominated me to get the prize?"

He shook his head and pointed to his car. "Sorry, Lacey, but I didn't know what else to do with her."

"Her?"

The back door of the patrol car opened.

Lacey watched the young woman step out with a tiny baby in her arms and a *so what* look on her face. Jay's strong hand gripped Lacey's arm, holding her tight as she drew in a deep breath and tried to focus. She pulled her arm free because she wasn't about to fall.

Or fall apart.

Even at twenty-two Corry still looked drugged-out, antsy and on the verge of running. Her dark eyes were still narrowed in anger—as if the world had done her wrong. The thrust of her chin told everyone she would do what she wanted, no matter whom it hurt.

Jay stood next to Lacey, his voice low. "She said she hitched a ride to Gibson and that she's your sister."

Lacey wanted to say that it wasn't true and that she didn't have a sister. She wanted to deny she knew the young woman with the dirty black hair and a baby in her arms.

The baby cried and Lacey made eye contact with Corry.

"She's my sister," Lacey said, avoiding Jay's gaze.

"Thanks for claiming me." Corry smacked her gum, the baby held loosely against her shoulder, little arms flailing. The loose strap of Corry's tank top slid down her shoulder, and her shorts were frayed.

Lacey sighed.

"I don't have to leave her here." Jay pulled sunglasses from his pocket and slid them on, covering melted-chocolate eyes. The uniform changed him from the cowboy that sat with the guys during lunch to someone in authority.

Lacey nodded because he did have to leave Corry. What else could he do? What was Lacey going to do? Deny her sister? The Samaritan had cared for the man on the side of the road, a man he didn't know. And Lacey *knew* Corry.

"She can stay. I'm off duty in thirty minutes."

"Do you have to make it sound like the worst thing in the world?" Corry handed Lacey the baby and turned to pick up the backpack that Jay had pulled from the trunk of his car.

Lacey looked at the infant. The baby, Corry's baby, was dressed in pink and without a single hair on her head. She was beautiful.

"Her name's Rachel." Corry tossed the information like it didn't matter. "I heard that in a Bible story at the mission we've been living in. We couldn't stay there, though. We need a real home."

A real home? The one-room apartment that Lacey rented from the owners of the Hash-It-Out was hardly a home fit for three.

She inhaled a deep breath of air that smelled like the grill inside the diner, and the lunch special of fried chicken. Corry and a baby. Family meant something. Lacey had learned that in Gibson, not in the home she grew up in. Now was the time to put it into practice. She could tell her sister to leave, or she could be the person who gave Corry a chance.

Like the people of Gibson had done for her.

But what if Corry ruined everything? Lacey tucked that fear away, all the while ignoring the imposing Officer Blackhorse in his blue-and-gray uniform, gun hanging at his side.

"You know, you two could help me," Corry tossed over her shoulder as she dug around in the back seat of the patrol car. "I haven't eaten since this morning. And then I get here and you aren't even glad to see me."

Continuous jabber. Lacey tuned it out, nodding in what she hoped were the appropriate places. She held Corry's baby close and took the car seat that Jay had pulled out of his car. His gaze caught and held hers for a moment, and his lips turned in a hesitant smile that shifted the smooth planes of his face. Jay with his perfect life and his perfect family.

She didn't want to think about what he thought when he looked at her and her sister.

"Need anything?" Jay took a step back, but he didn't turn away.

She shrugged off the old feelings of inadequacy and turned to face her sister. Corry shifted from foot to foot, hugging herself tight with arms that were too thin and scarred from track marks—evidence of her drug use.

"Lacey?" Jay hadn't moved away and she didn't know what to say.

* * *

Lacey Gould's dark, lined eyes were luminous with unshed tears. Jay hadn't expected that reaction from the waitress who always had a comeback. He held a grudging admiration for her because she never slowed down.

And he knew her secrets, just as he knew that her sister had prior arrests. Corry Gould had two drug convictions and one charge of prostitution. She was a repeat offender. A simple run through the state system was all it took to find out if a person had a criminal record. In Lacey's case, the Gibson police chief had filled him in. Jay hadn't been sure if it had been gossip or serious concern for his parents. They had spent a lot of time with Lacey Gould in his absence.

His parents hadn't appreciated his concern, though. They knew all about Lacey's arrest record, and they knew who she was now. That was good enough for them.

He'd been a cop for too long to let it be good enough for him.

Lacey shifted next to him, the baby fussing.

She was slight in build, but not thin. Her brown eyes often flashed with humor and she had a mouth that smiled as much as it talked. He tried to ignore the dark hair, cut in a chunky style and highlighted with streaks of red.

For the moment her energy and feistiness were gone. He couldn't leave her like that.

"Lacey, I can take her to the station," Jay offered, knowing she wouldn't accept. She scraped leftovers from plates at the diner to feed stray cats; he doubted she would turn away her sister and that baby.

Corry moved closer to Lacey. The younger sister had the baby now, holding the infant in one arm and the dingy backpack in the other. Her eyes, blue, rather than Lacey's dark brown, shimmered with tears.

Lacey was motionless and silent, staring at her sister and the baby.

"I have to take the baby somewhere, Lace. The guy who dropped me off at the city limits was going south, way south. I don't have a way back to St. Louis."

"I'm not going to turn my back on you, Corry. But as long as you're here, you have to stay clean and stay out of trouble."

"If it helps, I checked her bag and she doesn't have anything on her." Jay could tell when Lacey bit down on her bottom lip and studied her sister that this information didn't really help.

He shrugged because he didn't know what else to do. The two sisters were eyeing one another, the baby was fussing and his radio squawked a call. He stepped away from the two women and answered the county dispatcher.

"Sorry, I have to run, but if you need anything—" he handed Lacey a card with his cell phone number "—I'm just a phone call away."

"Thanks, Jay. We'll be fine." She took the card and shoved it into her pocket without looking at him.

"That's fine, but just in case." He shifted his attention to her sister. He had a strong feeling that Corry wasn't really here looking for a place to start over.

As he got into his patrol car and looked back, he saw Lacey standing on the sidewalk looking a little lost. He'd never seen that look on her face before, like she wasn't sure of her next move.

He brushed off the desire to go back. He knew he couldn't help her. Lacey was a force unto herself, independent and determined. He was pretty sure she didn't need him, and more than positive he didn't want to get involved.

* * *

Lacey watched Jay Blackhorse drive away before turning to face Corry again. The front door of the diner opened and Lacey's, Jolynn, stepped outside.

"Honey, if you need to take off early, go ahead. We can handle it for thirty minutes without you." Jolynn smiled at Corry.

Lacey wished she could do the same. She wished that seeing her sister here didn't make her feel as if her life in Gibson was in danger.

"I can stay." Lacey picked up the backpack that Corry had tossed on the ground.

"No, honey, I insist. Go home." Jolynn patted her arm. "Take your sister on up to your place and get her settled."

Lacey closed her eyes and counted to ten. She could do this. "Okay, thank you. I'll grab my purse. But if you need..."

"We don't need. You're here too much as it is. It won't hurt you to go home a few minutes early."

Lacey stepped back inside the cool, air-conditioned diner with Jolynn, and pretended people weren't staring, that they weren't whispering and looking out the window at her sister.

She pretended it didn't bother her. But it did. It bothered her to suddenly become the outsider again, after working so hard to gain acceptance. It bothered her that Jay Blackhorse never looked at her as though she belonged.

Jolynn gave her a light hug when she walked her to the door. "You're a survivor, Lacey, and you'll make it through this. God didn't make a mistake, bringing that young woman to you."

Lacey nodded, but she couldn't speak. Jolynn smiled

and opened the door for her. Lacey walked out into the hot July day. Corry had taken a seat on the bench and she stood up.

"Ready?" Lacey picked up her sister's bag.

"Where's your car?"

"I walk to work."

"We have to walk?"

Lacey took off, letting Corry follow along behind her. Her sister mumbled and the baby whimpered in the infant seat. Lacey glanced back, the backpack and diaper bag slung over her shoulder, at her sister who carried the infant seat with the baby.

As they walked up the long driveway to the carriage-house apartment Lacey had lived in for over six years, Corry mumbled a little louder.

Lacey opened the door to her apartment and motioned her sister inside. The one room with a separate bathroom and a walk-in closet was less than five hundred square feet. Corry looked around, clearly not impressed.

"You've been living in a closet." Corry smirked. "And I thought you were living on Walton's Mountain."

Ignore it. Let it go. Push the old Lacey aside. "I think you should feed the baby."

"Ya think? So now you're a baby expert."

The old Lacey really wanted to speak up and say something mean. The new Lacey smiled. "I'm not an expert."

Corry had done nothing but growl since they'd left the diner. Obviously she needed a fix. And she wasn't going to get one.

"Is there another room?"

"No, there isn't. We'll make do here until I can get

something else." Lacey looked around the studio apartment that had been her home since she'd arrived in Gibson.

The home she would have to give up if Corry stayed in Gibson. Starting over again didn't feel good. The baby whimpered. A six-week-old child, dependent on the adults in her life to make good choices for her.

Starting over for a baby. Lacey could do that. She would somehow make it work. She would do her best to help Corry, because that meant the baby had a chance.

Corry tossed her backpack into a corner of the room and dumped the baby, crying and working her fist in her mouth, onto the hide-a-bed that Lacey hadn't put up that morning.

Lacey lifted the baby to her shoulder and rubbed the tiny back until she quieted. Corry had walked to the small kitchen area and was rummaging through the cabinets.

"You know, Corry, since you're here, wanting a place to live, maybe you should try being nice."

"I am being nice." Corry turned from the cabinets and flashed a smile that didn't reach her eyes. "And your boyfriend is cute."

"He isn't my boyfriend." Lacey walked across the room, the baby snuggling against her shoulder. She couldn't let her sister bait her. She couldn't let her mind go in that direction, with Jay Blackhorse as the hero that saved the day. "Corry, if you're going to be here, there are a few rules."

"Rules? I'm not fourteen anymore."

"No, you're not fourteen, but this is my house and my life that you've invaded."

Lacey closed her eyes and tucked the head of the baby against her chin, soft and safe. Be fair, she told herself. "I'm sorry, Corry, I know you need a place for the baby."

"I need a place for myself, too."

"I know that, and I'm willing to help. But I have to know that you're going to stay clean. You can't play your games in Gibson."

Corry turned, her elfin chin tilted and her eyes flashing anger. "You think you're so good, don't you, Lacey? You came to a small town where you pretend to be someone you're not, and suddenly you're too good for your family. You're afraid that I'm going to embarrass you."

"I'm not too good for my family. And it isn't about being embarrassed." It was about protecting herself, and the people she cared about.

It was about not being hurt or used again. And it was about keeping her life in order. She had left chaos behind when she left St. Louis.

"You haven't been home in three years." Corry shot the accusation at her, eyes narrowed.

No, Lacey hadn't been home. That accusation didn't hurt as much as the one about her pretending to be someone she wasn't.

Maybe because she hoped if she pretended long enough, she would actually become the person she'd always believed she could be. She wouldn't be the girl in the back of a patrol car, lights flashing and life crumbling. She wouldn't be the young woman at the back of a large church, wondering why she couldn't be loved without it hurting.

She wouldn't be invisible.

Lacey shifted the fussing baby to one side and grabbed the backpack and searched for something to feed an infant. She found one bottle and a half-empty can of powdered formula.

"Feed your daughter, Corry."

"Admit you're no better than me." Corry took the bottle and the formula, but she didn't turn away.

"I'm not better than you." Lacey swayed with the baby held against her. She wasn't better than Corry, because just a few short years ago, she had been Corry.

But for the grace of God…

Her life had changed. She walked to the window and looked out at the quiet street lined with older homes centered on big, tree-shaded lawns. A quiet street with little traffic and neighbors that cared.

"Here's her bottle." Corry shoved the bottle at Lacey. "And since the bed is already out, I'm taking a nap."

Lacey nodded, and then she realized what had just happened. Corry was already working her. Lacey slid the bottle into the mouth of the hungry infant and moved between her sister and the bed.

"No, you're not going to sleep. That's rule number one if you're going to stay. You're not going to sleep while I work, take care of the baby and feed you. I have to move to make this possible, so you're going to have to help me out a little. I'll have to find a place, and then we'll have to pack."

Corry was already shaking her head. "I didn't say you have to move, so I'm not packing a thing."

Twenty-some years of battling and losing.

"You're going to feed Rachel." Lacey held the baby out to her reluctant sister.

Corry took the baby, but her gaze shifted to the bed, the blankets pulled up to cover the pillows. For a moment Lacey almost caved. She nearly told her sister she could sleep, because she could see in Corry's eyes that she probably hadn't slept in a long time.

"Fine." Corry sat down in the overstuffed chair that

Jolynn had given Lacey when she'd moved into the carriage-house apartment behind the main house.

"I need to run down to the grocery store." Lacey grabbed her purse. "When I get back, I'll cook dinner. You can do the dishes."

"They have a grocery store in this town?" Corry's question drew Lacey out of thoughts that had turned toward how she'd miss this place, her first home in Gibson.

"Yes, they have a store. Do you need something?"

"Cig…"

"No, you won't smoke in my house or around Rachel."

"Fine. Get me some chocolate."

Lacey stopped at the door. "I'm going to get formula and diapers for the baby. I'll think about the chocolate."

As she walked out the door, Lacey took a deep breath. She couldn't do this. She stopped next to her car and tried to think of what she couldn't do. The list was long. She couldn't deal with her sister, or moving, or starting over again.

But she couldn't mistreat Corry.

If she was going to have faith, and if she was ever going to show Corry that God had changed her life, then she had to be the person she claimed to be. She had to do more than talk about being a Christian.

She shoved her keys back into her purse and walked down the driveway. A memory flashed into her mind, ruining what should have been a relaxing walk. Jay's face, looking at her and her sister as if the two were the same person.

Chapter Two

Jay finished his last report, on the accident he'd worked after leaving Lacey's sister at the diner. He signed his name and walked into his boss's office. Chief Johnson looked it over and slid it into the tray on his desk.

"Do you think the sister is going to cause problems?" Chief Johnson pulled off his glasses and rubbed the bridge of his nose.

"Of course she will."

"Why? Because she has a record? She could be like Lacey, really looking for a place to start over."

"I don't know that much about Lacey. But I'm pretty sure about her sister."

"Okay, then. Make sure you patrol past Lacey's place a few times every shift. I'll let the other guys know." The Chief put his glasses back on. "I guess you've got more work to do when you get home?"

"It's Wednesday and Dad schedules his surgeries for today. I've got to get home and feed."

"Tomorrow's your day off. I'll see you Friday."

"Friday." Jay nodded and walked out, fishing his keys out of his pocket as he walked.

He had to stop by the feed store on his way home, for the fly spray they'd ordered for him. At least he didn't have to worry about dinner.

His mom always cooked dinner for him on Wednesdays. She liked having him home again, especially with his brother and sister so far away. His sister lived in Georgia with her husband and new baby. His brother was in the navy.

It should have been an easy day to walk off the job, but it wasn't. As he climbed into his truck he was still remembering the look on Lacey's face when she watched her sister get out of the back of his car.

He knew what it was like to have everything change in just a moment. Life happened that way. A person could feel like they have it all under control, everything planned, and then suddenly, a complete change of plans.

A year ago he really had thought that by now he'd be married and living in his new home with a wife and maybe a baby of his own on the way.

Instead he was back in Gibson and Cindy was on her way to California. She'd been smarter than him; she'd realized three years of dating didn't equal love. And he was still living in the past, in love with a memory.

As he passed the store, he saw his mom's car parked at an angle, between the lines and a little too far back into the street. He smiled, because that was his mom. She lived her life inside the lines, but couldn't drive or park between them.

Other than the parking problem, they were a lot alike.

He drove to the end of the block, then decided to go back. She typically wasn't in town this time of day. Something must have gone wrong with dinner. He smiled because something usually did go wrong.

He parked in front of the store and reached for the

truck-door handle. He could see his mom inside; she was talking to Lacey Gould. He let go of the door handle and sat back to wait.

He sat in the truck for five minutes. His mom finally approached the cash register at the single counter in the store. She paid, talked to the cashier for a minute and then walked out the door. Lacey was right behind her.

Talk about a day going south in a hurry.

"Jay, you remember Lacey." Wilma Blackhorse turned a little pink. "Of course you do, you saw her this afternoon."

"Mom, we've met before." He had lived in Springfield, not Canada. He'd just never really had a reason to talk to Lacey.

Until today.

"Of course you have." His mom handed him her groceries and then leaned into the truck, resting her arms on the open window. "Well, I just rented her your grandparents' old house. And since you have tomorrow off, I told her you would help them move."

"That really isn't necessary." Lacey, dark hair framing her face and brown eyes seeking his, moved a little closer to his truck. "I can move myself."

"Of course you can't. What are you going to do, put everything in the back of your car?" Wilma shook her head and then looked at Jay again.

Lacey started to protest, and Jay had a few protests of his own. He didn't need trouble living just down the road from them. His mom had no idea what kind of person Corry Gould was.

Not that it would have stopped her.

He reached for another protest, one that didn't cast stones.

"Mom, we're fixing that house up for Chad." Jay's

brother. And one summer, a long time ago, it had been Jamie's dream home. For one summer.

It had been a lifetime ago, and yet he still held on to dreams of forever and promises whispered on a summer night. His mom had brought Jamie and her family to Gibson, and changed all of their lives forever.

"Oh, Jay, Chad won't be out of the navy for three years. If he even gets out of the navy. You know he wants to make it a career." She patted his arm. "And you're building a house, so you don't need it."

He opened his mouth with more objections, but his mom's eyes narrowed and she gave a short shake of her head. Jay smiled past her.

Lacey, street-smart and somehow shy. And he didn't want to like her. He didn't want to see vulnerability in her eyes.

"I'll be over at about nine in the morning." He didn't sigh. "I'll bring a stock trailer."

"I don't want you to have to spend your day moving me."

He started his truck. "It won't be a problem. See you in the morning."

"Don't forget dinner tonight," his mom reminded.

"You don't have to cook for me. I could pick something up at the diner."

"I have a roast in the Crock-Pot."

That was about the worst news he'd heard all day. He shot a look past her and Lacey smiled, her dark eyes twinkling a little.

"A roast." He nodded. "That sounds good. Lacey, maybe you all could join us for dinner."

"Oh, I can't. I have to get home and pack."

He tipped his hat at her and gave her props for a quick escape. She'd obviously had his mother's roast before.

"Thanks, Jay." Lacey Gould backed away, still watching him, as if she wanted something more from him. He didn't have more to give.

"See you at home, honey." His mom patted his arm.

"Mom…"

His mom hurried away, leaving him with the groceries and words of caution he had wanted to offer her. She must have known what he had to say. And she would have called him cynical and told him to give Lacey Gould and her sister a chance.

Lacey woke up early the next morning to soft gray light through the open window and the song of a meadowlark greeting the day. She rolled over on the air mattress she'd slept on and listened to unfamiliar sounds that blended with the familiar.

A rustle and then a soft cry. She sat up, brushing a hand through her hair and then rubbing sleep from her eyes. She waited a minute, blinking away the fuzzy feeling. The baby cried again.

"Corry, wake up." Lacey pushed herself up off the mattress and walked to the hide-a-bed. Corry's face was covered with the blanket and she slept curled fetus-style on her side.

"Come on, moving day."

Corry mumbled and pulled the pillow over her head.

Lacey stepped away from the bed and reached into the bassinet for the pacifier to quiet the baby. Rachel's eyes opened and she sucked hard on the binky. Lacey kissed the baby's soft little cheek and smiled.

"I'll get your bottle."

And then she'd finish packing. She side-stepped boxes

as she walked to the kitchen. Nearly everything was packed. It hadn't taken long. Six years and she'd accumulated very little. She had books, a few pictures and some dust bunnies. She wouldn't take those with her.

Memories. She had plenty of memories. She'd found a picture of herself and Bailey at Bailey's wedding, and a note from Bailey's father's funeral last year.

She'd lived a real life in this apartment. In this apartment she had learned to pray. She had cooked dinner for friends. She had let go of love. She had learned to trust herself. Dating Lance had taught her lessons in trusting someone else. And when not to trust.

The baby was crying for real. Lacey filled the bottle and set it in a cup to run hot water over it. The bed squeaked. She turned and Corry was sitting up, looking sleepy and younger than her twenty-two years.

Life hadn't really been fair. Lacey reminded herself that her sister deserved a chance. Corry deserved for someone to believe in her.

Lacey remembered life in that bug-infested apartment that had been her last home in St. Louis. She closed her eyes and let the bad memories of her mother and nights cowering in a closet with Corry slide off, like they didn't matter.

She picked up the bottle and turned off the water. The dribble of formula she squeezed onto her wrist was warm. She took the bottle back to Corry and then lifted the baby out of the bassinet.

"Can you feed her while I finish packing?" Lacey kissed her niece and then lowered her into Corry's waiting arms.

Corry stared down at the infant, and then back at Lacey. "You make it look so easy."

"It isn't easy, Corry."

"I thought it would be. I thought I'd just feed her and she'd sleep, and stuff. I didn't want to give her away to someone I didn't know."

Lacey looked away from the baby and from more memories.

"I need to pack."

"I'm sorry, Lacey."

"Don't worry about it." Lacey grabbed clothes out of her dresser. "I'm going to take a shower while you feed her. You need to make sure you're up and around before Jay gets here."

When Lacey walked out of the bathroom, he was standing by the door, a cowboy in jeans, a T-shirt and a ball cap covering his dark hair. He nodded and moved away from the door. In the small confines of her apartment she realized how tall he was, towering over her, making her feel smaller than her five-feet-five height.

"Oh, you're earlier than I expected."

"I thought it would be best if we got most of it done before it gets hot."

"I don't have a lot. It won't take long." She looked around and so did Jay. This was her life, all twenty-eight years packed into a studio apartment.

"We should be able to get it all in the stock trailer and the back of my truck."

"Do you want a cup of coffee first? I still have a few things to pack."

"No coffee for me. I'll start carrying boxes out."

Lacey pointed to the boxes that she'd packed the night before. And she let him go, because he was Jay Blackhorse and he wasn't going to sit and have a cup of coffee with her. And she was okay with that.

Her six-month relationship with Lance Carmichael had taught her a lot. He had taught her not to open her heart up, not to share. She would never forget that last night, their last date.

I can't handle this. It's too much reality. His words echoed in her mind, taunting her, making a joke of her dreams.

"Are there any breakables in the boxes?" Jay had crossed the room.

Lacey turned from pouring herself a cup of coffee. He stood in front of the boxes, tall and suntanned, graceful for his size. He was all country, right down to the worn boots and cracked leather belt.

He turned and she smiled, because he wore a tan-and-brown beaded necklace that didn't fit what she knew about Jay Blackhorse. Not that she knew much. Or would ever know much.

Funny, she wanted to know more. Maybe because he was city and country, Aeropostale and Wrangler. Maybe it was the wounded look in his eyes, brief flashes that she caught from time to time, before he shut it down and turned on that country-boy smile.

"I've marked the ones that are fragile," she answered, and then grabbed an empty box to pack the stuff in the kitchen that she hadn't gotten to the night before.

Jay picked up a box and walked out the front door, pushing it closed behind him. And Corry whistled. Lacey shot her sister a warning look and then turned to the cabinet of canned goods and boxes of cereal. She agreed with the whistle.

Two hours later Lacey followed behind Jay's truck and the stock trailer that contained her life. Corry had stayed behind. And that had been fine with Lacey. She didn't need her sister underfoot, and the baby would be better in an empty apartment than out in the sun while they unloaded furniture and boxes.

From visits with Jay's mom, Lacey had seen the farmhouse where Jay's grandparents had lived. But as she pulled up, it changed and it became her home. She swallowed a real lump in her throat as she parked next to the house and got out of her car.

The lawn was a little overgrown and the flower gardens were out of control, but roses climbed the posts at the corner of the porch and wisteria wound around a trellis at one side of the covered porch.

Her house.

Jay got out of his truck and joined her. "It isn't much."

"It's a house," she whispered, knowing he wouldn't understand. She could look down the road and see the large brick house he'd grown up in. It had five bedrooms and the living room walls were covered with pictures of the children and the new grandchild that Wilma Blackhorse didn't get to see enough of.

"Yes, it's a house." He kind of shrugged. He didn't get it.

"I've never lived in a house." She bit down on her bottom lip, because that was more than she'd wanted to share, more than she wanted him to know about her.

"I see." He looked down at her, his smile softer than before. "You grew up in St. Louis, right?"

"Yes."

"I guess moving to Gibson was a big change?"

"It was." She walked to the back of his truck. "I want to thank you for this place, Jay. I know that you don't want me here…"

He raised a hand and shook his head. "This isn't my

decision. But I don't have anything against you being here."

She let it go, but she could have argued. Of course he minded her being there. She could see it in his eyes, the way he watched her. He didn't want her anywhere near his family farm.

Jay followed Lacey up the back steps of the house and into the big kitchen that his grandmother had spent so much time in. The room was pale green and the cabinets were white. His mom had painted it a few years ago to brighten it up.

But it still smelled like his grandmother, like cantaloupe and vine-ripened tomatoes. He almost expected her to be standing at the stove, taking out a fresh batch of cookies.

The memory brought a smile he hadn't expected. It had been a long time since his grandmother's image had been the one that he envisioned in this house. It took him by surprise, that it wasn't Jamie he thought of in this house, the way he'd thought of her for nine years. He put the box down and realized that Lacey was watching him.

"Good memories?" she asked, curiosity in brown eyes that narrowed to study his face.

"Yes, good memories. My grandmother was a great cook."

He didn't say, "unlike Mom."

"Oh, I see."

"I guess you probably do. My mom tries too hard to be creative. She always ends up adding the wrong seasoning, the wrong spices. You know she puts cinnamon and curry on her roast, right?"

Lacey nodded. She was opening cabinets and peeking in the pantry. She turned, her smile lighting her face and settling in her eyes. Over a house.

"I love your mom." Lacey opened the box she'd carried in. "I want to be like her someday."

She turned a little pink and he didn't say anything.

"I want to have a garden and can tomatoes in the fall," she explained, still pink, and it wasn't what he wanted to hear.

He didn't want to hear her dreams, or what she thought about life. He didn't want to get pulled into her world. He wanted to live his life here, in Gibson, and he didn't want it to be complicated.

Past to present, Lacey Gould was complicated.

And she thought he was perfect. He could see it in her eyes, the way she looked at him, at his home and his family. She had some crazy idea that if a person was a Blackhorse, they skipped through life without problems, or without making mistakes.

"It's a little late for a garden this year." He started to turn away, but the contents of the box she was unpacking pulled him back. "Dogs?"

"What?"

"You like dogs."

"I like to collect them." She took a porcelain shepherd out of the box and dusted it with her shirt.

"How many more do you have?" He glanced into the box.

"Dozens."

"Okay, I have to ask, why dogs?"

She looked up at him, her head cocked a little to the side and a veil of dark brown hair falling forward to cover one cheek.

"Dogs are cute." She smiled, and he knew that was all he'd get from her.

He didn't really want more.

* * *

Dogs are cute. As Jay walked through the front door of his house the next morning, he had a hard time believing that Lacey could be right about dogs. He looked down at his bloodhound and shook his head. Dogs weren't cute. Dogs chewed up a guy's favorite shoes. Dogs slobbered and chewed on the leg of a chair.

"You're a pain in my neck." He ignored the sad look on the dog's face. "You have no idea how much I liked those shoes. And Mom is going to kill you for what you did to that chair."

Pete whined and rested his head on his paws. Jay picked up the leather tennis shoe and pointed it at the dog. Pete buried his slobbery face between his paws and Jay couldn't help but smile.

"Crazy mutt." Jay dropped the shoe. "So I guess I keep you and buy new shoes. Someday, buddy, someday it'll be one shoe too many. You're too old for this kind of behavior."

The dog's ears perked. Jay walked to the window and looked out. A truck was pulling away from the house at the end of the dirt lane. Two days after the fact and he remembered what the Chief had told him: keep an eye on things at Lacey's. Well, now it would be easy, because Lacey was next door.

He turned and pointed toward the back door. Pete stood up, like standing took a lot of effort, and lumbered to the door. "Outside today, my friend. Enjoy the wading pool, and don't chew up the lawn furniture."

One last look back and Pete went out the door, his sad eyes pleading with Jay for a reprieve. "Not today, Pete."

Jay walked across his yard, his attention on the house not far from his. A five-acre section of pasture separated them. He could see Lacey standing in the yard, pulling on the cord of a push mower.

He glanced at his watch. He had time before he had to head to work. Pushing aside his better sense, he headed down the road to see if she needed help.

"Good morning, neighbor." She stopped pulling and smiled when he walked up. "Would you like a cup of coffee?"

"No, thanks." He moved a little closer. "Do you want me to start it for you?"

"If you can. I've been pulling on that thing for five minutes."

"Does it have gas in it?"

She bit down on her bottom lip and her hands slid into her pockets. "I didn't check."

He would have laughed, but she already looked devastated. Mowing the lawn was probably a big part of the having-a-house adventure. He wouldn't tease her. He also wouldn't burst her bubble by telling her it wouldn't stay fun for long.

"Do you have a gas can?"

"By the porch. Cody brought it. I just figured the mower was full." She went to get the can of gas. Cody was a good guy to bring it. Jay liked the husband of one of his childhood friends, Bailey Cross.

Jay opened the gas cap, pushed the machine and shook his head. "No gas. He probably filled the gas can on the way over, so you'd have it."

"Of course." She had the gas can and he took it from her to fill the tank.

"I can mow it for you."

"No, I want to do it. Remember, I've never had a lawn."

The front door opened. Lacey's sister stepped out with

the baby in her arms. The child was crying, her arms flailing the air. Corry shot a look in his direction. He tried not to notice the eyes that were rimmed with dark circles, or the way perspiration beaded across her pale face. He looked away.

"She won't stop crying." Corry pushed the baby into Lacey's arms.

"Did you burp her?" Lacey lifted the infant to her shoulder. "Corry, you have to take care of her. She's your daughter. You're all she has."

"I don't want to be all she has. How can I take care of her?"

"The same way thousands of moms take care of their children. You have to use a little common sense." Lacey made it look easy, leaning to kiss the baby's cheek, talking in quiet whispers that soothed the little girl.

He could have disagreed with Lacey. Not all moms knew how to take care of children. He'd been a police officer for five years. He'd seen a lot.

"I should go. I have to work today, but I wanted to make sure you have everything you need." He told himself he wasn't running from something uncomfortable.

"We're good." Lacey looked down at the baby. "Jay, thanks for this place."

"It needed to be rented." He shrugged it off. "But you're welcome."

"Hey, wait a minute." Corry moved forward, her thin arms crossed in front of her, hugging herself tight. "Aren't you going to tell him about the stove?"

Lacey smiled. "It isn't a big deal. I can fix it."

"Fix what?"

"One of the knobs is broken. I have to go to Spring-field tonight. I can pick one up."

"What are you going to Springfield for?" Corry pushed herself into the conversation.

"None of your business." Lacey snuggled the baby and avoided looking at either of them. And Jay couldn't help but be curious. It was a hazard of his job. What was she up to?

"I can fix the stove, Lacey," he offered.

"Jay, I don't want you to think you have to run over here and fix every little thing that goes wrong. I'm pretty self-sufficient. I can even change my own lightbulbs."

"I'm sure you can." He looked at his watch. "Tell you what. You pick up the knob. I'll have my dad come over and fix it tomorrow."

That simplified everything. It meant he stayed out of her business. And she didn't feel like he was taking care of her.

"Good." She smiled her typical Lacey smile, full of optimism.

He had to take that thought back. Her sister showing up in town had emptied her of that glass-half-full attitude. Maybe her cheerful attitude did have limits.

"Do you want to see if the mower will start now?" He recapped the gas can and set it on the ground next to the mower. Lacey still held the baby.

"No, I have to get ready for work now."

"See you at the diner." He tipped his hat and escaped.

When he glanced back over his shoulder, they were walking back into the house and he wondered if Lacey would survive her sister being in her life.

And if he would survive the two of them in his.

Chapter Three

"I can't stay out here all day, alone." Corry paced through the sunlit living room of the farmhouse, plopping down on the overstuffed floral sofa that Lacey had bought used the previous day.

Lacey turned back to the window and watched as Jay made his way down the road to the home he'd grown up in. A perfect house for a perfect life.

For a while he'd even had a perfect girlfriend, Cindy, a law student and daughter of a doctor. The perfect match. Or maybe not. He was back at home, and Cindy was off to California pursuing her career. Lacey knew all of this through the rumor mill, which worked better than any small-town paper.

And the other thing they said was that it was all because of Jamie. But no one really talked about who Jamie was and what she meant to Jay Blackhorse.

"Come on, Lace, stop ignoring me." Corry, petulant and high-strung. Lacey sighed and turned back around.

"You'll have to stay here. I have to work, and I can't entertain you."

"I'll go to town with you."

"No, you're not going with me."

"Why not?" Corry plopped down on the sofa and put her feet up on the coffee table.

"Because I said so." Lacey rubbed a hand across her face. "This is not what I want to do every day, Corry. I don't want to raise you. You're a grown woman and a mother. If you're going to be bored, we'll find a sitter for Rachel and you can get a job."

Corry frowned and drew her legs up under her. The baby slept in the bassinet someone from church had donated to their new home. They both looked at the lace-covered basket.

"You know I can't work," she whispered, for a moment looking vulnerable.

"You stay home with the baby, Corry. Be a good mom and let me worry about working."

"I'm not worried about it."

Of course she wasn't. "Fine, then you can be responsible for cooking dinner."

"I can't cook. Well, maybe mac-n-cheese or sandwiches. Not much else."

"You can learn. I have cookbooks."

At the word *cookbook* she saw Corry's eyes glaze over, and the younger woman looked away.

"I want to call my friends and let them know where I am." Corry plucked at the fabric on the couch. "They'll be wondering what happened to me."

Lacey shook her head, fighting the sliver of fear that snaked into her belly when she thought about the kind of friends that Corry had. She didn't want that old life invading Gibson.

"You can't drag the old in with the new, Corry."

"Just because you walked away from everyone doesn't mean that I have to."

"I didn't walk away, I started over."

"I don't see how you can like it here."

Lacey stood up but didn't answer. She picked up her cell phone and slipped it into her pocket, a way to let Corry know that she meant it when she said her sister couldn't contact people from her past.

"I'll be home by four o'clock. But after dinner, I have to go to Springfield for a few hours."

"Fine, have fun. Don't worry about me, stuck out here, alone, nothing to do."

"I won't."

Lacey grabbed the backpack off the hook on the wall and walked out the front door, letting it bang shut behind her. She heaved the backpack over her shoulder and glanced back, seeing Corry on the sofa, watching.

She couldn't tell Corry about the classes in Springfield, or what they meant to her. Corry wouldn't understand. Lacey was one month away from finishing high school. She would finally have a piece of paper to show that she had accomplished her goal.

As soon as the GED certificate was in her hands, she wanted to enroll in college. She wanted to be a teacher.

She wanted to help children who, like Corry, had never had a chance. Maybe if those children had someone to believe in them, their lives would take different paths than the path her sister had taken.

It was after ten o'clock Friday night when Jay saw headlights easing down the long drive to the old farmhouse that Lacey had rented. He dropped his book and went to the window.

"Who is it?" His mom turned down the volume on the news program she was watching.

"I'm not sure. Someone pulling into Lacey's."

Lacey's house was dark.

"You should go check on them. They don't have a phone yet." His mom had joined him at the window. She peered out into the dark night. Clouds covered the full moon but Jay could see stars to the south.

"Mom, I think they can take care of themselves." He shrugged off his own curiosity. "I'm not her keeper."

"You're also a nice guy. Don't try to pretend you're not." His mom gave him the mom look. "Jay, she's a sweet girl and she's worked hard to change her life."

"I'm sure she has. But I also don't think you can take in every stray that comes along."

"Okay, fine." She peered out the window again and then shrugged as if she didn't care.

"If it makes you happy, I'll go check on her. But I have a feeling she isn't going to appreciate it."

"Maybe not, but I will." She smiled at him, and he knew he'd lost the battle.

He grabbed a flashlight and his sidearm, sliding it into the holster he hadn't removed when he'd walked through the door thirty minutes earlier.

Pete woofed from the dog bed near the fireplace. The dog didn't bother getting up. He was retired from the police force and usually didn't care who did what.

Jay walked out the door and headed across a field bathed in silver light as the clouds floated overhead. Pete woofed again and he heard the dog door flap as the lazy animal ran to catch up with him. Obviously Pete had decided the action was worth getting up for. Five years of sniffing drugs and searching for lost kids, and now he spent most of his time sniffing rabbit trails and chewing up perfectly good shoes.

A shadow lingered in the front yard of the old farmhouse. Pete lumbered to Jay's side, growling a low warning. Jay's hand went to his sidearm and he walked more carefully, deliberately keeping an eye on the form that had stilled when the dog barked.

Pete took off, his long legs pounding and his jaws flapping. The person in the yard ran for the car and was scrambling onto the hood. The outdoor security light had been shot out by kids nearly a year earlier. As clouds covered the moon, Jay thought about the mistake of not getting that light fixed.

"Who's there?" He recognized the trembling voice.

"Pete, down." The dog immediately obeyed Jay's command. He walked through the gate and crossed the lawn to find Lacey cowering on the hood of her own car. He should have recognized the headlights of her Chevy.

"Where in the world did he come from?" She didn't move to climb down from the car. He almost laughed, but she had books and she might throw them.

"He's mine."

"Do you always sic him on people when they come home at night?"

He held a hand out and she refused the offer. Lacey Gould, afraid? How did he process that information? She always seemed a little like David, confronting the world with five stones and a lot of faith.

And she collected dogs. Of course, not real ones.

"I didn't know it was you. I saw a car pulling up to a dark house, late."

She grasped the books and shot him a "stupid male" look. "So, I can't come home late?"

"You were in Springfield this late?"

"Do you interrogate all of your renters?"

"No, I don't interrogate all of them. It was a question, Lacey. You were going to Springfield after work. It's late. We saw headlights down here and we were worried. Mom was worried."

Her shoulders slumped. "I have to get inside. I have the breakfast shift and I have to be at work at five in the morning."

"Let me help you down."

"Jay, do me a favor, grab your dog."

"He won't hurt you."

"He's huge and he has big teeth."

"You're afraid of dogs." More information to process. He reached for Pete's collar. "What about that dog collection of yours?"

He shouldn't have asked. Asking meant he wanted to know something about her, something that didn't quite make sense. He wanted to deny that she was a mystery to solve.

He definitely didn't want to get involved.

"I love collecting dogs." She stared at Pete. "The kind without teeth."

"Toy ones." He smiled and she glared.

"Don't tell anyone. How embarrassing would it be if everyone knew?"

"People can be afraid of dogs, Lacey."

"It's a ridiculous fear. Some dogs bite."

"Pete doesn't bite."

She smiled. "But if he did, he'd take a big bite."

"He chews on shoes, but he barely chews his own dog food."

"You chew it for him?"

"Now that's disgusting."

She slid down from the hood of the car, but stayed on the other side of the vehicle. "I need to get some sleep. Thank you for checking on us."

He nodded and in the sliver of moonlight that filtered through a break in the clouds he read the book in her hand. *Algebra 2*. She hugged it tight to her chest.

"You don't have to know all of my secrets, Jay. At least you know I wasn't in town and up to no good."

"I never thought that." But hadn't he wondered? When she'd said she was going to Springfield tonight, hadn't he suspected something?

"You did. And that's fine."

She turned and walked away. He held on to Pete's collar and watched her go. Her back was straight and her step was less than bouncy.

Pete pulled, trying to go after her. Jay almost agreed with the dog, but decided against it. One thing he didn't need was more information about Lacey Gould.

Saturday mid-morning and the diner was full. Every table. Lacey hurried to the table where the Golden Girls were having Saturday brunch. Not that the Hash-It-Out served brunch; for Gibson, that meant a late breakfast if Jolynn still had biscuits left.

"Lacey, honey, how are you doing?" Elsbeth Jenkins pointed to her coffee cup. She could chat as much as anyone, and Lacey knew the older lady really did care. But Elsbeth did have her priorities. Coffee first.

"I'm doing fine, Miss Jenkins." Lacey poured the cup of coffee and handed her a few more creamers. "Is there anything else?"

"No, honey, nothing else. We're just going to sit and

chat for a bit. Is Bailey working today?" Goldie Johnson asked.

"No, ma'am, she's not working today. She's only here
when we're short on help."

"How is she feeling?" Goldie nodded as she spoke.

"She's feeling great and she and Cody're excited about
the baby."

"Honey, did that grandson of mine ever write to you?"
Elsbeth stirred two creamers into the tiny coffee cup and
turned the liquid nearly white.

Lance had taken a job in Georgia shortly after the two
of them broke up. And she hadn't really missed him. She
realized now that she had been more in love with the idea
of love than in love with Lance. It had been wrong to start
a relationship based on a desire to be a part of this town,
a family and something that would last forever.

"No, Miss Jenkins, I haven't heard from him. Is he
doing okay in Atlanta?"

"Oh, I don't know. You know how men are, they don't
talk a lot. But I'm really sorry that things didn't work out
between the two of you."

The cowbell over the door banged and clanged. Lacey
looked up, glad for the distraction. And then not so glad.
Jay walked in, blue-and-gray uniform starched and
pressed. He looked her way and then looked the other
way.

She swallowed and started to move away from the
Golden Girls but one of them stopped her. "Honey, now
that's a boy that needs a good woman like you."

"No, I don't think so." Lacey smiled anyway.

Jay sat down with a couple of guys close to his age.
They were dusty from work and their boots had tracked

in half the dirt from the farm. Lacey had just finished sweeping up before the Golden Girls came in.

"Would you like coffee?" She asked because she knew he'd say no. He always did, and it was fun to watch his eyes narrow when she asked.

"Water, and a burger. No fries." He moved the menu to the side.

"Extra lettuce." *Health nut.* She smiled. "Be just a few minutes."

"Thanks." He didn't look at her.

"You roping tonight?" one of the other guys asked Jay as she walked away.

"Yeah, I'm working with a horse that a guy from Tulsa brought up to me."

"How does it feel to be home?" the other guy, Joey, asked.

Lacey paused at the door to the kitchen to hear him say, "It's always good to come home."

When Lacey took Jay his burger, he actually smiled. She refilled his water glass and turned, but a hand caught hers. Not Jay's hand.

"Hey, Lacey, how about you come to the rodeo with me tonight?" Joey Gaston winked and his hand remained on hers.

Lacey pulled her hand free. She could feel heat sliding up her cheeks and she couldn't look at Jay. "I don't think so, Joey."

"Oh, come on, we'd have a good time." He smiled, showing dimples that probably charmed a lot of girls.

"I'm not into a 'good time,' Joey." She wasn't good enough to take home to meet their families, but she was good enough for a back road on a Saturday night.

Lance had done that for her.

"Leave her alone, Joey." Jay's voice, quiet but firm.

Lacey couldn't look at Jay, but she knew that tone in his voice. And Joey knew it, too. He sat back in his chair, staring at Jay, brows raised.

"I was just kidding. I've got a girlfriend."

"Oh, that makes it *way* more amusing, Joey." Lacey walked away, pretending no one stared and that she hadn't been humiliated.

For six years she'd been accepted in Gibson. Dating Lance had been the mistake that changed everything.

She walked through the swinging doors into the kitchen and leaned against the wall. The doors swung open and Jolynn was there. "Honey, don't you listen to those boys. Remember, they're just young pups that need to have their ears boxed. The people who count, the people who love you, know better."

Lacey nodded, and wiped away the tear that broke loose and trickled down her cheek. "I know. Thanks, Jo."

"You can always count on me, sweetie. You know you're my kid and I love you."

The one tear multiplied and Jolynn hugged her tight, the way a mother would hug a daughter. The way Lacey had only dreamed of when she'd been a child growing up.

Chapter Four

Lacey pulled up the driveway to her house and then just sat in the car, too tired to get out. After a long breakfast and lunch shift at the diner, her feet were killing her and her head ached.

She didn't want to deal with Corry after dealing with Joey back at the diner. She didn't want to clean the house after cleaning tables all day. It would have been great to come home and sit by herself on the front porch.

Instead she knew she had to go inside and face her sister. She had to face that dinner probably wasn't cooked, and Corry probably wasn't any more appreciative today than she'd been yesterday.

As she walked up the steps a car drove past. Jay in his truck coming home from work. She waved and he waved back. He was going to the rodeo tonight. She used to go a lot, but not lately. Lately had been about work and classes, and when she had spare time, she studied.

She opened the front door and walked into the slightly muggy house, not completely cool because the window air conditioners were old. A huge mess greeted her.

"What in the world is going on here?" Lacey walked

into her beautiful new living room with the hardwood floors and cobalt-blue braided rugs. From the arched doorway she could see through the dining room to the kitchen with the white-painted cabinets.

Everything was a mess. Clothes littered the floors. Dirty dishes covered the counters and trash covered the floor. A radio blasted rock music and the baby was crying.

"Corry, where are you?" Lacey picked up the wailing baby and hurried through the house.

"I'm here." A voice mumbled from the back porch.

"What are you doing, taking a nap? You have a baby to feed. The house is a disaster and you were supposed to cook."

Corry was curled up on the wicker couch, hair straggling across her face. She was wearing the same clothes she'd worn the previous day. Lacey leaned over, looking into eyes that were blurry and a smile that drooped.

"What have you done?" Lacey reached for the phone, ready to call 911.

"Cold medicine. Just cold medicine."

"How much."

"Just enough. Get off my back."

"Did you have to trash my house?"

Lacey walked away, still holding Rachel close. Words were rolling through her mind, wanting to come out. She couldn't say what she wanted to say. She couldn't stand next to her sister, for fear she would hurt her. Corry was already hurting herself.

"I'm so angry with you, Corry. I can't believe you would do this. You have a baby." Lacey stopped in front of the corner curio in the living room and started picking up the few dogs that had been knocked off the shelves.

"Stop being a prude," Corry snarled.

"Stop being selfish."

"I have a friend coming to get me next week." Corry sat up, leaning forward, her stringy dark hair hanging down over her face.

"How did you call a friend?"

"I used your boyfriend's phone. His mother let me in."

"Leave Mrs. Blackhorse alone." Lacey crossed back to her sister, kneeling in front of her and turning Corry's face so that they made eye contact. "Stay away from Jay and his family."

"Why? Are you afraid of what they'll think of you if they meet me?" Corry smiled a hazy smile. "Too late. I think they were impressed."

Lacey stood back up. The baby cried against her shoulder, reminding her that it was time to eat. "I can't have you living here like this, Corry."

She couldn't let Corry destroy everything she'd built. Lacey had a life here, and friends. She belonged. For the first time in her life, she'd found a place where she belonged.

"I plan on leaving. I'm not going to stay and live like a hermit." Corry's words reminded Lacey of the phone call.

And the crying baby. "You can't take Rachel back to St. Louis. That isn't good for her. How are you going to take care of her if you can't take care of yourself?"

"I'll manage. Don't worry about me. Remember, I'm a woman and we know how to take care of babies. It's easy, right?"

"It isn't easy, Corry. I know that. But this baby deserves a chance. And it's her that I'm worried about, not you."

She walked away because she couldn't argue. And the

baby needed to be fed. She could concentrate on Rachel and let the rest go.

She was heating the bottle when Corry walked into the room. Rachel squirmed against Lacey, tiny hands brushing Lacey's face. Corry looked through blurry eyes, but maybe she was also sorry. Lacey wanted her to be sorry.

"Corry, this can't be the life you want for yourself."

"What's wrong with my life?"

"It doesn't include faith. It doesn't include you wanting a better life for yourself and your child."

"I'm here."

"Yes, you are here." Lacey tested the formula on her wrist and cradled Rachel to feed her. Corry only watched.

"Do you like that cowboy?" Corry leaned against the counter. She shoved her trembling hands into her pockets and hunkered down, defeated.

Lacey ignored the obvious signs of someone going through withdrawal. She knew that was the reason for the cold medicine. Her sister would have done anything for a high at this point.

"He isn't even a friend, just someone I know from town and from church."

For a minute it felt like a normal conversation between sisters. To keep up the illusion, Lacey kept her gaze averted.

"I think I could have more luck with him. You're too pushy." The normal moment between sisters ended with that comment.

Lacey lifted Rachel to her shoulder and patted the baby's back. "Stop it, Corry."

"Are you jealous?"

"There's nothing to be jealous of. I don't want him used. End of story."

"When did you get all righteous? Does he know what you used to be?"

Lacey turned to face her sister. She could feel heat crawling up her neck to her cheeks. "My past is behind me. And it wasn't who I…" She blinked a few times, wishing there weren't tears in her eyes. "It wasn't who I wanted to be."

She didn't belong. Not the way she really wanted to belong to Gibson. After all of these years, she wasn't really one of them. She wanted to be like these people, growing up here, having lifelong friends, family that never moved away, and a place that was all hers.

"Not so easy to be a goody-goody now, is it? Not with me here to remind you of what you used to be. What you still are."

Take a deep breath, she told herself. She wasn't that girl from St. Louis, not here in Gibson. Her past was forgiven. She had to remember who she was now, and who she was in Christ. *For God so loved the world that He gave His only begotten son.*

She was the "whosoever" who had chosen to believe in Jesus. She would not perish, but have everlasting life. They sang a song in church, "My Sins Are Gone." It was her song. Anyone could ask her why she was happy, how she could smile and go on, building a new life. The answer was simple: because her sins were gone, as far as east from west. Her sister could remind her, but she couldn't bring back what had been forgiven. Not really.

"I'm a Christian, Corry. I have faith. I have a new life, and that old life is no longer a part of me."

"Really? You might want to think it's gone, but it's still there."

"I am who I am because of my past, Corry. But God gave me a new life."

"And what makes you so special?"

"I'm not special. I made a choice that anyone can make."

"A past isn't that easy to get rid of." Corry shook her head and walked off, tossing the words over her shoulder. "You're the one living in a fantasy world. By the way, someone's here."

Jay knocked on the door because he had promised Cody and Bailey he would. They'd been trying to call Lacey, but she wasn't answering her cell phone. They were worried. He could have told them that Lacey Gould could take care of herself, but they wouldn't have listened.

They were a lot like his mom, determined to make sure Lacey was kept safe. As if she needed protection.

From the sounds coming from inside the house, he guessed that right now she wanted rid of her sister. He knocked again.

She opened the door, hair a little shaggier than normal and liner under her eyes a little smudged. She didn't smile.

"Bailey wanted me to stop and check on you."

"Why?"

"She's been trying to call and she can't get hold of you."

Lacey reached into her pocket and pulled out her cell phone. She frowned at it and then slipped it back into her pocket. "No signal."

"Okay, I'll let them know." He glanced past her. "What happened?"

"Nothing." Her eyes narrowed, and she shook her head a little, as if she really didn't understand his question.

"Lacey, is everything okay?"

"Fine." She glanced over her shoulder, at the mess, at the broken dogs, at the clothes scattered on the floor. "I'm sorry, I'll get it cleaned up."

"I'm not talking about the house. I know you'll get it cleaned up. I'm asking if *you're* okay."

The baby was crying, and the radio played from the kitchen. Lacey Gould's eyes watered and her nose turned pink.

"Let me help you clean up." He walked past her, into the ransacked house. "Is she looking for a fix?"

"She is." Lacey walked away from him. "Let me get the baby."

"I'll get a broom."

"You don't have to. You have somewhere you need to be and I'm here for the night. It won't take me long to clean up." She walked back into the room with the baby cuddled against her. Exhaustion etched lines across her face and her shoulders heaved with a sigh.

Jay offered her a smile that he knew wouldn't ease her worry or take away the burden. Instead he bent and started picking up the dog figurines that were still intact. The dogs meant something to her. He thought it was more about a life she had never had than a pet she wanted.

"We could get her help." He offered the suggestion as he put the last dog in place. "We could try for a seventy-two hour hold and maybe get her into a treatment program."

"She has to want help."

"I guess you're right." He stood up straight. He hadn't

realized before that she was a good half-foot shorter than his six feet two inches.

He felt as though he towered over her.

"Thanks for stopping by, Jay. If you see Bailey, tell her I'm fine."

"You could ride along and tell her yourself. It probably would be good for you to get out for a while."

"Ride along?" She stared and then shook her head. "I don't think you want to start that rumor."

"It won't start rumors."

"It would, and you really don't want your name linked to mine."

He didn't. She was right. He didn't want his name linked to anyone else's name because three years of Cindy had cured him of his dreams of getting married, having the picket fence and a few kids. He didn't want a woman that would only be a replacement for what he'd lost years ago. Somewhere along the way Cindy had figured that out.

The baby was crying. "I can't go, Jay. Corry is strung out and I can't leave the baby here."

"Bring the baby."

Her eyes widened. For a long moment she stood there, staring at him, staring at the door. Finally she nodded.

"I will go." She hurried into the kitchen and came back with a diaper bag and the baby still held against her shoulder. "But I have to change clothes first. I smell like a cheeseburger."

"Okay." He didn't expect her to shove the baby into his arms, but she did. The wiggling infant fit into the crook of his elbow, her hands grasping at the air. "Umm, Lacey, the baby…"

She had already reached the bedroom door. "What?"

How did he admit to this? Honesty seemed to be the answer, but he knew he wouldn't get sympathy. "I've never held a baby."

"You've never held a baby. Isn't your dad an OB-GYN? And you've never held a baby?"

"Never." He swallowed a little because his heart was doing a funny dance as he held this baby and he couldn't stop looking at Lacey Gould. And she had the nerve to laugh at him.

"Sit down before you drop her. You look a little pale."

He sat down, still clutching the tiny little girl in his arms. He smiled down at her, and man if she didn't smile back, her grin half-tilted and making her nose scrunch.

"Now aren't you something else." He leaned, talking softly, and she smiled again. "You're a little charmer. I think I'd just about buy you a pony."

"She wants a bay." Lacey was back, still smiling. She had changed into jeans and a peasant top that flowed out over the top of her jeans. Her hair spiked around her face and she had wiped away the smudged liner.

"Ready to go?" He handed the baby over, still unsure with her in his arms. And as he looked at Lacey Gould, she was one more thing that he was suddenly unsure about.

"I'm ready to go."

He held the door and let Lacey walk out first, because he was afraid to walk out next to her, afraid of what it might feel like to be close to her when she smelled like lavender.

Lacey leaned close to the window, trying not to look like an overanxious puppy leaning out the truck as they drove onto the rodeo grounds. Stock trailers were parked along the back section and cars were parked in the field next to the arena.

She had been before, more times than she could count, but never like this, in a truck with a stock trailer hooked to the back and a cowboy sitting in the seat next to her. Riding with Bailey and Cody didn't count, not this way. If other girls dreamed of fairy-tale dances and diamonds, Lacey dreamed of this, of boots and cowboys and horses.

Not so much the cowboys these days, but still…

"Don't fall out." Jay smiled as he said it, white teeth flashing in a suntanned face. His hat was on the seat next to him and his dark hair that brushed his collar showed the ring where the hat had been.

She shifted in the seat and leaned back. "I guess you're not at all excited?"

"Of course I am. I've been living in the city for eight years. Longer if you count college. It's good to be home full-time."

"What events are you in?"

"A little of everything. I mainly team rope. But every now and then I ride a bull."

"I want to ride a bull." She hadn't meant to sound like a silly girl, but his eyes widened and he shook his head.

"Maybe you could try barrel racing?" He made the suggestion without looking at her.

"Okay."

Anything. It was all a part of the dream package she'd created for herself. She wanted this life, with these people. For a long time she'd wanted love and acceptance.

She'd found those things in Gibson. Now she wanted horses and a farm of her own. Jay wouldn't understand that dream; he'd always had those things.

"Lacey, we're not that different. This has been my life, but I came home to reclaim what I left behind."

"And it cost you?"

"It cost me." He slowed, and then eased back into a space next to another truck and trailer.

"Are you team roping tonight?" She looked back, at the pricked ears of the horse in the trailer.

"Yeah, and I think I have to ride a bull. Cody signed me up. He says he needs a little competition from time to time."

"Because Bailey is keeping him close to home." She bit down on her bottom lip and looked out the window.

The truck stopped, the trailer squeaking behind it, coming to a halt. The horse whinnied and other horses answered. From the pens behind the arena, cattle mooed, restless from being corralled for so long.

Lacey breathed deep, loving it all. And the man next to her…she glanced in his direction. He was a surprise. He had invited her.

And she had to process that information.

Time to come back to earth, and to remember what it felt like to be hurt, to have her trust stomped on. Lacey unbuckled the baby and pulled her out of the seat, a good distraction because Rachel's eyes were open and she smiled that baby half-smile. Drool trickled down her baby chin.

"Do you think Corry will stay?" Jay had unbuckled his seat belt and he pulled the keys from the ignition of the truck.

The question was one that Lacey had considered, but didn't want to. It made her heart ache to think of Corry leaving, not knowing where she would take the baby.

Lacey shrugged and pulled Rachel, cooing and soft, close to her.

"I really don't know. I don't want to think about that." She kissed the baby's cheek. "But I guess I should."

"Maybe she'll stay."

"She won't. She's restless. She's always been restless."

"I understand restless." He stepped out of the truck.

Lacey, baby in her arms and diaper bag over her shoulder, followed. She met up with him at the back of the trailer. The small glimpse into his life intrigued her. He'd never been open.

"You don't seem restless." She stood back as he opened the trailer and led the horse out. Not his horse, he'd explained, but one he was training. The animal was huge, with a golden-brown coat that glistened.

He glanced at her, shrugging and then went back to the horse. He pulled a saddle out of the tack compartment of the trailer. Expertly tooled and polished, the leather practically glowed in the early evening light.

The lights of the arena came on and Lacey knew that the bleachers would be filling up. But she couldn't walk away because Jay had stories, just like everyone else.

"How could you be restless?" She pushed, forgetting for a moment that he was little more than a stranger.

"Why is that so unusual?" He had the saddle on the horse and was pulling the girth strap tight around the animal's middle. The horse, a gentle giant, stood still, head low and ears pricked forward.

"You don't seem restless."

"Really? And what makes you think you know anything about me?" He straightened, tall and all cowboy in new Wranglers and worn boots. His western shirt was from the mall, not the farm store.

Contradictions. And she loved a mystery.

"So, tell me." She waited, holding the baby in the crook of her arm, but dropping the diaper bag.

"I grew up on a farm in a small town, Lacey. I wanted to live in the city, to experience life in an apartment with close neighbors."

"And you loved it?" She smiled, because he couldn't have.

He grinned back at her. "I did, for a while. But then the new wore off and it was just noise, traffic and the smell of exhaust."

"So you came home because you got tired of city life?"

"I came home." And he didn't finish, but she knew that he'd come home because of a broken heart. Sometimes she saw it in his eyes. Sometimes he looked like someone who had been broken, but was gluing the pieces back together.

"Your parents are glad."

"I know they are." He slipped the reins over the neck of the horse. "And Lacey, before you start thinking I'm one of those poor strays behind the diner, I'm not. Cindy didn't break my heart."

He winked. For a moment she almost believed that his heart hadn't been broken. For a fleeting second she wanted to hold him. To be held by a cowboy with strong arms and roots that went deep in a community.

"I didn't…" She didn't know what to say. She didn't need to know? Or she didn't plan on trying to fix him?

"You did. Your eyes get all weepy and you look like you've found someone who needs fixing. I don't. I'm glad to be home."

He was standing close to her, and she hadn't realized before that his presence would suck the air out of her space, not until that moment. Her lungs tightened inside her chest and she took a step back, kissing the baby's head to distract her thoughts from the man, all cowboy, standing in front of her.

He cocked his head to the side and his mouth opened, but then closed and he shook his head. "I need to find Cody."

"Of course." She backed away. "I'll meet up with you later."

And later she would have her thoughts back in control and she wouldn't be thinking of him as the cowboy who picked up those silly dog figurines and put them back on the shelf while she swept up the pieces of what had been broken.

Chapter Five

Lacey hurried away, ignoring the desire to glance over her shoulder, to see if he was watching. He wouldn't watch. He would get on his horse, shaking his head because she had climbed into his life that way.

She had no business messing in his life; she was a dirty sock, mistakenly tossed in the basket with the clean socks. She couldn't hide from reality.

Jay was the round peg in the round hole. He fit. He was a part of Gibson and someday, he'd marry a girl from Gibson. And Lacey didn't know why that suddenly bothered her, or why it bothered her that when he looked at her, it was with that look, the one that said she was the community stray, taken in and fed, given a safe place to stay.

The way she fed stray cats behind the diner.

"Hey, Lacey, up here."

She looked up, searching the crowd. When she saw Bailey, she waved. Bailey had a seat midway up the bleachers, with a clear view of the chutes. Lacey climbed the steps and squeezed past a couple of people to take a seat next to her friend.

"I didn't expect to see you here." Bailey held her hands out and took the baby, her own belly growing rounder every day.

"Long story." Lacey searched the crowd of men behind the pens. She sought a tall cowboy wearing a white hat, his shirt plaid. She found him, standing next to the buckskin and talking to one of the other guys.

"Make it a short story and fill me in." Bailey leaned a shoulder against Lacey's. "You okay?"

"Hmmm?" Lacey nodded. She didn't want to talk, not here, with hundreds of people surrounding them, eating popcorn or cotton candy and drinking soda from paper cups.

"Are you okay?" Louder voice now, a little impatient.

"I'm great." Lacey leaned back on the bleacher seat. "My sister wrecked my house and she's passed out in my bed. The cowboy that lives down the lane treats me like an interloper. I'm living in his grandparents' house, and he doesn't want me there."

"He brought you tonight."

"He did. I'm a charity case. He felt bad because Corry broke my dogs."

Bailey nodded. "He's about to ride a bull. But since you've sworn off men, I guess that doesn't matter to you?"

"I have a reason for swearing off men. I'm never going to be the type of woman a man takes home to meet his family."

"Lance has problems, Lacey. That isn't about you, it's about him."

"It is about me. It takes a lot for anyone to understand where I've been and what I've done. I'm ashamed of the life I lived, so why should I expect a man to blindly accept my past?"

"You're forgetting what God has done in your life. You're forgetting what He can still do. You're not a finished product. None of us are. Our stories are still being written."

"No, I'm not forgetting." Lacey looked away, because she couldn't admit that sometimes she wondered how God could forgive. How could He take someone as dirty as she felt and turn them into someone people respected?

She worked really hard trying to be that person that others respected.

The bulls ran through the chutes. Lacey leaned back, watching as cowboy after cowboy got tossed. Each time one of them hit the dirt, she cringed. She didn't really want to ride a bull.

"Jay's up." Bailey pointed. Taller than the other bull riders, he stood on the outside of the chute. The bull moved in the chute, a truck-sized animal, pawing the ground.

"I really don't want to watch."

"It isn't easy." Bailey shifted Rachel, now sleeping, on her shoulder. "It doesn't get easier. Every time I watch Cody ride, I pray, close my eyes, peek, pray some more."

"Yes, but you love Cody."

"True. The cowboy in question is just your neighbor."

"Exactly." Lacey laughed and glanced at Bailey, willing to give her friend what she wanted to hear. "He's cute, Bailey, I'm not denying that. But I'm not looking for cute."

"Of course not."

"I'm not looking—period."

"But it is okay to look." Bailey smiled a happy smile and elbowed Lacey. "There he goes."

The gate opened and the bull spun out of the opening, coming up off the ground like a ballet dancer. Amazing that an animal so huge could move like that. The thud when the beast came down jarred the man on his back and Jay fell back, moving his free arm forward.

The buzzer sounded and Jay jumped, landing clear of the animal, but hitting the ground hard. The bull didn't want to let it go. The animal turned on Jay, charging the cowboy, who was slow getting up.

A bullfighter jumped between the beast and the man, giving Jay just enough time to escape, to jump on the fence and wait for the distracted animal to make up his mind that he'd rather not take a piece out of a cowboy.

Jay looked up, his hat gone. His dark gaze met Lacey's and stayed there, connected, for just a few seconds. Warm brown eyes in a face that was lean and handsome. And then he hopped down from the fence and limped away.

"Breathe," Bailey whispered.

Lacey breathed. It wasn't easy. She inhaled a gulp of air and her heart raced.

The rodeo ended with steer wrestling. Jay watched from behind the pens at the back of the arena, still smarting from the bull, and still thinking about Lacey Gould's dark brown eyes. He shook his head and walked away, back to his trailer and his horse.

"That was quite a ride." Cody slapped Jay on the back as he untied his horse.

"Thanks. I'm glad it made you happy."

"Oh, come on, you enjoyed it." Cody leaned against

the side of the trailer, his hat pushed back on his head. "You'll do it again next week."

"I'm thinking no." Jay tightened his grip on Buck's reins because the horse was tossing his head, whinnying to a nearby mare. "I think I'll stick to roping."

"Yeah, I think I'm done with bull riding, too. I've got a baby on the way."

"Right, that does sound like a good reason to stop."

"Yeah, it does." Cody smiled like a guy who had it all. And he did. He had the wife, a child, the farm and a baby on the way. Jay had a diamond ring in a drawer and a room in his parents' house. He had a box of memories that he kept hidden in a closet.

"Speaking of wives and babies, I'm going to find my wife." Cody slapped him on the back again and walked away.

Jay pulled the saddle off the horse and limped to the back of his truck, his knee stiff and his back even stiffer. He tossed the saddle in the back of the truck and then leaned for a minute, wishing again that he hadn't ridden that bull. Bull riding wasn't a sport a guy jumped into.

He tried not to think about Lacey's face in the crowd, pale and wide-eyed as she watched him scramble to the fence, escaping big hooves and an animal that wanted to hurt him.

The horse whinnied, reminding him of work that still needed to be done. He walked back to the animal, rubbing Buck's sleek neck and then pulling off the bridle, leaving just the halter and lead rope. The horse nodded his head as if he approved.

"I'm getting too old for crazy stunts, Buck."

"You stayed on." The feminine voice from behind him was a little soft, a little teasing.

"Yep."

He turned and smiled at Lacey. She wasn't a friend, just someone his mom had picked up and brought home. He had friends, people he'd grown up with, gone to church with, known all his life. He didn't know where to put her, because she didn't fit those categories. Someone that he knew? A person that needed help? Someone passing through?

He would have preferred she stayed in Jolynn's apartment, not the house his grandparents had built. Jamie's house. But she was there now, and he'd deal with it. He moved away from his horse and straightened, raising his hands over his head to stretch the kinks out of his back.

She was here tonight, in his life, because he'd brought her. He had been trying not to think about that, or why he'd extended the offer. Maybe because of the pain in her eyes when she'd looked at those silly dogs her sister had broken.

Who got upset over something like that?

Lacey took cautious steps forward. She held the sleeping baby in one arm and had the diaper bag over her shoulder. She didn't carry a purse.

"You actually did pretty well," she encouraged, a shy smile on a face that shouldn't have been shy. He had never seen her as shy. She was the waitress who never backed down when the guys at the diner gave her a hard time.

"I did stay on, but it wasn't fun and it isn't something I want to do again. I think I'll stick to roping."

"You won the roping event." She moved forward, her hand sliding up the rump of his horse. "Want me to do something?"

"No, I've got it."

She stood next to him, her hand on his horse's neck.

She didn't look at him, and he wondered why. Did she think that by not looking at him, she could hide her secrets?

"I'm going to put the baby in the truck." She moved away and he let her go. Buck pushed at him with his big, tan head, rubbing his jaw against Jay's shoulder.

"In the trailer, Buck." Jay opened the trailer and moved to the side. Buck went in, his hooves pounding on the floor of the trailer, rattling the metal sides as his weight shifted and settled.

"He's an amazing animal." Lacey had returned, without the baby. He was tying the horse to the front of the trailer. "When you rope on him, it's like he knows what you want him to do before you make a move."

"He's a smart animal." Jay latched the trailer.

"Thank you for letting me come with you tonight."

Jay shrugged, another movement that didn't feel too great. He stepped back against his trailer and brought her with him, because the truck next to them was pulling forward.

"I didn't mind." His hand was still on her arm.

She looked from his hand on her arm to his face. Her teeth bit into her bottom lip and she shivered, maybe from the cold night air.

It was dark and the band was playing. Jay could see people two-stepping on a temporary dance floor. Couples scooted in time to the music, and children ran in the open field, catching fireflies.

Lacey smelled like lavender and her arm was soft. She looked up, her eyes dark in a face that was soft, but tough. He moved his hand from her arm and touched her cheek.

She shook her head a little and took a step back, disengaging from his touch. But that small step didn't undo the moment. She was street-smart and vulnerable and he wanted to see how she felt in his arms.

He wanted to brush away the hurt look in her eyes, and the shame that caused her to look away too often. Instead, he came to his senses and pulled back, letting the moment slip away.

"We should go." Lacey stepped over the tongue of the trailer and put distance between them. Her arms were crossed and she had lost the vulnerable look. "Jay, whatever that was, it wasn't real."

"What?"

"It was moonlight. It was summertime and soft music. It was you being lonely and losing someone you thought you'd spend your life with."

"Maybe you're right."

"I am right. But I'm nobody's moment. Someday I want forever, but I'll never be a moment again."

He exhaled a deep breath and whistled low. "Okay, then I guess we should go."

He felt like the world's biggest loser.

Lacey woke up on Sunday morning, glad that she had a day off. If only she'd gotten some sleep, but she hadn't. Jay had dropped her off at midnight, and wound up from the night, she'd stayed up for two hours, cleaning.

She rolled over in bed, listening to the sound of country life drifting through the open window. Cows mooed from the field and somewhere a rooster crowed. He was a little late, but still trying to tell everyone that it was time to get up.

The baby cried and she heard Corry telling her to shush, as if the baby would listen and not expect to be fed. Lacey sat up and stretched. She had an hour to get ready before church.

When she walked through the door of the dining room, Corry was at the table with a bowl of cereal. Rachel was in the bassinet, arms flailing the air.

"Have you fed her?" Lacey picked up the tiny infant and held her close. The baby fussed too much. "Has she been to a doctor?"

"Give me a break. Like I have the money for that. She's fine."

"She's hungry and she feels warm."

"So, feed her, mother of the year."

"I'm not her mother, Corry."

Corry drank the milk from her bowl and took it to the sink. At least she did that much. Lacey took a deep breath and exhaled the brewing impatience. The baby curled against her shoulder, fist working in her tiny mouth.

"I'll feed her, you get ready for church." Lacey held the baby with one arm and reached in the drainer at the edge of the sink for a clean bottle.

"I'm not going to church."

"If you're staying with me, you're going to church."

"Make me go and you'll regret it."

"I probably will, but you're going." Lacey shook the bottle to mix the formula with the water. "I've already taken a shower. You can have yours now."

She turned away from Corry, but shuddered when the bathroom door slammed. "Well, little baby, this is probably something I'll pay for."

Rachel sucked at the bottle, draining it in no time and then burping loudly against Lacey's shoulder. She put the sleeping baby into the infant car seat and was strapping her in as Corry walked out of the bathroom. She wore a black miniskirt and a white tank top.

"You can't wear that."

"It's all I have." Gum smacked and Corry busied herself, far too happily, shoving diapers and wipes along with an extra bottle into the bag.

Rachel cried, a little restless and fussy.

"I think she's sick." Corry looked at the baby and then at Lacey. "What do you think?"

"She feels warm and her cheeks are a little pink. I don't know."

Corry unbuckled the straps and pulled Rachel out of the seat. "I think she has a fever."

"Do you have medicine for her?"

Corry nodded. "I have those drops. I'll give her some of those."

"And stay home with her. She shouldn't be out. You can stay here and let her sleep."

Corry's eyes widened. "Really? You're not going to make me go to church."

"I'm not going to make you." Lacey sighed. "Corry, no one can *make* you go to church. I only want you to try to get your life together and stay clean."

"And church is going to make it all better?"

"Church doesn't, but God does. He really does make things better when you trust Him." The act of going to church hadn't changed anything for Lacey. She had tried that routine as a teenager, because she'd known, really known that God could help, but each time she went into a church, thinking it would be a magic cure, it hadn't changed anything. Because she had thought it was about going to church.

In Gibson she had learned that it was about faith, about

trusting God, not about going to church wishing people would love her. She had learned, too, about loving herself.

She needed to remember that, she realized. Since Lance, she'd had a tough time remembering her own clean slate and that she was worth loving.

Corry pushed through the diapers and wipes in the diaper bag and pulled out infant drops. She held them out to Lacey. "How much do I give her?"

Lacey took the bottle and looked at the back, reading the directions. "One dropper. And don't give her more until I get home. I'll be late, though. You'll have to fix your own lunch."

"Where are you going?"

"After church there are a few of us that go to the nursing home to sing and have church with the people there."

"Ah, isn't that sweet."

Lacey let it go. "I'll see you later."

Today Jay would be joining them at the nursing home. She wondered how the return of one man to his hometown could change everything. For years Gibson had been her safe place. Jay's presence undid that feeling.

Chapter Six

Jay looked across the room and caught the gaze of Lacey Gould. She sat next to an older woman with snow-white hair and hands that shook. They were flipping through the pages of a hymnal and talking in low tones that didn't carry.

But from time to time Lacey looked up at him. This time he caught her staring, and he hadn't expected the look in her eyes to be wariness. She didn't trust him.

Distracted, he dropped his guitar pick. He leaned to pick it up and Bailey kicked his shin. He nearly said something, but the way she was smiling, he couldn't. She'd been teasing him for twenty-some years. She probably wasn't going to stop now.

For years she'd been the little girl on the bus that he looked out for, and sometimes wanted to escape. She'd sent him a love note once. She'd been thirteen, he was sixteen. When he told her it wouldn't work, she cried and told her dad on him.

"She's a good person, Jay," Bailey whispered.

"I'm sure she is." He remembered that Bailey also had a good left hook and he didn't want to make her mad.

He didn't doubt that Lacey was a good person. He had watched her at church, making the rounds and speaking to everyone before the service began. As soon as church ended, she said her good-byes and drove to the nursing home.

He had questions about her community service, but it wasn't any of his business. It should be up to Pastor Dan, or even Bailey, to explain to Lacey Gould that God wasn't expecting her to earn forgiveness through good works.

"What song do we sing first?" Lacey asked from across the room. The sweet-faced older lady had her arm through Lacey's.

Jay lifted his guitar and shrugged. He grimaced at the jab of pain in his lower back and Lacey grinned, because she knew that a bull had dumped him hard the night before.

"'In the Garden'?" He didn't need music for that one.

Lacey knew it; she was nodding and turning the pages of the hymnal. Her elderly friend clapped and smiled, saying it was one of her favorites, and then her eyes grew misty.

"My husband is there waiting for me in that garden." She said it in such a soft and wavering voice that Jay barely heard. He did see tears shimmering in Lacey's eyes, from compassion, always compassion. He wondered if she felt the emotions of everyone she met.

Lacey held the woman's hand and as Jay started to play, Lacey led the song, her voice alto and clear, the meaning of the words clearly written on her face. The wavering voice of her friend joined in, sweet and soprano.

Jay stumbled over the chords and caught up. Next to him, Bailey giggled, the way she'd done on the bus years ago. He was glad she was still getting enjoyment out of his life. He'd been gone nearly eight years, working on the Springfield PD, and it felt as if he'd never left.

Over the next thirty minutes, he found firm footing again. He forgot Lacey and concentrated on the music as the people gathered in the circle around them. He had missed Gibson. He had missed these people, some of whom he had known all of his life. The gentleman to his left had been his high school principal. One of the ladies had lived down the road from his family.

Most of the kids from Gibson had moved to the city or left the state. So many of the people in the nursing home were without close family these days, and this touch from their church made the difference.

Lacey made the difference, he realized. With her flashy smile and soft laughter, her teasing comments and warm hugs, she made a difference that he hadn't expected.

In the lives of these people.

"Not interested, huh?" Bailey teased as they finished up and he was putting his guitar away.

"Interested in what? Helping with this ministry? Of course I am."

"In Lacey."

"Go away, Bailey. You're starting to be a fifth-grade pest."

"Write her a note and ask her out."

"You stink at matchmaking. Matchmakers are supposed to be sneaky, a little underhanded."

Bailey laughed, her eyes watering. "Oh, thank you, now that I know the finer points of the art, I'll do better next time. Maybe you should learn the fine art of realizing when a woman is perfect for you."

"That's obviously a lesson I never learned." He closed

the case on his guitar. He saw Lacey walk out as if she had somewhere to be. "Bailey, I'm not interested. I really thought I'd found the right woman, and I dated her for three years only to find out she wasn't interested in a cowboy. So if you don't mind, I'm on vacation from romance and I'm boycotting matchmakers."

Bailey's laughter faded, so did her smile. "She didn't hurt you, Jay. You're still thinking about Jamie. Maybe it's time to let her go?"

Gut-stomped in the worst way, by a woman with a soft smile. He smiled down at Bailey, happy for her, and sorry that she knew all of his secrets.

"I'm trying, Bay. I really am. I guess that's why I decided to come home. Because I have to face it here, and I have to deal with it."

"I'm sorry, Jay. I thought that enough time had gone by and I was hoping you were ready to move on."

"You were wrong." He smiled to soften the words, because Bailey had been a friend his entire life. A pest, but a friend.

"So, you've given up on love?"

"For now. I want to build my house and get settled back into my life here. I'll be thirty this winter and maybe I'm just going to be a settled old bachelor, raising my horses and doing a little singing for church."

"What a nice dream." She patted his arm, not the slap on the back that Cody had given him the night before. She was getting all maternal. "See you later."

He nodded and picked up his guitar. When he walked out the front entrance of the nursing home, it was hot, unbearably hot. He pulled sunglasses out of his pocket and slid them on as he walked across the parking lot.

The sound of an engine cranking, not firing, caught his attention.

Of course it would be Lacey. They were the only ones left and she was sitting in her car with the driver's side door open.

Jay put his guitar in the front of his truck and walked over to her car. "Won't start?"

"Nope." She tried again. "It always starts. Why won't it start now?"

He shrugged. Probably Bailey did something to it, something less conspicuous than just telling him he should ask Lacey out. He smiled at the thought, because he could picture Bailey out here removing the coil wire from Lacey's car. But she wouldn't do that. He didn't think she would.

"Pop the hood and I'll take a look."

She did and he walked to the front of the car to push the hood up. The coil wire was there. He smiled. Nothing looked out of place.

"Lacey, it isn't out of gas, is it?" He peeked around the raised hood at her.

"I don't think so." And then she groaned. "First the mower and now this."

"I'll drive you home and we'll come back later with gas."

"I can't believe I did that." She got out of the car and closed the door. "I always make sure it has gas."

"Not today."

She shook her head. "I'm not sure what's wrong with me."

"You have a lot going on in your life." He opened the passenger-side door of his truck. "Maybe having today off will help."

"Maybe."

Jay closed the door and walked around to the driver's side with a quick look up, wondering what God was thinking. He got in and started his truck. Lacey kept her face turned, staring out the passenger-side window.

He wondered if she was crying.

The front door of the house was open. Lacey sat in Jay's truck, her stomach tightening, because it didn't look right. She glanced at Jay, who had remained silent during the drive home. She hadn't had much to say, either.

What did you say to a stranger whose life you felt like you were invading?

"Do you always leave the front door of the house open?" He turned off the truck.

"Of course I don't. Something's wrong." She reached for the door handle and started to get out of the truck.

Jay's hand on her arm stopped her. "No, let me go in first."

"Don't say that." Her skin prickled with cold heat. "Don't say it like something has happened."

"Nothing has happened, but we're not taking chances."

She nodded, swallowing past the lump that lodged between her heart and her throat. Jay got out of the truck and walked up to the house. He eased up to the front door and looked inside. Then he stepped through the opening into the dark house.

Lacey waited, her heart pounding, thudding in her chest. She should have known that something like this would happen. Whatever *this* was. She didn't even know, but she knew without a doubt that something was wrong.

Jay walked back onto the porch and shook his head. He motioned her out of the truck. Lacey grabbed her Bible and got out. She walked to the front porch, not wanting to hear what she knew he would tell her.

"There's no one in here."

"Maybe she went for a walk. Or she might have gone to use your phone." Grasping, she knew she was grasping at straws.

And Jay was just being the nice guy that he was by staying, by not making accusations.

"That's possible," he finally said.

"She might have left a note, telling me where she went."

"Okay. We can look." But he didn't believe it. Lacey didn't know why that hurt, but it did. Because it felt like he didn't believe her, or trust her. She was an extension of Corry, because they had come from the same place.

She walked into the house and he followed, slower, taking more time. "I knew I should have made her go to church."

"You can't force someone."

"I know, but if I had, she'd be here and Rachel would be safe."

Lacey wouldn't feel so frantic, like some unseen clock was ticking, telling her she was nearly out of time. And she didn't know why, or what would happen when the time ran out.

"Lacey." He stood in front of the desk where she kept her bills and other paperwork. "You know she has a record, right?"

Lacey turned, and he was watching her, pretending it was a normal question. "I do know."

She wanted to ask him if he knew that *she* had a record. Did he know what she had done to put food on the table, to pay the rent to keep the roof over her younger siblings' heads? She looked away, because she didn't really want answers to those questions from him.

It was too much information, and it would let him too far into her life, and leave her open to whatever look might be in his eyes.

It might be too much like the look in Lance's eyes when he'd said he could love her no matter what. With Jay it was different; they hadn't stepped into each other's lives that way. He just happened to be here with her now.

"Lacey, do you know who she's been in contact with?"

"No." She stood in the doorway of Corry's room. The bedding was flung across the bed and dragged on the floor, and a few odds and ends of clothing were still scattered about.

Jay walked into the room, an envelope in his hand.

"She's gone. This was on the table." He handed her an envelope.

Lacey's fingers trembled as she took it from him. She ripped it and tore the paper out. Eyes watering, she read the scribbled lines, trying to make sense of misspelled words and her sister's childlike handwriting. But she got it. She crumpled the note in her hand. She got it.

"She's gone." She held out the note and Jay took it from her hand.

"Let's take a drive and see if we can find her. She couldn't have gotten far."

Optimism. Lacey had worked hard on being an optimist. She had worked hard on finding faith in hard times. She didn't know what to think about Corry leaving with the baby.

She glanced at her watch. "Jay, if they left right after I left, they could be back in St. Louis by now."

He inhaled and let it out in a sigh. "That's true. Let's go inside and we'll see if she left anything behind."

"We should call the police."

Dark brows lifted and he sort of smiled at her. "Lacey, I am the police. And unless she's committed a crime, there's no reason for going after her. She's a grown woman who left your house with her own child."

"But she can't take care of Rachel. She can barely take care of herself."

"She's an adult."

"An adult who reads and writes at a first-grade level." Lacey looked away from his compassion, his sympathy.

"Can she take care of Rachel?"

Lacey walked through the dark, cool interior of the house, her house. She kept her eyes down, thinking of what to do next. She couldn't face the empty bassinet or thoughts of Rachel with Corry.

"She can, but I don't know if she can keep her safe." Lacey spoke softly, because if she said it too loudly, would it seem harsh? "My mother and Corry make a lot of bad decisions."

"We could hotline her with family services and maybe they could intervene on behalf of the baby." Jay walked through the kitchen. He stopped at the canisters.

"What do you keep in these?"

"Sugar, flour, coffee. Normal stuff. Why?"

"This one is empty and the lid was next to it." He lifted the smallest canister.

The air left her lungs and the room felt too hot, and then too cold. Never in a million years would she have thought…

But then again, she should have. Because she knew

Corry, knew what she was capable of. She was capable of stealing from her own family.

"It wasn't coffee?" He set the canister down and replaced the lid. "Money?"

Her chest ached and her throat tightened. "I can't believe I was so stupid."

She wouldn't cry. She wouldn't be the person he pitied. She had survived worse than this, and she would survive again.

"You aren't stupid."

"I should have put it in the bank." She shook her head, looking away from Jay so she wouldn't see his compassion and he couldn't see her tears. "I put my tip money in there, and lived on my hourly wages. It was for land."

"For land?" Soft and tender, his voice soothed. He took a few steps in her direction, and she wanted to rely on the strong arms of a cowboy to hold her and tell her everything would be okay.

He wasn't offering, and she knew better.

"Yes, for land. I want a place of my own." Dreams, snatched away. "But I can start over, right? It isn't the end of the world."

"No." He stood in front of her now, tall and cowboy, with eyes that seemed to understand. "It isn't the end of the world, but it probably feels like it is."

"It feels more like I might never see my niece again. Rachel is more important than land. I don't want that baby to live the life we lived in St. Louis. I want her to have a real family and real chances."

"She'll be okay with her mother."

"No, she won't. Jay, you don't get it. You've lived here all your life, in a cocoon that sheltered you from the outside world. You don't know what it's like to always worry about who's walking through the front door and what they're going to do to you."

The words spilled out and so did the tears, coursing down her cheeks, salty on her lips. She brushed them away with her hand and shook her head when he tried to hold her.

"Don't look at me like that," she whispered, staring at the floor because she couldn't look him in the eyes. "I don't want to be someone you feel sorry for. I'd much rather you resent me for being here."

"I don't resent you."

She smiled then and wiped at her eyes. "You do, but it's nice of you to say you don't. Look, I'm fine. I survived and I have a great life here. And if you keep looking at me like that, you're going to make me cry again. I don't want to cry anymore."

"We'll find Rachel." He made it sound like a promise she could believe. She'd been promised a lot in her life.

"I hope so."

"Lacey, growing up in Gibson doesn't guarantee anything." He walked to the door. "Let's see if we can find your sister and the baby. At least now we have a reason to call the police."

The stolen money. Lacey picked up her purse and followed him out the door, still hurting over what Corry had done, and ashamed because she knew that life held no guarantees for anyone.

Not even for Jay Blackhorse.

Chapter Seven

Jay cruised past the church on Tuesday afternoon. He'd been past a couple of other times, and each time, Lacey's car had been parked out front. It was still parked out front. Maybe she'd heard from her sister.

Probably not. He didn't expect Corry to suddenly have a conscience and feel guilty for what she'd done to Lacey. He pulled into the church parking lot and parked. But he didn't get out.

Instead, he questioned why he was there. He asked God, but didn't hear a clear answer. It felt a lot like getting involved in Lacey's life, and that was the last thing he wanted to do. He didn't want involved, he didn't want tangled up. He didn't want to understand her life in St. Louis and what she'd done there.

Pastor Dan walked out of the front of the church, taking the steps two at a time, because that was just Dan. He was always in a hurry to get somewhere. And he was always smiling. Dan had a lot of joy. Joy was as contagious as someone's bad mood, but a lot easier to take. Jay got out of his truck and waited.

"Got business, or are you just here to pass the time?"

Dan stopped, still smiling, but with a curious glint in his eyes.

"Passing time." Jay reached into the truck and pulled out two plastic bags with Styrofoam containers. "I doubt she's eaten anything."

And that was the entangled part that he hadn't wanted. He'd noticed her car at the church for the last few hours, and he'd started to think that maybe she hadn't eaten. She wasn't his problem, but his mom had made her their problem. On her way out of town, Wilma had even called and asked him to make sure Lacey was okay.

"I don't think she's eaten since Sunday," Dan admitted. "She's done a lot of praying, though. I would guess that most of it's for other people, not herself. Sometimes life is that way, we can't see the trees for the forest."

Jay pushed the truck door closed. "I'm not sure I'm catching what you mean."

"It's simple, Jay. We look at life, at things that go wrong, and we just see things that went wrong, that didn't go our way. And sometimes they went wrong for the right reason, because God has a better plan."

Jay smiled. "I got dumped for a reason that I don't yet understand."

"Bingo." Pastor Dan gave him a hearty slap on the back. "You'll find Lacey in the youth room. She's mopping, so don't step on the floor. It really irks her if you step on her wet floor."

"Does she work here every week?"

"She volunteers. Our cleaning lady moved and Lacey considers this one of her ministries."

"Has anyone bothered to tell her that God doesn't require works?" He sighed, because he hadn't meant to say the words.

Pastor Dan only laughed. "It isn't about works. It's about love and the works grow from that love, and from her faith. You know that, Jay. When you've gone through what Lacey has gone through, you're a little more appreciative of a new life."

"Maybe so."

"Get that meal in there before it gets cold." Dan nodded to the bags. "Oh, any news on Corry?"

"None."

Pastor Dan shook his head. "I hate that for her."

Jay nodded and headed on up the sidewalk, carrying the meals that were still warm, and telling himself that he was doing what his mom would want him to do. He was taking care of Lacey.

He found Lacey standing in the hall outside the youth room, her hair in a dark auburn ponytail. Her skin glowed, glistening with perspiration.

She turned and smiled at him, the smile hesitant. "Have they found her?"

He shook his head, not surprised by the question. Of course her thoughts were focused on Rachel and Corry. He lifted the bags of food.

"You should eat."

"I'm not hungry."

"I am, and I don't like to eat alone." He handed her one of the bags. "We could sit outside."

"Shouldn't you be at home?"

"My mom is staying in Springfield for a few days. Dad has a pretty serious workload this week and can't make it home, so she's with him."

"You have chores to do at home."

"I'll do them when I get there." He nodded toward the door, amazed that it took so much convincing to get one woman to sit and eat with him. That was a pretty harsh blow to his ego and he'd never thought of himself as prideful.

"People will talk." She continued her objections, but she followed him out the side door to the playground and the pavilion.

"Talk about what?"

"You know, they'll talk about us. I promise you, that isn't what you want."

He sat down on the top of the picnic table and she sat next to him. "It might not be what you want."

She opened the plastic bag and pulled out the container. She lifted the lid and smiled at the club sandwich and fries. "I promise you, Jay, being seen with you could only be good for me. And thank you for this. You either made a good guess, or Jolynn made the sandwich."

"Jolynn." He opened his container. "I asked her what you liked."

She groaned and he glanced sideways. She looked heavenward and shook her head. "Jolynn, she's the main contributor to the rumor mill, bless her heart."

"We'll deal with it." He didn't want to deal with it. Lacey squirted mayo on her plate and dipped a corner of her sandwich into it before she took a bite. He pulled the onions off his burger.

"Thank you for the sandwich." She spoke after a few minutes. Jay nodded. The quiet between them had been nice. He didn't really want to admit it, not even to himself, but she was easy to be around.

"You're welcome. Tell me something, Lacey, why and how do you do it all?"

"Do it all?"

"Work doubles, go to school." He shrugged. "You're going to school, right?"

"I never graduated from high school." She turned a little pink and took another bite of sandwich.

"Okay, work, school, church, the nursing home, cleaning and nursery. Why?"

"Because I…" She looked away, the summer breeze picking up dark hair that had come loose from her ponytail. She brushed it back with nails that were painted dark pink but were chipping at the ends.

She smiled at him. "Because it makes me feel good to be a part of this community."

He didn't buy it.

"I've always tried too hard, too," he admitted. "It isn't easy, being a Blackhorse and knowing people expect a lot from you."

She choked on her last bite of sandwich. As she gasped for air, he handed her a clean napkin. She wiped her eyes and took a deep breath.

"I'm not trying to do anything."

"Okay." But she was.

He sighed and let it go, because he couldn't explain what Lacey didn't want to hear. They were fighting a battle that had already been fought and paying for sins that were already paid for. They were forgetting the grace that covered a multitude of sins.

"Jay, if you want to say something, say it. I'm really tired and not in the mood for games." She looked at him like he really had just fallen off the turnip truck. "What exactly are you trying to tell me?"

"That you don't have to work so hard to be accepted, or worry that God will kick you out of His house."

Her eyes widened and she moved away from him,

picking up her empty Styrofoam as she went. "You do know."

"Lacey, that isn't…"

She lifted a hand, a hand that shook. "I don't want to hear it. I don't want to hear what you think of my life or what I've done, or how it was okay. You don't know how I feel."

No, he didn't. He shook his head and she walked away.

Bailey answered the door on the third knock. She opened the door, eyes a little sleepy and blond hair wispy. Lacey shoved trembling hands into her pockets.

"You were sleeping."

"No, I wasn't." Bailey yawned, proof that she had been asleep. "Come in, I could use company."

"Good, because I'm looking for a place to hide."

"You've come to the right place. I'm here alone. Cody and our little angel went to a horse auction in Tulsa. They won't be back until tomorrow."

"I don't really want to fall apart in front of Cody and Meg."

"You, fall apart?" Bailey motioned her into the house that she and Cody had built earlier in the spring. They had just moved in last month.

"Me, fall apart, never." Lacey followed her friend into the kitchen and pulled out a bar stool at the island.

"Have they found Corry and Rachel?"

Lacey shook her head. She wrapped her hands around the glass of iced tea that Bailey put on the counter before she sat down across from Lacey.

"Well?"

"Jay knows."

"Knows where they are?"

"Knows about me." She slid her hands up the glass and they came away wet and cold from condensation. "I guess I knew, but I wanted to believe that only the people I wanted to tell would know."

"He won't tell anyone."

"I know he won't." Or did she? She could only remember the look on Lance's face when he learned the truth. He had been shocked and disgusted. Jay had shown pity.

She wanted to cry, because the past couldn't be undone. What she had done couldn't be forgotten. It was in black and white, for anyone to find. She had been arrested for prostitution. It had felt dirty then, and it still felt dirty.

"God forgives, Bailey, I know that. But forgetting and forgiving myself is the real trick. People are so quick to judge, and to walk away. Everyone thinks they know the story and how to fix it."

"I know." Bailey shrugged slim shoulders. "Okay, I don't know. But in a way, I do. I came home from Wyoming pregnant. It wasn't easy, and it obviously couldn't be hidden."

Lacey nodded, because she had met Bailey when Meg was just a baby. The two had become friends because they'd both felt a little lost and alone that first year of Meg's life, and the first year of Lacey's life in Gibson.

"I don't want Jay to look at me the way Lance looked at me."

"He's a different person."

"True, we're not dating and he doesn't feel like I've kept something from him. I should have been honest with Lance from the beginning."

"Maybe, but if he'd loved you, he would have taken time to understand. Just remember, Jay and Lance are two different people."

Lacey smiled, and it wasn't hard to do, not with her best friend sitting next to her. "You can give up the matchmaking, my friend. I'm not going to be the dirty sock in the Blackhorse family's clean sock drawer."

"That's the most absurd statement."

"I like a touch of absurdity from time to time. But you have to admit, it's a fitting analogy."

"It's not. And because you made such a ridiculous statement, you have to make us a salad."

"Bailey, can I really stay in Gibson if everyone finds out the truth?" Lacey looked at her friend, hoping for answers. The thought of leaving left a wound in her heart because this town really was home.

"You can't leave, Lacey. What would we do without you?"

"Make your own salad?"

"See, I'd be lost without you in my life."

Lacey hugged her friend and then hopped down from the stool. "I'll make your salad, but you have to make ranch dressing. That's what friends do for each other."

Her cell phone buzzed. Lacey pulled it out of her pocket and groaned. "It's Jay."

"Answer it."

"I don't want to talk to him. He can leave a voice mail."

Bailey grabbed the phone and flipped it open. "Hi, Jay."

She talked for a minute and then handed the phone to Lacey. She wasn't smiling, and Lacey's heart sank with dread.

"Jay?"

"Lacey, Corry is in Springfield."

"Okay. Where in Springfield? What about Rachel? Are they okay?"

"I'm afraid that's all the news that I have. They haven't caught them."

"Caught them?" She took shallow breaths and sat back down on the stool. "What does that mean?"

"She and her boyfriend robbed a convenience store. Lacey, they had a gun."

"Rachel?"

"I'm sure she's still with them."

Lacey closed her eyes, fighting fear, fighting thoughts that told her that Rachel would be hurt, or worse. She didn't want to think about what this meant for her sister. "They don't know for sure?"

"They don't. Do you want me to come and get you? If you can't drive, I can come over there."

She could drive, of course she could. Her hands shook and she didn't want to think, to let it sink in.

"I can drive myself home. Will you call if you hear something?"

"You know I will."

"Okay." She sobbed a little, not wanting him to hear. "Jay, thank you."

"You're welcome. And I'm sorry."

She closed her phone and slipped it into her pocket. Bailey's hand was on her shoulder. "It'll be okay."

"I don't know how."

"Let Jay drive you home." Bailey sat down across from her, their salads forgotten.

"No, I'm fine. You need to eat. Little Cody Junior can't go without food."

"I'll eat, but you need to let friends help you through

this. Lacey, you've always been there for me. Let me be here for you. Let Jay be a friend."

Jay, a friend? It felt like a mismatched shoe. It didn't fit. It was a little tight. A little uncomfortable.

Jay hung up from the call to Lacey and concentrated on driving, on not getting distracted. As he pulled up to the barn, he noticed his parents on the porch. They were home. He hadn't expected that.

His dad greeted him as he got out of the truck.

"I wondered if you were coming home any time soon." Bill Blackhorse smiled and winked, talking the way they had talked to one another a dozen years ago.

"Did you think I would pull a stunt and miss curfew?" Jay smiled back.

"Nah, not really. But as we came through town we saw your truck and Lacey's car at the church."

"I was just doing what Mom asked, making sure Lacey was okay."

"Lacey is a wonderful young woman."

So that's the way this was going. Not that Jay was surprised. His dad had introduced him to Cindy, too.

"Dad, we're neighbors, maybe friends, nothing more."

His dad patted him on the back and they walked into the barn together. "Jay, it's okay to fall in love again."

"Is it, Dad?" Jay pulled his saddle out of the tack room. "I need to work that black mare."

"Working the black mare isn't going to undo what's happening to you. You're letting go. I guess maybe you feel guilty."

Jay shrugged. He faced his dad, and it wasn't comfortable. He wanted to let it go, the way they'd been letting it go for years now.

"Dad, I can't forget Jamie. I can't forget that I loved her."

"No one said you had to forget. But let someone else in. That's all I'm saying."

Jay walked out the back of the barn. At the gate he whistled and the horses, ten of them grazing a few hundred feet away, turned to look at him. A few went back to grazing. He whistled again and they headed in his direction.

"What you're saying is that I should let Lacey in." Jay smiled, glancing at his dad in time to catch a shrug and a little bit of a sheepish look. "Dad, you can't push us together. From what I hear, Lacey is still getting over Lance. I still have a wedding ring in my dresser drawer."

"I'm asking you to pray." Bill reached out to pet his favorite gray mare. "I'm asking you to let God heal your heart. Maybe that's why you came home. Time to face what happened and move forward."

"I think I am moving forward." Time to let go of the girl he loved? He didn't know if he could.

The black mare, Duckie, a strange name for a horse, was at the fence. Jay slid the halter over her head and clipped on the lead rope.

His dad opened the gate and Jay led the mare through, moving fast to keep the other horses from following. Bill closed the gate behind him. A car door closed. Jay led the horse to the barn and tied her.

Lacey walked through the doors, her face a dark silhouette with the setting sun behind her. He heard his dad behind him.

"I'm going to the house." Bill patted him on the shoulder as he walked away, greeting Lacey with a hug.

"I'm sorry. I should have called." Lacey looked a little

lost, like she wasn't sure. She stood a few feet from him, from the mare. "She's beautiful."

"You don't have to call." He looked over the mare's neck at the woman leaning against the wall. "You okay?"

"I'm fine. I was on my way home from Bailey's and I realized I really didn't want to go home. There's no one there."

"The police will find her, Lacey."

"And take her to jail."

"They won't take Rachel to jail."

She reached to slide her hand down the neck of the mare. Jay slid the saddle pad into place and then lowered the saddle onto the mare's back. The mare turned to look at him, but she stood still.

"Do you want to ride her?" He tightened the girth strap and knotted it.

"Could I?"

"I think so. I'll show you how to rope."

"No way!"

He smiled and it felt really good. "Yeah way!"

"I'd love it."

It would keep both of their minds off what they didn't want to think about. He didn't want to think about letting go of Jamie. She didn't want to think about her little sister going to jail.

"Come on, we'll take her out to the arena." He led the horse and Lacey walked a short distance away. "You do know how to ride, right?"

"Of course. You can't live around here for six years and not know how to ride."

He laughed because she bristled like an angry cat.

"Let me ride her first and then she's all yours."

Chapter Eight

Lacey felt like a rodeo queen on the back of the black mare. The horse was gaited, so her trot was smooth and easy. Jay stood on the outside of the arena. She kept her eyes focused on the point between the mare's ears and tried not to look at him.

But she did look at him. He smiled and pushed his hat back, crossing his arms over the top rail of the vinyl fence of the arena.

"Bring her over here." He opened the gate and walked through, a rope in his hand. "Here you go."

"You really think I can do this?"

"Why couldn't you?"

"I'm clumsy and uncoordinated."

He laughed again and she wanted him to laugh like that all the time. When he laughed she forgot that her sister was in the biggest trouble of her life, her niece was in danger…no, maybe she didn't forget. It distracted her for a few minutes and the knots in her stomach relaxed a little, but she couldn't forget.

He put the rope in her hand, his hand closing over hers. His hands were strong and warm. He looked up, like that touch meant something, and she couldn't look away, not this time.

She realized she had one more problem she was going to have to deal with: Jay. Because his smile did something to her heart, shifting what had been numb and cold and for a moment making her believe in something special.

"Here you go." His voice was a little quiet and rough and she wondered if he felt it, too. "Take it like this and make easy loops. Don't work it too hard. You have to look at your target. That's what works for me." He nodded to the horns on a post. "Give it a try and remember, she's going to do some of the work. She knows what to do. Don't panic."

"I won't." If only she could breathe. Breathing would be helpful.

"Relax."

"Okay." She wished. But relaxing was probably going to happen when she managed to rope those horns. Never.

She rode twenty feet out from the target and stopped. The mare responded to her leg pressure; just a squeeze and she came to a halt. Amazing.

"You can get a little farther away," Jay encouraged.

"Umm, no." Lacey smiled and lifted her arm. "I thought it would be easier, and lighter."

"Come on, Lacey, cowgirl up." He winked.

"Okay, here we go." She did it the way she'd seen it in the movies and at rodeos, raising her arm and swinging the rope. It seemed to fly, to soar, and then it dropped.

She never expected it to drop on the mare's head.

But it did. And the mare didn't appreciate it. She sidestepped and jumped back. Lacey fell to the side a little and she felt the horse hunch beneath her, like something about to explode. Lacey had no intention of getting thrown, so she jumped. As she flew through the air, she knew she was hitting the ground face first.

She hit the ground with a brain-jarring thud that rattled her teeth. The hard impact of the ground socked her in the gut and knocked the wind out of her. She tried to draw in a breath and couldn't.

"Lacey, are you okay?" Jay was at her side, kneeling and not hiding his smile the way she would have liked.

"Can't breathe," she whispered.

His smile dissolved. "Does anything feel broken?"

She glared. "Everything."

"Let me help you sit up and you need to take slow, easy breaths. It knocked the wind out of you, but I think you're okay."

"Easy for you to say."

Lacey rolled over and looked up at the sky, and then at Jay. He sat back on his heels and his lips quivered. Lacey laughed a little, but her head hurt and so did her back. Her whole body hurt.

"I don't think I did it." She leaned back again, thinking maybe she'd stay on the ground.

"I think maybe you're not going to be George Strait anytime soon."

"He does rope, doesn't he?"

"Yep."

"I stink. Tell Duckie I'm sorry."

Jay's smile dissolved. "Come on, let me help you up. You sound a little loopy and I want to make sure you're okay."

"I don't sound loopy. I'm fine." She eased herself to a sitting position, aware of his arm around her back and that cinnamon-gum scent.

If she turned he would be close, really close. And

being near him upset her balance more than the fall she'd taken.

"You're not fine. That was a hard spill."

"Help me up." She stood, slow and steady, and a little sore. "Nothing broke."

"Jay, is she okay?" Bill stood at the gate. Lacey smiled at Jay's dad and saluted.

"She's fine." Lacey answered. "My pride is hurt. I really thought roping would be easy."

"Come on out here so we can take a look at you."

Jay's arm was around her, holding her close like she mattered. "Why in the world did you jump?" he asked.

"I thought it would be better than being thrown."

Jay and his dad both laughed. Jay shook his head. "Did you really?"

"Yes, I really did. And I was wrong. I can admit that."

"Next time grip her with your legs and hold steady on the reins. She spooked, but she wasn't going to throw you."

"I'll remember that. Stay on horse, don't try to jump. Got it."

Jay's arm tightened around her waist and he pulled her against his side. "Lacey, I haven't smiled…"

And then he was quiet and Lacey didn't know why he didn't smile. But she was glad it was time to go home.

Lacey's phone rang late the next afternoon. She was stiff from the fall and from working all day. As she reached for the phone she grimaced a little. Bailey was sitting at the dining room table and she laughed. But she had promised not to mention the fall again.

"Lacey, they've got Corry in custody."

Lacey closed her eyes. "Okay. What now?"

"I'll pick you up and take you to Springfield. Family Services has Rachel."

"Will they let me have her?"

"We're making phone calls." Jay paused. "It'll work out. I'll be down there in a few minutes."

Lacey hung up and then turned to Bailey. "They have her in custody."

"Jay's taking you to Springfield?"

"He is." Lacey tossed her cell phone in her purse. "I'm scared to death."

"Don't be. This is going to work out. Call me when you get home, so I know you're okay."

Lacey nodded. "I'll call."

Five minutes later Jay's black truck pulled up in front of the house. Lacey had popped a few ibuprofen and she met him at the front door. He stepped out of the truck, leaving his hat behind.

He was the one there for her.

No, not for her. She pushed that thought away, because it was dangerous to her heart. That thought didn't even belong. It was like a kid's activity book, *one of these things doesn't belong.* The thing that didn't belong was Jay Blackhorse in her life.

This was about Corry in trouble, the baby and the police. Jay wasn't in her life. He was…

She wasn't sure and now wasn't the time to deal with suspicion, worrying that he had other motives for helping. She didn't want to get caught up in questions, prodding her to ask why he was involved in her life and what he wanted.

"Call me." Bailey stood behind her. "And stop looking like the sky is falling. That isn't you, Lacey. You're my sunshine friend, not a dark cloud."

Lacey turned and smiled at Bailey, remembering a time when they were on opposite sides of this fence and Lacey had been the optimist. "You're right."

"Ready to go?" Jay stood in her yard, Wrangler jeans, a button-down shirt and his puka-shell necklace. She smiled, because she couldn't help herself. She liked that he had these two sides of his personality.

"I'm ready to go." She smiled when Bailey kissed her cheek. "Thanks, Bay. You mean the world to me."

"Ditto, chick."

Bailey walked down the steps, punching Jay a little on the arm. "Take care of her. She's my best friend."

"Will do." He shifted a little and looked down, his cheeks red.

Lacey pulled her door closed and twisted the knob to make sure it was locked. And then she walked across the lawn with Jay.

It felt worse than a first date.

It was anything but.

"Climb in." Jay opened the passenger-side door and she obeyed, really not seeing the running board, and then falling over it. A strong hand caught her arm from behind and held her steady.

"Very graceful." He said it with a smile that she could hear. "You're two for nothing on the accident scale."

Lacey turned, frowning, and he was still smiling, a smile that showed dazzling teeth and the tiniest dimple in his chin.

"Thanks." She smiled back.

"You're welcome. Do you need help?"

He was teasing and that helped, for a second she forgot the case of nerves that was twisting her insides.

"I'm fine, and you can let go now." She slid into the seat, aware of the place his hand had rested on her arm.

The truck was still running and Casting Crowns played on the CD player, songs of worship, loud and vibrant. She fastened her seatbelt and leaned back, waiting for him to get in. He did, bringing with him that freshly showered and spicy-cologne scent of his.

"Lacey, you have to stop thinking I'm the enemy." He reached to turn the music down. "I'm sorry for knowing about you, about…"

"My record." She looked out the window, watching farm-land slip past them. Gentle hills, green fields, a few houses and barns. Not St. Louis, city streets and crowded neighborhoods of people getting by the best way they knew how. Some did better than others.

Lacey's family had been one of the families not making it at all. Never any security or hope, just scraping and trying to survive.

"We've all done things." Jay tried, she knew he really tried. He didn't get it. He couldn't.

"What have you done?" She turned away from the window to look at him. "Well?"

He didn't answer, but he smiled a little smile, keeping his eyes on the road ahead of them. Both hands on the wheel in driver's-ed position. He did everything by the book.

"Did you maybe sneak behind the barn and smoke once, years ago? It made you choke, might have made you sick, and you never tried it again?"

He laughed. "Were you watching?"

"No, but I can picture your skinny little self out there with a friend, sneaking around with your contraband, your little hearts racing, hoping you didn't get caught."

He laughed, and Lacey laughed, too. And it felt good. It felt like a moment of normal in a crazy, mixed-up world. A world that for a time had been on its axis, turning smoothly.

"You picture me as a skinny little kid, huh?"

"You weren't?"

"I was."

"I know. Your mom showed me pictures."

He groaned at that and shook his head. "Of course she did. So you see, we've all done things."

He didn't understand feeling dirty. He didn't know what it meant to walk down the aisle of the Gibson Community Church, wondering if it would be like the other times she had gone to church, wanting to be loved and walking out lonelier than ever.

She closed her eyes, remembering that first week in Gibson, when she'd gone to church and she had gone forward, looking for love. And for the first time, finding it. She found perfect love, and redemption. She found forgiveness.

"Do you know what I learned when I moved to Gibson?" She looked at him and he shook his head, glancing her way only for a second.

"No, what?"

"That the love I had been looking for wasn't real love. I had tried church quite a few times over the years, but I'd had the wrong idea and each time I went, I left unhappy."

"Okay." He waited. She liked that he really listened. He got that from his mom.

"I wanted love from the people in those churches. And when I didn't get the love I needed from them, I left. Not that some of them didn't reach out to me, but they couldn't give me what I needed."

"Forgiveness?"

"Exactly. I needed God's love, and I craved His love, I just didn't know it."

"I know."

"Really?"

He nodded. "I've had my angry moments with God and a few years of wild rebellion because I thought he'd let me down."

"You really were a bad boy?"

"I was."

Lacey looked away, because she didn't know how to go farther with the conversation. She didn't know how to accept that Jay could actually understand her.

They were fifteen miles from Springfield. Jay turned the radio up a few notches and let the conversation go. Lacey was staring out the window. A quick glance and he could see her reflection in the glass, big dark eyes and a mouth that smiled often. But she wasn't smiling. She wasn't crying, either.

She reminded him of a song, a song about a young woman seeking love. And she found it at the cross. Lacey was that song.

"I guess I can't bail her out." She spoke as they drove through the city.

"If you have the money. I don't know how much her bail will be."

"Since she stole my savings, I guess she'll have to spend her time in jail."

"It might do her some good." He didn't want to be harsh. He also didn't want to see Lacey go through this exact same scenario again. And he thought she would if her sister was released.

"I know." Still no tears. "But the baby. I really don't like to think about Rachel being taken from her mother."

"It isn't always the worst thing for a kid." He didn't know what else to say. They'd said pretty much everything on the drive to town. "Lacey, is being with Corry the best thing for Rachel?"

She didn't answer for a long time. Finally she shook her head, but she was still looking out the passenger-side window. "No, it isn't."

He slowed and pulled into a parking lot. "We're here. You can probably see your sister for a few minutes. And then we'll see if we can't get you custody of Rachel."

She turned away from the window, her brown eyes wide. Troubled. "Do you think they won't let me have her?"

"I think they will, but you know that isn't up to me."

"I know."

He parked and neither of them moved to get out. Lacey stared at the police station. Her eyes were a little misty but she didn't cry.

"Okay, let's go." She got out of the truck and he followed.

"Before I picked you up I had one of our county social workers call the family services workers up here. I don't know if that will help, but we can hope."

They walked side by side. Jay's shoulder brushed Lacey's and his fingers touched hers, for only a second. He wondered about holding her hand, but didn't. She didn't need that from him. He didn't believe that she wanted it.

He pulled his hand back and pulled a pack of gum out of his pocket. "Would you like a piece?"

"Please." She took it from him, unwrapping it as they walked. "I don't want to do this."

"It won't be easy."

"Thanks, that makes me feel better."

"Anything to help." He slid the gum back into his pocket. "She's going to try and make you feel guilty."

"It wouldn't be the first time."

"Remember, you haven't done anything wrong."

"Maybe I did." Her voice was soft.

Jay opened the door and she stepped in ahead of him. He took off his hat and breathed in cool air, a sharp contrast from the heat outside. "How did you do anything wrong?"

"I could have taken her with me when I left St. Louis. She might not be going through this." She walked next to him again, her shoes a little squeaky on the tile floor and his boots clicking. "She was about sixteen when I left. She could have been saved."

"You were just a kid." He pointed down the hall. "What were you, about twenty-one or two when you moved to Gibson?"

"Twenty-two."

"You can't keep looking back at all of the things you could have done differently." He stopped at a window and smiled at the woman behind the glass. "We're here to see Corry Gould."

"Oh, yes, just a minute please." She slid the glass closed and talked on the phone. She opened it again and smiled. "Have a seat."

Lacey crossed the room and stood, glancing out the window and not really seeing the view of the city. She sat down next to Jay. The plastic chairs placed them shoulder to shoulder. After a few minutes she got up and walked across the room to look at magazines hanging in a case on the wall.

The door opened. Lacey turned, meeting Jay's gaze first, and then her attention fell on the woman walking through the door. And Rachel.

Lacey choked a little, dropping a magazine back into the rack and hurrying to the woman that held her baby niece. Only a few days, but it had seemed like forever.

"She's a little bit sick." The lady handed Rachel over. "I'm Gwenda Price."

"Thank you, Ms. Price. Thank you so much." Lacey lifted Rachel and held her against her shoulder, feeling the baby's warm, feverish skin. "Is she okay?"

"She probably needs to see a doctor. Her temp is a little high and she's stuffy."

"Okay." Lacey looked up, her gaze locking with Jay's, as it hit home. "I get to take her?"

"We need to fill out some paperwork, and we'll have one of the case workers in your area do a home study."

"What about my sister?" Lacey shifted the baby, who slept through all of the movement.

"I can't answer that question." Ms. Price smiled a little smile. "I'm just here to deliver the baby."

Lacey turned to Jay. He had moved to the window and was speaking in quiet tones to the lady behind the glass. His words didn't carry. Lacey walked a little closer and he turned away from the window, shaking his head.

"Corry doesn't want to see you." He slipped an arm around her waist and she didn't pull away. The comfort of his touch was unexpected. Her need for it, more unexpected. Rachel was cuddled close, smelling clean and powdery, and Jay was strong, his arms hard muscle and able to hold them both.

"What do I do?"

"I think you should concentrate on your niece." He

touched Rachel's cheek. "Take her home and do your best for her. Give her a chance. Corry might come around, if she gets lonely enough."

"I can't do this." Lacey bit down on her lip, her eyes getting misty as she stared at the tiny little girl, now dependent on her for everything. Everything.

"You *can* do this."

"I don't know."

"You do and so do I." Jay moved his arm from her waist and pulled back. He looked down at her, his brown eyes kind and gentle, encouraging her with a smile.

He touched Rachel's hand and little fingers wrapped tight around his thumb. He glanced back up at Lacey and something soft and compelling sparked between them. It had to be her imagination, because Jay was a Blackhorse, and she was the girl from St. Louis that had wandered into town one day.

Jay could hold her close and show compassion. That didn't make him a part of her life. It didn't even make him a friend.

"You can do this, Lacey." He spoke softly.

"I can." She kissed the pink and ivory cheek of her baby niece. "I can."

"You'll have a lot of help. The entire town of Gibson will be behind you."

"Yes, I know."

"We'll need to spend a few minutes talking," Ms. Price reminded, looking at her watch as she spoke. "If you'll come with me."

"Oh, of course." Lacey followed her into a small room, white walls with white tables and bright lights. She glanced back at the door closing behind her. Six, almost seven years in Gibson, and the memories returned full force.

If they'd meant for the room to put someone on the defensive, it worked.

Lacey sat down in the chair Ms. Price indicated, keeping the baby close and praying they wouldn't look at her record and take the baby away. What would she do if she couldn't keep Rachel?

The windows were high on the wall. Ms. Price was between her and the door. Lacey inhaled the cold air of the room, the strong scent of the cleaners used to keep it so white.

"Relax, Lacey, we're not here about you, we're here about your niece. At the moment, you are the person most suited for guardianship." Ms. Price looked over the papers in her folder, glasses perched on the end of her nose. She looked up, smiling. "We would much rather keep the child with a relative. It's easier on them if they're with someone like you, someone familiar, who can provide what they need."

"I can provide. I'll do whatever I can for her."

"Where do you work?"

Lacey gave all of her information. Job, address, income, and even that she was going to school to get her high school diploma. Ms. Price smiled again, her hands sparkling with too many rings and red-painted nails.

"Lacey, you're not on trial." Ms. Price put the paperwork down. "But more than likely we'll have to move toward permanent guardianship if your sister is found guilty. That'll require a court hearing."

"I don't mind." Lacey's heart thumped against her ribs and her lungs felt tight in her chest. "Do I need a lawyer?"

"Not yet. But I would like to know who will be watching Rachel when you're at work."

She hadn't thought that far ahead. "I'm not sure. I mean, I know that I can find someone."

"Is there a day care in Gibson?"

"Yes, there is."

Could she afford it? That was the other problem. All money she'd saved was now gone. She smiled, at Ms. Price, and then at her niece.

"It'll work out, Lacey. There are programs to help you with child care, even with formula and other things you might need. This doesn't have to be a huge burden."

"Thank you. I just want her to have stability."

"That's what we want for her as well. So, you take her home tonight and tomorrow we'll visit with your county workers." Ms. Price stood up. "Do you have everything you need?"

Lacey held Rachel tight and thought of all the things she didn't have, all the things she needed. And she smiled because she had the most important thing. She had her niece.

"We're good."

Chapter Nine

"I don't know how I'll do this." Lacey buckled the baby into the car seat in Jay's truck. He started the truck but didn't say anything. "How can I be the best person for her?"

"Lacey, I can't think of anyone better to take care of her."

She nodded but couldn't look at him, because they both knew what a stretch those words of comfort were. She buckled herself into the passenger side of the truck.

"I need to get medicine for her. I don't know what to give her, though."

"I'll call my dad."

"Thank you."

She touched her niece's tiny hand, warm from the fever. Jay spoke into his cell phone and then he was talking to his dad. She dug around in her purse for paper to write down instructions when he gave them to her.

"Thanks, Dad."

He ended the call and she wondered what it was like, having people to rely on. She brushed aside the thought that could only bring her down. Besides, she had people.

She had Bailey, Jolynn and other friends in Gibson that she counted on.

The one thing she didn't have was family that she counted on. No real blood ties that she could call on in an emergency. But Corry had Lacey, and so did Rachel. That was the change Lacey had made in her family. She'd given them someone to call.

She glanced sideways, catching the shadowed profile of the man sitting next to her. It was dark and streetlights glowed orange as they drove through Springfield. And he was the one who had been there for her. She hadn't even had to ask.

"Thank you." She smiled when he glanced at her, his brows raised, a question in his eyes.

"What?"

"For taking me to Springfield. Thank you for this."

"I didn't do anything."

It was that easy for him to shrug off the fact that he'd done something good for her. "You don't get it, do you? I wouldn't have her if you hadn't stepped in. I'm sure they wouldn't have just handed her over to me, not without you backing me up."

He was a Blackhorse. A name did count for something. Good character counted, too. A part of her remembered that she had walked away from her old life and that she'd made the best of her second chance.

Some people change. She thought of the words of a song that sometimes made her cry, because she saw herself in the hollow lives of the people in the words, people at the end of their ropes, hopeless. And then full of hope, knowing that life could be better, they could change. It started on their knees, reaching up to God.

"Lacey, stop being so hard on yourself."

"I guess maybe you're right."

"Of course I'm right." A quick glance in her direction and then his attention went back to the road. "Listen, I haven't walked the straight line my entire life. I know what it's like to live with regrets."

"Really?"

"If you don't already know them, I'm not going to share my sad stories with you. I think life has too many good moments that we miss if we're constantly looking back, thinking about what went wrong."

"So, I'm not the town optimist, you are?"

"If optimism is faith, then I'm pretty optimistic." He pulled into a pharmacy. "If you give me that list, I'll go in and get what you need."

"I can do it."

He was already opening the door. "Let me. I'd rather you stay with the baby."

She remembered that he didn't like to hold babies. He was afraid of them, of their size and his big hands and awkwardness with them. She gave him the list and watched as he walked across the lighted parking lot, long strides, confident.

Rachel cried, eyes blinking and glazed. Lacey spoke to her, stroking her cheek and leaning to kiss her brow. The baby quieted, but her breathing was raspy. Lacey knew how to feed a baby. She knew how to change one.

But a sick baby? This was new territory and her confidence felt like an empty place inside her.

Jay walked across the parking lot, the bottles of fever reducer in a bag with a few chocolate bars. Because he knew one thing about women; chocolate made everything better. He remembered back to chocolate peanut butter fudge made by his mother and Jamie.

He opened the door of the truck, still fighting to let go of memories, and handed the bag to Lacey. When she smiled, he knew he'd done the right thing. He couldn't take it back.

"How is she?" The baby was restless in the seat next to him. He glanced down, smiling at the little girl, at the pretty yellow dress the social worker had dressed her in.

"I'm not sure. I mean, it's probably just a virus, right?"

"I'm not the doctor in the family." He sighed, because those words didn't comfort. "Dad said to take her home, keep her fever down and if you can't keep it down, she should go to the emergency room or urgent care."

"Okay, that does help." She chewed on her bottom lip and looked less than confident. "So, you didn't want to go into the family business?"

"Nope, the medical field wasn't the place for me. Linda is a nurse. Chad is in the navy because he wants to get his medical degree that way."

"It wasn't the thing for you?" Lacey wasn't letting go, he knew she wouldn't. He smiled, because she was tenacious.

"No, it wasn't the thing for me."

"What was the thing for you?"

"I have a counseling degree." He shifted gears, deciding how far to let her into his life. Not far. He didn't want her taking up spaces that were comfortably empty. "I went to the police academy after I finished college."

Her eyes widened a little. He caught the look before he turned his attention back to the road. "Surprised?"

"No, not really."

The tires hummed on the pavement and the road that

wound through the country was dark except for the white beams of his headlights and the occasional security light illuminating a farmhouse.

Lacey remained quiet in the seat next to him.

When he pulled up to her house, she didn't move. He turned the engine off and looked at her in the dim light of the truck. Her eyes were closed and her head leaned against the window.

"Lacey."

She jumped a little, rubbed a hand across her eyes and turned to look at him. She smiled a little, embarrassment flitting across her face. "Sorry about that."

"No need to be sorry. You're probably going to need the sleep. What time do you go to work in the morning?"

She groaned and looked at the clock on the dash. "Too early. Six a.m."

"You're going to be tired."

"Yep. But the bigger problem is what will I do with the baby? It's a little late to call around and find a sitter."

"I have to work tomorrow." He didn't know what else to say. He couldn't watch a baby. He wouldn't know the first thing to do with Rachel.

Lacey's soft laughter answered him. She shook her head as she unhooked the infant seat from his truck. "Jay, don't worry, I won't dump the baby on you. I have a feeling that wouldn't be good for either of you. Since she's sick, I'll probably call Jolynn and take tomorrow off. She's probably still up watching TV."

"A day off wouldn't hurt you."

"No, probably not." But he saw her look away, and he knew she was thinking of the money that Corry took. Money she would never get back.

"Let me help you get her inside." He took the infant seat, snapping the handle up.

"You don't have to."

"In a hurry to get rid of me?" He winked as he got out of the truck, and he knew that empty spaces were filling up with this woman, and a baby.

The two were pulling him in. Without meaning to, they were involving him in their lives. He tried to think back, to three years with Cindy and never feeling as if she was really a part of his life.

Because he hadn't really let himself be in hers. He'd kept the empty spaces empty, filled only with old memories that were fading to glimpses of a smile, a soft touch, a scent that brought it all back.

"Jay, are you with me?" Lacey stood next to him, the diaper bag over her shoulder and the bag from the pharmacy in her hand.

"I am." But he wasn't, not really. He smiled and she nodded, letting it go.

"I asked if you wanted a cup of coffee." She swallowed and he wondered about the flicker of doubt, the shadows of what looked like fear in her eyes.

Lacey had empty spaces, too. He had thought of her as the person taking on the world, alone and strong. That was before he'd really known her, before he'd seen beneath the surface.

"I should go." He waited for her to open the front door. She didn't respond.

She opened the door and walked through ahead of him, flipping on lights as she went. It was muggy because the air was turned down. She adjusted the setting on the AC unit and turned back around, her smile, her confidence in place.

He couldn't stay.

She was looking for someone to lean on, to be strong for her. That wasn't him. Not in this house. He'd gone as far as he could, done as much as his heart would allow for tonight.

He realized it was a step forward, in forgetting. A small step, but in his heart he knew that it mattered.

He put the baby down on the couch and Lacey unbuckled her, pulling her from the seat and holding her close. She had given her medicine in the truck. He watched as she kissed the child's cheek, closing her eyes as she held the baby against her.

"Has her fever gone down?"

Lacey nodded. "I think so."

"If you need anything…"

Another Lacey smile, too bright and too confident. "We're fine. And, Jay, I really do appreciate what you did today."

He nodded and walked to the door, Lacey with the baby behind him. "I'll see you tomorrow."

"You don't have to."

"I know that."

He was on the porch and she stood in the doorway, the soft glow of lamplight behind her. And he had a strange urge to lean and kiss her. He took a step back, said goodbye and walked away.

It was much easier that way. Easier to walk away than to get involved and then have someone leave.

Lacey woke as dawn broke across the eastern horizon. She had called Jolynn the previous night and gotten the day off. And more time if she needed it, Jolynn had said. Lacey appreciated it, but she couldn't take more time off.

She had today to take care of details. First off, a sitter. And of course, the meeting with Family Services.

She wanted to go back to sleep and put it all off. Maybe another hour of sleep? The baby cried a little and that question was answered. Lacey sat up and looked in the bassinet. Rachel's eyes were open, but watery, and her cheeks were pink, too pink. Lacey touched the baby's face and then leaned to kiss her forehead, the way she'd watched Wilma do in the nursery at church.

"Sweetie, you're burning up." She picked the baby up and walked into the kitchen, where she'd left the medicine.

The chocolate bars were on the counter. Her heart lifted a little, because the gesture had been kind and Jay didn't have to be kind to her. She felt a sharp jab to her conscience, because she had doubted his motives, wondering what he was after when he'd stepped in to help.

Because she had known too many people who only helped when they thought they'd get something in return. Those days were so far in her past, it hurt that the old insecurities sometimes sneaked back in.

She opened the medicine bottle and squeezed the rubber end of the dropper to get the right amount of medicine.

"Okay, Rachel, my dear, time for medicine and then we'll take your temperature." She held the baby in the crook of her arm and squeezed the pink liquid into the tiny mouth.

Rachel fussed, but it was a weak attempt. No smile, no baby grin, no hand reaching for Lacey's hair. "Please God, don't let her be sick."

Lacey lifted her niece and carried her to the living room. She set her down on the couch to take her temperature. And she was right, the fever was high. It hurt, the feeling that she couldn't do anything. She looked at her watch. She'd give the medicine thirty minutes to work.

It was a long thirty minutes. When Lacey took Rachel's temperature the second time, it was higher than the first.

"Baby, baby, what do we do now?" She looked at her watch again, and then picked her niece up. "A damp cloth. We'll try that."

Lacey held a hand towel under lukewarm water and then wrung it out. She carried the baby back into the living room and wiped her bare back and belly. Rachel cried, weak and pitiful.

And then her body stiffened. Lacey froze as her little niece convulsed, her body jerking, her eyes rolling. "No. Rachel, no."

She grabbed the phone and with fingers that shook, dialed 911. Rachel stopped convulsing. Lacey picked her up and held her close, crying silent tears and her heart aching. She couldn't do anything. She was powerless.

And she felt like she was eighteen again, and unable to change her life, the lives of her siblings. Powerless.

"911, what is your emergency?"

"My niece is two months old and she's having seizures."

"Has she had seizures before?"

"No, she has a high fever. I gave her fever reducers, but her temperature is going up."

"What is her condition now?"

"She's sleeping."

"I have a unit on the way and first responders should be there in less than five minutes."

Lacey nodded wordlessly and hung up. She looked

at the phone, not sure if the operator had ended the call. She couldn't think about the call, only about her niece.

Rachel slept against her, hot from fever and motionless. But breathing. Lacey heard the sirens of first responders, the community volunteers that always arrived before an ambulance could reach them in the country. She walked to the door, seeing Jay's truck behind the emergency vehicle.

She breathed in deep, her heart letting go of the tightness, just a little. She unlocked the door as the first responders hurried toward the house.

And Jay. Wilma was with him. Lacey's body shook in a sob that she hadn't expected, relief hitting her hard, because she did have people who would come to her aid. She had people.

"What happened?" Jay walked through the door, in his uniform, his jaw set. Wilma took hold of his arm and he breathed in, deep, letting go. And Lacey didn't understand.

The first responder took Rachel from her arms and held her, using a stethoscope to listen to the baby's chest. The other first responder radioed directions to the ambulance. Lacey waited, her body hot and cold, fear holding tight to her heart.

Wilma wrapped a motherly arm around her. "It'll be okay. Now, tell us what happened."

"She has a fever, and I thought it was a virus." She shrugged and let Wilma pull her close. "I thought you were in Springfield?"

"We came home last night. We hadn't planned to, but…" Wilma watched the baby in the arms of the first responder. "Maybe God wanted us at home."

God had known that Lacey would need them.

"She had a convulsion?" The first responder asked. "Her fever is still high. Did you give her something?"

Lacey nodded. "I have it in the kitchen. Do you need it?"

"The amount and time you gave it to her."

Jay stood to the side, motionless, watching the baby. The words of the first responder brought him back to life. "I'll get the medicine."

The ambulance pulling up in front of the house brought a new fear, a new moment of reality. Lacey watched as the paramedics rushed up the steps and Wilma motioned them inside. And then it was a blur of activity, of monitoring the baby and whispered conversations.

"We're going to transport her to Springfield," the paramedic explained. "Do you want to ride with us?"

Lacey nodded. "Please."

Wilma patted her arm and Lacey looked past her, to Jay. He looked away, and she didn't understand. But Wilma took over. "You go, Lacey. I'll follow in my car so I can bring you home."

Jay glanced at his watch and frowned. "I have to be on duty in thirty minutes. I'm sorry…"

This is what distance felt like. She knew this moment, and she couldn't think about it, or why it was happening.

"Don't be. I know you have to go to work. I don't expect…" Lacey let go of the words that would have been harsh and she hadn't meant because she was just glad that he was there at that moment. "You don't have to go with us. We'll be fine."

"Of course we will." Wilma smiled, a little too brightly, a little too big. "Go, Lacey, and don't forget that I'm praying. It's a fever. Sometimes babies have seizures when their temperature gets too high."

"Okay." Lacey breathed in deep, the first deep breath she'd taken in thirty minutes and let it out. She relaxed a little. "I'll see you at the hospital."

Wilma nodded and Lacey followed the paramedics and her tiny niece, just a baby and already going through so much. And Lacey had wanted to change that. She had wanted to make things better for Rachel. She didn't want her niece to grow up in a world that was always chaotic, always full of doubts and questions.

Like her own childhood. Lacey climbed into the back of the ambulance and sat where they told her to sit. She tried to push aside thoughts of being a little girl, of fear in the darkness of her bedroom, her sister and brother cuddled against her sides.

Her years in Gibson had started a healing process. It began with faith, and forgiving. But healing didn't mean forgetting.

But maybe forgetting wasn't necessary. The memories of her childhood provided a backdrop, a place to begin the changes that would make life better. She knew who she didn't want to be.

And she knew what she didn't want for her niece.

As the ambulance pulled away, she saw Wilma in her car, and Jay standing next to his truck, watching them leave.

Chapter Ten

Jay stepped onto the hospital elevator and rode up in silence, people around him talking in quiet tones. One lady laughed at something the man standing next to her said. And Jay couldn't smile, not when he remembered too clearly a trip in this same elevator.

The door slid open. He walked onto the pediatric floor, much the same, but changed. There were murals on the walls now. The bright colors depicted children playing in a park. It was the best the hospital could do for the patients who were here, who couldn't go outside.

They could watch painted children playing in a painted park. They could solve puzzles in a playroom, or watch a clown make animals from balloons.

His stomach tightened into a familiar knot. He stopped at the desk, got a name tag and signed the log-in sheet. The lady behind the desk smiled and buzzed the door for him to enter.

She had given him the room number for Rachel on a slip of paper that he crumpled in his hand without thinking about it. He walked down the hall, breathing in the antiseptic air of the hospital. Oxygen that smelled like medicine. It was cold and clean.

The door to the room was open. He peeked in. Lacey was sitting in a chair, her eyes closed. His mom sat next to the bed where Rachel slept, hooked to IVs. She put a finger to her lips to silence him.

He stepped softly, hoping he wouldn't wake Lacey. As he got closer to the metal crib, he realized that Rachel was awake. Her bright blue eyes were open and clear, not glazed as they had been that morning. She even smiled a little.

"She's much better." Wilma patted the seat next to hers. "But Lacey is worn out. She was up a lot last night, checking Rachel and giving her medicine."

He nodded, but he didn't know what to say. The last few days hadn't been easy for Lacey. He took that back. Since Corry arrived in town, Lacey's life had been turned upside down.

"She's strong," he told his mom. "She'll be fine."

"Even strong people need help." Wilma said it with soft but firm tones that he couldn't argue with.

"I know." He touched his mom's arm. "Why don't you go home? I'll be here for a while."

"Are you sure you don't mind? The doctor said that if Rachel's fever stayed down, he'd let her go home this evening."

"I don't mind." He glanced again at the sleeping Lacey, amazed by the softness of her features when she slept. "Does Bailey know?"

"She came up earlier. So did Pastor Dan and Lillian."

"That's good."

She leaned and kissed his cheek. "I'll see you at home."

He watched her go and then he sat back in the seat, his legs stretched out in front of him, but not relaxed.

Rachel cooed. He reached through the bars of the crib and rubbed her arm softly, careful of the IV. "Little baby, life isn't always easy."

She didn't realize that she'd already found out that life wasn't easy. In her short little life, she'd experienced more than some adults. He prayed that as she got older, it would get easier and she wouldn't have to suffer. If life was fair, she would remain in Lacey's custody where she would be loved and kept safe.

He didn't know Lacey very well, but he knew that she would take care of this little girl. He glanced her way, and she was still sleeping, her mouth open just a little. Street-smart and tough. The description didn't fit her today.

He leaned back in the seat and thought about a girl who hadn't been tough. She'd been sweet and full of faith, with a smile that lit up his day. And she hadn't been able to win her fight.

The memories of losing her were still a sharp ache. Sometimes it felt as though everyone had forgotten but him and her parents, but they'd left years ago.

Jamie hadn't had a chance to become a part of Gibson. She came and left the summer of his twentieth birthday. His mother had brought her to the white farmhouse after his grandparents moved to town. And for a few short months, she'd been a farm girl. The dream of her life.

Lacey moved in the chair, but didn't wake up. She was spending a summer in the country, too. Because she wanted to live on a farm. And because his mother had the habit of bringing home strays.

Lacey and Jamie were nothing alike.

* * *

Lacey woke up and the sun was an orange ball on the western horizon. She heard a noise and turned. Wilma was gone. Jay had taken her place in the chair next to the bed. He was sleeping, too.

She stood, stretched and walked to the bed where her niece had been since that morning. Rachel slept, her cheeks pale but not flushed pink with fever. It was a virus, the doctor said, that had gotten out of control. She would be fine, but from this point on, Lacey would have to monitor when Rachel had a fever.

The baby would probably outgrow the seizures, brought on by the high temperature. Lacey lifted her from the bed, careful with the IV.

"Sweet girl," Lacey whispered, and kissed Rachel's cheek. "I'm going to take care of you. You'll never have to wonder what is happening in the other room. You'll never be hungry."

Telling secrets to a baby. Lacey closed her eyes and held her niece close.

The door opened. A nurse, soft shoes, quiet on the floor and a smile that put people at ease. She bit down on her bottom lip when she saw Jay sleeping.

"I came to give you good news." The nurse had a handful of papers that she placed on the table. "You get to take this little girl home. Her temperature has been down all day, she's hydrated, and there's no sign of seizures."

Lacey swallowed objections. How could she tell this nurse that she was afraid to take the baby home? What if she couldn't handle this alone?

Jay moved in his chair, his brown eyes a little sleepy and his hair messy. He ran his hand over his head, smoothing the distracting strands. Lacey met his gaze and he smiled, like she could do it, and she didn't need to be afraid.

She didn't have to handle this alone.

"I don't have my car or the car seat." She didn't look at Jay this time.

"We can give you an infant seat that we give to newborns," the nurse assured her.

"And I can give you a ride home," Jay offered. He stood and stretched, his shirt pulling tight across his chest, and then he shoved his hands into his pockets and waited.

Lacey nodded. "I think we'd rest better at home."

"Of course you would." The nurse removed the IV from Rachel's arm and placed an adhesive strip on the tiny spot. Rachel didn't cry, but her mouth twisted down and tears welled up in her blue eyes.

Lacey picked her up again and the nurse smiled. "Let me go over the release papers with you." The nurse moved the table in front of Lacey. "And then I'll get the infant seat."

She read the instructions, the doctor's diagnosis and treatment and then she handed Lacey a pen. Lacey held the pen over the area for parent or guardian and the words brought it all home, the significance of what had happened in her life.

She was no longer responsible only for herself. The tiny little person in her arms depended on her, for wise choices, for safety, for nurturing.

And Corry was in jail. Her hand shook as she lifted the pen and signed.

"She'll be okay." The nurse meant the words to encourage, and Lacey nodded. "I'll be right back."

Jay had started packing the diaper bag, a guy in faded

jeans and a T-shirt, a man used to being in control and taking care of situations. He didn't look at her.

When he looked up, he smiled. "You're going to be able to do this, Lacey. You're not alone."

She nodded, but couldn't respond. How had he known that she felt alone?

"Do you need anything from the store before we head back to Gibson?" He zipped the diaper bag.

"I'm good."

The door opened again. The nurse walked in, holding up the infant seat. "Found one. And I have some medication for you, with the instructions on the label. She'll need this when you get home."

"Thank you." She had been saying that a lot lately. She buckled her niece in the seat and Jay had the diaper bag. Time to go. She paused, not really wanting to leave the secure environment of the hospital, where people who knew what they were doing were on hand.

"Let's go." Jay reached for the infant seat. "I'll carry her."

"Okay." Lacey said good-bye to the nurse, and followed Jay from the room. She had the diaper bag. He had Rachel in the infant seat.

When they got to the elevator he turned to face her.

"Lacey, it really is okay."

"What if I can't do this?" She asked, not able to look at him, instead studying the pattern in the tile floor. "It was so easy telling my sister what she needed to do. It was easy to help. Now, it's all on me."

She looked up, smiling, because he looked so serious, taking in her words, her rambling fears. Did he ever get riled up, or frightened? Did he ever lose it?

Probably not. He made black-and-white decisions,

dealt with facts, and he probably never took chances. He had it all together. Lacey was still not there, and she probably never would be.

For a while she had embraced herself. She was who she was and she was okay. God had done something in her life, was still doing something. But being around him, she felt like her flaws were magnified.

"Come on, Lacey, stop looking like you're about to run out on me." Jay held the door of the open elevator. "Let's go."

"I'm not about to run." She stepped on the elevator ahead of him.

"I didn't think you were. That was just a little well-planned prodding. I figured if I got your hackles up, you'd kick back into gear."

"How sweet of you to think of me."

The sun had set and the sky was a deep lavender with a touch of pink on the western horizon. The sounds were urban and familiar. The hum of city traffic, a siren in the distance and across the parking lot, someone shouted to get the attention of a friend. Lacey breathed in the smell of exhaust and from somewhere, the sweet perfume of a mimosa tree.

Jay held the infant seat in one hand and reached for Lacey's elbow. She followed his lead and he guided her across the parking lot to his truck.

"I'm keeping you from work, or from your horses." She waited for him to unlock the door and set the baby inside his truck.

"You're not keeping me from anything."

"Why are you doing this?"

He set the baby on the seat between them and pulled the seatbelt through to fasten it. When he turned around, he wasn't smiling.

"My mom is paying me."

Lacey opened her mouth, not sure what to say. He laughed. She frowned and stepped away from him. "That was mean."

"How do you think I feel when you question my motives?"

"I'm not trying to insult you, but people tend to have ulterior motives." The words slipped out, more truth than she had planned.

Jay sighed. "Yes, Lacey, people do have motives. I can't deny that you're right. People use others, and they hurt them. But sometimes a guy is being nice, with no ulterior motives. End of story."

A soft spot in her heart latched onto his words, wanting to believe that he really was just a nice guy, and that he might be a friend. She told herself that he'd proven that fact by being there, by helping.

And then that other part of her, the part that had been around a little more, told her that everyone had ulterior motives. He could hurt her. As she doled out more and more trust, he could take that and use it to his own advantage.

She had trusted before. Not just Lance, but other people along the way who had let her down. He wanted her to say she trusted him, she saw it in his eyes, the way he looked at her, waiting. She squeezed the bridge of her nose and tried to think beyond tears, beyond what the moment felt like.

"Lacey, don't make this so difficult." He held the door to the truck and motioned her inside. "You either trust me, or you don't."

"I'm trying." She shrugged. "Jay, you feel like a friend. I hope that's good enough for now."

"That's good enough for now."

* * *

Jay didn't know why he had pushed Lacey, or what he wanted her to say to his questions. He started his truck and pulled out of the hospital parking lot, guilt prodding him to apologize. He had pushed her to admit she didn't trust him.

He shouldn't have done that to her. And then he shouldn't have felt so let down when she said he felt like a friend. His ego felt smacked down, like a bad dog chewing shoes. Pete must feel like this on a regular basis.

It wasn't as if Pete really liked shoes. He didn't go looking for shoes. He found them lying around the house and he chewed on them. Jay didn't really like Lacey Gould. Maybe, like she said, she could be a friend.

But he definitely didn't want to step foot into another relationship. He had learned from his failed attempt with Cindy that it wasn't worth it. He had tried to turn a good dating relationship into love, into a marriage.

It had been comfortable.

At least Lacey wasn't comfortable.

"Could we go through a drive-thru?" She had her window down and warm summer air invaded the truck, overwhelming the air conditioner. "I hope you don't mind the window down. After being in the hospital all day, I need fresh air."

"And real food, I bet." He hit his turn signal. "Food, coming right up. What do you want?"

She gave him her order and dug money out of her purse. "I'm buying."

"I can get it, Jay. You've driven me all over the county the last two days. You've spent two evenings in Springfield because of me."

"It feels a lot like friendship." He winked and then wished he hadn't. "I'm sorry."

"No, don't be. Friendship is a good thing. Who can't use more friends? And really, I'm the one who's being too sensitive."

He ordered and she let him pay. He took that as a move toward the trust she had talked about. She knew that he could buy her dinner and he wasn't expecting anything in return.

They pulled over in the parking lot to eat. Lacey had slipped her shoes off and she ate the burger as if he had bought her steak and lobster. He laughed a little and she gave him a sideways look.

"Can't a girl enjoy a burger and fries?" She shot the comment with a look that put him in his place.

"Of course she can. I just didn't know a girl could be happy with fast food."

"You were hanging with the wrong kind of girls, Blackhorse." And then her cheeks turned pink and she looked away.

"You're right. I did hang out with the wrong women. I almost married one of them." Before Lacey, girls in college, young and flighty, impressed by a cowboy with a wealthy father. They hadn't been looking for long term. He hadn't wanted a long-lasting relationship, either.

Until he met Cindy, he had kept the promise he'd whispered on a summer night. Cindy had been comfortable, the opposite of Jamie in so many ways. Come to find out, he hadn't truly wanted forever with Cindy. And neither had she.

"What happened?" She rubbed her cheeks and glanced sideways at him. "Sorry, that's crossing the line."

"No, it's okay. Cindy was a friend and we were comfortable with friendship and with each other."

"Were you in love?"

"Not really. Disillusionment when she turned me down, yes."

"So, you think a woman can't turn you down, cowboy?"

He felt heat crawl up his neck. It was his turn to blush and cringe a little. "That isn't what I meant. I thought we were perfect together. Come to find out, we were just comfortable in our friendship."

"Slick." She laughed. "So, you're not a ladies' man."

"Not at all."

He could laugh now, a little. His heart was healing. Time had taken care of that. He hadn't realized until she'd scoffed at his ring and his proposal that he was moving on.

"Why do you look like she broke your heart, then?"

He finished his soda and shoved it into the bag with her trash, and shrugged. "It's a long story."

"That you don't want to share."

"That I don't want to share." He didn't know why he couldn't. Maybe because he still remembered whispered promises of forever with a girl who didn't have forever.

He had held that summer inside himself along with secrets they had shared. If he talked about Jamie, would she vanish from his memory, be poured out like water from a pitcher and never return? He knew better.

Empty places were filling up. He looked at the little girl in the infant seat next to him. A little girl with a new beginning to her young life.

Something good to pour himself into. And that included Lacey, in ways he hadn't expected.

Chapter Eleven

Lacey rushed to the waitress station at the side of the dining room and refilled the pitcher of water for the third time since the lunch shift had started. A yawn pulled at her jaw and she covered it with her hand. Three days since Rachel came home from the hospital and Lacey was still adjusting to sleepless nights. The baby ate at least twice every night.

"Honey, you look wiped out." Georgia, who had started working the day shift a week ago, rubbed Lacey's back as she scooted through to the coffeepot.

"I am wiped out," Lacey admitted, yawning again. "But I'll adjust. And at least Rachel is feeling better."

"That had to be a frightening thing for you as a new mom."

New mom. Lacey still felt a tingle of fear at the word. She wasn't a mom. She hadn't given birth to this child. She wasn't ready for this, not at all. But instead of the litany of excuses, she smiled.

"It was pretty scary."

"Who's watching the baby?" Georgia turned with the coffeepot.

"Bailey part of the time, Wilma the rest."

"It's good to have friends like that. I had to leave mine in a day care when they were little. It wasn't easy, but you do what you gotta do."

"Yes, I guess so." And a person adjusts when they have to adjust. They learn to live with changes and they learn to take new paths.

She remembered what Pastor Dan had told her: *"Lacey, nothing surprises God. You have to remember, He knew what was ahead of you, and He has a plan to help you deal with it."*

"Hey, you know you've got company at tables two and three."

"I have company?" She peeked and saw the Golden Girls. "Oh goodness!"

"They're a sweet bunch, aren't they?"

"They are, but they're in your section."

Balloons rose from the center of the table and presents were piled up and down the length of it. Someone was having a birthday. Lacey smiled. Those ladies had more fun than any other group of women Lacey knew.

Georgia moved Lacey forward, a hand on her back. "Honey, they're in my section because you're taking a break. This is what we call a baby shower."

"A baby shower?" Lacey planted her feet and tried to stay at the waitress station. Georgia gave her a firm push in the small of her back.

"Get out there, girl. They're having a shower for you and that baby."

"But…"

"Come on, honey, it's time to show you we love you." Jolynn came from the kitchen, wiping her hands on a towel. "We put a lot into keeping this a secret and surprising you."

The cowbell clanged and Bailey walked through the door with Wilma and Rachel. Lacey brushed at the tears streaming down her cheeks, because she had people, and they loved her. These women knew where she'd been and what she'd done, and they loved her.

It made loving herself a little easier.

Bailey brought Rachel to her, and after handing the baby over, she hugged Lacey tight. "Smile, sweetie, this is fun. This is about you and this baby."

"I know." Lacey took the tissue that Jolynn pushed into her hand and she wiped her eyes and then her nose. "I can't believe you all are doing this for me."

Pastor Dan's wife stood from where she'd been sitting with the Golden Girls. "Lacey, you deserve this, honey. We love you. You're such a part of this community and our church. We wanted to do this for you, and for that sweet little girl you're holding."

Lacey held Rachel close and kissed her soft, powdery cheek. And then she realized that her niece was wearing a new dress. The orange-and-pink outfit fit perfectly, unlike some of the baby's other clothes. A little orange bonnet covered her bald head.

"She looks beautiful."

"I dressed her." Bailey pointed her toward a chair that put her in the center of the activity. "Come on, we have games."

"But I really don't need all of this." Lacey sat down, because Bailey was standing behind her, insisting.

"Oh, Lacey, you're going to need all of this and more. You just don't know it yet." Wilma smiled, serene and comforting.

"Here we go." Jolynn passed out paper for a game.

The game took five minutes. Occasionally Jolynn rushed off to take care of customers, and Georgia would excuse herself from time to time. Lacey laughed as the Golden Girls got into the games, laughing and cheering one another.

A memory sneaked up on Lacey; for a brief moment it almost robbed her of this moment. Because she remembered St. Louis six years ago, the summer she left. She remembered a soft cry and empty arms.

"Okay, open the gifts." Bailey stopped the third game before it could start. She shot Lacey a look that asked if she was okay. "I want to see the pretty baby stuff."

Jolynn heard and laughed. "You're wondering if we're going to throw you a surprise shower and what kind of great baby stuff you'll get."

"I definitely want my shower here, with all my friends." Bailey reached for Lacey's hand, giving it a light squeeze. And then she handed Lacey the first gift.

A bouncy seat. Clothes came next, and then diapers, toys and more clothes. Lacey watched as the pile of gifts grew. The last gift was money. She wiped at her eyes as she read the card from an anonymous friend. She looked at Bailey, who shook her head, then looked down, not giving away the identity of that gift-giver.

"You all overwhelm me." She smiled at the group. "I'm so blessed."

"Honey, you've blessed us." Jolynn, hair frosted a light blond and careful makeup hiding her age, smiled big. "You're our kid."

Lacey looked around. The diner had cleared out while the party went on. She stood and looked at the mess left behind. "We should get this cleaned up."

"You can't clean. You're the guest of honor." Elsbeth smiled sweetly. The look she bestowed on Lacey said she meant it and she wouldn't be argued with.

"Look, the law is here."

"Not again," Bailey muttered, and then she laughed, but the laughter was nervous.

Lacey watched Jay's patrol car come to a stop in front of the diner. He got out of the car, tall and yet a little nervous. He glanced around and then he reached into the back of his car.

"Well, what do you know, he's delivering a gift." Elsbeth talked a little under her breath about something in the air.

And Lacey couldn't let them think that the something in the air was a relationship between herself and Jay Blackhorse. She glanced at Wilma, a woman so giving and kind. Lacey would never hurt Wilma.

It was one thing to throw a shower for Lacey. It was another altogether to have her dating one of the favorite sons of the community. Dirty socks and clean socks. Some things just didn't match.

"Stop looking like a train is about to derail right in front of you." Bailey pinched her arm and Lacey yelped.

"Don't do that."

"You have that look on your face. I know what you're thinking. You're thinking you don't fit. Look around you, Lacey, at the love these people have for you."

"I know."

"You know—" Bailey pulled her aside "—you're stoning yourself. You have to stop doing that and remember what happened when those people wanted to stone that girl. Jesus said for the one who hadn't sinned to cast the first stone. But you're saving people the trouble by stoning yourself."

Lacey looked away from the window, away from the cowboy cop that was walking up to the door. He had caught her eye and smiled, but something on her face must have warned him because his smile faded.

"Stop stoning yourself, Lacey."

Lacey nodded and the cowbell clanged. Jay walked through, a little red-cheeked when all of the ladies smiled and said hello with knowing tones in their voices. Matchmaking was alive and well in Gibson.

"I heard about the shower. I wasn't invited, but I wanted to bring a gift." He held it out to Lacey. Hands trembling, she took the large bag.

Bailey laughed. "Of course you weren't invited. We weren't about to ruin a good time by inviting men."

"Thank you, Jay." Lacey slid her finger under the tape.

"It's clothes." He shrugged. "I hope they're okay. I bought winter things, because I knew that everyone would buy cute summer dresses for a little girl."

Lacey blinked a few times and looked into the bag. A coat, pants, warm dresses and sweaters. She smiled at the man standing in front of her, at ease, army-style, but definitely not at ease in the middle of the women of Gibson.

"Thank you." Lacey took a step back, because he was tall and strong. "They're perfect."

"Good, okay, I have to go." He tipped his hat to the women, and nodded to his mother. "I'll cook tonight, Mom."

A few giggles. He shook his head and explained. "I'm only cooking on the grill."

Lacey wanted to walk him to the door. She wanted to slip her hand into his and pretend she could be the person that someone like Jay Blackhorse loved forever. Because it felt good, watching him walk through a door and knowing his smile was for her.

Even if it was barely friendship.

"Okay then, I think I'll clean up." Jolynn smiled a little too big, a little too bright. "Bailey, help Lacey carry this stuff out to her car, would you? Georgia and I will clean up and then we can all have a cup of coffee and another piece of cake."

Lacey picked up the bags and boxes, and Bailey followed with more bags. As she hit the sidewalk, Lacey stopped to take a deep breath.

"That was awkward." Bailey spoke as the door closed behind them.

"What do you mean?" Lacey walked around to the back of the building and when they reached her car she fumbled to get the door open, dropping a couple of bags in the process.

Bailey laughed a little. "You. Jay. The zing when you look at each other."

"Stop." Lacey turned from shoving bags into the back of her car. "Bailey, it isn't fair. Please don't try to make something happen with him. He's closed off, getting over his girlfriend from Springfield. He's a Blackhorse. I don't want to be rejected again. I don't want to see that look in his eyes, like I'm a mistake that he made one night."

"Lacey, I can't believe you. Do you ever stop to consider what God has done in your life? You act like you're defiled in some way and you can't touch what is clean. And that's crazy."

Words poured out, fireworks of anger, sharp and painful. Bailey ended her tirade, a little breathless and her cheeks tinged with pink. Blond hair blew around her face and she had crossed her arms.

"Okay."

"That's it?" Bailey drew in a deep breath and let it out. *"Okay?"*

"What more can I say? Maybe you're right. I have a lot of hang-ups. I don't want to be hurt again."

"Maybe he'll hurt you, maybe he won't. At least let him be your friend."

Lacey nodded and reached to hug her friend. "I'm okay with friendship."

"You're a lot like Jay. Friendship is safe. It doesn't hurt. God couldn't have planned this any better."

"You're really very funny. I think you should go home to your husband and leave me to take care of this little mess myself."

"Leave, without more cake? You've got to be kidding." Bailey hooked her arm through Lacey's. "Have you heard from Corry?"

"She doesn't want to talk to me."

"She'll come around."

"Maybe, maybe not. I'm afraid. What if something happens and they won't let me keep Rachel?"

"That won't happen. We won't let it."

Jay's truck cruised past. He waved, but he kept on going. Lacey watched until the truck turned and drove out of town.

"Interesting, very interesting." Bailey laughed a little and wouldn't release Lacey's arm.

"Let it go, Bay. You're like a coon dog on the wrong scent."

Jay led the bay gelding into the center aisle of the stable and cross-tied him. The horse shied a little to the left but calmed down when Jay ran a hand down his neck. He touched the horse's front left leg and the animal lifted his hoof off the ground for Jay.

He'd been trimming hooves for the last week, a few horses a night. He'd put off this guy until the end because he was still green and wasn't always so easy to get along with.

"Good boy." He leaned into the horse and filed the hoof. The gelding moved a little, but Jay kept hold of him.

A car drove down the drive and pulled up in front of his mom's house. Lacey. She'd gone home after the baby shower. His mom still had Rachel. If he knew his mom, she'd invite Lacey for dinner. Burgers on the grill, nothing fancy, but at least he didn't add strange seasonings.

The horse shied a little, brushing against him. Jay tapped him on the shoulder to get his attention. "None of that, buddy."

From the drive he could hear Pete woofing, loud and a little frightening. Especially if a person was afraid of dogs.

"Afraid of dogs. Oh, man." He untied the gelding and led him to an empty stall. "Stay there. Not that you have a choice."

Jay hurried out of the barn. Lacey was where he knew she'd be, sitting in her car, windows up. She didn't look happy. Pete looked like he'd just discovered a new favorite game.

"Pete, down," Jay yelled. Pete sat down and waited, but he didn't take his attention off the car. "Pete, to the house."

Pete turned and hurried to the front porch. Lacey opened the car door and got out, not too quickly. She glanced at the dog, and then at him.

"Are you okay?" Jay stopped in front of her, realizing he still had the file. "Need your nails done?"

She sort of smiled. "I don't. But your dog took five years off my life."

"You're going to have to get to know him better."

"Does he dislike all women, or just me?"

"He doesn't dislike anyone." He took her by the hand, a gesture he hadn't intended. But he didn't let go, because her fingers wrapped around his, and it didn't hurt. "Come on, let me introduce the two of you."

"That can wait. Really, I don't want to know him."

He felt her pulling back. He stopped and she stopped.

"You collect dogs." He didn't get it.

"They don't have teeth. They're not real. You understand that, right? Stuffed, porcelain, resin, not real. But Pete, he is real and he has real teeth."

"Once again, I have to remind you that you collect dogs. People typically collect things they like, not things that scare them." He laughed. "They scare you, so you collect them?"

"I got bit when I was five. A neighbor's dog." She lifted the heavy veil of bangs that parted on the left and covered her brow. "I still have the scar."

A jagged line above her brow. He nodded, understanding. "Okay, I get it. But not all dogs bite."

"I know that. I always wanted one and we couldn't have pets in our building. Fear was easier than…"

"Wanting?"

She glanced away from him, and he wanted to turn her, to look into her dark eyes and read the other secrets. But he knew the deepest of her secrets, the guarded past that she tried to hide behind her cheerful waitress persona.

He knew about wanting.

"Pete." He whistled and Pete lumbered off the porch. "Come on, boy, meet our new friend."

Her hand had dropped back to her side, but it slid back into his, seeking, and he tightened his fingers around hers. Pete ambled in their direction, a lumbering red beast with slobber hanging from his mouth, but eyes so kind Jay couldn't imagine anyone being afraid of him.

"He's big."

"He's afraid of the kittens in the barn."

"Kittens? Now that's more like it." She smiled up at him. "Soft, fuzzy kittens?"

"Have you never had a pet?" Jay led her a few steps and when he raised his hand, Pete sat in front of them.

"No, I haven't ever had a pet. Bailey's dog runs in fear of me, because I scared him one time, screaming because he got close to me. Seems silly, doesn't it?"

"Everyone has a fear. Some are big fears, some are small."

"And how do we overcome our fears?" She said it in a soft voice and he didn't have an answer. He feared losing someone again.

He feared forgetting.

It had once been a larger-than-life fear. Now it was subtle, but still clinging to the dark corners of his mind. He shook it off to watch as Lacey conquered her own fear, reaching to touch his dog.

Pete's long, slobbery tongue came out and he slurped her hand and then her arm.

"Disgusting," she said with feeling.

"Yeah, it is." He got the words out, and then he smiled.

"Hey, you two," his mom called from the front porch. "I have the baby asleep in here. Why don't you take Lacey for a ride down by the creek? It wouldn't hurt her to have a break."

Jay waved at his mom, and when he looked at Lacey, her eyes were bright, her smile huge. She wanted to ride a horse. He wanted to sigh.

"You want to go for a ride?"

"Can the dog stay here?"

"Still don't like him?" He nodded at Pete and Pete sat. If only the dog could be trained not to chew up shoes.

"I kind of have a friendship with Bailey's dog now, it's called ignoring one another. So I might start to like him, but let's not push it." She smiled at the dog, his tongue hanging out and his soulful gaze on her. "But he is cute."

"Another nice feature is he's softer than a stuffed animal or a porcelain dog, and he can even keep a person safe at night, or find a lost child."

"He does have positive traits." She reached, her fingers close to the dog's nose, and then she stroked his face. "But he still can't go with us."

"Pete, stay here." This time he did sigh. "Lacey, come with me."

Chapter Twelve

Lacey settled into the saddle of the gray mare. Bailey had taught her to ride, and Lacey never tired of the experience. A horse, a slow canter across a field. She glanced to the side and watched the cowboy who owned the horse as he tightened the girth strap on his big buckskin.

He wore jeans, boots and a plaid shirt. His hat was pulled low over his brow, putting his face in shadow. He turned, smiling at her, but the smile wasn't the real thing. There were shadows in his eyes, too.

He didn't want to take her for this ride.

"Jay, we don't have to do this. Or I could go alone."

He pushed back the brim of his hat and cocked his head to the side. He leaned against the horse, his smile a little soft. "I don't mind, Lacey."

"You look like you mind."

Jay put his foot in the stirrup and swung his right leg over the saddle, settling with ease that came from a lifetime of riding. "It isn't that I mind…"

"Then what?" She loosened the reins and her horse moved next to his, through the open gate and into the

empty hay field where red clover bloomed and scented
the air with a soft fragrance.

"I'd rather not talk. Let's ride down by the creek. I'll
show you the old swimming hole." And he looked away,
like there was more to say but he couldn't.

Lacey felt uneasy, like she had invaded private places
in his heart, or his life. He didn't want her next door, or
riding his horse. He didn't want her in the private places
of his life.

"Stop worrying." He rode close to her, close enough
she could have reached out to touch him. And she wanted
to. She wanted to reach for his hand, to tell him she understood.

Shadows lengthened as they rode. The sun was setting
and the creek was in a valley where it was cool and dark,
shaded by hills and trees. The temperature dropped and
cicadas started their evening song, wings brushing, the
sound loud and to some people annoying.

"The cicadas are like crickets on steroids down here."
Jay shook his head.

"I love them."

He laughed.

"You would." He had moved a little ahead of her on
the trail and he glanced back over his shoulder. "They're
not bad."

They rode to the edge of the creek. It widened at a
bend and a rope hung from a tree branch that extended
over the rippling waters. Jay's horse stopped. Lacey's
stopped next to him, no command needed. She watched
the cowboy dismount, and then he reached for her horse.

"Come on, we'll walk for a while." He smiled up at
her, those shadows still in his eyes.

Lacey slid off the horse, her legs a little wobbly. She

reached for the reins that he held and he handed them over, his hand brushing hers, his gaze not wavering, not looking away.

Lacey looked away, because she couldn't catch her breath and the moment wasn't real, it was created by the creek, the music of cicadas and a cowboy.

Think of something to say, something safe and neutral. She looked at the water, the grassy banks. "I bet you spent a lot of time down here when you were a kid."

"I did. We loved this place."

"We? You and your family?"

"Yes, me and my family." He dropped the reins of his horse and the buckskin lowered his head and seemed to doze. Lacey looked from him to the horse she had been riding.

"You can drop the reins. She'll stay." He took the reins from her hand.

"I'm sure she will, but it scares me to let her go. What if she runs off?"

"We'll walk back to the house and she'll be there waiting for us. But she won't run."

Lacey glanced back; the horse was still standing in the same spot. Jay's hand reached, his fingers taking hers. Lacey's breath caught in her lungs, a combination of fear and expectation.

This felt like falling in love, and she wasn't, couldn't, be falling in love with Jay. It was a moment, just a moment created by a setting sun and soft shadows.

It still felt like falling in love. A lingering ache in her heart reminded her of rejection and what it felt like to not be the woman that a man wanted forever.

"It's a great picnic spot." Jay spoke, his words soft.

"I'll bring you down here sometimes. We can bring Rachel."

"That would be nice." Lacey stopped at the edge of the creek, Jay at her side. She looked up and he looked down. And then his head lowered, and she couldn't breathe. Cicadas were singing and a bird dipped over their heads, and she couldn't think, couldn't find a way to tell him no.

His mouth touched hers, their lips connecting. His hands held her shoulders and then moved to her back. His lips moved to her neck, lingering for a few seconds and she felt his warm breath and a heavy sigh like he felt too much. His lips returned to hers. Lacey closed her eyes and melted into the softness of the moment.

A moment, she reminded herself, so it wouldn't hurt later.

It was just a moment.

Jay sighed as he pulled away. "I'm not sure what to think about you, Lacey."

She shrugged and closed her eyes, because she was a *moment*, not a *forever*.

Jay wanted to pull Lacey back into his arms. He wanted to ask why she looked as if her world had come to an end with their kiss. But he wouldn't. If he knew her secrets, she would want to know his.

Memories of Jamie were fading, being replaced by this woman, her smile, her quick wit and her shadows.

He had promised Jamie that he would love her forever, and he would never forget her. At twenty the promise had meant everything. At almost thirty, he realized that it was the promise of a kid to a dying girl who had wanted to feel something that resembled forever.

Jay leaned in again, this time kissing Lacey's cheek,

and cupping the back of her head to hold her close, to comfort her. His fingers weaved through soft strands of hair. He saw the tears in her eyes and wanted to bring back her smile. He didn't want to hurt her.

"We should go." She turned away from him and walked back to her horse. Foot in stirrup, she swung into the saddle.

They rode to the house in silence. Jay knew that they were both lost in thoughts they didn't want to share. He stopped his horse next to the barn and dismounted. Lacey stood next to her horse. He took the reins she held. She smiled and she didn't move away. He had kind of expected her to make a run for it.

"Thank you for taking me riding." She reached for the reins of the horse. "Shouldn't we unsaddle them?"

"I'll do it. You go ahead and get Rachel. Tell Mom I'll start the burgers when I come in." He held her gaze, wondering if she had felt the things he'd felt in that kiss. "You're staying for dinner, aren't you?"

"No, I should go home. It's been a really long day."

"I'm cooking," he teased.

She smiled a little. "I know, but I'm about wiped out."

"Lacey, I'm sorry."

"Sorry?"

"The kiss. The ride wasn't supposed to be about that."

That didn't come out the way he had planned. He shook his head, amazed that he could be so dense. From the look on her face, she had to be thinking the same thing.

"Don't worry about it." She let him off the hook too easily and then she walked away.

He led the horses to the barn, his thoughts scrambled

inside him. Past and present were colliding. He didn't know how to let go of the one to find the other.

"Why did Lacey look like she was going home to cry?"

His mom's voice. Almost thirty and living at home was not a good plan, he realized. He felt as if he was eighteen again. Jay pulled the saddle off his buckskin and carried it into the tack room. His mom was waiting, her hand on the horse's neck, her other hand holding carrots. Buck took a bite and chewed, his ears pricked forward.

"Do we have to talk about this?" He remembered conversations as a teenager, when he'd poured out his confusion and she had listened, always silent, letting him talk.

Back then he'd thought how great it was, to have that relationship with his parents, when his friends were struggling just to understand growing up.

Today he didn't want to talk about it.

He heard a car. His dad, home from work. That was close, but now he had a way out of this conversation. He smiled a little and his mom shook her head. "I'm not giving up that easily. You were supposed to take her for a ride so she could relax a little, not send her back to me in tears."

"Now you're exaggerating."

She shrugged. "A little."

"Bad matchmaking job, Mom." Did the entire town get together on certain days and plot the futures of single victims? Didn't God have a say in all of this?

"I wouldn't dream of matchmaking." She wiped her hands on her jeans. "Jay, she's a wonderful girl. She isn't Jamie and never will be. And maybe that's a good thing?"

"Maybe." He remembered a kiss that had changed

everything. He hadn't thought of Jamie when he kissed Lacey.

"She's been hurt a lot in her life."

"I don't plan on hurting her."

What did he plan? It had seemed easy, to be her friend, to help her in the situation with Corry. That had felt safer than this.

"Jay, you know her past." His mom clicked a lead rope onto the halter of the mare that Lacey had ridden. "I'm not sure if you know how often she's been hurt or how strong she is. Not everyone can come from where she's been and survive it, and still smile."

"I am aware."

"Not everyone can handle where she's been."

"I know that, too." He took the mare and led her to the end of the stable and released her into the field. As he walked back to his mom he glanced in at the gelding he'd planned to work with, whose hooves were half-trimmed. The horse's ears twitched and he chewed on a mouthful of hay.

"I want to make sure." His mom returned to the conversation, not letting it go. "She doesn't have family to look out for her."

"She has you." He smiled at his mom and leaned to kiss her cheek. "I love that you want to take care of everyone."

"And I love you. I love you first, and I want you to be happy." She reached into the stall with the gelding and patted the horse's neck. "You look happier than I've seen you look in a long time."

"I've always been happy."

"No, for a long time you were pretending. You were

too young for what you went through with Jamie. If I had known then what I know now, I might not have…"

"Brought her here?" They walked outside and Pete lumbered across the yard to walk with them back to the house. Jay could smell the grill and knew that his dad had started the coals.

"I guess if I could take it back, maybe I wouldn't have brought her, because I would have spared you losing her."

"I don't think we can second-guess. I think we have to accept that God has a plan for all things. And now, I think it's time to find out the next path, the next direction for my life."

"I'm glad you didn't marry Cindy."

"That wouldn't have been God's plan." He could admit that now, and a month ago, he couldn't have. A month ago he had felt rejected. Not brokenhearted.

"No, it would have been wrong. What about Lacey?"

"I've seen her a few times in the last six years and known her for two months. I can't really tell you what I think about Lacey. But she makes me smile."

"That's a start."

It wasn't enough. He knew that. His mother knew it, too. You couldn't build forever on a smile.

The message had been on the answering machine when Lacey got home from Jay's. She was still thinking of the kiss—trying to decide what it meant—when she learned that her sister wanted to meet with her the next day.

Bailey went with her so she wouldn't be alone. Lacey walked down the hall of the jail facility, Rachel in her arms and Bailey at her side. She kept remembering the voice on the answering machine, young and unsure. Apologizing.

"Do you think she meant it, that she's sorry?"

"Of course she's sorry, Lacey." Bailey hitched her purse over her shoulder, bumping it against her seven-month belly. "She's either truly sorry, repentant, or she's just sorry that it didn't work out. Either way, she's sorry."

"It makes me sick to my stomach."

"Me, too. I want this to all work out for you, and for Rachel. At the same time, I want Corry to find a way to make her own life better."

Without hurting Rachel. Lacey wanted to add those words, but it felt selfish, not compassionate. She had started over in Gibson, running from pain, heartache and guilt. It should work for everyone.

It worked because she had found faith and forgiveness. She had forgiven herself and the people who had hurt her. Even her mom. She'd struggled with that one; her mother had been the hardest to forgive.

"Thank you for coming with me." Lacey handed Rachel to Bailey. "I don't think it will take long. They said visiting times are limited."

Bailey kissed Rachel's pudgy cheek. "We'll be fine. And Lacey, you'll be fine, too. This will all work out."

"I know it will. It isn't easy."

God had a plan. She had to keep telling herself that. Believing had highs and lows. Sometimes it was hard to believe, harder to find faith. But it was there; if she kept searching, she found herself knowing that God was in control. Even of moments like this.

They parted at the waiting room. Lacey followed the female officer to the room where she would talk to her sister. The walls were pale blue, the lights fluorescent. It was like every other jail; it felt cold and it twisted a person's confidence. Even a person from the outside.

Lacey sat down and a moment later the door opened and Corry was there with another female officer. This one stood at the door while Corry took a seat.

Corry looked gaunt and pale, but her hair was clean and her eyes were clear. She wasn't high; she wasn't looking for a fix. Her hands were clasped in front of her on the table and she finally looked up.

"I'm sorry." Two words and then tears streamed down pale cheeks.

Lacey reached for her sister's hands. The guard cleared her throat and Lacey sat back, hands in front of her, like Corry's, but without handcuffs. "I know."

"I want to tell you that I am sorry for what I did to you. And what I did to my baby." Corry sobbed, lowering her face into her hands. "I'm not a bad person."

"I know you're not."

"You know, sometimes I feel like I never had a chance to be good or to do the right thing. I never had a chance. No one ever believed in me." Corry looked up. "Except you."

Lacey nodded, but she couldn't talk. Her throat tightened around the words she wanted to say and her eyes burned as tears surfaced. She had prayed so hard, so often for her sister to have a chance. A few years ago she had even tried to bring Corry back to Gibson with her. Corry hadn't wanted to leave her friends.

"Lacey, please adopt Rachel."

"What?"

"I've been talking to this minister guy that comes here. He explained your faith, and why you've changed. I never understood. I guess I was jealous. But now, I'm starting to get it, and I know that Rachel needs you."

"You're her mom."

"I'm guilty, Lacey. My lawyer says I'll probably get five or ten years. More likely ten. Rachel doesn't need a mom who went to jail. She needs to be able to go to school and say that she has a mom who works for a diner and has a diploma." She laughed a little. "She needs to have you for a mom and your cowboy boyfriend for a dad."

Normal moments between sisters in an unlikely place. Lacey regretted that it couldn't have happened sooner.

"He isn't my boyfriend."

"You're a little slow, but you'll get it."

"Time's almost up." The voice of the officer.

Corry bit down on her lip and shook her head. "You have to do this, Lacey. I don't have time to argue. You have to be her mom. She can take the place of…"

"Don't."

"No, you're right, she can't. But she needs you, and you need her. I've already signed a paper with my lawyer, giving you custody. Now you have to go and get it legal, so she can be your daughter."

"Oh, Corry."

The officer walked to the table and Corry stood.

"It's the right thing to do, Lacey. For once, I'm doing the right thing." She whispered that she loved Lacey and then the guard led her out.

Lacey cried. She couldn't stop the tears. She couldn't stop the mixture of hurt and joy that mixed inside her heart. Joy, because Corry was finally growing up, pain, because it had to be now, like this.

She left the room and walked down the hall, through

security and back to the waiting room where Bailey held Rachel. A month ago Lacey had thought she had life figured out.

Lance had been a wound that was healing, but his rejection had taught her something about herself and it had cemented in her mind that she could make it without a man. She would live her life in Gibson, taking up space in Jolynn's studio and waiting on farmers who came into the Hash-It-Out for coffee and steadily dished-out banter from their waitress.

She had made a plan for herself that included getting her GED and maybe taking college classes because she wanted to be a teacher.

Everything had changed that day Jay walked through the doors of the diner, Corry in the back of his police car, and a baby that needed someone to keep her safe.

"What happened?" Bailey stood, a little slower getting up with a baby on the inside and Rachel holding her hair in both hands.

"I'm not sure." She held her hands out and took Rachel. Bailey had to untangle baby fingers from her hair.

"You're not sure."

"She wants me to adopt Rachel. She wants her baby to have someone who will make the right decisions for her, and give her a chance." Lacey held her niece close. "What if I'm not that person?"

Bailey walked next to her, down the hall and out into bright sunshine and heat. "Of course you're the right person. And you can give her something else that Corry couldn't. You give her community and people who love her. You give her stability."

"I know you're right, but it isn't the perfect plan, is

it? The perfect plan would include Corry getting her life together and making the right decisions."

"That isn't going to happen right now. And right now is what needs to be taken care of."

"I guess you're right." Lacey unlocked her car and Bailey opened the back door so she could put the baby in the car seat.

"Of course I'm right." Bailey spoke with a soft smile. "Remember, when we're giving each other words of wisdom, we're always right."

"Of course, how could I have forgotten?"

"Momentary lapse." Bailey buckled her seat belt. "Lacey, it'll all work out."

"I know it will. It's a little scary at the moment, but I know it'll work out."

It was still early. Her mind turned to easier thoughts: a day off and weeding her flower gardens. But somehow Jay entered into those thoughts, because lately he had done that a lot.

No matter how much she told herself it was wrong, that it wouldn't work, her silly heart still insisted on thinking about him and what it felt like to be held in his arms.

No one had ever made her feel as safe, or as threatened.

Chapter Thirteen

Jay walked out of the barn and looked toward the old farmhouse. Lacey's sedan was back. His mom had told him that Lacey went to see Corry. He had wondered about the meeting, and worried. He knew that Lacey could hold her own, but he worried that Corry would manipulate her.

The movement of the mare inside the barn drew him back inside, into the dark interior that smelled like hay and horses. A cat ran past him, chasing a mouse that ran up a post. The horse turned, her sides heaving and her head down.

"It won't be long, Lady." He leaned his arms on the top of the gate. The horse looked up, eyes sad, and then she turned again. Away from him.

She would have the foal any time. But she didn't appreciate his presence. He walked back to the door, to sunlight and heat. It felt good to take his hat off. There wasn't much of a breeze, but enough. At least the mare had the fan that he had plugged in and hung outside her stall.

"Be back in a little while. Don't have the baby while I'm gone." He looked back inside. The horse didn't seem to care that he was leaving.

Lacey would probably love to watch the mare give birth. He had a feeling she was all about newborns. He walked to his truck and jumped in, starting it with the key that he never took out of the ignition. He should; it wasn't as if Gibson was completely crime-free. But they didn't have a lot of car thefts in the area.

When he pulled behind her car and parked, he saw her weeding flower gardens that hadn't been taken care of in a couple of years. The last renter hadn't been interested. And then the house had been empty for a year.

He got out of his truck and walked across the yard. A playpen was set up in the shade of a big oak tree. Next to it, Pete. So that's where the dog had gone off to. Jay shook his head and gave his dog a look. It didn't do any good. Pete looked pretty happy with his spot under the tree. And he had a rawhide bone.

"Looks like you have company." He spoke as he walked up behind Lacey. She jumped a little and turned.

"Don't do that."

"Sorry. I thought you heard me."

"I did, but I didn't realize you were behind me already." She pulled off gardening gloves and brushed hair back from her face. Somewhere along the way she had gone from cute to beautiful. Maybe it was her smile, or the way her eyes lit up.

He was as confused as Pete obviously was. He shook his head. "Sorry. I came down to see if you wanted to watch my mare give birth. It'll probably happen in the next couple of hours."

"I'd love to watch."

"How did it go with Corry?"

She glanced at the baby in the playpen, holding a rattle and cooing. "She wants me to adopt the baby. She's been meeting with a minister and she's decided Rachel should have stability. With me."

She looked away, cheeks flushed. He wondered, but didn't know how much to ask, about what this meant to her.

"I'm going to do it." She pulled a weed, continuing to talk, but not looking at him. She moved a little and pulled crabgrass that was spreading through the flowers.

"You'll be a great mom."

"I hope. I don't know."

"Lacey, I don't get it. This seems like an easy decision to make. Actually, I can't imagine that it would really require a decision. Do you not want her?"

She leaned back on her heels and looked up at him.

"Of course I want her. I want her more than anything. I'm just afraid. And I don't want to make mistakes with her life."

"I think my mom would tell you that every parent makes mistakes. And I'm telling you, that little girl will be better off with you. And Corry knows it. So stop worrying."

She nodded a little, biting down on her lip, the pulled crabgrass still in her hand. "Jay, I had a baby."

He stared, too surprised to say anything. He kneeled next to her, reaching for a dandelion. She slapped his hands away.

"Not the dandelions." The words caught on a sob.

"What?" It didn't make sense. They were talking about babies, not dandelions.

"The dandelions are my favorite flowers."

"They're weeds." He wanted to talk about babies and the stark sadness in her eyes, the loss. He could tell her that he knew how it felt, to let go of someone.

"They're not weeds. They're sunny, happy flowers and I love them. People are always trying to get rid of them, yanking them out by the roots and tossing them. But they survive because God designed them with a purpose. He made them strong." Tears rolled down her cheeks.

"Strong, like you."

She wiped at her eyes. "I don't feel strong. Dandelions are survivors. They can grow anywhere. They fill up bare places."

Filling up bare places. He sighed, because she was a dandelion and she didn't know it. He didn't know how to tell her that, or what to say about a baby she had given up.

She smiled up at him, tears clinging to dark lashes, smearing liner under her eyes. "Did you know dandelions have a lot of vitamin A?"

"I see. That's probably why my grandmother wilted dandelion greens with bacon grease and made me eat them every summer." Jay reached for hands that were busy pulling weeds while tears fell. "Lacey, I'm sorry."

She nodded, tears sliding down her cheeks and dropping onto the dry earth. Sad tears watering her dandelions.

"I gave her up for adoption. I knew that I wasn't prepared to be a mother, not the mother she needed. So a family in Ohio adopted her."

"You gave her life. That's an amazing thing. It isn't always the choice that a woman makes when she feels like her back is against the wall."

"I wanted her to have life, and to have a life with a family that loves her and takes care of her. Everything I never had and couldn't give her. And now Corry thinks I can give her daughter that life."

"I believe you can, too."

"I'm single. I work at a diner and live on tips."

He wanted to tell her he would help, but he couldn't. He had already done that once, proposed because it seemed like the thing to do. He had actually proposed twice. The first had been accepted.

"You have people who will help you, Lacey. You can do this."

She looked up, eyes red and tears trickling down her cheeks. He wiped the tears away, and then he kissed her, because it felt like the thing to do. She was looking at him as though she believed it when he said she could raise Rachel.

She kissed him back, soft and easy like a spring day, and then she moved, out of his embrace and out of his reach.

"You have to stop doing that. You're confusing me. We're friends, and then you kiss me like that. I don't want to be this woman that you kiss when the moment feels vulnerable. I'm not…" She stood up. "I'm better than that."

He stood next to her. "Yes, you are, and I'm sorry. I didn't mean to hurt you."

"Why can't life be simple? Why couldn't I have been the girl who grew up in this town, making the right choices and living the life I wanted?"

"Because life isn't predictable and we all have a path. What we go through makes us who we are. And now God is replacing what you lost, with Rachel."

Replacing what was lost. He faltered at those words and looked away from Lacey, to the fields and the distant stable. He needed to escape the sweet tangle that was Lacey Gould.

"Let me get Rachel." Lacey dropped her gardening

shovel and gloves into the nearby wheelbarrow. "I still want to see that baby horse."

No way out. He smiled and walked across the yard with her. He watched as she gathered the baby and her bag. She pointed to the playpen.

"Can you grab that?"

"I can." He folded it, or at least he figured it out after two or three tries. Lacey stood next to him, smiling again. It didn't take her long to bounce back.

"Let's go." He walked back to the truck and as he stowed the playpen in the back and lowered the tailgate for Pete to jump in, she strapped the baby into the car seat she'd pulled out of her car.

She'd make a good mom.

Lacey loved the stable, with the dust, the smell of hay, horses moving restlessly in their stalls and the cats climbing around, looking for mice. It felt like a comfortable place that a kid could have hidden in while playing hide-and-seek.

She asked Jay if he had played there as a kid.

"We did. Linda, Chad, me and a few neighbor kids would hang out in the barn. It wasn't this barn, not back then."

Lacey closed her eyes, remembering her own childhood, riding bikes down busy streets and staying away from her mom as much as possible. That had been a game of hide-and-seek she would have gladly not played.

She was a whole person, though. And happy. She looked at the baby sleeping in the playpen, the dog on the ground next to her. He'd taken up the job of protector. Lacey smiled. Jay, in the lawn chair next to hers, moved.

They were sitting in a stall opposite the stall where

the mare was laboring. Jay stood and walked out into the aisle. He came back shaking his head.

"She's stubborn."

"I'm not sure why you're watching her. Won't she give birth on her own?"

"She will, but this is her first foal and we've only had the mare a month. I bought her at the auction."

"At the auction?"

"She was cheap and I was bidding against guys that wouldn't have taken her to a nice home. She's part Arabian and sometimes they have thicker placenta and the babies need help breaking through the sac. Especially if she's been on a fescue-grass diet."

"That's a lot to remember."

"It's all information you pick up as you go. Sometimes you pick it up through a bad experience."

"A lot like life."

"I guess. Yes."

Pete lifted his head and looked at the wide open doors of the barn. Wilma Blackhorse walked through the opening, her smile wide. "There you two are."

"We're waiting for Lady to have her foal." Jay got out of his chair and motioned for his mom to sit.

"I wanted to see if you need anything." Wilma glanced in the direction of the baby, her smile soft. "I thought I might see if Lacey wants me to take the baby to the house."

"Are you sure?" Lacey had to ask. "I don't want you to feel like you have to constantly watch her."

"Lacey, I love you and that baby. Remember, I have a grandchild that lives hundreds of miles away that I can't see or hold every day."

Wilma was already gathering baby stuff. Lacey lifted

the infant from the playpen, kissing her cheek before handing her over to Wilma.

"Now, we'll just go on up to the nice, cool house and you two stay and make sure that foal is safe." Wilma smiled as she walked out the barn door, holding Rachel close and talking to her.

Lacey watched them go, watched the horse, watched cats playing and finally sat down. Jay sat next to her. Neither of them talked. Lacey avoided looking at the man next to her, because he had to know that his mom was starting to think of them as a likely match.

"She's never been subtle." Jay finally spoke, legs stretched in front of him, his jeans bunched over boots that were scuffed.

Lacey looked down at her worn sneakers, dirty from gardening. She tried not to think of all the differences between them.

"She means well. She just doesn't understand."

Jay looked at her, eyes narrowed. "What?"

"Me, the girl next door who is anything but the girl next door. Jay, I'm not naive. I know that I'm not the type of woman a man thinks of when he thinks of a wife and mother for his children."

"You're selling yourself short, Lacey. I'm not interested in a relationship with anyone. If I was…"

She waited, wondering for a moment why she was holding her breath, why she wanted to hear him say something that would make a difference. When she looked into Jay's eyes, she saw acceptance. And he knew all of her secrets.

"Lacey, I'm not ready to share deep, dark secrets. Maybe because I'm a man and we're not geared to talk about our feelings—" he flashed a cowboy grin and wink that lightened the moment "—but I couldn't imagine being ashamed to take you home to meet my family."

"You know that I dated Lance?"

"I know."

"I'm over him. I'm over whatever was between us. I'm getting over being rejected and dealing with the reality that he thought it was okay to date me, but all of our dates were in Springfield and never here, where people could see."

"Maybe it's time for you to forgive yourself."

"What?"

"You're still holding on to what you did in St. Louis. You're still punishing yourself and telling yourself you can't have what other people have because you made mistakes."

Lacey looked away from questioning eyes that were warm and compassionate. "I know. But Jay, people don't always let go of what they know about someone. I sold myself, and in the process I lost part of my self-worth. It isn't always easy to look in the mirror. It isn't easy to feel clean when for so long I felt dirty."

"You've asked for forgiveness. Maybe it's time to forgive yourself and to realize no one is perfect or sin-free."

Lacey nodded, because he made her want to believe in herself, but she couldn't tell him that. She couldn't take that step into his life and make a connection that would only lead to a broken heart.

Movement from the stall across from them brought both out of their seats. Jay walked to the stall and Lacey followed. Neither of them spoke.

The mare moved to the corner of the stall, head down. Lacey held her breath, watching as the foal slipped to the ground, dark and slimy on the straw-covered floor. Jay opened the stall door and moved quietly, talking to the mare. He helped the mother free her baby from the sac that covered its body. He used a towel to wipe the face, the nose and ears. When he stepped back, the mare took over, cleaning the dark, still-wet baby.

"It's a girl." He smiled over his shoulder, but the smile didn't reach his eyes.

"Jay, I'm sorry. I don't want things between us to be complicated." She shrugged. "I like having you for a friend."

He nodded and stepped back to lean against the wall. He draped the dirty towel over the gate and his gaze remained on the mare and foal.

"Lacey, I just got out of a relationship. It took me three years and a rejection to realize it would have been a mistake. I didn't love Cindy. She was easy to be around." He turned to Lacey, his brown eyes serious, his smile gone. "I won't do that to another woman. It isn't fair to slide into another relationship because it is easy."

"You don't have to explain."

"That isn't an explanation. It's a fact, and it's hard for a man to admit he nearly messed up someone else's life to make his own a little easier."

"I can't picture you looking for an easy relationship. You've got a big house nearly framed, a good life here, and it seems like you'd want to fill that life with a wife and kids."

"It seems that way, doesn't it?" He moved out of the stall door and stood next to her, resting his arms on the door. His shoulder brushed hers. "I'll tell you all about it someday."

"Okay."

Lacey focused on mother and baby. The little foal,

still too wet to tell her true color, tried to stand again. She would get up on hind legs, front legs still bent, and push. And down she'd go. The mother horse nuzzled her, encouraging her to try again.

It took a few minutes. Finally, on wobbly legs, she stood next to her mother.

"She's beautiful." Lacey leaned, looking in at the most miraculous event of her life.

"I'm going to name her Dandelion." Jay winked as he spoke. "And when she's weaned, she's yours."

"Jay, I can't take a horse."

"She's a gift. Lacey, I bought her mom for almost nothing, just to save her life. The baby was a bonus. She's yours. Just call her Dandelion, okay?"

"Dandy for short."

"Okay." He stepped out of the stall. "And don't let the Gibson matchmakers bother you too much. They've been at it for years. Probably for decades. A long time ago they wanted me to marry Bailey. Think about what a mistake that would have been."

A mistake. She nodded and let her gaze drift back to the mare and her foal. Lacey didn't want to be anyone's mistake.

"I should go." She stepped back, not really wanting to leave the mare and the little filly, Dandelion.

"Don't." Jay remained next to her. "Lacey, I have stories, too. I'm just not ready to share."

"You don't have to share." She folded the playpen, smiling a little because Jay watched, shaking his head like he had more to say.

"You make that look easy." He meant the playpen, she knew.

Chapter Fourteen

Three days after a foal named Dandelion was born and she'd learned that Jay had secrets, secrets Lacey didn't want to know, she stood on the porch and watched the county social worker drive away. Lacey felt a little sick to her stomach, not knowing what the lady had meant by *hmmm* and *um-hmmm*.

As her car pulled away, Bailey's pulled in. Lacey let out a sigh of relief that only Pete heard. Pete. She still didn't love the dog, but he was growing on her. She looked at him, frowning a little, a gesture he obviously didn't get. His tail thumped the wood porch.

"Was that the case worker?" Bailey walked up to the porch. "And isn't that Jay's dog?"

"It is Jay's dog, and yes, it was the case worker. She did the home study."

"How'd it go?" Bailey glanced at the dog again and shook her head. "Why is Pete here? You don't like dogs."

"He's a little like his owner, kind of clueless sometimes."

"Jay, clueless?" Bailey walked into the semi-cool interior of the house. "I love this place."

"Practice." She carried the playpen out of the stall they'd been sitting in and he took it from her.

"You can't walk home with all of this stuff and the baby."

She groaned, because she hadn't thought of that. She had ridden down in his truck. And she had the baby. It was no longer just her, taking care of herself.

"I'll get Rachel." She let him take the playpen from her hands. In some circles this would have been running away. Maybe it was. She didn't want to hear personal stories that would lead her further into his life, and she didn't want to be anyone's mistake.

"Me, too." She led Bailey to the kitchen. "Thank you for watching her tonight."

"I don't want you to quit school."

"Again." Lacey turned and smiled as she pulled a pitcher of lemonade out of the fridge. "Want some?"

"Homemade?"

"Of course."

Bailey nodded and got glasses out of the cabinet. "So, Jay is clueless?"

"Of course he is. We have this strange friendship that only exists because he brought Corry to the diner and I moved in here. He didn't want that, but now we're friends and I don't know."

"He's drop-dead…"

"Stop." *Gorgeous* wasn't a word that Lacey needed supplied in order to picture the cowboy with the dark hair and stomach-tilting smile.

"Okay, I'll stop. So, his dog likes you."

They sat down at the table. Lacey pushed a plate of cookies to her friend. Bailey took one, and then took another.

"Yes, his dog likes me." Lacey smiled at the baby sleeping in the playpen. "And I like Jay. As a friend. As a neighbor."

"I'm glad to hear you're opening that door."

After a drink of tart and sweet lemonade, Lacey explained, "I told him about my little girl."

Bailey's eyes watered and a few tears spilled out. That hadn't been Lacey's goal. Tears should be behind them.

"Oh, Lace, I'm sorry. I know this can't be easy for you, with Rachel and the memories."

"It's easier than I thought it would be. It's been years, and I'm a different person. And that little girl has a life with a family that loves her. It's the way it's supposed to be." She smiled. "I never thought I'd be able to say that."

"So then, what's the problem with Jay?"

"I'm okay with my past. I don't want for someone else to have to be okay with it."

"I guess that make sense."

"Not only that, but I don't want to be his rebound girl. He got rejected by someone he dated for three years. That has to leave a few wounds."

"He wasn't in love with her. *She* was the rebound girl."

"He told me he wasn't in love with her, but that's all I got from him."

"You don't know about Jamie?"

"I guess not."

"She lived here. In this house."

Lacey closed her eyes. "Wonderful. Now I understand why he didn't want me here."

"They were—"

Lacey raised her hand. "I don't think I want to hear this."

"She came here—"

Lacey stopped her friend. "Bailey, I mean it, I don't want to hear. This is his story, and I don't want his story. I don't want to hear his secrets. I don't want to be connected to him that way. I don't want…"

"To have your heart broken?"

She nodded. "I don't want to fall in love with him, because I'm fine the way I am. I have Rachel now. I love this town and I love my friends here. It's taken me a long time to get to this place."

"You're absolutely right, you have made it. You're a bigger part of Gibson than you realize."

* * *

Jay reached for his phone the next morning. Without thinking his plan through, he dialed Lacey's number, knowing she was up, even after her late night at school.

He'd made the mistake of stopping by Lacey's the night before, and he'd gotten stuck talking to Bailey.

Bailey, who had questioned him about his intentions toward her friend. He had to smile at the protectiveness that had been evident. He didn't plan on hurting Lacey. He had told Bailey that he didn't have *intentions*.

She answered on the third ring, a little out of breath, her voice soft.

"Lacey, are you busy?"

"No, why? Is everything okay?"

He sat down in the rocking chair on his mom's front porch and watched as the construction crew worked on the roof of his new house. "Everything is fine. I just thought I'd see if you wanted to go riding."

"I don't know." Hesitation. "Jay, what's going on?"

"They did the home study yesterday. I thought you might need to be distracted."

"Thank you."

"So, riding?"

"I want to be here when they call, so I really can't go riding."

"How about if I come down there. We can water the dandelions."

"That isn't nice, making fun of a girl because she shared something with you."

"You're right. So, how about a picnic and Pete can play with Rachel."

"A play date with the kids, how fun." Her tone teased and he smiled. It sounded like a normal conversation

"I know, but I guess I'm always waiting for the floor to drop out from under me. It only takes one person bringing it up, making a big deal of it, and then people start to talk."

"True, but you're a part of this community now. Lacey, people know you and love you. Everyone gets talked about, people do gossip, but there are more people who love you than who would want to hurt you."

"You can be right about that." Lacey smiled, and it was easier to smile now. "But I'm right about relationships."

"Okay, if that's the way you want to play, I'll let you be right about relationships. I get to be right about everything else."

"Deal." Lacey looked down at her watch. "And if I don't get going, I'm going to be late for class."

"Go. We'll be fine. Oh, did you talk to the lawyer?"

"Yep. We have to go to court and have a judge approve everything." She reached for her books. "As long as the home study comes back okay and no one contests the adoption."

"It will work out."

"Bailey, I want to be an optimist, but I have to be realistic on this. I have a record. What happens if they don't approve me for this adoption?"

"We'll make sure she stays here."

"How?"

"Cody and I will adopt her."

Lacey hugged her friend for that out-of-character impulsiveness. "I love you, Bailey. See you later."

Lacey hurried to her car, trying not to look at the truck that drove past, or the cowboy who waved without really looking in her direction.

she was spunky and beautiful. The rough edges he used to imagine had softened and her smile teased.

"The kind of food women like. It usually contains nuts and fruit."

"Is that the definition in Webster's?"

"It's the Jay definition." He kissed Rachel's cheek and then looked at Lacey. "Chicken salad, croissants, salad with some kind of fruity-tasting dressing and cheesecake."

"Wow, it *is* chick food."

"Mom bought it at some *homemade but not* deli in Springfield."

"You're willing to eat such chick food? For me?"

"For you."

She turned a little pink and he didn't comment. He felt as if the picnic mattered in ways he couldn't begin to understand.

"I'm going to take it in the house for now." Lacey stepped back, away from him and the baby. "You hold Rachel. I'll put this in the fridge. The last thing we need is food poisoning. And I'll make lemonade."

He smiled because she was rambling.

"I'll sit here in the shade with Miss Rachel." He watched Lacey go and then he sat down on the swing, the baby in his arms, her fingers wrapping around his, and she cooed.

"Little girl, you are one special creature. You know, I think your aunt is special, too. Don't tell her that." He leaned back, the baby sort of standing in his lap, her slobbery mouth on his shoulder. "It isn't easy, moving forward. It isn't easy to let go of promises."

He sat Rachel back on his lap and she gave him a

between a man and a woman. Then Jay knew that he shouldn't have called.

Too late now. She was silent on the other end, waiting for him to say something.

"Yes, a play date."

"Come on down."

Jay drove down to Lacey's with a picnic basket on the seat next to him and Pete in the back of the truck. When he pulled up to Lacey's she was sitting in the backyard on a canopy-shaded swing. The baby was sitting in her lap.

He got out, Pete hurrying ahead of him. The dog sat at Lacey's feet, nuzzling her hand and then sniffing the baby. Jay reached them, smiling a little because they were quite a trio, that dog, the baby and Lacey.

He wasn't sure where he fit in. That thought didn't make sense. He wasn't supposed to fit in here.

"Have you heard from the lawyer?"

She shook her head, standing with the baby. "Not yet. I'm a little nervous."

She handed him the baby girl. In the short time Rachel had been at Lacey's she'd grown and she smiled more. Drool slid down her chin and she touched his cheek with her tiny hand.

"She likes you." Lacey took the picnic basket.

"Good thing she doesn't know that I'm scared to death of her."

"Good thing. But I think babies are like dogs. They smell fear." Lacey pulled a cloth off her shoulder and wiped the drool off the baby's chin. "What's in the basket?"

"Chick food."

"Chick food?" Her brows arched and he thought that

Footsteps on the floor in the kitchen. She turned as Jay walked into the room, and she answered the phone.

"Miss Gould, this is Lynette McCullough from Family Services. I wanted to let you know that the review for your home study was positive and we can proceed with the adoption. We'll go to court in two weeks."

"Court in two weeks?" Lacey turned and smiled at Jay. He was leaning against the door frame, watching her. "That soon?"

"In a situation like this, with the parent giving up her rights, the process is a little easier and definitely takes less time."

She looked away, focusing on the call, the details and the baby that would be hers. She said good-bye and hung up, knowing that Jay had moved closer, that he was behind her.

"Good news?"

She nodded as she finished putting the new diaper on Rachel. "Court in two weeks. They approved the home study."

It felt like they had approved her. She felt a little lighter, a little freer.

"Would you like me to go with you?" He took the dirty diaper she handed him and she pointed to the trash. He cringed a little and held the diaper as if she'd handed him a poisonous snake. He had delivered calves and foals, cleaned stalls, and he couldn't handle a diaper. She smiled, because he had offered to go to court with her and she wanted to forget how it had felt when Lance broke her heart.

"You don't have to go." She wiped her hands with baby wipes and picked up Rachel. How could she tell him that each time he moved a little further into her life, crooked grin. "Yes, like you know exactly what I mean. It's easy to tell you secrets. Who are you going to tell?"

The baby blew spit bubbles and he lifted her to kiss her cheek. "I know exactly what you mean. Life is definitely complicated."

She grinned again, and then her face turned red and she made another face. "Oh, well, that's not pleasant."

He looked from the baby to the house. No sign of Lacey. He held the baby out a little and wrinkled his own nose. Rachel smiled, obviously thinking his face was part of a game to entertain her.

The back door slammed shut. Pete got up and walked away, choosing a place under the shade tree. Lacey laughed as she crossed the yard. "Is she suddenly toxic?"

He nodded and held the baby out to Lacey. "I think she is."

Lacey took her niece and held her, not bothered, obviously. "I'll change her and be right back. Try not to look so offended."

He laughed a little. "You have to admit, it isn't nice."

"I admit, it really isn't. But you're a country boy, you've seen worse."

"I'm not sure if I've smelled worse."

Lacey walked through the back door, Rachel cooing against her shoulder, and smelling really unpleasant. She put the baby down on the changing table in the tiny spare bedroom and reached for the diapers. The phone rang.

Of course it would ring while her hands were full with a messy baby, diapers and wipes. She held Rachel and reached for the phone, knocking the wipes off the table in the process.

she thought about what it would feel like to be loved by the cowboy next door? She thought about how it would feel to watch him walk away.

She wanted to hear about Jamie, from him, not from Bailey or someone else.

"I think we should eat." She grabbed the bouncy seat for the baby and handed it to him.

"Good idea." Letting go of secrets, of wanting something she couldn't have. He hadn't told her about Jamie, and that meant something. It meant he didn't want her to share that part of his life, or know about that broken piece of his heart.

As they walked out the back door she wondered if he thought of Jamie when he visited. Was he thinking about the memory of a girl he had loved, who owned his heart?

She stopped herself, because she didn't know the story. She hadn't let Bailey share his secrets. Anything she came up with was speculation.

"You okay?" He stood under the cherry tree where she'd placed a picnic table she had bought at the local flea market. She had painted it bright yellow.

"I'm fine, just hungry. Do you want to get the food out of the fridge and I'll buckle Rachel in the bouncy seat?"

Did he want to tell her about Jamie? She bit down on her bottom lip and tried not to imagine what she read in his dark eyes. She wouldn't let her heart be broken again.

Jay turned and walked away, straight back and dark blue T-shirt. Two months ago he had been a stranger. When he came back with the picnic basket and lemonade, he still wasn't smiling.

"Lacey, we can be friends."

"I know that." She really did. She looked away, sliding

the pacifier back into Rachel's mouth, and then opening the basket that Jay had placed on the table.

He moved behind her, close. Too close.

His hands brushed her arms and he leaned, kissing her neck from behind, his hands still resting on her arms. "Turn around."

He whispered the words into her ear and she turned, aware of his cologne, aware of mint and the sweet scent of summer clover as bees buzzed. He cupped the back of her neck and his lips met hers, tasting like mint—and forever.

Lacey's mind played tricks on her, reminding her of a girl who had done things to feed her family, to keep her siblings in a home through the winter. And this cowboy, strong and sure of himself, he had never had to make those hard decisions.

She backed away. "No."

"What?"

She shook her head, feeling ridiculous for even letting herself believe in forever. "I'm a dirty sock."

He smiled just a little. "A dirty sock?"

"You're a clean sock and I'm a dirty sock. We're not a matched set. We're not…I'm not going to play games and kiss you on a summer day, believing in fairy tales and forever. I know who I am and what I am. I know that I'm not someone's forever. I'm just the girl that's easy to kiss on a summer day. I'm just a friend."

"Lacey, you have the oddest way of putting things. I'm not playing games. I don't play games."

"Then tell me about Jamie."

He backed away, looking wounded, as if she'd slapped him. "Keep the food. I have to go."

"Jay, wait. I'm sorry."

He turned and stopped. "For what? For thinking such ridiculous thoughts about yourself, or for listening to gossip?"

"I didn't gossip."

"Then how do you know about Jamie?" He took a few steps toward her and her breath caught in her lungs, hopeful, thinking he might not walk away.

If he shared, what would that mean?

"Someone tried to tell me, and I wouldn't let them."

"I don't want to talk about Jamie."

"Okay." She bit down on her lip and told herself she wouldn't cry. She wouldn't let her heart be broken over the closed look on his face.

He hadn't shared. What did that mean?

"I'm not ready for this." He shrugged. "I'll talk to you later."

Not ready for what? She wanted to throw the question at his retreating back. Not ready for a relationship, or not ready to tell her about Jamie?

Chapter Fifteen

Lacey didn't see Jay again until Sunday. He was in his uniform, getting out of his patrol car, and she pulled into the church parking lot. He was leaning against the car parked next to hers when she opened the door of her car.

"Need some help?" He reached for the back door. "I can get Rachel."

"Oh, okay." But not really okay. Not when there was an incredible distance between them.

"You should come and see Dandelion today. I have a halter on her and she could use some attention. The more we mess with her now, the easier she'll be to handle as she gets older."

"I can do that."

"Lacey, I'm sorry about the other day. I thought I could do the picnic."

"Don't apologize, Jay. It was a mistake on both our parts. We should stick to friendship. I think we might be good at being friends."

He nodded and smiled again, but then his gaze shot past her. "I don't recognize that car."

A cop. She'd somehow forgotten that he was a cop.

She turned, wondering why a car would intrigue him. It was church, and the whole idea was for people that didn't normally come to attend. That was a good thing.

The car in question was moving too fast and the right front tire was a spare, the doughnut kind that looked like it belonged on a bike. And the woman behind the wheel was Lacey's mother.

"This can't be happening," Lacey muttered. Her heart did a painful, nervous squeeze.

"Who is it?"

"My mother." Or the woman who claimed the title. *Forgive.* The word rolled through her mind, because it was necessary to let go, and to forgive.

"I'm with you." His voice was strong, and he didn't move away from her.

He was with her. A friend. And yet he didn't share secrets. She blocked thoughts of Jamie, previously a name whispered in connection with his, but not a real person. Now she felt very real. She was living, in a surreal way, in Lacey's dream house.

Lacey's mom parked her car and got out. Deanna Gould was nearly fifty, but still tried to look like a woman in her twenties. In short skirts and tank tops, her hair dyed a brassy blond, she didn't pull off the younger look. Her makeup was garishly bright and her smile was stiff. A hard life had aged Lacey's mother.

"That's my grandchild," Deanna yelled as she approached them. "And don't think your cop friend scares me."

"I'm not here to frighten you." Jay still held the car seat that carried Rachel. Lacey stood close to him, feeling a little protected because he was near. For the moment she pushed aside the hurt she'd felt when he walked away.

"Well, I'm here to get that baby." Deanna crossed skinny arms in front of her.

"You can't take her." Lacey found her voice and her strength. "I have custody of Rachel. She's not going with you."

Movement out of the corner of her eyes. She turned and saw several people standing in the doorway of the church. Her stomach tightened with dread. Her old life had invaded Gibson.

"She's my granddaughter and you're not the good little girl you want these people to think you are."

"Maybe not, but she's with me and she's safe."

"She's my grandchild." Deanna's face crumpled and she looked ten years older. Lacey felt sorry for her.

"I'm not going to keep you from seeing her. I'm also not going to let you take her."

"I'll get a lawyer." Deanna took a few steps closer, looking as if she might really try to grab Rachel and run. Her gaze glued to the baby, and then traveled up, to Jay's face. "You can't keep me from getting her."

"We're going to court, Mom. I'm going to adopt her."

"You? With your record?" Deanna laughed, a harsh laugh.

"That was a long time ago."

"Why don't we all go into church and we can talk about this later?" Jay, calm, in control. Lacey felt like her insides were shaking as badly as her legs.

"Go in there?" Deanna looked past them, eyeing the church and looking less than sure. "Well, if it means seeing my grandchild, I guess I can."

Wonderful.

Jay touched Lacey's back. She wanted to move closer to his side. She didn't. Instead she walked a little taller,

telling herself she could do this. She could walk through the doors of this church with her mother. She could face people who had become like family to her. These people who had prayed for her mom, for her brother and sister.

It had been easy, praying for a mother who lived four hours away. Having her here, walking through the doors of the church, wasn't as easy. This was reality, and it was glaringly bright, like a spotlight in the dark, shining into the corners of Lacey's past, highlighting who she had been before she came here.

Reality.

She shuddered and Jay reached for her hand. His hand was warm and strong, his fingers clasping hers. The security of his touch was undone by the look her mother shot at her, a look that accused and mocked. Lacey knew that this day changed everything.

"You must be Deanna Gould, Lacey's mother." Pastor Dan reached for Lacey's mother's hand, greeting her with a smile that was genuine. It was the smile that Lacey couldn't work up to.

"That's me." Deanna looked past him, no longer smiling, no longer looking confident.

"Welcome to Gibson, and to our church."

"Yeah, thanks." Deanna peeked through the doors into the sanctuary. "I've seen enough and I'm not going in there. Lacey, I'll be waiting in my car for you to finish up your little charade here."

"It isn't a charade, Mom."

"Oh, I think it is. Why don't you let me keep Rachel while you're in church?"

"No, she's going with me." Lacey took the baby from Jay. "You can see her later."

Deanna Gould shrugged, and with a smile, she walked

away. She had always walked away when things got tough. Lacey watched from the doorway as her mom got back in her car. And instead of waiting, she started the old sedan and drove away.

For some reason, Lacey had convinced herself that her mother would be gone when she got out of church. Deanna wasn't gone. Her car was back in the parking lot, windows down. Deanna was drinking a soda and blowing smoke rings out the window.

Lacey felt the stares of people she considered friends as she crossed to her car parked next to her mother. She tried to block her imagination from telling her what people would say about her. She tried to block thoughts of dinner tables and comments about Lacey Gould.

"Hey." Bailey hurried toward her, blond hair free, skin glowing with the health of her pregnancy. "Don't run off."

"I have to go." Lacey held the seat with Rachel. What had she thought? That this would be easy? That she'd be able to take this baby and raise her with no one objecting?

"Do you want us to come with you?" Bailey glanced in Cody's direction. Her husband stood a little distance away, Meg at his side. He nodded and smiled. Friends who wouldn't let her down.

She didn't want to think about other people seeing her there with her mother, hearing her mother's accusations.

"I can handle it." Lacey smiled because she felt stronger now. She could do this. "She wants to see Rachel, that's all."

"You call if you need us." Bailey gave her a quick hug. "Don't forget that you have friends."

"How could I forget?"

Lacey buckled Rachel's seat into the back of the car

and walked around to her mother's open window. Deanna Gould blew another puff of smoke and dropped her cigarette out the window. Lacey stepped on it.

"Ready to go?"

"Do you have something for lunch?" Deanna lit another cigarette.

"I put a roast on this morning. I take it you're staying?"

"Where's your Christian charity, Lacey?"

"It's here, don't worry." She pulled her keys out of her pocket. "Follow me."

"My car won't start."

Lacey resisted the urge to sigh. "You can ride with me."

The Lord won't give you more than you can handle. Pastor Dan had preached that sermon a month ago. It had been a fresh message on verses sometimes tossed around to help cover someone else's troubles. But the meaning was strong, that God would help us through whatever situations we faced. He would give us the strength and grace to make it through trials and tribulations.

God wouldn't leave us to drift alone.

He even had a plan for Deanna Gould being in Gibson. Lacey couldn't think of what the plan might be, not at that moment. Maybe it would be one of those hindsight things that she would figure out later.

Later, when she wasn't thinking how her mother's presence would rock the boat that was her life.

"Stop looking like I'm the worst news you've ever had. I think giving that baby of yours up would qualify for that. And here you are, thinking you can replace that kid with Corry's baby."

"Stop." Lacey started her car. She watched Jay's patrol

car leave the parking lot, lights on. He must have gotten a call. "Stop trying to beat me down."

Her mom buckled her seat belt. "I'm not beating you down, just being honest. You are who you are, Lacey. You're not someone that a guy like that cop dates, not for real."

"Stop." Lacey pulled out of the parking lot, her foot a little heavy on the gas. "Keep this up and I'll take you back to the church and I won't let you see Rachel."

"I'll get a lawyer and make sure you don't get to adopt her."

Lacey couldn't stand to lose more. She couldn't handle the thought of losing her heart, losing the baby and losing the community that she loved. "You can't do that. I have an approved home study and Corry signed over custody."

Deanna Gould looked out the window, shrugging as if it didn't matter. "I need money to get home."

It all came back to money. Lacey didn't hold back the sigh, not this time. "I don't have a lot of money."

"I can't get home with a broken-down car and ten bucks."

"Fine, I'll give you some money. And there's a mechanic in our church who can probably get the car running. I'll buy you a used tire tomorrow, to replace the spare."

"Don't forget to let me know that you'll pray for me. Isn't that what you always say when you call? When you used to call, that is." Was that hopefulness in her mother's tone?

Lacey's heart thawed a little. "Mom, I pray for you all the time."

And someday, someday she knew God would answer those prayers. Maybe this was a start.

* * *

Lacey's car was at home. Her mom's car was still parked at the church. Jay pulled his truck down the drive and parked behind her sedan. He didn't get out. He felt as if he was tangled in a spiderweb of emotion and the more he tried to untangle, the stickier it got.

He didn't know how to be in Lacey's life, and all day he'd thought about how to walk away without either of them getting hurt.

And here he was, parked in her drive, waiting for her to come outside. He opened the door and stepped out of the truck as the front door of the house opened. He told himself he had just stopped by to check on her. People were worried. He was worried.

She was dressed in shorts and a T-shirt, her auburn-streaked hair pulled back with a headband. She smiled and wiped her hands on her pants.

"I was doing dishes." She shrugged.

"I wanted to check on you. Pastor Dan and a couple of other people called this afternoon. They were worried."

"I'm fine." She glanced over her shoulder, looking less than fine and a little worried. "Her car isn't running and I need to find a tire to replace the spare so she can go home."

"I'll go take a look at the car."

"You don't have to do that." She spoke as if he was a stranger, less than a friend. That didn't add up.

"Lacey, are you sure everything is okay here?"

She smiled then and glanced over his uniform. "I don't need police backup, Jay. I'm used to dealing with her games. She wants money to go home, to leave Rachel and me alone. I'll give her what she wants if it means an end to this."

"Don't let her manipulate you that way."

She shrugged slim shoulders and smiled a little. "You make a great hero. But really, she's not going to hurt us. And after everything she said about me today, it's better if I stick to myself for a while until this blows over."

"What does that mean?"

"It means that people will talk. I'm not the church Sunday-school teacher or the nursery worker. I'm not Lacey who works at the Hash-It-Out. I'm Lacey from St. Louis and I have a police record. I'm a fraud who sneaked into this community and pretended to be someone I'm not. And now everyone knows."

Jay brushed a hand through his hair and sighed. "Lacey, you can't believe that's true. The people here care about you. You're a part of their lives." His life. He cared. He looked away, getting his thoughts together. "And you didn't hide who you are. You told the people closest to you, and the rest didn't really need to know."

"My heart knows that. My brain only knows that my mother is here and now everyone is looking at me like I'm someone they don't know."

"It'll blow over."

"And if it doesn't blow over?"

"It will. Right now you feel like it won't, but if you think back, nothing like this lasts forever. It settles down in time. That's how a small town works."

"Thank you, Jay. I'm glad we became friends."

He nodded and walked away. Friendship. He had a lot of thinking to do. Lacey thought they had friendship, and that would have been an easy option for them both. Friendship didn't include strings. Friendship should have made walking away easy to do.

This felt anything but easy.

* * *

Lacey walked back into the house and found her mother on the sofa with Rachel, hugging the baby close. Had Deanna Gould ever held her own children that way? Lacey couldn't remember. She remembered boyfriends, drunken parties and men that she and her siblings hid from.

Lacey remembered an empty pantry and selling herself on a street corner because her siblings were cold and hungry and she had exhausted every other avenue of hope.

They had all escaped in whatever way worked for them. Lacey ran. Corry turned to drugs. Chase joined the marines when he turned eighteen.

For years she'd had nightmares of that life. Now she had dreams that included Gibson and a small house in the country. Maybe even a cowboy. Someday.

"She's a beautiful little girl." Deanna kissed Rachel's pink baby cheek. "I really messed up our lives, didn't I?"

Lacey shrugged and sat down in the easy chair across from her mom. "I don't know, Mom. I guess you did. It wasn't an easy way to grow up."

Deanna's eyes watered. "I'm not sure if I can change my life. I'm too old. I really am glad you found something better. It makes me so angry sometimes, that you chose this place over your own family, but I guess it makes you happy."

"It does make me happy. And this will be a good place to raise Rachel. She won't have to worry…"

"I know, I know. Don't accuse me, okay?"

"I'm not. Mom, I forgive you."

"I didn't do anything wrong."

Let it go. Lacey sighed. "Jay is going to look at your car."

"Are you in a hurry to get rid of me?"

"No." She knew that was a lie. "Mom, I don't mind you being here, but I don't want you to cause problems."

"I'll mess up this pretty life you've built for yourself?"

"Maybe that's what I feel. I don't know. But I won't let you have Rachel and I won't let you manipulate me."

"Lacey, I don't have a house to go back to."

Lacey wanted to cry. She wanted to hit something and scream that it wasn't fair. Her mom shouldn't be able to come here and do the same thing she'd been doing all of Lacey's life: create instability. Lacey had her life organized and settled, the way she'd craved during her childhood.

"I guess you don't want me here?"

"I don't know. We'll figure something out." Lacey stood up and reached for Rachel. "But what about you taking Rachel? What kind of game was that?"

Her mom shrugged. "I knew I couldn't take her. I guess I thought if you had money, you'd give me some to get rid of me."

"I don't have money. Corry already stole it all."

Lacey walked out the front door to the porch, Rachel cradled and protected against her chest. She heard laughter and glanced in the direction of the Blackhorse house. Wilma Blackhorse stood in the yard watering her flowers, and from the way Jay jumped and ran, Wilma must have sprayed him with the water hose.

A normal family. Lacey's heart ached, empty because she wanted that space in her life filled with people that would be that for her. She wanted a family that didn't

crash and burn as often as other families sat down for dinner together.

She wanted people to come home to, to share dreams with and to lean on. She didn't want to lose what she had in Gibson.

Chapter Sixteen

Lacey sat down to roll flatware in paper napkins at the end of her shift on Monday. She glanced up as Jolynn walked out of the kitchen, two cups of coffee and a plate with a slice of pie on a tray. She set the tray down on the table next to Lacey.

"Let's chat, sweetie." Jolynn scooted out the chair next to Lacey's. "We'll figure out this situation with your mom."

"I don't know if there's a solution."

"Of course there is. I haven't rented the studio. We'll put your momma there and she can do something. I'll have her wash dishes and maybe we can have her clean up around our place."

"But…"

"But you don't want her to stay in town? Lacey, stop worrying about what people will think."

"That's easier said than done. You have no idea what it was like growing up with her. Imagine her at school, talking to your teachers, or attending Christmas programs with her latest boyfriend."

"She attended?"

Lacey rolled a set of flatware in a napkin and nodded. "She did attend."

"That must mean something."

"I guess."

Jolynn scooted the napkins and covered Lacey's hand with her own. "Lacey, everyone has dreams, even people who don't seem to. Your mom might have made wrong choices, but she had dreams. Give yourself a little credit and God a little credit. We all love you and your mom showing up isn't going to change that. Maybe this is the answer to all of your prayers for her."

"I know."

Lacey wanted to tell Jolynn about secrets and dreams. She wanted to explain that her heart wanted to let Jay in, to trust him, and she couldn't. She couldn't let herself fall in love. She couldn't expect him to look at her as anything more than a friend.

"You're still frowning. Is this about Jay Blackhorse?"

Lacey looked up. "Maybe."

"And do you love him?"

She took a bite of the pie that Jolynn had set in front of her. Chocolate pie, not her favorite, but she ate it anyway. Did she love Jay? The question made her heart ache, because she wanted to let herself love him.

"I can't love Jay. Wilma and Bill are great and they've helped me so much. Helping me is different than having Jay bring me home…"

"What in the world are you talking about?"

"I heard a few ladies talking the other day, about me living down the road from Jay, in Jamie's house. I don't even know who Jamie was, but I feel her presence every single day and I know I can't compete."

"You need to ask Jay."

"I asked and he doesn't want to talk about it. Besides, he's just a friend and he doesn't owe me explanations."

Jolynn clucked a couple of times. "Lacey, Wilma and Bill would be blessed to have their son bring you home. You're everything a woman wants for her son. You're bright, warm and loving."

"I have a record for prostitution. I'm not the girl next door. I'm the woman that a guy takes out a few times, and then he doesn't call her anymore."

"Jay isn't Lance."

"No, and I'm not asking him to make me promises. He's a friend. I want to keep him that way."

"That might not happen." Jolynn stood and before she walked away she leaned and kissed Lacey on the top of her head. "You're a beautiful girl, Lacey, but sometimes you're a little slow when it comes to figuring things out. Give it time."

Give it time. Lacey nodded, as if she could do that.

The cowbell clanged and her mom walked through the doors. She had dyed her hair a natural shade of brown. Some things did change. Lacey smiled, because she wanted her mom to have a chance at a new life.

It wouldn't be easy, but she really did want that.

Jay drove past Lacey's house a little slower than usual. He had heard the talk in town, about her and her mom. He knew that she had to be hurting over old wounds re-opened. And the comments about her living next door to him.

He hadn't responded well to those accusations. Even now his blood boiled a little when he thought about the guys at the livestock auction making jokes about her and him. He'd left, not bothering to bid on a bull his dad had

been interested in. Still in his uniform, he'd parked his patrol car at the station and driven home.

Lacey's car wasn't at home. He hadn't seen her at the diner, either. He had even stopped. Jolynn had told him that Lacey had left an hour earlier. She had also let him know that Lacey had heard talk similar to what he'd heard at the auction.

When he pulled up to his parents' house, Lacey's car was there. He got out, stretching the kinks from his back. It had been a long day on the job, and a long day of hurting families.

Lacey's included.

He wanted a shower and clean clothes. He didn't see Lacey as he walked through the house. His parents had her somewhere, probably in the backyard. His mom had planned to grill pork steaks for dinner. He cringed a little. He'd picked up a burger from the concession stand at the auction because he knew about the curried pork. He wouldn't escape the leftovers.

On the way to the bathroom he glanced out the window of the sitting room. He saw Lacey and his dad walking to the barn. Probably to see the foal.

Fifteen minutes later he walked through the doors of the stable, his hair still a little damp. He had changed into a cotton shirt and shorts.

"Jay." Lacey walked out of a stall, the baby in one arm and a kitten in her other hand. "Look what we found."

"Great, the world needs more cats." He took the kitten that she held out to him. "Do you want me to put her back with the rest of the litter? Or do you want to take her home?"

"She isn't ready to be weaned." She looked up, uncertainty shadowing her eyes. "Maybe in a couple of

weeks. I'd like for Rachel to have a kitten. And maybe even a puppy."

"I think we can find her a puppy." He walked into the stall and put the kitten with the others. When he walked out, Lacey was waiting. "Did you see Dandy?"

"I did. She's beautiful. Your dad helped me put a lead rope on her and she's wonderful."

"She is a beautiful little thing."

"You don't have to give her to me. I mean, she's probably going to be a great horse."

"She's going to be a great horse for you. I really don't have any use for her. I think I'll put her and the mare on the two acres next to your place. You can mess with them all you want."

"Really?" Her eyes were huge and soft brown.

At that moment, he would have given her the world. The thought took him by surprise. He had to stop for a second and refocus.

"How's your mom?" He walked to the back of the barn with her. His dad was there, saddling his gelding. "Going for a ride, Dad?"

"I thought I'd check those back fences to see if I can figure out where the cows are getting out onto Seth's place."

"Good luck. I rode the four-wheeler out there a few days ago and didn't see anything."

His dad shook his head. "It's that one Angus heifer that's causing most of the problems. For all we know, she's climbing the fence."

Jay laughed. "I kind of wondered that myself. She's going to the auction next week. I don't feel like spending all my time chasing her down."

"Sounds like a good idea. I'll still take a ride and see if I can figure where she's getting out."

Jay watched his dad ride away and then turned back to Lacey. She had her fingers through the fence and her foal had approached with cautious steps and curious ears pricked forward. He didn't repeat his question about her mom. Instead he watched as she ran her fingers along the foal's muzzle. Rachel leaned against Lacey's shoulder, wrapping tiny fingers in dark hair.

"I think my mom is moving to Gibson." Lacey turned to face him when the foal pranced away, skittish because a cat had walked out of the barn. The mare nuzzled her foal and the baby leaned into her mom and started to nurse.

Lacey's mom was staying. Jay leaned on the fence and watched the mare and foal, not Lacey.

"I wondered. Are you okay with that?" He stood next to her, and he realized that she wasn't a girl in need of someone to make her dreams come true.

"I am, but I'm not. I've prayed for her for so long, and it was easy to pray. I wanted God to send someone who would be a witness to her. I wanted it to happen in St. Louis, so that I could stay here in my safe life." She brushed a hand across her eyes. "What kind of person does that make me?"

"A person who has dealt with enough."

"Maybe." She sighed. "Let's talk about you. How was your day?"

His day. He leaned against the fence, watching the mare and foal. "We had a drug bust and it ended with two little kids being taken into protective custody. No matter how low people get, or what mistakes they make,

it always rips their hearts out when you take their kids. That dad…"

Her hand was on his arm and he smiled down at her.

"It had to be hard to do." She spoke softly, encouraging. When was the last time he'd talked to someone the way he talked to her?

Never. The one word took him by surprise. Not even with Jamie. He and Jamie had shared a fantasy world that made letting go easier.

"It was," he admitted. "The parents were crying. The kids were crying."

Standing next to him, Lacey was crying. Tears trickled down her cheeks and she brushed them away. "Life without faith."

"Yes."

"Jay, I know what people are saying. I'm sorry. I'm not even sure who Jamie is, but I'm not trying to take her place. I'm sure that no one could do that. I'm the last person to try and fit into someone else's place in your life."

He nodded in the direction of the gazebo in the yard. "Let's go sit down in the shade."

"Okay."

Jay led the way, not sure what he would say, or how he would say it. He only knew that she deserved the truth. As a friend, she needed to know about Jamie.

Lacey walked up the steps into the gazebo. It was cooler there, with a ceiling fan spinning from the rafters, moving the summer air. Hummingbird feeders hung on hooks. A tiny bird buzzed past them, landing on a feeder and drinking for a long time from the nectar.

"My mom keeps the feeders full and sometimes there

are dozens of hummingbirds out here." Jay sat down on a bench and Lacey sat across from him.

She wanted to sit facing him, not next to him, touching him and breathing in the scent of soap and peppermint toothpaste. But sitting across from him presented other problems. Looking at him made her think of the kiss and how it had felt when he walked away from her.

She didn't want to think about him walking away.

He stretched long, tan legs in front of him and smiled. She smiled back, but Rachel fussed against her. She turned the baby so she could look around. Immediately Rachel looked up, mesmerized by the ceiling fan.

"Lacey, I was married."

It was really hot and she was positive she hadn't heard him correctly. He had proposed and Cindy had rejected him. *Married?* She couldn't process the word.

"Lacey, are you with me?" He leaned forward, tan, lean cheeks, a mouth that smiled hesitant smiles that nearly always did something to her heart.

She took in a deep breath and nodded. "You were married?"

"To Jamie." He clasped his hands and looked up, like Rachel, at the ceiling fan. The memory she couldn't compare to. Now she understood. At least she understood a little more than she had.

"You don't have to do this. I told you, it's your story and you don't have to share." She took a shallow breath that hurt.

"I want you to know. I want you to understand. It was the summer I turned twenty. I came home from college and my mom had brought home a family. She met them in Springfield and they wanted a place in the country for the summer. She gave them the farmhouse, where you live."

"Jamie?" It was hard for Lacey to say the word, to know that he had loved someone enough to marry her.

And her heart knew that this was his way of telling her what she already knew, that she didn't belong in his life.

"Jamie. She was eighteen and a patient in the clinic where my dad works. She had six months to live and she had always dreamed of living on a farm. Mom made that dream come true for her."

"And you fell in love with her?"

He didn't answer. Not right away. His eyes were closed and he nodded. When he opened his eyes she saw his broken heart.

"I fell in love with her. She was perfect and innocent. She was full of joy and faith. She had a dream of loving someone forever. And she knew that she wouldn't have forever. So we had three months."

"Jay, I'm sorry."

He nodded and his eyes filled with tears. He didn't cry. "I promised her that I would only love her. Forever. It was all I could give."

"What about Cindy?"

"Friendship. We had a great friendship and a lot of fun together. We got tangled up in something that became a habit. It was an easy relationship that didn't require a lot from either of us. She wanted a career, and I had memories of someone else. It wasn't love and she was smart to say no when I proposed."

"I'm not sure what to say."

"You don't have to say anything. I just wanted you to know the truth, before you hear it from someone else. I wanted you to know that it wasn't about you living in that house. It isn't about who you were in St. Louis."

"That isn't true, Jay. I'll always be that girl from St.

Louis. Our past makes us who we are. Remember?" Her past made her someone who couldn't compete with the memory of a perfect summer.

He didn't want anyone in that house. She understood now. She understood that he was telling her that he had already loved and lost. He had loved someone perfect, someone innocent. Someone who was nothing at all like Lacey.

She got it. She finally got it.

Our past does make us who we are. He agreed with that. That summer with Jamie had changed his life.

Lacey was looking at him, looking a little lost, looking hurt and he didn't know how to change that. He had given her the truth, it was all he had.

"I have to go now." Lacey stood, holding the baby. Rachel was still trying to look at the fan.

"Don't. You really don't have to leave."

"I know, but I can't stay."

She walked away without looking back, and without telling him she'd catch him later.

Jay stood in the gazebo and watched her go, watched her take a little of his heart with him. He didn't know how to call her back. He had never dreamed of this day, when he would want to call her back, because calling her back felt more important than holding on to a perfect summer.

He walked back to the barn, slow steps, thinking about why it had been necessary to tell her about Jamie and the promise. His dad was back from checking fences. Jay took the reins of his dad's gelding and led the horse into the stable.

"Did you find the hole?" he asked, his back to his dad.

"I found a place with loose barbed wire. That has to be it. Not a hole, just an empty space."

Empty spaces. Jay tied the horse. Empty places that Lacey and a baby had started to fill. And that had scared the daylights out of him. It had felt like a broken promise to a girl who hadn't had a chance to live, to really dream, to be.

"What's up?" His dad pulled the saddle off the dozing horse.

"Not much."

"That's more than a *not much* look on your face."

"I guess it's a look of pretty much total confusion."

"Got a girl on your mind?" His dad handed him the saddle and reached to pick up the brush he'd brought out of the tack room.

"A girl on my mind? Dad, I'm not sixteen."

"Sorry, but I wish it was as simple as that. You're a grown man. That's hard for a dad to handle. And you're going to have to let go of something that happened when you were a kid."

"'Something that happened'?" What an easy way to characterize a marriage that had ended three months after it started.

"Jamie was a long time ago, Jay. It's time to move on and to let someone else into your life. That doesn't mean you should replace her with someone you don't love just to fill the void."

"Cindy?"

His dad shrugged. "You know the answer to that better than I do."

"I guess I do. But I made a promise to love Jamie forever."

His dad stopped brushing the horse. Jay looked away

from a face so similar to his own that people often called them carbon copies. His dad hadn't known about the promise. Jay had kept that to himself, because it had seemed too private, too important.

Now it did seem like something a kid had done a long time ago.

His dad went back to brushing the horse, smooth, easy strokes. The horse twitched and stomped at flies that buzzed around his legs.

"That was a big promise to make."

"I guess it was."

"You can keep room in your heart for her and still make room for someone else. You made a promise to a dying girl. That's noble but a little unrealistic. I haven't said much over the years because I knew you'd work it out on your own."

Jay smiled at his dad. "So, why now?"

"Because I don't want you to make a mistake."

Mistake? It was up to Jay to figure that one out. Would loving Lacey be a mistake? Or would walking away from her be the mistake?

"Jay, do you care about Lacey?"

"I care about her. But I'm not sure if she's ready for a relationship any more than I am."

"I guess you've got to think about this and where you want it to go from here."

He nodded and reached for the halter of the gelding. Where to go from here? He remembered Lacey walking away. She wasn't a girl of eighteen looking for someone to fulfill her dreams. She was a woman who knew how to deal with life.

And she had walked away from him.

Chapter Seventeen

"Here you go, Mom." Lacey set the suitcase on the hide-a-bed in Jolynn's studio. "Remember, you have to work in the morning."

"I know, I know." Deanna sat down, clasping her hands at her knees. "I haven't worked in a long time, Lacey."

"You'll be fine. Show up and do what Jolynn asks you to do."

"Thank you for doing this for me. I hadn't expected you to be this good to me, not after everything I've done to you."

"I forgive you." The words were getting easier. "Are you sure you don't want to go to the rodeo with us?"

"I'll stay here and put things away. Do you want me to watch Rachel?"

Lacey shook her head. "I'm not ready for that, Mom. You have to understand that forgiving and forgetting are two different things. I can't trust you with Rachel, not yet."

"That isn't really fair. I'm not going to hurt her."

"I know." But Lacey didn't know. "I'll see you tomorrow."

She hugged her mom at the door to the apartment and she walked down the sidewalk that used to be hers, past flowers she had planted. Her place. A few months had changed everything.

She put Rachel in the car seat and buckled it, pretending her mom wasn't at the door to the apartment, watching, wanting her to feel guilty. Someday she'd leave Rachel with her mother. Not yet.

When she drove onto the rodeo grounds, past lines of cars and trucks, she saw Jay's truck and trailer. Of course he would be there.

She parked next to Bailey's truck and got out. She turned with Rachel and saw Bailey walking across the parking area, her belly round and her top stretched tight. Lacey waved and Bailey smiled a greeting.

"I didn't know if you would come tonight." Bailey reached for Rachel. "Give me this baby girl."

"Are you sure? She's heavy."

"She really has grown." Bailey held the baby close and slipped an arm around Lacey. "How are you?"

"Good, I guess. You know people talk and you just let it go because there's nothing you can do to change the past. And talk doesn't change who I am now."

"You're finally starting to get it."

"I guess. It's easy to say. I'm working on actually feeling that confident."

"And what about Jay?"

Lacey shrugged and didn't mean to look for him. But she did. He was on his horse, a lariat in his gloved hand and his hat pulled low. Cowboy. He was a cowboy all the way.

"Lacey?"

"Bailey, I can't do this. I can't be the woman he rejects.

I can't be a second-best replacement for a memory that has lived untarnished in his mind. I've worked too hard on my life to make that mistake."

"Is that what you think about him?"

"It's what I know. Now, let's go watch some cowboys rope some steers, okay?"

"You got it." Bailey sighed, like the conversation wasn't over.

They climbed the steps of the bleachers and sat midway up, away from dirt that would be flung through the fence, and close enough to see the action.

As they sat down, Bailey handed Rachel back to Lacey. She made a face and leaned a little forward.

"Bay, you okay?"

"Contraction. Don't worry, just one of those 'getting ready' kind, not the real thing."

"It looked like the real thing."

Bailey smiled. "It wasn't. Believe me, I'll let you know if it is the real thing. And then you can yell for that cowboy down there because he is not missing the birth of this child."

"I won't let him miss it."

Bailey took another deep breath and relaxed. "Court is next week. Are you ready for that?"

"I am ready. I'm a little afraid of the future, of raising her by myself."

"You'll be fine. Look at Meg down there. We managed with her, didn't we?"

Lacey smiled at Meg, sitting on the saddle in front of her daddy, her blond hair in a braid and a wide-brimmed hat on her head. The little girl waved at them.

"She's such a great kid." Lacey smiled and kissed the

top of Rachel's bald little head. "Cody is a lucky guy to have the three of you."

"We're blessed. And remember the days when I didn't think that would happen?"

"I do remember."

"Remember when I was the talk of the town, coming home from Wyoming pregnant?"

"We're two different people, Bailey."

"I know that, but I'm saying to you that you shouldn't sell yourself, God or this community short. Or that cowboy with the sweet smile and brown eyes. Don't sell him short, either."

"I'm not going to do that. I'm also not going to sit and dream of something that isn't going to happen. I'm a friend. I'm someone he helps. I'm not someone he loves."

"You're still living in the past, Lacey."

"I'm all about today and the future. I'm all about raising this baby the best I can and being the best person I can be."

She held the baby close as Jay Blackhorse rode into the arena on a horse that knew every move a calf would make. Jay loosened his arm and let the lariat fly. The circle of rope dropped over the calf's neck and the horse immediately backed up as Jay dismounted and ran to the calf, flipping it and tying its hooves the way cowboys had done for centuries.

"He's pretty amazing." Bailey said the words with a tight smile. "And eventually you'll have to admit that you love him."

"I don't love him."

"Umm-hmm," was all Bailey said, and then she gasped.

"Jay, where's Cody?" Lacey's voice, screaming over the crowds. He glanced her way as he tied his horse to the back of his trailer.

"He's running bulls through the chutes. Why?"

"Baby!"

"Rachel?"

She shook her head. She had Rachel in her arms. "The baby is coming. Bailey's water broke about five minutes ago. We need to get Cody."

"I'll get him. Why don't you go back to Bailey? Get her down here to his truck."

Calm. He had to be calm and not think about babies and about Lacey five feet from him, her lips soft pink and her eyes brown and sparkling with excitement. He swallowed emotion that stuck like day-old bread.

"I'll get Bailey. Jay, it's too early." She said it so softly he nearly didn't catch the words, but when he turned, she was retreating, back to Bailey in the bleachers and a new baby on the way, too soon.

Jay hurried through the crowds and found Cody near the bulls that were penned and about to be driven into the chutes for the riders. "Buddy, you've got to come with me."

"What's up?" Cody opened a gate and waved for one of the other guys. "Let me finish this up and I'll be right there."

"Cody, Bailey's water broke."

"Water broke? Why?"

"I think it means a baby on the way."

"She's a month from her due date." Cody stood his ground, his face a mess of emotion and nerves. Meg, on the other side of the fences, started to yell for him to "cowboy up, Dad. We're gonna have a baby."

Jay laughed, because of the shock on Cody's face and the excitement of the little girl. They were making a family out of something that hadn't been a family until a short time ago. And it was working. Jay didn't want to envy, but he did.

His mind switched back to Lacey and Rachel. He didn't have time to think about promises, about Lacey. Instead he motioned for Cody to follow him.

"Cody, someone else can do this job. You're the only guy that can take Bailey to the hospital."

"I'm coming. Can you make sure someone gets my livestock home?"

"I'll get them home."

"Thanks, Jay." Cody climbed a gate and grabbed Meg. Jay watched them go, kind of wishing it was him.

"Hey, need some help?" Lacey stood behind him. He smiled and shrugged.

"I've got to get Cody's livestock home. You've got Rachel and I bet Bailey wants you at the hospital."

He wanted distance between them, because he couldn't think with her standing this close, smelling like spring. He really needed space to think.

"They took my car." She walked a little closer. "I can help you, Jay. I can drive a trailer. Bailey taught me how. I can help you get your horse home. Whatever you need me to do. There's one thing I do know, babies take time and I don't need to hurry to the hospital."

She'd had a baby. He remembered, and he knew from shadows in her eyes that she was remembering. And he saw that she wasn't letting him in, she was shutting him out.

He pushed his hat back on his head and nodded. "Okay, you can help. If you want to drive my truck and trailer home with my horse, I'll take Cody's livestock home."

"Do you want me to put your horse in the field or in a stall?"

"He's usually in the field, but it'll be easier for you to put him in a stall."

"I don't mind…"

"I know you don't, but I'd feel better if you put him in the stall. I don't want to worry about you out there in the dark."

"Okay, I'll put him in the stall. So, show me how to drive your truck."

He coughed a little. "You can't drive the truck?"

"Gotcha."

Yes, she had gotten him. He smiled a little weakly and handed her his keys. "I'll be over in a sec to put him in the trailer."

"I can do that, too."

"I know, but…"

"But he's your animal and you want to make sure. I don't blame you."

She walked away, suddenly a cowgirl and not the city girl who waited tables at the Hash-It-Out. He didn't turn away for a long second because he realized that once upon a time he had been in love with a girl.

And Lacey was a woman. She was someone a guy could count on. She didn't need a cowboy to be strong for her. She could be strong for a cowboy.

He processed that newly found knowledge because he didn't know what to do with it, or how to let go of promises he had made.

Lacey gripped the steering wheel of Jay's truck and said a lot of prayers as she drove the back roads to the farm. She had driven a truck and trailer, but this ride, this night felt different. Bailey was having a baby and Jay's horse was in her hands.

She prayed for her friend and the baby as she drove, and by the time she parked in front of the stable, her back was stiff from being tense and her jaw felt permanently clenched. She hopped down from the truck and landed on wobbly legs.

As she unloaded the horse, lights came on in the house. A door closed and someone crossed the lawn to the barn. Lacey heard Rachel's quiet whimpers in the truck and hurried to get the horse in the barn and unsaddled.

"Lacey, you okay in here?" Wilma walked up, robe flapping and hair in curlers. "Jay called. He wanted to make sure you made it."

"Worried about his horse?" The wrong words. She regretted them immediately, even if she had meant them to be funny.

"No, sweetie, he was worried about you. Let me get the baby and you put that horse in the stall. There's grain in the feed room."

"Thank you, Wilma."

"Don't mention it. It was sweet of you to do this for Jay, especially with Bailey in labor. As soon as you get finished, come up to the house. I'll give you my keys, so you don't have to drive that truck to the hospital, and I'll keep the baby."

"You don't have to do that."

"I want to." Wilma touched Lacey's arm. "Honey, we love you. I know that there has been talk and you've been hurt by that. But I want you to know, I would never be ashamed to have you as part of my family. I'm only sorry that Jay can't let go of the past and see what's in front of him now."

Lacey turned into the dark, hiding tears and choking back a sob that almost escaped. "Wilma, that means a lot to me. More than you could ever know."

"Lacey, stop telling yourself that you're the only one who has made mistakes. I made my share back in the day. As a matter of fact, I made one that nearly killed Jay's dad. But he forgave me. It wasn't easy, but we worked through our troubles and we came out stronger than ever."

"I didn't know."

"No one but Bill knew, until right now. It isn't something I'm proud of. Bill was in medical school and gone all the time. I was young and lonely and we had a neighbor that had a habit of saying all the right things. And he convinced me that Bill didn't appreciate me. Of course that wasn't true, but I was lonely and let myself believe that it was."

"I…"

"You don't know what to say." Wilma smiled as she spoke. "Pretty houses and fancy cars hide a lot of sins that we'd all rather not talk about, but we need to face and work through our sins. The Blackhorse family isn't perfect. But we're happy and we love each other. We've never pretended to be perfect. Temptation doesn't pay attention to class or location. It isn't a respecter of persons."

Wilma cleared her throat. "Now, enough of that. You have to go see a new baby into the world. And I need to get Rachel out of the truck."

"Wilma?"

Wilma turned. "Yes, Lacey?"

"I'm glad you shared that with me."

"I am, too. I wanted you to know, you're someone I would want my son to bring home to meet his family."

As Lacey unsaddled the horse and put him away, tears

flowed and she didn't try to stop them. She was good enough. Wilma wouldn't be ashamed of her. Whatever happened between Lacey and Jay, she had that knowledge and it felt good.

It felt a lot like love. It wasn't the love of a man, but the love of a family and a community. And that was enough.

Chapter Eighteen

Lacey left the hospital the next morning, blinking against the bright sunlight. Bailey had given birth two hours earlier, to a tiny little guy with dark hair and a big cry. He was small, but healthy. Lacey sighed with relief and exhaustion as she got into the car for the drive home. Back to Gibson.

She tried not to think of Jay at the hospital, and the two of them not speaking. It had felt a lot like losing a friend. And more. She hadn't expected that.

She hadn't expected silence between them.

As she drove past a new apartment complex her mind turned in a completely foreign direction. She could move to Springfield.

She could get an apartment and take college classes.

Of course that was running away. But hadn't she run away before, and it worked out for her? She had run away and ended up in Gibson.

She had found faith and love. She had found herself in that small town. And now it was all crumbling and falling apart. Her mom had invaded her life. Jay had invaded her heart.

The drive to Gibson took a little more than thirty minutes. When she pulled up in front of the Blackhorse home, she breathed a sigh of relief because Jay's truck was gone.

As she walked up the front steps, the door opened. Wilma smiled and motioned her inside. "You look beat."

Lacey tried for a smile. "I am. It was a long night. But worth it. The baby is beautiful."

"I can't wait to meet him." Wilma motioned her inside. "And your own little angel is still sound asleep. Why don't you leave her here and go home for a nap?"

It was tempting, very tempting. The thought of sleep brought a yawn that Lacey covered with her hand. "I started to say I don't need to sleep."

"Of course you need to sleep. Unlike Jay, at least you admit that. He came home, changed into his uniform and went to work."

"He's going to be sorry." She didn't want to talk about Jay, not with his mother.

"He'll be tired tonight. Oh, that reminds me, I wanted to make sure you knew about the ladies' meeting at church tomorrow night. Will you be able to make it?"

"I might. I usually have classes on Thursdays, but since Bailey is in the hospital, I probably won't go. She usually takes care of Rachel for me."

"If you need me to take care of her, I can."

"Thank you, Wilma. But I can't keep taking advantage of you that way." She pulled her hand back from Pete, who had ambled onto the porch and nudged her. "I'm actually thinking of renting an apartment in Springfield. I realized that it would be easier for me to take classes at the university if I lived there and didn't have to spend so much time away from Rachel, driving back and forth."

"You would leave town?" Wilma frowned. "Lacey, has something happened between you and Jay?"

"No, nothing." Only moments, and moments didn't make forever. Moments didn't equal something. Especially when the man in question was now ignoring her.

She couldn't tell Jay's mother what it felt like to be a stolen moment and nothing more. She knew she could never compare to a perfect summer, a perfect memory.

"Please don't rush into this decision. We all love you and we'd be heartbroken if you left like this. And what about your mom? Jolynn said she's doing a great job at the diner. She even accepted a dress Jolynn gave her to wear to church this Sunday."

"I know, and you're right, I won't rush."

"Go home and sleep, honey. You're just tired and things always look bad when you're tired. You probably feel like you're coming apart at the seams, with everything you've been through lately."

Lacey nodded, because if she opened her mouth to agree, she might cry. How had her perfectly structured life changed in such a short amount of time?

And in five days she would go to court to finalize the adoption of Rachel. That counted as one of the good things in her life. She didn't want to forget the good things. Everything falling into place and falling apart, all in a matter of weeks.

Nearly a week after Bailey gave birth, Jay drove down a paved country road, windows down and his radio blasting Kenny Chesney. And he couldn't stop thinking about Lacey. He wished he could go back and undo whatever had gone wrong between them. Maybe it couldn't be undone. She had been hurt by memories that he'd held on to for too long.

He hadn't been able to explain why he needed distance and time to think.

Yesterday she had told his mom that she had gone to Springfield to look at apartments. Her plans were to make a decision after her court date. He let out a sigh and gripped the wheel a little tighter. Letting go.

He drove down the road to the familiar drive that led to the cemetery. He hadn't been there in a few months. He hadn't really thought of going lately.

He was letting go. And that felt wrong. He felt guilty for the memories that were fading, becoming more a part of his past.

He stopped his truck and got out, walking up to the grave with flowers from his mom's garden. He stood for a minute staring at the headstone. *Jamie Collins. She loved to laugh.* She loved life.

For a very short time.

She wasn't buried here. Her parents had taken her home for a real funeral. This place was for Jay, to remember, to have a place to go. Her parents had bought the marker. They had insisted on keeping Jamie's last name the same.

He placed the flowers in the vase attached to the granite marker and stepped back. It was time to move on, to let someone else into his life, and into his heart. It had been time for a while now, but he realized the other day that the right person just hadn't come along.

Lacey had filled the empty spaces in his heart, spaces that even Jamie hadn't filled. It hadn't been easy to accept that.

"How do I move forward?" he whispered. But he

knew the answer. Jamie had been a kid. He hadn't been much more than a kid when they married. He had loved her because she had been soft and vulnerable. She had needed him.

"Son, you move forward by letting go of the past."

Jay turned, surprised that he wasn't alone. The older man leaned on a cane and tears rolled down his wrinkled cheeks.

"I'm sorry?" Jay took a step back, facing the man that had appeared out of nowhere. But a quick glance around the cemetery and Jay saw the car a short distance away.

"You move forward by letting go. Or you miss out. I missed out." He wiped his faded blue eyes. "I lost my wife six years ago. She was the love of my life and no one could replace her. But I met this sweet gal at the seniors' center. She was a little younger than me, about sixty, and she had this laugh. I loved her laughter."

"What happened?"

"I didn't ask her out. My kids were hurt by the relationship. They thought I wasn't being loyal to their mother's memory. They didn't understand how lonely I was, and I didn't want to hurt them. So I didn't date my gal friend. We still had coffee from time to time, and occasionally we sat together, but we didn't date. And now she's gone."

"She passed away?"

"Nope, she married someone else." The older gentleman smiled and winked. "I'm really sorry I wasn't the one to marry her. Now, what's your story?"

"I promised my wife I'd love only her, forever."

"You were young, weren't you?" The older man nodded at the granite marker. "I remember being that young.

You can love her forever. But make room in your heart for other people, other love and more experiences."

"I think you're right about that."

"Well, if you've got a sweet gal that you could love, I think I'd make an effort to work things out with her."

"I'm going to try, if it isn't too late."

"Unless she's married another man, it probably isn't too late. Or maybe you don't have the courage?"

Jay smiled. "I think I have the courage."

"Does she know how you feel about her?"

"No, she doesn't."

"It seems to me you need to work on relationships. Communication. They talk about that a lot on those afternoon talk shows. You might want to watch one." The older man took a few steps with his cane, leaning heavily for support.

Jay laughed at the man's comment. "Yes, I guess I probably do."

"If not with her, then with someone else."

"Thank you. I guess I needed to hear that."

"Yes, you probably did need to hear that. Sometimes our hearing takes a while to kick into gear. It was nice talking to you, Jay Blackhorse."

Jay blinked a few times and the man laughed again.

"You're wearing a name tag. You're a little jumpy, aren't you?" He held out an aging and wrinkled hand. "Gordon Parker. Maybe I'll see you around some time."

Jay watched Gordon Parker walk back to his car, and then he sat down on a nearby bench. His mind went back to that summer that Jamie entered his life. She had needed him in a way that no one else had ever needed him.

Need.

He leaned back and looked up into the green canopy of leaves above him. She had been a girl, innocent and desperate to live.

In the months of their marriage he had helped make her dreams come true. And now he was tangled in memories that had faded, but he had worked to keep alive.

Coming home had changed everything, because Lacey had shown him the difference between loving a girl and loving a woman.

He closed his eyes as he thought those words. Loving a woman. A woman he had pushed away, and who thought she wasn't good enough to be loved forever.

Jay's phone beeped, signaling a text message. He flipped it open and read a message from Bailey.

Have you forgotten what today is?

He had.

Lacey had made the decision to go to court alone. So it was her, Rachel and the attorney who walked up the courthouse steps. Bailey was at home with the new baby, and Deanna had taken Lacey's shift at the diner. She could have asked Wilma to come with her, but that would have meant possibly seeing Jay. She'd been avoiding him for the last week, trying to let go of dreams she should never have allowed to form.

Why, after all of these years, had he been the one to make her dream of forever? She didn't want to think about that, not now. Thinking about Jay brought a tight lump to her chest and tears that stung her eyes.

If she could do this alone, she could do anything. Even sign the contract for the apartment in Springfield. She could go to college and be a teacher.

"It'll all be over in less than an hour." Her attorney

patted her arm in a fatherly gesture. She smiled at him, thankful that he'd taken this case and thankful that Bill Blackhorse had paid the legal fees. She didn't know how she would ever thank them for all they'd done for her.

"Will my sister be here?"

"She will."

Lacey nodded, because it was okay that Corry would be at court. They'd seen each other a few times and Lacey knew that her sister really was trying to get her act together. She was clean, because she had no other options in jail. And she was still attending the church services with the minister that visited the inmates.

The lawyer pushed the door open and motioned Lacey inside. The building was old and smelled of polished wood and history. It was the smell of a government building, or a library. Lacey blinked to adjust to the dim light.

"This way."

He pointed and she followed him to the elevator. They waited a few minutes and the doors opened. Lacey stepped inside with Rachel. The lawyer, Mr. Douglas, followed.

"Lacey, you're going to be a good mother to that child. You really need to feel good about this."

"I do." She smiled to prove it. "I do feel good about what I'm doing. It's just hard."

Because she had given up her own child. She smiled through eyes that blurred with tears because she couldn't share that with her lawyer. He knew about that other baby, that little girl. It had been brought up because it did affect the outcome of this case. She had given up a child and now she wanted to adopt one. That had to be clarified so that the ruling would go her way.

She prayed it would go her way. Her stomach tight-

ened with thoughts of losing Rachel because the judge
or the social workers, or someone, thought she might
not be a suitable mother. What if they took Rachel from
her today?

She couldn't lose the baby. She thought about losing,
and Jay. She really couldn't lose any more, could she?
But then, hadn't Job lost everything and more? And he
had continued to have faith, even when it wasn't easy.

What if God wanted her to lose everything?

Her thoughts were spiraling down and she couldn't
let that happen. "Mr. Douglas, would you pray for me?"

He nodded and as the elevator climbed, he prayed. The
prayer didn't stop her heart from breaking.

Jay pounded the steering wheel of his truck as he
cruised the overcrowded parking lot. Not an empty space
in the place and he knew that the hearing started in less
than ten minutes. Lacey was alone. He didn't want her
to be alone.

Ever.

But if he didn't find a parking space, that was exactly
what would happen. Besides that, what guarantees did
he have that she would want him to be there with her?

A group of people walked across the intersection and
toward a car in the parking lot. Like a vulture, he watched
them get out keys and get into the car. He circled, waiting for them to back out, and praying no one else would
challenge him for that spot.

The car backed out and he zoomed into the empty
space with barely enough room to get his door open. As
he hopped out, he reached back into the truck for the bun-
dle of flowers he'd picked when he went home to change

clothes. He smiled, a little embarrassed by the scraggly bouquet. No one but Lacey would understand.

He ran up the stairs of the courthouse and through the front doors. The courtroom was up the stairs or the elevators. There was a crowd at the elevator so he picked the stairs. He ran, taking the stairs two at a time. A few people in the stairwell slid to the side to get out of his way. He apologized and kept going.

The bailiff at the doors to the courtroom stopped him.

"Court is already in session." The uniformed officer stood in front of the door.

"I know, and I'm sorry that I'm late, but I need to be in there with Lacey Gould." Because she was adopting a little girl and he wanted to be that child's father. His heart raced in his chest and he wanted to rush the gates to get past the armed officer.

"Sorry."

"Please, I know you're not supposed to do this, but it's an adoption and I really need to be in there."

The officer looked at the bouquet, his eyes scrunching. "You're taking that in there?"

"It isn't hiding a weapon, I promise."

"No, I'm just saying, couldn't you have done better?"

"Nope, this is the best."

The officer shook his head and stepped back. "Good luck. You're going to need it."

Jay smiled and nearly laughed as he pushed the door open and stepped into the courtroom. The judge turned, staring and not happy. Jay pointed to Lacey and the judge gave a short nod.

Lacey's mouth dropped and then closed again. She smiled just a little and he held up the bouquet, wilted and more scraggly than ever. But dandelions could survive anything, and Lacey would get it.

Her smile trembled on her lips. He loved her. He had known it for a while, but now, seeing her there with Rachel and knowing that her smile was for him alone and that she was a woman who could love a man forever, he knew without a doubt that he loved her.

The judge pounded his gavel on the desk and Lacey turned away from Jay, back to the proceedings. But she couldn't stop smiling. She couldn't stop the little dance in her heart. Jay had showed up. That meant something.

Dandelions meant something.

"I see no reason for not approving this adoption," the judge decreed. He looked at Corry, in a jumpsuit and handcuffs. "I believe you've made one wise decision in a life full of unwise decisions and I hope that this is a starting place for you."

She nodded and tears trickled down her cheeks. But she didn't speak. Lacey wanted to go to her, like she had when they had been young girls hiding from their mother. She wanted to hug her sister and tell her it would be okay and they would take care of each other. But Lacey could only promise to take care of Rachel and to be there for Corry.

"Lacey Gould, this child, Rachel Gould, is now your child. Love her and protect her. Do your best to be a good mother for her." The judge took off his glasses and rubbed his eyes. "And do something about this man in my court. I think he must have something to say to you."

Lacey turned and smiled at Jay. He stood next to her, a cowboy in faded jeans. His sleeves were rolled up and he carried the most pitiful handful of dandelions she'd ever seen.

But it was the most beautiful bouquet ever. Because it was for her.

"I really hadn't planned on doing this here, with a judge and lawyers as witnesses." He held up the scraggly, wilted bouquet of yellow flowers.

"Jay?"

"Lacey, I'm so in love with you I can't sleep at night. You've filled the empty spaces in my heart and in my life. I want to be a part of your life, and a part of Rachel's life. Forever."

"Forever?"

He handed her the dandelions. "Forever. I realized the other day that you've changed my life. You're strong and beautiful and I love you."

"You love me?" Tears streamed down her cheeks, salty on her lips. She brushed them away.

"I love you."

"I love you, too."

"That's good, because it works better that way."

The judge cleared his throat. "I could marry the two of you right now and put his name on the birth certificate if you'd like."

Lacey didn't know what to say, or if she could say anything. Jay had hold of her hand and when he leaned to kiss her, she couldn't think. Because this was more than a moment. It was forever.

He kissed her for a long minute, his lips exploring hers, and his arm around her and Rachel. Lacey leaned into that kiss and his embrace, feeling safe and knowing he would protect them and cherish them.

She wasn't a replacement. She saw in his eyes and

knew in that kiss that she didn't have to compete with a memory. They would make their own memories.

When he pulled away, he cupped her cheek, looking steady into her eyes. "Lacey, marry me today."

"I would love nothing more, Jay. But I think we have family and friends who might be upset with us if we didn't invite them to the wedding."

He smiled and kissed her again.

"I don't care when the wedding is," he whispered in her ear, his breath soft. "I just want to make sure you'll marry me."

"I will, but I do think we need time." She leaned into his embrace and around them people clapped. Her cheeks heated and she buried her face in his shoulder.

"You're right, Lacey, dandelions are about the most beautiful flower. They're like us. They can make it through anything."

Lacey walked out of the courtroom at his side, no longer alone. She had a family now. She had a little girl that clung to her neck and cooed happy sounds, and a cowboy that had promised to love her forever.

* * * * *

Dear Reader,

Life sometimes feels like a puzzle that isn't quite coming together the way we want it to. We have all the pieces, we know what it is supposed to look like and we know how we want it to go together, but for some reason we can't make it work.

As things crumble, as pieces fail to fit and nothing seems to work, we begin to see the edges of the puzzle come together. The framework is there, it just takes time and patience. Sometimes we have to move on, and then later, when we look back, we suddenly see that what we thought was a plan falling apart was actually God's plan coming together.

Jay and Lacey, like so many of us, thought they had their lives all planned out. God had something totally different in mind, and when He started to work in their lives, they first thought that things were falling apart and their own plans were coming unraveled.

Like us, Jay and Lacey had to learn to let go of what they thought would be best for them, and realize that God had something even better in mind.

I love to hear from my readers. Please visit my website, brendaminton.net, and drop me an email.

Blessings,

Brenda Minton

JENNA'S COWBOY HERO

In his heart a man plans his course,
but the Lord determines his steps.
—*Proverbs* 16:9

This book is dedicated to all of the people who keep climbing mountains and to those who want to climb mountains. To my family for putting up with me. To my friends who keep answering the phone (Haven't you learned your lesson?). To Janet and Melissa, for the continued support and encouragement.

Chapter One

"What do you mean, there's no money in the account?" Adam Mackenzie shouted into his cell phone.

His manager, Will, sighed from five hundred miles away. "The money is gone, Adam. Fortunately, a lot of the work on the camp has already been done."

Adam gripped the steering wheel a little tighter and went through the list of reasons why this wasn't the worst thing that could have happened to him. He had been through worse things.

The most important thing to remember: the camp wouldn't be his problem for very long. But how could the money be gone? He'd given his cousin Billy more than enough to build the camp.

"What happened to the money?" Adam leaned and flicked his gaze to the left, looking for a road that he was starting to question the existence of. Not one internet map had directions for Camp Hope on the outskirts of Dawson, Oklahoma, population fifty.

For the last few miles, since he'd left the main highway, he'd seen nothing but fields of grazing cattle, a few small oil wells, and a smattering of aging farmhouses.

Will cleared his throat, the way he did when he didn't want to give the answer.

"What do you mean, what happened?" Will said, avoiding the answer. Adam came close to smiling, because he knew his agent that well, and he liked him that much.

"You know what I mean." Adam slowed when something moved into the road a short distance ahead. "Where did my money go?"

"It looks like Billy took a few trips, bought a car for his girlfriend and lost a big chunk of cash in Vegas." Will paused at the end of the list. "I really am sorry about this."

"It was my money." Adam wanted to yell but he didn't—this time. It wouldn't do any good to lose his temper. But it sure would have felt good.

He'd learned from experience that giving in to what feels good can get a person into a lot of trouble. He'd learned from the experience of losing contracts, being pushed off on other teams and having his face on tabloids. He'd learned that he didn't have a lot of real friends.

"I know it was your money. And now it's your camp," Will said with conviction and probably a smile, judging by his tone.

"I get that. But no way is this *my* camp, or *my* problem. I'm trying to rebuild my reputation so that the Sports Network sees the new me, not the old me, when I interview for the sportscaster job. That's my problem, Will. The last thing I need is the responsibility of a camp and a bunch of kids."

"Sorry, Adam, the camp is now your problem."

"Of course it is."

Billy had lied. Like so many other people had lied.

People liked to use him. Adam's family used him. Women used him. Billy had used him.

He reminded himself of one important fact. Will, his manager for the last few years, had never used him. He had never lied.

"What am I going to do with this place?" Adam asked as he reached to flip the visor and block the setting Oklahoma sun.

Before Will could answer, something at the side of the road caught Adam's attention. A dog. *Don't move, dog. Don't make this day worse.* Worse happened to be two kids holding the leash attached to the dog. Two small boys wearing shorts, and T-shirts. Adam honked the horn. The dog looked up, but continued to back into the road, away from the boys who stood in the ditch.

"This can't be happening. Gotta go, Will." He slammed on the brakes.

The car veered and Adam held tightly to the wheel, trying to see where the kids had disappeared to. The car spun and then jolted, slinging him to the side as it came to rest against a tree with a thud.

His brand-new car. The thought barely registered when he heard the whoosh of the air bags. Other words slipped through his mind. And he still didn't know if he'd hit those kids or their dog.

His phone rang. He pushed at the air bag and freed himself from his seat belt. The phone rang again. Will's ring tone. Adam lifted it to his ear as he leaned against the headrest, waiting for his heart to stop hammering against his chest.

"I'm fine, Will."

"Do I need to call 911 for you?"

"Like I could give directions to this place. Talk about…"

"No such thing as Godforsaken, buddy."

Adam groaned as he pushed past the pain in his shoulder. "Save the sermon for my funeral. I have to make sure these kids are okay."

"Kids?"

"There were two kids out here. I swerved to keep from hitting them and their dog."

He pushed at his driver's side door. It wouldn't open. Will was still on the other end, asking questions.

"I can't get out of my car."

"I can call for help." Will sounded a little too amused. "Doesn't that car have one of those fancy talking computers that asks if you need assistance?"

"I had it disconnected. I don't need a bossy female asking me if I'm lost or need assistance. I'll call you later."

He pushed and then kicked the passenger's side door. It opened and he climbed out of the car, stumbling as his feet hit the ditch. Thorns from a wild rosebush caught his arms and sleeves. He untangled himself and waded through tall weeds to reach the road.

The boys were standing at the edge of a gravel drive. The dog, a black-and-white border collie, sat next to them, tongue hanging out and ears perked. They watched him, eyes big and feet moving nervously—like they were getting ready to run for their lives.

He probably looked like a giant coming up out of that ditch. Especially to two little boys.

"What are you boys doing by the road?" He glanced up the drive to the old farmhouse not two hundred feet away. The house was old, but remodeled, the white siding wasn't green with moss, and the windows gleamed.

The boys shifted in front of him, tugging on the dog's leash, keeping it close to their side.

"Our dog needs to learn to walk on a leash," the heftier of the two boys, obviously twins, answered. They weren't identical, but they were close.

"Well, that dog won't do you any good if you get her hit, or get yourselves hit." He spoke as softly as he could, but it still came out in a growl. They had scared ten years off his life.

He stood at the edge of the road, thinking he should march them up to the house and let the parents know what they'd been up to.

Or he could leave and forget it all.

A glance over his shoulder and he knew he wouldn't be driving away, not in the car that was lodged against a tree, two tires flat.

He'd had some bad days of late. This one took the cake. He didn't even like cake.

"Our dog's a him," the bigger boy muttered, his gray eyes wide, not looking away. "Are you a giant?"

"No, I'm not a giant. Where are your folks?" Adam eyed the smaller boy, the one with the thumb in his mouth. The kid was shaking. Adam took a deep breath and lowered his voice. "And what are your names?"

The bigger twin started to answer. The little one nudged his brother with a bony elbow that prompted him to say, "We don't talk to strangers."

Both boys nodded and the bigger twin chewed on his bottom lip, obviously wanting to break the no-talking-to-strangers rule. Adam wanted to laugh, and that took him by surprise.

"Well, this stranger wants to let your parents know what you were up to."

A screen door slammed, reverberating through the quiet of an Oklahoma afternoon. He glanced toward the house and knew he was in big, big trouble, because he didn't have the skills for dealing with mad wet hens. She came off the front porch and stomped toward him, brown hair with streaks of blond, bouncing, lifting in the soft breeze. Faded jeans and a T-shirt, her face devoid of makeup, and he was suddenly sixteen again.

He let out a breath and remembered who he was and why he was here. And he remembered to be angry about his car and everything else that was out of his control.

"What's going on here?" She came to a stop behind the boys, her accent an Oklahoma drawl, half Southern belle and half redneck woman. She was pretty, but looked like a scrapper, like she wouldn't be afraid to come at him if he messed with her or the boys.

And the dog was growling now.

"Your dog was in the road, and the boys were pretty d—"

She raised a hand and her eyes flashed fire. "Watch it."

"Your boys were close to getting run over, and you're worried about my language?"

"Yes, sir, I am."

"Great, total insanity."

"Only partial." She smiled. Huge brown eyes lit with golden flecks caught and held his gaze. She took a few more careful steps and he realized that she wasn't much bigger than her two boys. Five feet nothing, and he felt like a giant towering over her.

Adam stamped down the desire to ask her name. He pushed aside old habits that had gotten him into more trouble than he could handle. More gossip than real trouble, but to the world, it might as well be true.

"I'm really sorry about the boys, and the dog." She had

rounded up all three and they gathered close, in a tight-knit huddle at the side of the road.

"It's okay. I just wouldn't want them to get hurt."

"You're right, of course. I'm Jenna Cameron." She held out a small hand with pink-painted nails. "Welcome to Dawson."

"Yeah, thank you. I'm looking for a half-finished summer camp."

"You sound happy about that."

"Real happy." Because he never expected to lose his cousin, and he hadn't expected the camp to be unfinished. He pulled the directions out of his pocket and read them off to her. "Do you have any idea where that is?"

She stepped to the edge of the road and pointed. Three hundred feet ahead, on the other side of the road and barely visible due to shrubs and grass, was a gravel drive. "That's your place."

"You've got to be kidding." He took a step closer to her and the dog snarled, raising an upper lip in a pretty convincing warning. Adam backed away.

"Sorry, he's my guard dog." Her hand rested on the dog's head. "I'm afraid I don't reprimand him for doing his job."

"No need, as long as he doesn't bite me." He didn't want to add dog bite to the things that had gone wrong today. He looked at the overgrown drive and the address on the crumpled paper in his hand. "Are you sure that's it?"

It was a cow pasture dotted with trees. He couldn't see much of the property because trees lined the fence row that ran parallel to the road.

"That's it. Earlier this summer they were working up

there, until…well, anyway, they built a barn and a dorm.
They even hauled in a single-wide mobile home."

"At least he did that."

"So, *you're* the owner."

"I'm the lucky guy." He shoved the paper back into his
pocket and walked back to his car. She followed, slower,
taking it easy over the rocks. The boys and the dog remained at the edge of the road, all three looking at him
like he might be public enemy number one.

He was used to that look, more used to the look than
to kids. He had made a careful choice not to date women
with kids. Or at least he'd had that policy since Morgan.

"You're probably going to need help getting your car
out of that ditch." She walked closer, eyeing the car. She
smelled like soap and peaches, not Chanel.

"I don't think this car is going anywhere anytime soon."

"I can give you the number of the local garage," she
offered, looking up at him. "They can tow it for you."

"Are you going to pay the tow bill, seeing as it was
your kids who caused the wreck?"

"If you insist."

"No, I don't insist. Forget it." He glanced back at the
boys and the dog. "They're cute."

"Thank you, Mr. Mackenzie, and I really am sorry."
She bit down on her bottom lip and averted her gaze
back to his car.

He didn't know what to say. She knew him, which
meant that even here he couldn't find anonymity. And
it wouldn't be long before his family knew that he was
back in Oklahoma.

Jenna looked away from the pale blue eyes of the man
towering over her. She'd get a crick in her neck if she

kept looking up at the six-and-a-half-foot giant, whom she knew well from watching football with the guys in her unit. His face was all smooth planes beneath a sandy-brown goatee, and when he smiled, there was something about it that changed his eyes, making her think a light was hiding inside his heart. It was a kind of shy smile, almost humble, but powerful.

Maybe it wasn't real. It could be a part of his lady-killer image. As an optimist she liked to think that it was something else. It was the real person hiding inside the public image, hidden by tabloid stories of models and actresses.

She'd like to know the real Big Mac Mackenzie.

But of course, she wouldn't. Getting to know a man wasn't on her five-year plan. Or her fifteen-year plan. She would get her boys and walk back up the drive to her house, away from the temptation to ask him questions about his life and why he was here now.

He had finished checking out the wrecked car and walked back to her, shaking his head.

"Is it bad?" She was mentally calculating what a car like that would cost, and how much the repairs would cost her.

"No, I don't think so. Two tires are blown, and there's a good dent in the driver's side door."

"Do you want the number for the garage?"

"I guess I have to." He pulled a cell phone out of his pocket.

"Sorry, you'll have to come up to the house for the number." Jenna gathered the boys and looked back over her shoulder.

He was standing in the road, looking unsure, like this was all some malicious trap on her part. He looked like a giant, but he looked lost and a little vulnerable. She shook off the thought that compared him with David, her smallest twin, after he'd had a bad dream.

Big Mac Mackenzie wasn't a lost child. He was a grown man standing in the road wearing faded jeans, a loose white shirt with the top three buttons undone and a black cowboy hat firmly in place.

"Are you coming?" She waited. "I'll get you a Band-Aid for the cut on your head."

He finally nodded, let out a sigh and took long-legged strides that soon put him next to them. And then he walked slower, keeping pace with them as they made their way up the drive to the house.

Horses whinnied from the barn, reminding Jenna that it was feeding time. She glanced in that direction, thinking of work that needed to be done, and how she'd rather be sitting on the front porch with her leg up and a glass of iced tea on the table next to her.

She loved her front porch with the ivy and clematis vines climbing the posts, drawing in bees and butterflies. She loved the scent of wild roses in the spring. Like now, caught on the breeze, the scent was sweet and brought back memories.

Some good, some bad.

"What are your names?" Adam Mackenzie asked the boys, his deep voice a little scary. Jenna gave a light squeeze to their hands to encourage them.

"Timmy." The bigger of her two boys, always a little more curious, a little more brave, spoke first. "And we don't talk to strangers."

He also liked to mimic.

"Timmy, mind your manners," Jenna warned, smiling down at him.

"Of course you don't, and that's good." Adam Mackenzie turned his attention to the smaller of her two boys. "And what about you, cowboy?"

"I'm David." He didn't suck his thumb. Instead he pulled his left hand free from hers and shoved his hands into his pockets. He looked up at the tall, giant of a man walking next to him. "And we have a big uncle named Clint."

A baritone chuckle and Adam made eye contact with Jenna. She smiled, because that light was in his eyes. It hadn't been a trick of the camera, or her imagination. She had to explain what David had meant to be a threatening comment about her brother. Leave it to the boys to think they all needed to be protected from a stranger.

"My brother lives down the road a piece."

"Clint Cameron?" Adam's gaze drifted away from her to the ramp at the side of the porch. Her brother had put the ramp in before she came home from the hospital last fall.

"Yes, Clint Cameron. You know him?"

"We played against each other back in high school. What's he doing now?"

"Raising bucking bulls with his wife. They travel a lot."

Jenna grabbed the handrail and walked up the steps, her boys and Adam Mackenzie a few steps behind, watching her. The boys knew the reason for her slow, cautious climb. She imagined Adam wondering at her odd approach to steps. In the six months since she'd been home, she'd grown used to people wondering and to questioning looks. Now it was more about her, and about raising the boys. She was too busy with life to worry about what other people were thinking about her.

It hadn't always been that way. Times past, she worried a lot about what people thought.

She opened the front door, and he reached and pushed it back, holding it for them to enter. She slid past him, the boys in front of her.

"Do you want tea?" She glanced over her shoulder as she crossed the living room, seeing all of the things that could make him ask questions about her life. If he looked.

He stood inside her tiny living room in the house she'd grown up in. A house that used to have more bad memories than good. For her boys the bad memories would be replaced with those of a happy childhood with a mom who loved them.

There wouldn't be memories of a dad. She wasn't sorry about that, but then again, sometimes she was.

The walls of the house were no longer paneled. Clint had hung drywall, they'd painted the room pale shell and the woodwork was white now, not the dark brown of her childhood. The old furniture was gone, replaced by something summery and plaid. Gauzy white curtains covered the floor-to-ceiling windows, fluttering in the summer breeze that drifted through the house.

Everything old, everything that held a bad memory, had been taken out, replaced. And yet the memories still returned, of her father drunk, of his rage, and sometimes him in the chair, sleeping the day away.

Adam took up space in the small house, nearly overwhelming it, and her, with his presence. As she waited for his answer to the question about iced tea, he took off his hat and brushed a hand through short but shaggy sandy-brown hair.

"Tea?" He raised a brow and she remembered her question.

tions of staying here. He'd find a way to get out of it. He pushed his hat down on his head and walked off the porch, still holding the phone.

"Billy said the chicken-fried steak was to die for." Will the optimist.

"Billy died of a heart attack. Talk to you later."

Jenna picked her way across the overgrown lawn. Adam Mackenzie stood next to the porch, staring at the barn and the dorm. He looked a little lost and kind of angry. Angry didn't bother her. Neither did tantrums— she had the twins.

"Bad news?" She stopped next to him and looked up, studying his face.

"Nothing I can't handle." He tore off a piece of fescue grass and stuck it between his teeth. "My agent thinks I should stay. This sure wasn't where I wanted to spend my summer."

"Really?" She looked out at land that, with a little care, could be a premium piece of property. And she thought of the kids, the ones who were so much like herself, who could come here for a week or two and forget the abuse or poverty at home. Couldn't he see that? "It looks like a great place to me."

"What do you see that I don't?"

"Promise. I see kids finding a little hope and maybe the promise of a better future. I see kids escaping for a week and just being kids."

He groaned and tossed the grass aside. "Another optimist."

"I call it faith."

"So does Will." Adam had turned back to the steps that led up the porch. "But how does faith help me solve this problem? Does faith clean this place up, or finish it so that it can be used?"

"Prayer might be the place to start."

"Right."

She followed him up the steps, right leg always first. It was getting easier every day. Ten months ago she had wondered if anything would ever be easy again. Adam turned when he reached the top and gave her a questioning look she ignored.

"I'm sorry, it really isn't my business." She answered his question, pretending the look was about that, about him wanting an answer. "I just happen to believe that God can get us out of some amazingly bad situations."

"Well let's see if God can help us get into this trailer."

She watched as he shoved a credit card into the door. The boys were in the yard playing with the dog. "Guys, stay right here in front of the trailer. Snakes are probably thick right now."

"That's another positive." He pushed the door open and stepped inside. Jenna followed.

He looked around, focusing on the phone and answering machine. Jenna waited by the front door, not sure what she should do. Maybe she should go home? Maybe now was the time to remove herself from his presence and this situation.

While she considered her options, he pressed the button on the answering machine. Messages played, mostly personal and a little embarrassing to overhear knowing that Billy was gone and this was his legacy. There were messages from a distraught girlfriend, creditors asking for money, and his mom wondering why he didn't call.

Adam replayed the last message.

"Billy, this is John at the Christian Mission. I wanted

"Yes, iced tea."

"Please. And the phone book?"

"The number for the garage is on my fridge." She led him down the hall to the kitchen with a wood table in the center of the room.

She loved the room, not just the colors—the pale yellow walls and white cabinets. She loved that her sister-in-law, Willow, had decorated and remodeled it as a way to welcome Jenna home. The room was a homecoming present and a symbol of new beginnings. They had worked on the rest of the house as Jenna recovered.

Jenna poured their tea while Adam dialed the phone. When she turned, he was leaning against the wall, watching her. She set the tea down on the table while he finished his conversation.

"Is it taken care of?" She pulled a first-aid kit from the cabinet over the stove.

"They'll be out in an hour. They wanted to call the police to write up an accident report."

Jenna swallowed and waited for him to tell her how he'd responded to that. Accident. She hadn't really thought about that. Her boys had caused an accident. She pulled out the chair and sat down, stretching her legs.

"I'm so sorry. You really could have been hurt."

"Your boys could have been hurt."

She nodded. "I know. The rule is that they don't go down the drive. They're usually very good boys."

"I'm sure they are." He picked up the glass of tea. "I'm going to need to rent a car."

"Not around here. And I want to finish talking about the accident report. You'll need to let them call the county so you can get this covered on your insurance."

He drained half the glass of tea in one gulp and set it down on the table. "I'll take care of it."

"Just like that, you'll take care of it?" She bit down on her bottom lip, waiting, because it couldn't be this easy. "My boys caused an accident and major damage to an expensive car."

"They didn't really cause the accident. I saw their dog backing into the road...."

"And that caused the wreck. They were holding the leash of the dog that backed into the road."

"Wow, do you plan on making this difficult?"

"No, I'm just trying to do the right thing."

"You can give me a ride down to that Godfor—"

She lifted her hand and shook her head to stop him. "Watch your language."

He shook his head. "Great, another Will."

"Excuse me?"

"My manager, Will. Did he hire you to keep me in line?"

"Sorry, no, you're a big boy and you'll have to keep yourself in line. Now let me put a Band-Aid on your cheek. You're bleeding." She motioned to the chair as she stood up and opened the first-aid kit. "Sit."

"I'm fine."

"I can't have you get an infected cut on my watch."

The boys hurried into the room. They must have heard her mention that he was injured. They were wide-eyed and impressed as they stared at the cut.

"It's gonna need stitches," Timmy informed their victim, peering up, studying the wound.

"Do you think so?" Adam asked, reaching to touch the cut.

"Yes, iced tea."

"Please. And the phone book?"

"The number for the garage is on my fridge." She led him down the hall to the kitchen with a wood table in the center of the room.

She loved the room, not just the colors—the pale yellow walls and white cabinets. She loved that her sister-in-law, Willow, had decorated and remodeled it as a way to welcome Jenna home. The room was a homecoming present and a symbol of new beginnings. They had worked on the rest of the house as Jenna recovered.

Jenna poured their tea while Adam dialed the phone. When she turned, he was leaning against the wall, watching her. She set the tea down on the table while he finished his conversation.

"Is it taken care of?" She pulled a first-aid kit from the cabinet over the stove.

"They'll be out in an hour. They wanted to call the police to write up an accident report."

Jenna swallowed and waited for him to tell her how he'd responded to that. Accident. She hadn't really thought about that. Her boys had caused an accident. She pulled out the chair and sat down, stretching her legs.

"I'm so sorry. You really could have been hurt."

"Your boys could have been hurt."

She nodded. "I know. The rule is that they don't go down the drive. They're usually very good boys."

"I'm sure they are." He picked up the glass of tea. "I'm going to need to rent a car."

"Not around here. And I want to finish talking about the accident report. You'll need to let them call the county so you can get this covered on your insurance."

He drained half the glass of tea in one gulp and set it down on the table. "I'll take care of it."

"Just like that, you'll take care of it?" She bit down on her bottom lip, waiting, because it couldn't be this easy. "My boys caused an accident and major damage to an expensive car."

"They didn't really cause the accident. I saw their dog backing into the road…."

"And that caused the wreck. They were holding the leash of the dog that backed into the road."

"Wow, do you plan on making this difficult?"

"No, I'm just trying to do the right thing."

"You can give me a ride down to that Godfor—"

She lifted her hand and shook her head to stop him. "Watch your language."

He shook his head. "Great, another Will."

"Excuse me?"

"My manager, Will. Did he hire you to keep me in line?"

"Sorry, no, you're a big boy and you'll have to keep yourself in line. Now let me put a Band-Aid on your cheek. You're bleeding." She motioned to the chair as she stood up and opened the first-aid kit. "Sit."

"I'm fine."

"I can't have you get an infected cut on my watch."

The boys hurried into the room. They must have heard her mention that he was injured. They were wide-eyed and impressed as they stared at the cut.

"It's gonna need stitches," Timmy informed their victim, peering up, studying the wound.

"Do you think so?" Adam asked, reaching to touch the cut.

"Don't touch it, just sit." Jenna pointed again to the chair.

He sat down at the kitchen table, giving her easier access to his face. His eyes were closed and when she touched his cheek he flinched.

"That hurts. What are you putting on it, alcohol?" He pulled away from her fingers.

Her fingers stilled over the small cut and he opened his eyes, looking at her. She glanced away. "I'm cleaning it. It doesn't hurt that bad."

He looked at the boys. Jenna glanced over her shoulder and smiled at them. They were cringing, twin looks of angst on their suntanned faces.

"It's really bad," David whispered.

"Does it need stitches?" Adam asked them, not her. As if they were the authority.

The boys were nodding. "It has a lot of blood."

Timmy and David stepped closer.

She shook her head. "Don't listen to them. It won't even leave a scar."

She pulled the backing off the Band-Aid with fingers that trembled as she put the adhesive strip in place. She felt like a silly teenager watching the star football player from across the dining room of the local Dairy Bar. She'd never been the girl that those football players dated.

"Finished?" He touched his cheek and pushed the chair back from the table.

"Finished. Now, if you want, I'll drive you to the camp."

"That sounds good. I'll make a call to the rental company and have a car delivered."

Settled, just like that.

With Adam "Big Mac" Mackenzie behind her, she

walked out the back door. As she headed for her truck, she walked slowly, hoping he wouldn't notice if she stumbled.

But what did it matter? She was who she was. And Adam Mackenzie was passing through.

The boys were climbing into the backseat of her truck squabbling over who sat on what side. She smiled, because that's who she was, she was Timmy and David's mom. But as she opened her truck door, she caught Adam Mackenzie's smile and she was hit hard by the reality that she was more than a mom. She was obviously still a woman.

Chapter Two

Adam slid into the old truck and slammed the door twice before it latched. He glanced sideways and Jenna Cameron smiled at him, her dimples splitting her cheeks and adding to her country-girl charm. He knew a dozen guys that would fall for a smile like that.

He knew he'd almost fallen when he looked up as she dabbed salve on his face and caught her staring with brown eyes as warm as a summer day. She'd bitten down on her lower lip and pretended she wasn't staring.

The boys were buckled in the backseat of the extended-cab truck. They were fighting over a toy they'd found on the floorboard. He wondered where their dad was, or if they had one. Jenna Cameron: her maiden name, so she wasn't married. Not that he planned on calling her. He had long passed the age of summer romances.

The truck, the farm, a country girl and two little boys. This life was as far removed from Adam's life as fast food was from the restaurants he normally patronized. He kicked aside those same fast-food wrappers in the floor of the truck to make room for his feet. A toy rattled out of one of the bags and he reached to pick it up.

"This should stop the fighting." He reached into the back and the boys stared, eyes wide, both afraid to take the plastic toy. "I'm not going to bite you."

They didn't look convinced. Jenna smiled back at them. He would have behaved, too, if that smile had been aimed at him. The smaller twin took the toy from his hand. Another look from Jenna and the boy whispered a frightened, "Thank you."

The truck rattled down the drive and the dog ran alongside. When they stopped at the end of the drive, the dog jumped in the back. What would his friends think of this? And Morgan—the woman he'd dated last, with her inch-long nails and hair so stiff a guy couldn't run his fingers through it—what would she say?

Not that he really cared. They'd only had three dates, and then he'd lost her phone number. How serious could he have been?

"You grew up not far from here, right?" Jenna shifted and the truck slowed for the drive to his *camp*. He couldn't help but think the word with a touch of sarcasm. It was the same sarcasm he typically used when he spoke of *home*.

"Yeah, sure."

"Are you staying with family?"

"Nope." He rolled his window down a little farther. He wasn't staying with family, and he didn't plan on talking about them.

He'd taken his father into the spotlight he craved, and now it was over. Retirement at thirty-three, and his father no longer had the tail of a star to grasp hold of. They hadn't talked since Adam announced his retirement.

Over the years his relationship with his family had crumbled, because they'd made it all about his career.

His sister had faded away a long time ago, probably before high school ended. She'd yelled at him about being a star, and she wasn't revolving around his world anymore. And she hadn't.

The truck bounced over the rutted trail of a drive that had once been covered with gravel. Now the rain had washed away the gravel and left deep veins that were nearly ditches. The truck bumped and jarred. Overgrown weeds and brush hit the side panel and a coyote, startled by their presence, ran off into the field. The dog in the back of the truck barked.

"This can't be the place."

"Sorry, it is." Jenna flashed him a sweet smile that didn't help him to feel better about the property, but he smiled back.

She reminded him of girls who'd wanted to wear his letter jacket back in high school. The kind that slipped a finger through a guy's belt loop as they walked down the hall and kissed him silly on a Saturday night.

"If it makes you feel better, there are plenty of people around here looking for work." She broke into the silence, speaking over the wind rushing through the cab of the truck and country music on the radio. "Take a drive into town and there are half a dozen guys who will mow this with a Brush Hog."

"That's good to know." Not really.

He sighed as they continued on. Ahead he could see a two-story building with rows of windows. Probably the dorm. To the left of the dorm was a stable, and to the right of the dorm, a large metal-sided building. Jenna parked in front of a long, single-wide mobile home.

"Home sweet home." She pushed the door open and

jumped out. "It really is a good quality mobile home. And there's a tornado shelter."

She pointed to a concrete-and-metal fixture sticking up from the ground. A tornado shelter. So, the manager would duck into safety while fifty kids huddled in a dorm. He didn't like that idea at all. Billy probably hadn't given it a second thought.

Billy had lived a pretty sketchy life for the most part. A few years ago he'd found religion and then a desire to do something for troubled kids. Adam had thought Billy's plan for the camp was legit. Maybe it had started out that way.

Adam walked toward the mobile home, wading through grass that was knee-high. The boys were out of the truck and running around, not fazed by grass or the thought of snakes and ticks.

He would have done the same thing at their age. Now, he was a long way from his childhood, not far from home, and the distance had never been greater.

"Do you know a Realtor?" He looked down, and Jenna Cameron shook her head.

"Drive into Grove and pick one. I couldn't tell you the best one for the job, but there are several."

His cell phone rang. He smiled an apology and walked away from her, leaving her looking toward the stable with a gleam that was undeniable. Most women loved diamonds, not barns.

"Are you there?" Will's voice, always calm. That's what he got paid for. Will was the voice of reason. Will prayed for him.

Adam had bristled when Will first told him that a few months back. Now the knowledge had settled and he sometimes thought about why his manager would think he needed prayer.

"If this is it, I'm here. And I'm…"

"Watch it, Adam." Will's endless warning.

"Fine, I'm here. It's paradise. Two hundred acres of overgrown brush, a drive with more ruts and ditches than you can imagine and my living quarters are a trailer."

"It could be worse."

"So you always say. Is that a verse in the Bible? I can't remember."

Will laughed. "Close. The verse says more about not worrying about today's troubles, tomorrow's are sufficient in themselves."

"Is that supposed to make me feel better? Can't you think of something more optimistic?"

"Has it been so long since you've been to church?"

"Your kid's dedication when she was born."

"She has a name."

"Yeah, she does. Kate, right?"

"You're close. It's Kaitlin."

"See, I'm not so shallow and self-centered."

"I never thought you were. So, about the camp…"

"I'm going to contact a Realtor."

"No, you're not. Adam, you can't ditch that place."

Adam glanced in the direction of the cowgirl and her two kids. They were tossing a stick for the dog and she was pretending not to listen. He could tell she was.

"Why am I not selling?" He lowered his voice and turned away.

"Because you need this patch on your reputation. You need to stay and see this through. You need to be the good guy."

"My reputation isn't bad enough for this to be the punishment."

"Look, Adam, let's not beat around the bush. You have money in your account, a nice house in Atlanta and a shot at being a national anchor for one of the biggest sports networks in the world. Don't mess it up."

Adam walked up the steps to the covered porch on the front of the mobile home. He peeked in the front door, impressed by the interior and the leather furniture his cousin had bought with his money.

"Adam?"

"What do you want me to do?"

"Is this compliance?" Will sounded far too amused and then he chuckled, as if to prove it. "Stay there. Clean the place up and make it a camp for underprivileged kids. Show the world what a good guy you are."

"I'm not a good guy, I'm self-centered and macho. I'm a ladies' man. I worked hard on that reputation and now you want me to change it?"

"I didn't ask for the other reputation, it's the one you showed up with. This is what I'm asking for. That you stay for the summer, show the world the real you, and be nice to the neighbor."

Adam glanced in her direction, blue jeans and a T-shirt, two little boys. "How do you know about her?"

"Billy told me she's a sweet girl."

"You talked to Billy?"

"He called to ask a few questions, just advice on the property."

"I don't like this. You do realize, don't you, that I'll have to live in this trailer and eat at a diner in Dawson called The Mad Cow?"

Will laughed and Adam smiled, but he had no inten-

to confirm that we have the third week of June reserved for fifty kids. Can you give me a call back?" The caller left a number.

Adam turned. "What's today?"

"The sixth of June."

He groaned and tossed his hat on a nearby table. "I can't believe this."

The message replayed and he scribbled the number on a piece of paper.

"What are you going to do?" Jenna sat down on a bar stool at the kitchen counter.

"Cancel this camp."

"And let those kids down?"

"I didn't let them down, Billy did. I can't have someone bring fifty kids to this place."

"But…" She bit down on her bottom lip and told herself it wasn't her business. Not the camp, not his life, none of it. She was just the mom of the kids who ran him off the road.

"Fifty kids," he repeated, like she didn't get it. "I don't even know if the buildings are finished."

He sat down on the stool next to hers and it creaked. "Obviously the bar stools aren't one size fits all. Look, I'm not a bad guy, but this isn't my thing. Summer camps, Oklahoma, none of this is me."

"I know you're not a bad guy. And you're right, this isn't my business. You have to make the decision that's right for you."

He smiled, and she liked that smile, the one that crinkled at the corners of his eyes. "You're slick, but you're not going to work me this way."

"I wasn't trying."

"Of course not." And his smile disappeared.

"I would help you." She hesitated, at once sorry, but not. "I mean, it wouldn't take much to get the camp ready."

"Don't you work?"

"I have two boys and ten horses. That's my work. But with the help of the community…"

She hopped down from the stool, momentarily forgetting, and she stumbled. A strong arm caught her, holding her firm until she gathered herself. Her back to him, she closed her eyes and drew in a deep breath.

"Are you okay?" He stood next to her, his hand still on her arm. Looking up, she realized that his face was close to hers, his mouth a gentle line.

"Of course I am."

He laughed, the deep baritone filling the emptiness of the dark and shadowy trailer. "Of course you are. You waited a whole five minutes after meeting me to involve yourself in every area of my life, and I can't get a straight answer on if you're okay. I know a knee injury when I see one. Remember, I've spent a lot of years getting plowed over and pushed down."

"It's an old injury." She smiled but it wasn't easy in the face of his unexpected tenderness, the baritone of his voice soft, matching the look in his eyes. "I need to check on the boys."

He released her. "And I need to check on the barn and the dorms to see how much more money I'm going to have to spend to make this place usable."

"But I thought you weren't going to run the camp."

"I'm not running it. I'm going to get it ready for someone else to run. I'll let you and my noble agent, Will, run it. Or I'll put it up for sale."

Jenna grabbed a tablet off the counter and the pen he

had tossed down. "We'll drive down there. I can help you make a list for what you might need."

Because she didn't feel like making the long walk through the brush on the overgrown trail that used to be a road. The boys were sitting on the porch steps, holding a turtle they'd found.

"Can we keep it?" Timmy poked at the turtle's head.

"No," she answered as she walked down the steps of the porch.

"Why not?" all three guys asked.

"Because it wouldn't be happy in a box. It belongs here, where it can travel and find the food it likes, not the food we toss to it every day."

The boys frowned at the turtle and then at Jenna. "We just want to keep it for a little while."

David touched the back of the box turtle, fingers rubbing the rough shell. "I like him."

Adam sighed and walked back into the house. He came back with a permanent marker. "Guys, there is a way you can keep an eye on this bad boy. We'll write your names and today's date on the bottom of his shell. When you're out here, you can find him and see how he's doing."

And that's how he became a hero to her boys. Jenna watched, a little happy and a lot threatened. She couldn't let Adam into their lives this way.

Herself in his life, that was different. Making sure this place became a camp was important to her. It was important to kids who were living the same nightmare childhood she had lived.

It was about the camp, not about Adam "Big Mac" Mackenzie. She honestly didn't need to understand his smile, or the way his eyes lit up. It had been easy, imagining his story when he'd been a football player she and the guys cheered for. Now, with him so close and his story unfolding, she didn't want to know more.

Adam climbed back into the truck. The boys piled in with them this time because it was a short ride across a bumpy drive to the barn. He glanced sideways, catching a glimpse of Jenna Cameron with her sun-streaked brown hair windblown and soft.

He wasn't staying. He wouldn't be pushed into this by her, or by Will. They'd have to understand that he was the last person in the world who ought to be running a camp, dealing with children, especially in Oklahoma.

As soon as he could figure out what to do with this place, who to turn it over to, he'd head back to Atlanta, back to his life. Back to what?

He sighed and she flicked her gaze from the road to him. That look took him back more than a dozen years, to pickup trucks and fishing holes, summer sun beating down on a group of kids just having a good time.

There hadn't been many times like that in his childhood. His dad had always been pushing, always forcing him onto the practice field. He had sneaked a few moments for himself, enough to make a handful of memories that didn't include football.

And she brought back those memories, most of which he had forgotten.

The truck stopped in front of the barn. She shot him a questioning look. "It needs a corral."

He nodded, like he knew. A long time ago he would have noticed. The barn sat on an open lot, no fences, no arena, no corral.

"It's probably going to need more than that."

"Horses wouldn't hurt." She smiled and then reached for the door handle to get out of the truck.

He followed her, walking behind her into the shadowy interior of the barn. One side was a stable. The other side was for hay, equipment and a room for tack. It creaked in the Oklahoma wind.

She looked up, questions in her brown eyes. The boys shrieked and she glanced in their direction. They were outside, the dog next to them barking.

"Timmy, David, what are you doing?"

"Snake!" the two shrieked at the same time. And Adam noticed that they didn't scream in fear, but in obvious boyhood delight.

"Get them." She looked up at him, expecting him to be the one to run to the rescue of her offspring. And he didn't think they wanted to be rescued. "Please, Adam."

She couldn't run to them, and she wanted to. He could see it in the tight line of pain around her mouth. Ignoring the fact that the running he wanted to do was in the direction of Atlanta, he ran to the end of the stable and gathered the boys in his arms, pulling them back from the coiled snake. A garter snake, nonpoisonous and no threat to the boys or the dog.

"It's a garter."

The boys wiggled to get free. He set them down, knowing that they'd go back to the snake. The reptile slithered along the side of the barn now, in search of a warm place to rest. The dog had lost interest and was sniffing a new trail.

Jenna was leaning against the barn, watching them, a soft and maternal smile turning her lips.

"Come on, guys. I think you've caused enough commotion for one day." She motioned them to her side. "Mr.

Mackenzie, don't give up on the camp. I know someone would buy it, live here, raise some cows. But a camp. Not just everyone can do that."

"Probably true, but I'm not the person who can."

"But you have to." She turned a little pink. "I'm sorry, you don't have to."

He wanted to smile. He wanted to ask how a person became so passionate about something, so willing to fight for it.

"Why does it mean so much to you?" As the words slipped out, he thought he probably didn't want the answer.

"It isn't about me. Not really. I think you shouldn't give up on something that could mean so much to so many people. Including you. And, believe it or not, I think it meant a lot to Billy."

"But it doesn't mean that much to me. I'm not looking for good deeds to do. This was about my cousin, something he wanted to do, and something that I had the money to help him with."

"If you didn't believe in this when Billy proposed it to you, why did you give him the money?"

"I don't know." And he didn't. He looked out the open doors of the barn and fought the truth. Maybe he did know why. Maybe he hadn't run as far from his roots as he'd thought.

"It's too bad that it won't be a camp. Come on, boys, we're going home. It was nice to meet you, Mr. Mackenzie." She said it like she was disappointed in him, as if she had expected better from him. But she didn't know him.

Before he could say anything, she was walking away, the boys running a little ahead of her. The dog went in another direction, chasing a scent that interested him more than the direction his family was going.

As she climbed into her truck, not looking in his direction, he felt strangely let down. A thought that took him by surprise. She wanted this camp, not for herself but for the kids it could help.

At least it meant something to her. To him, it was just another way he'd been used.

He headed back down the driveway, toward the road, because the tow truck would arrive soon and the rental car he had ordered would be delivered in an hour.

The Mad Cow Diner was starting to sound pretty good, another sign that he was nearing the end of his rope. The lifeline he had to hold on to was the reality that he could take care of what needed to be done, hand it off to someone else, and leave.

Jenna Cameron's truck rattled down the rutted driveway, slowing as she reached the road, and then pulling onto the paved road in the direction of her house.

Chapter Three

"What's up with you?" Vera sat down at the table across from Jenna. The Mad Cow wasn't crowded in the afternoon and the boys were enjoying slurping up chocolate shakes.

Jenna had fallen into a stupor. The black-and-white, Holstein-spotted walls of the diner had become a little hypnotic as she'd sat there, her elbow on the black tabletop, her chin on her hand.

Vera, dark hair pulled back in a bun and a smock apron over her white T-shirt, filled Jenna's cup and set the coffeepot down on the table.

Jenna picked up the sugar container and poured a spoonful or more into her coffee. "Why do you think something is up?"

Vera smiled as if she knew everything that was going on, and even what might happen. "Oh, honey, we all know that Adam Mackenzie crashed into your ditch the other day."

"It wasn't my ditch." She stirred creamer into her coffee. "It was the ditch across from me."

"He came in for my chicken-fried steak last night, and the night before."

And that made him Vera's hero. He would be Jenna's hero if he kept Camp Hope alive. That didn't seem too likely. Besides, she didn't need a hero. She had two little boys who were slurping up the last of their shakes and eyeing someone else's French fries.

"I think those boys need fries." Vera slid out of her chair. "Don't despair, Jenna dear. It'll all work out."

"I know it will, but I really want that camp."

Vera's brows went up in a comical arch. "*You* want it?"

"For kids. Can you imagine what a treat that would be for children who don't normally get to attend camp?"

Kids like her, when she was ten or twelve, and broken, feeling like no one cared and God was a myth, meant only to keep naughty children on the straight and narrow.

She'd had a hard time with *straight and narrow*.

"I can imagine." Vera's hand rested on her shoulder. "Give it time. I don't think he'll ditch it. If he isn't going to run it, someone else will."

But would someone else run it at no cost for the kids attending, the way Adam's cousin had planned? She wished she had the money to buy it. But wishes were vapor and her bank account was barely in the black.

"Mom, how does a person get to be a football player on TV?"

Timmy's question shook her from her thoughts. She smiled at him. His lips were back on his straw and Vera had left, pushing through the doors, back into the kitchen.

"Lots and lots of work," she answered, and then pulled the cup away from him and pushed the small glass of water close. "The shake is gone, drink some water."

"Vera's making us some fries." He grinned, dimples making it even cuter, even harder to resist. "She whispered that it's 'cause we're the best boys she knows. She's putting cheese on them, the way we like."

He added the last with a lilt of an accent that was meant to sound like Vera. Jenna kissed his cheek. "You're the best boys I know, too. And we might as well order burgers, since you won't want supper now."

David's eyes lit up. He pushed away the empty shake glass and sat down in the chair that he'd been perched on, sitting on his knees to better reach his glass.

"Do you think I could be a pro football player someday? I'd make a lot of money and you could have a big house in, well, somewhere." Timmy was out of his chair, standing next to it. He didn't like to sit still, a reality that had caused problems in school last year.

First grade was going to be rough for him, a whole day of sitting still, listening.

"I don't need a big house and you should only play football if you love it, not because you think I want a big house." She didn't think Adam Mackenzie loved the sport. She wondered if he ever had.

She had asked Clint, because her brother had known Adam years ago. Clint said he really couldn't say. Adam had seemed intent, serious, but he didn't know if he had loved it.

Vera returned with their fries. "What else, kiddos?"

"Go ahead and bring us three burgers, Vera. We'll let you cook for us tonight."

Vera was all smiles. "You got it, sweetie. Three Vera specials coming up."

The door opened, letting in heat and sounds from outside—a train in the distance and cars driving down Main Street. Vera's eyes widened. Jenna glanced back, over her shoulder and suddenly wanted to get her order to go.

* * *

"Jenna Cameron, imagine seeing you here." Adam stood next to Jenna's table, smiling at the two boys because it was easier than smiling at her, easier than waiting for an invitation to join them and easier than dealing with the reality that he wanted to join them.

He told himself it was just pure old loneliness, living at that trailer, not having his normal social life. He was starved for company, that's all.

"You knew I was here. My truck's right out front." She smiled up at him, a mischievous look in eyes that today looked more like caramel than chocolate.

He laughed. "You got me there. I thought I'd swing in for Vera's meat loaf and I wanted to tell you something."

"Have a seat." She pointed to the chair on her left.

He hesitated, but her wide eyes stared up at him, challenging him. He sat down, taking off his hat as he did. He hooked it over the back of the empty chair on the seat next to him.

The boys occupied the two chairs across the table from him. Blond hair, chocolate milk on their chins and suspicious looks in their eyes, they stared at him in something akin to wonder.

"So, what's your news?" Jenna leaned back in her chair, hands fiddling with the paper that had come off a straw.

"You get your camp."

"Excuse me?"

"I'll be staying, at least through the end of July. My agent thinks I should stay and help get the camp running." He wouldn't expand on Will's words, which had been a little harsher than what he was willing to admit to Jenna. "I called the church that left the message and told them I might be able to get something going in time, or close to it. If they can be flexible."

Her eyes widened and he could see the smile trembling at the corners of her mouth. "I can help."

"I thought you might."

Vera pushed through the swinging doors of the kitchen carrying a tray of food and avoiding eye contact with him. Probably because she'd been listening in. At least she didn't have a camera or an agenda.

Or did she have an agenda? Probably not the one he was used to. More than likely Vera had only one agenda. She had matchmaking on her mind. She had the wrong guy if that was her plan.

"Did I hear someone mention my meat loaf special?" She set down plates with burgers in front of Jenna and the boys and pulled a pen and order pad out of her pocket. "I've got that chocolate chess pie you like."

"No pie tonight. If I don't start cutting myself back, you'll have me fifty pounds overweight when I leave Dawson."

Vera's brows shifted up. "Oh, don't tell me you're still in a hurry to get out of here?"

"Not anymore. I'm going to stay and make sure things are taken care of at the camp."

Across from him the boys stopped eating their burgers and looked at each other. It was a look that settled somewhere in the pit of his stomach, like a warning siren on a stormy afternoon. Those two boys were up to more than seeing who could get the most ketchup on their fries.

At the moment David was winning. He had a pile of ketchup on top of two fries and he was moving it toward his open mouth. Adam held his breath, watching, wanting the kid to win, and maybe to break into that big grin he kept hidden away.

Just as David started to push the fry into his mouth, the front door to Vera's opened. David looked up and his fry moved, dropping the ketchup. Everyone at the table groaned, including Adam.

"That isn't the reaction I normally get when I walk into a restaurant." The man stepping inside the door was tall, a little balding and thin. The woman behind him smiled, her gaze settling on Jenna.

"No, it's usually the reaction you get when you tell one of your jokes on Sunday morning," the woman teased with a wink at Jenna, punctuating the words.

"Pastor Todd, Lori, pull up another table and join us," Jenna offered a little too quickly and Adam got it. She wasn't thrilled with the idea of Adam Mackenzie at her table. He sat back, relishing that fact.

A little.

Until it got to him that she wasn't thrilled to be sharing a table with him. Jenna cleared her throat and a foot kicked his.

"Excuse me?" He met her sparkling gaze and she nodded to Pastor Todd.

"Could you help him move that table over here, push it up against ours?"

"Oh, of course." Adam stood up. And he remembered his manners. "I'm sorry, we haven't met."

"Pastor Todd Robbins." Todd held out his hand. "My wife, and obviously better half, Lori."

"Adam Mackenzie."

And they acted like they didn't know who he was. Maybe they didn't. Not everyone watched football. He reached for the table and helped move it, pushing it into place as Jenna had directed. And Vera still watching, smiling, as if she had orchestrated it all.

"So, what first?" Jenna wiped her fingers on a paper towel she'd pulled off the role in the center of the table.

"What?" Adam looked surprised, like he'd forgotten the camp. She wasn't going to let him forget.

"The camp. You'll need beds, mattresses, food…"

He raised his hand, letting out a sigh that moved his massive shoulders. "I don't know where to start. I don't see any way this can be done in a matter of days."

"Weeks."

He didn't return her smile. "Yeah, well, my glass of optimism isn't as full as yours. We have less than two weeks. And then we have kids, lots of them, and they need activities."

"Not as many as you might think. I think if you talk to their church, they have lessons planned, chapel services, music. You need the beds, window coverings. They'll bring their own bedding." She stopped talking because he looked like a man who couldn't take much more. "Oh, horses."

She whispered the last, in case he was at the end of his rope and about to let go.

"Horses?"

"Clint can help you with that."

"Is there some way that I can help with this project?" Todd broke in. "I'd be glad to do something."

"We'll need kitchen help, and people to clean the grounds and the cabins." Jenna reached for her purse and pulled out a pen. She started to write, but Adam covered her hand with his.

She looked at his hand on hers and then up, meeting

a look that asked her to stop, to let it go. He turned to Pastor Todd.

"Let's talk about it later, maybe tomorrow. Not now."

He was in denial. Poor thing. And so was Jenna if she thought she was immune to a gorgeous man. She moved the hand that was still under his, and he squeezed a little before sliding his hand away.

"Okay, tomorrow." But she was no longer as sure as she had been. Adam smiled at her, like he knew what she was thinking. So she said something different to prove him wrong. "Clint will be back tomorrow."

With that she let it go, because it hit her that she had just invited this man into her life. He was the last person she needed filling space in her world, in her days.

The horse tied in the center aisle of the barn stomped at flies and shook her head to show her displeasure with the wormer paste they'd pushed into her mouth. The tube said green apple. Jenna had no intentions of trying it, but she doubted it tasted anything like an apple. She patted the horse's golden palomino rump and walked around to her side, the injection ready with the animal's immunizations. Clint stood to the side. He and Willow had come home early and he'd surprised Jenna by showing up this morning to help with the horses.

"Why are you so quiet today?" Clint slipped the file back into the box of supplies he'd brought in. This horse's hooves hadn't needed trimming, which meant he had just stood back and watched as Jenna did what she needed to do.

And now she wished she had more to do so she could ignore his question. He knew her far too well.

"I'm not quiet."

"Yes, you are. Normally when we get home from a trip you have a million questions. 'How did Jason do this week?' He did great, by the way. Got tossed on his head."

She looked up. Leaning against the horse's back, watching from the opposite side of Clint. "Is he okay?"

Jason was one of her best friends. She sometimes regretted that they'd never really felt anything more than friendship. He'd make a great husband for someone. He was kind, funny, wealthy. And not the guy for her.

"He's fine. And Dolly has gone ten outs without being ridden."

"That's great. I bet Willow is proud."

"She is. They're considering him for the finals at the end of the year."

"Great."

"And then we flew home in the pickup."

"I'm so glad."

"And you're not listening to me."

Jenna stared out the door at the boys, watching them play in the grassy area near the barn. The dog was sitting nearby, watching, the way he watched cattle in the field. If he had to, he'd round the boys up and drive them to her. They loved it when he did that. Sometimes they wandered away from her just to see if the dog would circle and move them back to Jenna. The nature of a cow dog was to herd. Jenna was glad she'd brought home the black-and-white border collie. It had been a cute, fluffy puppy, and was now a great dog.

"Jenna, is everything okay?"

"Of course it is. I'm just tired." She smiled back at her brother. "Let's get this horse out of here and bring Jinx in."

"Who is that?" Clint walked to the door as the low rumble of an engine and crunch of tires on gravel gave an advance warning that they had company. And then the dog barked.

Dog. She really needed to name that poor animal. It was probably too late. The boys called him Puppy and Jenna called him Dog. He came to either name so it seemed wrong to call him something like Fluffy or Blue.

"I don't know." Jenna tossed the used needle into the trash.

"Big, blue truck."

She groaned and Clint shot her a look. "You know who it is? Did you sell that roan gelding?"

"Jenna?"

"It's Adam Mackenzie." She untied the horse, rubbing her neck. "Come on, girl."

"That's it? Adam Mackenzie is pulling up to the barn and you act like you expected him?"

"He's the mystery owner of the camp."

"Adam is building a youth camp?" Clint followed her to the barn door with the mare. "The mystery deepens."

Jenna laughed. "It isn't a mystery. Billy was his cousin and he convinced Adam to buy the land and start this camp."

"Sis, you know he's trouble, right?"

"I don't think he's trouble. I think he's confused."

Clint shook his head. "Remember when you thought a baby skunk would be a good pet because it didn't spray you?"

"I remember."

She laughed at the memory. Because eventually the skunk did spray her. She gave it to a zoo and missed school for a week. She really did learn by her mistakes. Sometimes it just took a few tries before the lesson sank in.

Men were included in the list of mistakes she'd learned

her lesson from. The father of her boys had walked out on her. He went back to California, and she let him go because she knew she couldn't force him to stay and love them. The soldier she'd fallen in love with, he'd written her a Dear Jane letter after her surgery.

She would never again own a pet skunk. She would never again fall for a pretty face and perfect words. She had a five-year plan that didn't include falling in love.

"He's getting out of his truck," Clint warned as he took the halter off the mare and slapped her rump to send her back to the field with the rest of the horses.

Jenna nodded. "He wants to talk to you about buying horses. And since he's here to see you, I'm going to the house."

"Are you running?" Clint followed her to the front of the barn. And the twins were no longer sitting in the grassy area with their toy cars.

"Nope, just leaving."

"Are you afraid of him?" Clint caught hold of her arm. "Jenna, did he say something to you?"

"No, and I'm not afraid." *Much.* "I have to check on the boys. They've abandoned the road they were building for their toy trucks. I need to see where they went."

"That's because they're showing Adam something." He nodded in the direction of the blue truck that was parked a short distance from her house.

"Great." She watched the boys open their hands. Two blond-headed miniatures with sneaky grins on their faces, and dirt. They needed baths.

The giant in front of them jumped back from their open hands, either feigning fear or truly afraid. The boys laughed, belly laughs, and then they ran off.

Adam Mackenzie turned toward the barn, his smile

a little frazzled. He wasn't used to kids. She had to give him points for trying. And she wasn't going to escape because he was heading their way.

Who could escape that moment when they felt as if their insides had jelled and their breath caught somewhere midway between lungs and heart?

All due to a cowboy in faded jeans and a T-shirt. Not a cowboy, she reminded herself. A football player with a life so far removed from this small community that she couldn't imagine what it was like to live in his world.

"Adam." She greeted him with a wavering smile.

"Jenna." He held his hand out to her brother, his white hat tipped down, shading the smooth planes of his suntanned face. "Clint Cameron. I haven't seen you since we played against each other our senior year."

"Fifteen years." Clint shook Adam's hand. Jenna waited, wondering what came next. "Jenna said you're back to take care of the youth camp."

This time Adam smiled at her, that slightly boyish yet wicked grin that made his blue eyes dance. "Yeah, something like that. It looks as if I'm in charge, and I need horses. Maybe a dozen or so, with tack."

"Got it. I think I can round them up. It might take a few weeks."

"I don't have a few weeks." The edge was back in this voice.

Jenna looked up. She watched as her brother considered the words of the other man. And she made a way to escape.

"I need to get supper started. I'll let the two of you take care of business."

Chapter Four

Adam watched Jenna go, surprised that she was leaving. Let down? No, of course not. He wanted space, time out from relationships. He wasn't let down by her walking away.

He was surprised, and a little bruised by her lack of interest. Typically she was the kind of woman he ran from. The kind that was looking for a husband and a father to her kids. She didn't seem to be looking, though.

Horses. Clint's one word brought Adam back to his surroundings, and his gaze shifted back to the man standing in front of him, away from the retreating back of a cowgirl.

"A dozen, at least." He followed Clint into the barn. "She runs this place by herself?"

"She does."

"Impressive."

Clint shrugged and walked into the tack room. He hung up halters and lead ropes that were tossed on a shelf. "She's always been strong."

"It has to be tough, raising two boys alone."

"It is, but she has family and friends who help."

Adam picked up a currycomb and ran the sharp metal over his hand. "High school was a long time ago, Clint. If you're still holding a grudge about Amy, I'm sorry. I didn't know she was playing a game with the two of us."

Clint turned, smiling in a way that felt a lot like a warning snarl from a dog. "Amy is fifteen years of water under the bridge and I have no regrets. I have a wife that I love and a baby that we adopted a few months ago. My concern now is for my sister."

"You don't have to be concerned on my account. I'm here to get this camp mess cleared up, and then I'll be leaving. I'm not here looking for a relationship."

Clint shook his head and walked out of the room, switching the light off as he went, leaving Adam with just the light from outside. When he stepped out of the tack room, Clint was waiting.

"Adam, Jenna's an adult. She's also my sister. Don't use her. Don't mislead her. Don't hurt her."

"She's not a kid."

Clint took a step closer. "She's my kid sister."

Adam lifted his hands in surrender. "I don't plan on hurting your sister. I don't plan on getting involved with her at all. She's offered to help me get this camp off the ground so I can leave. Believe me, my only goal is to get this done and get out of Oklahoma."

"Okay, as long as we understand each other." Clint grabbed a box and walked out of the barn. "I'll get back to you on the horses."

"Thanks." Adam watched Clint Cameron drive away and then he turned toward the two-story farmhouse, a small square of a house with a steep, pitched roof. The boys were playing in the front yard and a sprinkler sprayed a small patch of garden. The few trees were tall and branched out, shading the house, a few branches brushing the roof.

The boys. He couldn't remember their names, and he'd had dinner with them yesterday. He walked in the direction of the house, thinking about their names, and not thinking about why he was still here. Timmy and David. He remembered as he walked up to them.

He smiled when the bigger boy looked up, a suspicious look on a dirt-smudged face and gray eyes like his uncle Clint's. The little boy, wearing shorts, T-shirt and flip-flops, sat back on his heels. He picked up his toy soldiers and nudged his other brother.

Adam knew their names, but couldn't remember which was which. "One of you is Timmy, the other is David."

"I'm David." The one who sucked his thumb. The little guy wouldn't look up.

"I'm Timmy." The bolder of the two. "And we still don't talk to strangers."

It was a long way down to the ground. Adam sighed and then he squatted. "I'm not really a stranger now. Aren't we sort of friends?"

David looked up, gray eyes curious. "Are you friends with my mom?"

"I guess."

"Did you know her in the army?" The little guy pushed his soldiers through the dirt. "Were you there?"

"No, I wasn't in the army."

He hadn't known Jenna was in the army. But did he ask little boys about their mother, and about the military? He didn't think so.

"She was in Iraq." Timmy solved the problem of Adam asking for more information.

"That's pretty amazing." More amazing than he could

imagine. She wasn't much bigger than her boys, but he had pegged her right. She was tough. She had something that so many women he'd met lately didn't have. She had something…

"Boys, time to come in for supper."

She had two boys and no interest in him.

Adam stood and turned. She was standing on the porch, leaning on a cane. He didn't know what to do. Had she heard their conversation? Her face was a little pink and she avoided looking at him.

He should go. He shouldn't get involved. He didn't ask the women in his life if they were okay. He didn't worry that they looked more wounded emotionally than physically. He didn't delve into their private lives.

He had easy relationships without connecting because if he didn't connect, he didn't get used. The girl in high school, Amy, had used him against Clint. She had used them both for her own games that he still didn't understand. As much as he had lived life, he still didn't always get it. Maybe because his childhood and teen years had been spent on the football field guided by his dad, and without a lot of social interaction off the field.

"Do you want to stay for supper?" It was Timmy, holding a hand out to him, not Jenna offering the invitation.

"I should go." He looked down at the little guy and tried to remember when he'd last had supper cooked in a farmhouse and eaten at an oak table.

"You can stay." Jenna walked onto the porch, her brown hair pulled back in an unruly ponytail. "I have plenty. It's nothing fancy."

He pushed his hat back and stared up at her, a country girl in jeans and sneakers. He resented Billy for putting him in this position and Will for telling him to stay.

Because this felt like home. And he hadn't been home in a long time.

It had been so long that he'd forgotten how it felt, that it felt good here, and safe.

"Adam?"

"I shouldn't…"

"What, shouldn't eat? Are you afraid it'll ruin your boyish figure to eat fried chicken?"

"Fried chicken, you say?" His stomach growled. "I think I might have to stay."

He couldn't remember the last time he'd had fried chicken. Or the last time he'd known a woman that cooked fried chicken.

Timmy pulled his hand, leading him up the stairs. Jenna limped back into the house. He followed her slow pace, telling himself that questions weren't allowed.

He had rules about women, rules that included not asking questions, not getting personal. Because he knew how much it hurt to be used, to be fooled. But he couldn't admit that, because he was Adam Mackenzie, he could take a hit and keep going.

"What can I do?" He pulled off his hat and hung it on a nail next to the back door.

Jenna turned, her face flushed. "Pour the tea? I have glasses with ice waiting in the fridge."

"I can do that." He opened the fridge. Four glasses. She had expected him to stay. Did she think she was going to have to take care of him while he stayed in Oklahoma? He'd have to make sure she understood that he didn't need that from her.

But not today. Today there were shadows in her eyes. Today his heart felt a lot like that grassy field behind his trailer—a little empty, kind of dusty.

And Jenna Cameron looked like the person that needed to be taken care of.

He poured the tea and carried the glasses to the table. The boys were setting out the plates and flatware. He smiled down at them. They, unlike their mother, smiled back.

As Jenna came to the table with the chicken, the boys dropped into their seats. Jenna sat down, sighing like it was the biggest relief in the world to sit.

"David, pray please."

Pray? Adam watched as the boys bowed their heads. He followed their example, remembering back to his childhood and meals like this one.

The prayer was sweet, really sweet. The way only a kid can pray—from the heart. The little boy had prayed for their meal, and for soldiers and for the new baby that Willow said wouldn't let her sleep. And he prayed for Adam because he was a new neighbor.

Adam smiled at Jenna as she stood again, going for something on the counter. He should have offered. Before he could, she stumbled, catching herself on the counter.

He started to stand, but Timmy shook his head.

"Are you okay?" He scooted his chair back.

"I'm fine."

"My mom got injured in the war," David whispered. "But she's good now. We take care of each other."

A warning if ever he'd heard one.

"Maybe you need to take a few days off. I can find other help."

She put a basket of rolls on the table. "I don't need a day off, Adam. There are no days off from life."

She was one tough lady. He had to give her that. And when he left that night, he knew that she was different than anyone he'd ever met. He drove away from her house, relieved that his stay here was temporary. And he ignored the call from his sister, a call that would have required explanations.

Jenna awoke with a start, her heart hammering in her chest and perspiration beading across her forehead. It took her a minute to place this dark room—her room in the farmhouse she'd grown up in, not the dark room in Iraq that had been her hiding place. As the fear ebbed, she became more aware of the knife-sharp pain in her leg. It throbbed, and she couldn't close her eyes without remembering the sweet lady who had tried so desperately to fight the infection and save the limb.

Jenna had survived, though. Her prayers that she would live, that she would come home to her boys, had been answered. Every day she remembered those prayers and she was thankful. Even on nights when she couldn't sleep.

Fear and pain tangled inside her, both fighting to be the thing that took over, that consumed her thoughts, forcing her to focus on them, not on the good things in her life.

She could control it. She had learned ways to deal with it, even on nights like tonight when it hurt so much she didn't know if she would ever be okay again.

She closed her eyes, breathing deep, thinking about being home, and her boys, and God. The pain lessened, but her heart still ached because the dream tonight had gotten mixed in with the memory of Jeff, the last time she'd seen him. He hadn't been able to look at her.

He had sent her a letter to say goodbye.

The next day the counselor had asked her to write a

five-year plan. She hadn't included love or marriage. Nor had she included them in her fifteen-year plan. Her plan included raising her boys, dedicating herself to making them young men that she could be proud of. Her plan included being at home, alive and healthy with her family. And her plan included thanking God every day for giving her a second chance at life and faith.

The list had included never having a man look at her like that again, that look that wavered between pity and horror, as if he couldn't get out the door fast enough.

The throbbing pain continued, bringing an end to the trip into the past and the return of her convictions. She reached for crutches and pulled herself out of bed. Slow, steady and quiet, she left her bedroom and eased through the house.

At the front door she stopped, looking out at what was left of the night, and watching as the eastern horizon started to glow with the early-morning light of sunrise. The trees and fields were still dark, making a perfect silhouette against the sky as it lightened into pewter and lavender.

She walked out the door, easing it closed so it didn't bang against the frame and wake the boys. Outside the air was cool, but damp with morning dew. Horses whinnied and somewhere in the distance dairy cows bellowed in the morning as they stood in line at the barn to be milked.

She hobbled down off the ramp and across the lawn, greeting the day and praying as she went. The pain faded to a less intense throb, rather than the breathtaking pain that had kept her awake.

She stopped, letting the world come into focus. Unafraid.

As she walked, the dog joined her. She reached down,

petting his dark head. He froze, whining and then snarling low.

"Stop that, silly Dog." Jenna spoke with a lightness she didn't feel at the moment. Her heart picked up speed, because she heard it, too. Footsteps on the road, coming fast, much faster than she could run.

"Shhh, Dog, quiet." Jenna patted the dog's head, calming him, wishing she could calm herself as easily. The footsteps were closer. And then she spotted the figure of a man. The dog barked at the shadow standing at the end of her drive.

"Jenna?"

Adam Mackenzie. Her heart was pounding and cold chased up her arms. She froze, knowing she couldn't escape. She waited, the dog no longer snarling at her side.

"Jenna?" He called out louder. She could see him clearly now, coming up her drive.

He wore shorts and a T-shirt. She was in cutoff sweats and a T-shirt. She stared down at her foot, waiting. When she looked up, he was in front of her. His gaze lifted from the lost leg to her face.

"You're pale."

Not the first words she expected from him, but it gave her a minute to gather herself. "Because you scared the life out of me."

"What are you doing out here?" He hadn't turned away. He was still looking at her.

"The same as you, taking an early-morning run."

He looked like he didn't know if he should laugh or not. She smiled, wanting him to be the way he was yesterday, before he knew. But if she had a wish, she wished she could go back further in time than yesterday. A year, maybe more. She'd make wiser choices. She would be more careful.

But this was her reality and it couldn't be changed. Deal with it. And Adam needed to deal with it, too.

"Adam, that was a joke."

"Oh, okay."

"Please, don't do this. Don't get weird on me."

He nodded.

"I mean it." Anger put power behind her words. "Don't look at me like that."

"I'm not. You can give a guy a minute or two to adjust, right?"

"Fine, but I'm heading for the house and I'm making coffee."

"Is that an invitation?"

"Not really." She smiled up at him, glad that he was still talking, still being real. The tightness that had gripped her heart was letting go, releasing. "Yes, I guess it is."

"What are you doing out here at this time of the morning?" He walked next to her as they neared the house. "Or is that question off-limits?"

"I couldn't sleep." She stopped. "Some nights are worse than others."

"Pain?"

He opened the back door and motioned her inside.

"Yes." She flipped on the kitchen light and reached for the coffeepot. He leaned against the counter and watched. His shirt was stained dark with perspiration. She remembered jogging. Someday she'd be fitted with a limb that made it easier to run. Now, she wore one that worked for riding horses and living on a farm.

Her life hadn't ended on that summer day in Iraq. It

had started over, with new obstacles, and new moments when God proved Himself. She had met Him there, in the desert, as far from church and Sunday-school lessons as a person could get.

She poured water into the coffeemaker and added fresh-ground beans, leaning on the crutches, but her hands free. She was good at this now, at balancing, at moving and continuing with everyday duties that had always seemed like second nature. Before. Her life was cut into chapters. This chapter was about learning to be the person she really wanted to be. The last chapter was the "Jenna who was whole" chapter.

But she hadn't really been whole. She had been missing something vital. Faith.

The coffee started to brew. She turned and Adam was waiting, watching her.

"What happened?" Adam pushed out a chair for her and took the one next to it. He looked like a giant at her table. A big golden-tan giant with hair that glinted in the soft overhead light.

"We were in a convoy and we were attacked." She closed her eyes as the memories came to life. "I remember being on the ground and the sand was hot and I could feel that I was bleeding. I knew the enemy was close and I didn't think I'd live to see my boys again."

"Jenna, we don't have to do this." Adam's big hand covered hers.

She looked up, and he was looking straight at her. His gaze held hers and he didn't look away. She didn't know how to feel about that, about him here in her kitchen, coffee brewing and the rooster crowing in the morning.

She smiled. "It's okay, I don't mind. I've told the story before. I have to tell people what God did for me that day."

"Oh."

Was that him discounting God, and disconnecting? "Oh?"

"I'm sorry, go ahead."

"I managed to move a short distance from where I'd been hit, but then I couldn't move any farther. I had one of those moments. You know how they say your life flashes before your eyes? Well my life hit me between the eyes. Good memories and bad came at me. I remembered stories from Sunday school. I remembered being picked up by various neighbors or by church buses and hauled to nearly every church in the county. I remembered oatmeal cookies with butterscotch chips. And I remembered those stories of Jesus. I had never really thought that He loved me enough to die on a cross for me. No one ever loved me that much, except maybe Clint. At least that's what I thought when I was eight." She looked across the room at the blurping coffeepot. "The coffee is ready."

"I'll get it, you talk." His chair scooted on the tile and she watched him pour coffee and then add sugar to hers.

"You really want to know all of this?"

"Yep."

"Okay, I'll keep talking." Because maybe that was the reason for his early-morning jog and her early-morning walk. Maybe God had brought Adam all the way to Oklahoma for this moment. "I had all of those thoughts and I thought of my boys and I knew that I couldn't die. And I knew that I could no longer deny God. After that I passed out and I don't know when I woke up again."

She took the coffee and added more sugar from the bowl on the table. His eyes widened as he watched her add the two spoons and creamer.

"Want coffee with your sugar?"

"Only a little." She sipped and it was just right.

"What happened next?"

"An elderly lady saw the attack and she sent her nephew out to rescue me before the insurgents found me. He dragged me back to their shack and they hid me. The lady had once been a nurse and she knew enough to keep me alive."

"Not enough…"

"To save my leg." Jenna sipped her coffee. Out the window the sun peeked over the eastern horizon where the sky was streaked with pink against blue. It promised another beautiful June day with clear skies.

She couldn't look at Adam Mackenzie.

"It had to be hard for you."

"It wasn't easy," she whispered, holding the hot cup of coffee between her hands.

"Is it easy now?"

"It's getting easier all the time. I have faith, my life and my boys. I have a career training reining quarter horses."

She didn't stop to think of the things she didn't have, and wouldn't have. Willow had told her those were self-imposed "can't haves." If that was the case, so be it. She wouldn't have a man in her life. Especially when he looked at her with pity. She wouldn't have a man in her life when she knew she couldn't let him look at her. And what man would want to look at her?

"It's that easy?" He shook his head and she smiled, because she could hear that he didn't believe it.

And she had to be honest with him. "It isn't always that easy. I get angry. I get down. I give up. And then…"

"You pick yourself up again. You would have made a great football player."

"Thank you." And she no longer wanted to talk about

her. "Now do me a favor, let's talk about you. How does it feel to be home?"

"This hasn't been my home for a long time."

"Of course not. I understand that because I left as soon as I could get away. I went into the military so I could live anywhere but here. But family and roots have a way of bringing us home."

"Family and roots didn't bring me home. Unless, I guess, you consider Billy dying."

"Why haven't you gone home to see your family?"

"Because I..." He laughed. "You almost got me. All of this emotion, and you almost pulled me in."

"You're right, it was a trap. I shared my sad, pathetic little story just to get you to engage with your inner child. But there is no child in there. The tough guy squashed him."

"Exactly. And I have been home, just not in a few years."

"I hear the boys." Jenna stood, wobbling a little before she got her balance.

"That's my cue to go?"

"It is. They wouldn't understand that it's morning and..."

"I get it." He stood in front of her, towering over her. He smiled, but then the smile faded and he leaned.

Jenna choked a little and leaned back. "I don't think so, cowboy. I'm not a woman who plays games."

Adam looked startled, his head tilted to the side a little like the dog when she smacked his nose for messing with her garden or chasing the cat.

"You're right. I'm sorry." He reached for his ball cap and walked out the back door. On the step he paused. "Will you still be over later?"

"An almost kiss doesn't mean that I'm not going to

help you. I'm not going to give you an excuse for backing out of helping those kids."

He nodded, and she watched as he jogged away, her dog running alongside him. She listened as the boys scuffled around upstairs, the sound of a normal day starting. But she knew that today was anything but normal.

Today Adam Mackenzie was her neighbor and she stood at the screen door, looking out at the morning, wondering what that meant to her life. Or if it meant anything at all.

Chapter Five

The Dawson Farm and Home Store was pretty close to empty at mid-morning, two hours after Adam nearly made a big mistake. Kissing Jenna would have been that, and more. He could think of a dozen reasons why.

But he didn't have time for thinking. He walked down the aisle that held horse tack and livestock vitamins, looking for what he thought he might need in the coming weeks. He hadn't bought farm supplies in a few years.

Instead of shopping for farm supplies, he should have been at home in Atlanta, preparing for a new career. Billy should be here, buying supplies, talking to locals and getting the camp ready to go. Not Adam, a guy who had spent less time with children than almost anyone he knew.

"You might want to grab mineral blocks." A familiar voice.

Adam turned from the shelf of vitamins and insect repellants. Clint Cameron stood next to him, comfortable with his life of cowboy and local hero. Adam's boots were still too new to be comfortable.

"Yeah, there's a lot to get done, a lot to buy." Including the mineral blocks, Adam realized. And if he needed them, that meant Clint had come through for him.

"I have ten horses." Clint's hat was tipped low. "I'm still looking for two more."

"That's good. Can you deliver?"

"Yeah, this afternoon if that works for you. I bought tack for them. I'll bring the bill."

"I'm sure you will."

Clint picked up a few cans of fly spray. Adam wondered if he should do the same. But if he did, he'd look like he didn't know what he was doing, like he was taking cues from Clint. And he didn't want to look like a novice. He had grown up on a farm. He knew what he needed and what he didn't.

Clint tossed him a can of the fly spray. "You'll probably need this."

"I know that." His collar felt really tight on his neck.

"Adam, we're not enemies, just guys who used to know each other and we had a few run-ins. That was a long time ago. Now we're two guys doing business, and I'm part of the community that wants to help you get this camp off the ground. Maybe you could give us all and yourself a break in the process."

"Yeah, of course." He grabbed another can of the fly spray. "I guess I'll see you this afternoon."

"Sure, at about two."

The front door chimed. Clint waved and Adam's collar felt a little tighter. Jenna, her blond-streaked brown hair pulled back in a ponytail. She smiled at her brother and then at him. Her smile for Adam was different, it was strained. He knew how she felt.

This morning he had wanted to kiss her. Good thing she'd reminded him of the boys and her desire not to get sidelined with someone like him. Good thing, because Clint Cameron was two feet from him, giving him a look that nailed him into the floor.

She adjusted easier than he had, shifting her attention away from him, sweeping that look from her eyes that said she remembered.

"Are you two up to no good?" She had a cheeky expression and a Southern drawl.

"I'm up to good. I can't speak for your brother." Adam smiled back. How did a smile change everything?

"He's always up to good." She slipped an arm around her brother. "He's just that way. I'm the bad one in the family."

"I don't buy that."

"It's true. I'm the rebel. But I'm a rebel with a cause. We're making a schedule for when people will start showing up to work at the camp."

"I appreciate that."

She laughed. "No, you don't. You're thinking it's going to cost you."

He was, but he shook his head to deny her accusation. "Not at all."

"It's going to cost you big-time. Church, this Sunday. You need to be there and thank people, maybe tell them your plans for the camp."

"I don't really have plans." He had plans, but the plans were about his life, his future, not a camp in Dawson, Oklahoma.

"You have to have plans. Oh, and I have a catalog where you can order what you need for the dorms. Do you want me to do that?"

"This afternoon. If you want to come over, we can use my phone and get that wrapped up." How did he tell her no? She was a pint-sized dynamo, intent on her mission. He nearly smiled.

She hugged Clint and winked at Adam before turning to walk away. He watched her go, but turned when Clint Cameron cleared his throat to get his attention.

"She's my sister, Adam."

"I know she is. Don't worry, I'm just looking to get this camp taken care of so I can leave."

"This is a real inconvenience for you, isn't it?"

"It definitely isn't convenient, Clint. Look, I didn't set out to run this camp. I'm not a bad guy. I'm not unfeeling. I gave money to my cousin because he wanted to help kids who couldn't afford camp. He wanted to do something good with his new Christian life. What he did was swindle me and then he had a heart attack."

Clint smiled. "Adam, sometimes God has a plan that we can't even begin to imagine. Maybe you coming here was His plan all along."

"Right, thanks for the sermon." He walked off, leaving Clint standing in the aisle with fly sprays and vitamins. He couldn't wait to get out of a store that smelled like chemicals, dusty grain and molasses.

As he stood at the counter paying, he watched Jenna Cameron walk across the parking lot that the farm store shared with The Mad Cow.

Jenna could have imagined a thousand scenarios as she pulled up the drive to the half-finished summer camp that afternoon. She never would have imagined Adam Mackenzie on the back of the big bay that Clint had decided to sell. She eased off the gas and let her truck coast to a stop. The boys jumped up from the backseat to lean into the front and watch the man on the back of the big red horse, black tail flagging proudly as it trotted around the yard.

He looked good on a horse. A tall giant of a man, his white cowboy hat pulled low, his jaw set as he held the reins and controlled the barely broke gelding.

The horse sidestepped, prancing and then bunny hopping as he tried to convince the man in the saddle that he might actually buck. Adam kept the reins tight and his legs visibly tightened around the animal's middle.

"Let's get out, Mom. I want to see if that mean old horse starts to buck." Timmy climbed over the seat and fell into the spot next to Jenna. David remained in the back. She glanced back at him. His eyes were wide and his mouth a firm line of seriousness.

"We're not going to get out. We don't want to spook Ready." The horse had been named *Ready, Set, Go* as a foal, because Willow thought he always looked like he was about to race.

"It might be fun to see him spooked," Timmy mumbled.

"That isn't nice."

"I don't want Adam to get hurt. I wanna see if he can stay on."

Jenna didn't laugh. Instead she hugged her son and motioned for David to climb over the seat and join them. She loved them so much. And her heart still ached when she thought about how close she came to not coming home to them. She didn't want to close her eyes, because when she did, it came back—the fear, the darkness, the thoughts of not being there to watch them grow up.

Adam reined the horse in and slid off. Jenna opened her door to get out. "Come on, guys, let's go see what we need to do around here today."

"We need to find our turtle." David slid out of the truck, already searching the grassy area around them. "We might want to feed him some bugs."

"As long as *you* don't eat bugs, that's fine," Jenna teased, ruffling her fingers through David's blond hair as he stood next to her.

The boys looked up at her, eyes wide and twin looks of serious contemplation. Timmy held her gaze for a moment and then looked down, kicking at a clump of grass.

"Boys, we don't eat bugs." Because they really looked like they might have already tried. "Do we?"

"Not anymore." And then they ran off. She laughed and watched them go.

No more distractions. Nothing else to keep her from joining the men.

Adam was standing next to the horse, tall, making the sixteen-hand horse look small, and talking to her brother with a hint of a smile on his face. She likened him to Goliath. And she really felt as if he had come to devour her kingdom.

Of course he hadn't, though. That was just her imagination. He couldn't hurt her. He couldn't hurt the people she loved. She didn't know why she had put him in that category to begin with.

He smiled at her and pushed his hat back. "Nice horse, isn't he? Clint brought ten, and this one."

"I thought he might like something for himself," Clint explained.

"You're just looking for someone to take that grain-eating beast off your hands." Jenna rubbed the massive head of the bay gelding. "He's a pain."

"He's not. I just don't have the time to ride him the way he needs to be ridden," Clint explained, and she wanted to tell him he could have brought the horse to her. But he wouldn't do that, she knew. He didn't want her to get hurt.

"Come into the office and I'll write you a check." Adam motioned them all to the trailer that had become his residence. Jenna followed the men, their longer strides eating up the ground. She wasn't in a hurry. A summer breeze swirled through the overgrown lawn, rustling last year's leaves, and the smell of a freshly cut hayfield carried on the wind. Days like this were for enjoying, not rushing through.

Inside would be stuffy. And crowded.

The boys were playing at the corner of the trailer. They were looking for the turtle, searching the grassy area as if they'd lost a treasure. Of course it was a treasure; it was a turtle. And what boy didn't consider those a treasure?

Girls liked them, too. Jenna had had her share of box turtles as a kid. She stopped to watch the boys for a second. They talked in whispers about the turtle and Adam falling off Ready. And then they looked up and smiled, a little guilty, too cute.

Adam cleared his throat. "Are you coming inside with us?"

"Oh, sorry, I was watching the boys. They're still looking for that turtle."

"I saw him the other day. He's still around."

"I hope they find him, not another snake."

Clint laughed. "It wouldn't be the first snake they found."

She nodded and reached for the rail to climb the stairs. "Did they eat bugs when they stayed with you?"

"No, but I did feed them hot dogs. Come on, Jen, you know I wouldn't feed your kids bugs."

"I didn't mean that you fed them bugs. I wondered if you *caught them* eating bugs."

"Never. Why?"

"Oh, something they said." She smiled, letting it go. "Never mind."

"I ate part of a worm once," Adam said as he opened the front door for them. "I turned out okay."

"Thanks, that makes me feel so much better. I want them to grow up to be…" She wouldn't say driven and detached.

"Strong?" He supplied a word that she hadn't planned to say, and she nodded.

"Sure, strong."

The trailer was dark and the furniture was dark. Jenna closed her eyes to give them a second to adjust from bright afternoon sunshine to the shadowy interior of the trailer. When she opened her eyes she could see clearly that it was a mess. Paper plates littered the coffee table and cans of soda sat on the end tables.

"What in the world have you done to this place?" She started gathering trash.

"It's my mess. I can clean it up." He took the paper plates from her hands. "I'm sure not asking you to be my maid."

"You need one."

"Check, please." Clint tapped the paper in his hand and held it out to Adam, who handed the plates back to Jenna.

She grumbled and walked into the kitchen, where the trash was overflowing. Had the man ever picked up after himself? She doubted it. He'd probably always been a superstar, even when he was in diapers.

"Jenna, I'll clean it up later," he called out as he scribbled his signature on a check.

"I don't mind. If we're going to get any work done, I need a clean space to sit down."

"It's clean."

"Give it up, Adam, she's going to win." Words of wisdom from Clint. He smiled at her, winking before he turned his attention back to Adam. "I've lived with her, and she's not going to put up with clutter, trash or dirty dishes. Have you seen her place?"

"I'm right here, stop talking about me." Jenna bumped her fist against her brother's arm. "Don't you have a wife that needs you for something?"

"Yeah, she wants me to do the dishes," Clint admitted with a wry grin.

"I know, when I picked up the boys, she asked me to come down here and make sure you didn't hang out too long." Jenna sat down on the sofa, spreading the catalog she'd brought on the table in front of her. "Time to get busy, Mr. Mackenzie."

"Yeah, busy." He sat down next to her, the sofa cushion sinking a little with his weight. "Where do we start?"

"We'll need to order mattresses, and supplies for the kitchen."

"See you later." Clint paused at the door. "Jen, call me when you get home."

She nodded and waved, not wanting to look at him, to see the worry in his eyes. He was too protective.

And Adam Mackenzie knew it. She felt him slide away, putting space between them. He didn't need to. There was already space between them. His goals. Her need to focus on her boys and living her life.

Those things equaled a chasm the size of the Grand Canyon. And she didn't have any desire or need to close the distance.

* * *

Adam's phone buzzed in his shirt pocket. He pulled it out and glanced at a familiar number with a local area code. He slid it back into his pocket and ignored the curious glances of the woman sitting next to him.

"So, we need mattresses. Can we get them in time? What about curtains?" He flipped through the catalog as she wrote down numbers.

"Mini blinds, not curtains. You won't have to take them down to wash them. I've called a company about mattresses and I think it is doable if we order them today."

"Where am I going to find enough people to work here?"

She put her hand on a page and pointed to a model of mini blind. "That one will work. I measured. It's the right size, a good price and neutral color."

"Okay, back to workers. I need more than help getting the beds made and the lawns mowed."

She pulled a paper out of her pocket. "I know. You need people in the kitchen, a few in the stables, we need cleaning crews before—"

"Could you slow down?" He took off his hat and brushed his hands through his hair. She was smiling at him, that cheeky grin he'd seen a few times. Someone should do something about her cheekiness. Not him.

She was the kind of woman looking for long-term, for a father for her boys. He wasn't the guy she was looking for. He didn't do relationships.

"Of course I can slow down. What's wrong?"

"What do you mean?" He scrambled, wondering if he had missed something. He ran his finger over the catalog, trying to remember what she'd just said.

"You mean, because you're looking dazed, staring at the wall and kind of mumbling?" She laughed a little.

"Have you already planned the entire camp?" He tossed his hat on the nearby chair. She was bossy. He didn't like bossy. It felt like she was taking over his life.

He'd had enough of that. His dad, agents, coaches, a few girlfriends—they'd all had plans for him. Other than Will, he kept a safe distance from people who wanted a piece of the Adam Mackenzie pie.

He knew what she wanted. She wanted this camp.

Another of her smiles, this one sheepish. Her eyes were amber and a sprinkling of freckles on her nose caught his attention. She cleared her throat, like she knew the direction his thoughts had taken. "I wrote out a schedule, a tentative menu and how much food I think we'll need and how many workers. I'm not really taking over, just getting you on track."

"Fine, you're hired."

"I didn't ask for a job." She flattened the papers on the table, covering the catalog. "I offered to help. This is volunteering and I'm not asking for anything in return."

Right. He didn't mean to sigh, and he didn't need the look she gave him. But he had a hard time believing she was simply volunteering out of the goodness of her heart.

"You're better suited for this than I am. You take over and I'll go back to Georgia."

"Nope." She stared him down.

He tucked away the strong urge to look deeper into eyes the color of caramel, but flecked with gold. He wouldn't move his hand and slide that strand of hair back behind her ear.

She did it, brushing her hair back and looking away from him.

The camp. He didn't want to run a camp. He wanted to go home before his family caught on, realizing he was a short thirty-minute drive from the home he'd grown up in. He definitely didn't want to take that journey home, not even in his imagination.

A quick look out the window and he saw twin boys following a turtle, their dog barking. That was what a childhood should be.

"Hello, are you still with me? You've forgotten to keep arguing." Her hand was on his arm.

"Sorry, just thinking back. Your boys are having a great childhood. Every kid should have that."

"Which is why you should be excited about this camp. Think of kids coming here, finding turtles, chasing lightning bugs and being kids. Some of them will be able to laugh and play like they've never laughed and played before."

He glanced back out the window, and let her words run through his mind, because she made it feel different. Her words made him think about what this camp meant. It meant children playing, having fun. He could give those kids something every child should have.

It made the pill of running the camp a little less bitter.

His phone buzzed again. He pulled it out and looked at it. Jenna's curious gaze caught his. She didn't ask questions.

"We need to get these orders placed." He picked up her papers she'd taken time to write out. Schedules, workers, menus. He shook his head and folded the papers. "I'll look over these later."

"Okay, but don't put it off. We have a little more than a week."

"Got it."

She held out her hand. "Phone, please. I need to place the order for the mattresses and other things we need in this catalogue."

He handed her his phone. "Do you think I can order the food we'll need from the grocery store?"

"Yeah. But I'd talk to Vera at The Mad Cow. She can look at the menu and the ingredients and make sure you get enough of everything for the amount of kids and workers."

"She won't mind?"

"She won't. I can go with you, if you'd like."

He was starting to feel tied to her. He'd been independent for as long as he could remember and now he needed this woman to keep him on track and help him get things done. That was great for his ego.

Somewhere out there was his life, the one he'd worked hard at building for himself. A house, a life, friends that probably wondered if he'd fallen off the face of the earth and a career he'd been working toward for the last few years.

There were also back issues of magazines and articles categorizing every mistake he'd ever made. Which was why he couldn't leave this mistake undone.

"Adam?"

"I'll stop by tomorrow afternoon and pick you up before I run into town."

"And then we'll go by and speak to Pastor Todd. He has the list of people we can contact for kitchen help, music, activities."

"This is way too much work. I shouldn't let the church bring kids here. We can't have dozens of children roaming this place with nothing to do."

"Have a little faith." She was dialing his phone with the catalog in front of her.

"Yeah, faith."

And then she was talking, ordering dozens of mattresses with his money and giving his credit card number. He felt used all over again, because she wanted this and she was willing to do whatever she needed to do to make it work.

No, she wasn't using him. She was finishing what Billy had started, and what Adam didn't want to finish. He had to remind himself that it had felt good when Billy had asked him for the money to buy this land and start the camp. Billy had sold him on the idea of helping kids.

The camp was a good thing. He stood, leaning against the bar that separated the kitchen from the living area of the trailer and watched Jenna Cameron on his phone, talking, smiling, writing down numbers. Her hair fell forward a little. She had taken it out of the ponytail holder and she pushed it back with a small hand, nails painted light pink.

She'd told him to have faith, and she said it lightly, as if it was a given. Faith was something he hadn't given a lot of thought to over the last ten or fifteen years. Faith was connected to home, to his childhood, and hadn't been included in his adult life.

Why? The question took him by surprise, because he hadn't questioned himself on too many of the choices he'd made. But church. He couldn't remember when he'd stopped going. Maybe college, when he'd realized that he'd had a faith born of his dad's job as pastor. His own connection to God had shorted out.

The trailer was suddenly hot and stuffy. He glanced

out the door, to the field, wind blowing the grass that needed to be mowed.

"I'll be outside."

As he walked out the door, he saw the boys playing with the turtle, and the dog sniffing a trail across the open field. The boys turned and ran toward him, not getting that he didn't know a thing about kids.

The phone beeped as Jenna was finishing the order. She switched to the incoming call and then realized she shouldn't have. It wasn't her phone, or her business.

A woman's voice said, "Hello," and then repeated the greeting when Jenna didn't respond. "Adam, don't ignore me. I know you're in Dawson."

"I'm sorry, this isn't Adam." Jenna glanced out the window. "Hold on and I'll get him."

"Who is this?"

"Jenna Cameron. I'm a neighbor."

"No, don't get him."

"It isn't a problem, he's right outside." Jenna stood, revisiting the idea of calling Adam in to get the call. She glanced out the window, watching as he crossed the lawn. "He isn't busy. You can talk to him."

"No, he obviously doesn't want to be bothered by his family, and that's fine." A short pause. "I'm his sister, Elizabeth."

Too much information, too personal. Jenna didn't want to be in the middle of a family problem. She was here because this camp was a good thing. End of story.

"I can give him a message," Jenna offered.

"No, don't give him a message."

"I can give you directions if you want to come by. I'm sure he'd love to see his family."

The sister laughed a little. "You don't know him very well, do you?"

No, she didn't. Jenna glanced out the window again. Adam had David on his shoulders and he was trotting around the yard. She smiled at the sight and wondered about a man who gave piggyback rides to little boys but didn't want to see his own family. Then again, the twins had a way of getting what they wanted. Adam might not be a willing participant in the piggyback rides. As a matter of fact, if she looked closely, he probably looked a little trapped.

"I'll give you directions, in case you change your mind." Jenna continued to watch out the window as she gave the directions and the call ended. And then she regretted what she'd done. A past was a difficult thing to deal with. Jenna knew that as well as anyone.

She also knew that dealing with her childhood had helped her to move forward. She had dealt with her own anger, her resentment of God that had caused her to push away the people who wanted to help.

Maybe, just maybe, that was the reason Adam Mackenzie had crashed into her life.

She walked outside and watched as he switched boys. It was Timmy's turn for a ride on Adam's shoulders. As they went in circles, the dog chased after them, jumping and barking. Jenna leaned on the rail of the porch, watching and worrying. She didn't want for worry to be the emotion she felt.

"The orders are placed," she called out, ending the ride, because she didn't want her boys to be hurt when he left. Adam put Timmy down and walked in her direction, his smile so natural it looked as if it should always be on his face, in his eyes, directed at her. And she knew better than to let her thoughts go there, to think about how good it felt when he smiled at her like that.

For the right woman, that smile would mean everything. It promised things he didn't even realize it promised.

"They're great kids." He had a hand on each of the twins, rubbing their heads and mussing blond hair that needed to be cut.

"They are great. They also need baths. So, you can pick me up tomorrow?"

"I can."

"Guys, time to go." She motioned the boys to her side.

"Do we have to?" Timmy moved with reluctance, shooting a glance back at Adam.

"We have to." Tomorrow she'd leave the boys with Clint and Willow. The less time they spent with Adam the better.

But what about her? How safe was it for her to spend all of this time with a man who planned to leave in six weeks?

Chapter Six

Adam pulled up in front of Jenna's house the next day, parking under the shade of a big oak, and watching as she came out the front door, locking it behind her. She eased herself down the steps and crossed the yard, watching the ground as she walked, but occasionally looking up, smiling at him.

This all felt like a time-out from his life, as if it wasn't even real. It wasn't a vacation, either. But there were good things about all of this. He got out of his truck and walked around to open the door for her, because that's what a gentleman did. His dad had taught him that.

"Where are the boys?" Adam waited for her to get into the truck, but she paused, watching as a car came up her drive. He shifted his gaze in that direction as she answered.

"They're with Clint. He bought a mule and they can't get over the fact that he bought that long-eared thing."

She kept talking. He listened, but the conversation was about the mule being able to jump a fence, the dog chewed up her new rosebush and one of her horses threw a shoe.

"By that, I mean that his shoe came off." She still wasn't getting in the car.

"I know what that means." He stepped to the side as the old sedan pulled up and stopped next to his truck. "Who is that?"

"Jess Lockhart. I'd say we're in trouble. He has his nasty face on."

"Good, we need trouble." Wasn't his life trouble?

Jess Lockhart, a farmer in overalls and work boots, got out of his sedan, still wearing what Jenna had called his nasty face. And he had his angry eyes on to go with it.

"Jess, how are you?" Jenna greeted the man with a smile that was a little tight.

"Well, I'd be a lot better if I knew the rumors I'm hearing around town were wrong."

"What does that mean, Jess?" Jenna tossed her purse into the cab of the truck, like she planned on leaving without finishing the conversation.

"Well, I heard we're going to have a camp with a bunch of juveniles roaming around." Jess turned his censoring gaze on Adam, and Adam was pretty sure he knew what the old farmer meant, and what he was there for.

"I don't think there will be juveniles," Adam defended, and he didn't even care about the camp. He let out a sigh. "The camp isn't a juvenile facility, just a summer camp."

"For kids from the city. They'll be out running through my fields, running my cattle, vandalizing my property."

"Oh, Jess, you know that won't happen." Jenna leaned against the side of the truck, her face a little flushed.

"You can't guarantee it won't, Jenna Cameron. And I plan on stopping it. I'll go to the county commission and I bet they'll find that you don't even have a permit for this thing, or the proper zoning, Adam Mackenzie.

I don't care who you think you are, around here that doesn't mean much."

"I'm sure it doesn't." Adam had never felt the truth to those words quite like he did now. Who he was just didn't really matter. What he wanted mattered even less.

"Jess, take a few days and think about this." Jenna patted the old farmer's arm. "This camp could be such a good thing for kids. It'll keep them off the roads. Remember me when I was sixteen? I bet you wish there'd been a camp to keep me in."

Adam watched the older man change from frowning to smiling, but he didn't think that meant the older man's opinion about the camp had changed. Maybe it didn't matter. Maybe this would put a stop to the camp and Adam would be able to leave without feeling guilty.

"You were a handful, Jenna. You weren't a juvenile delinquent running loose, tearing up my fields."

"Mr. Lockhart, I'm not sure why you think that will happen."

"I watch the news. I know what kids are like today."

"There are good kids, too, Jess." But her soft words weren't working. Adam touched her arm, stopping her.

"I don't want this camp in my backyard." Jess got into his car and slammed the door.

"Well, that went over well, didn't it?" Jenna looked up at him, her smile a little wavering. Adam nodded and he didn't let go of her arm. He knew he couldn't walk away from this camp, not without finishing it. Because it meant a lot to Jenna.

That shouldn't matter to him, it really shouldn't. But it did.

"It went well," he teased, standing behind her as she

climbed into the truck. "Don't worry about it. I'll work it out with him."

"Will you? It seems like this would be the perfect opportunity for you to say you tried, but it didn't pan out. You can leave and no one will blame you for going."

"I know." He leaned into the cab of the truck, resting his arms on the roof, and her face was close, close enough that he could smell the light scent of her perfume. "I know I could walk away, but I have a feeling you'd be my biggest nightmare if I did."

He winked and backed away, escaping from whatever had pulled him close to her, whatever it was that made him want to give her this camp, and make her smile.

"Let's go to lunch." He hadn't planned on offering the invitation, but it was close to noon.

"I don't know."

"We can sit at separate tables if you're worried about what people will say."

She smiled, a little sheepish and kind of shy. He shifted and pulled onto the road. Two miles to Dawson. Two miles of her sitting next to him, his mind framing a picture of a woman with a smile that he wouldn't soon forget.

"I guess you can sit with me." She looked out the window. "But you can't talk to me."

"Okay, that's a deal."

"You know I'm kidding, right? And besides that, we need to start at The Mad Cow, so Vera can help us with the specifics of the menu before we go to the store. We have to get this done before kids show up."

"I do know you're kidding, and yes, we have to get this done." He shifted again, slowing as they turned from the paved road they lived on, onto the highway that led to Dawson.

"We could have brought the boys." He wondered why she had decided to leave them with her brother.

"We can do this without them. It'll be easier."

"Okay." He accelerated and the tires hummed on the road. The wind whipped through the cab of the truck and Jenna rolled the window up.

"Adam, they're little boys and you're a hero who isn't going to be here long. I don't want…"

She looked away, brushing a hand through long hair that had gotten tangled by the wind.

"You don't want them to be upset when I leave?" He got it. He should have thought of it himself. They weren't a couple, the boys knew that, but boys got attached to people. They could even get attached to him.

He could get attached to them. That thought took him by surprise. He shifted gears and let the feelings go, because this wasn't real. This was Oklahoma in the summer, a return to his youth for a few short weeks, and soon he'd return to reality.

The woman next to him was a reminder that this was reality. She sang along to the radio and her scent, peaches and soap, filled the cab of the truck, whipping around him with the breeze from his open window.

He slowed the truck as they drove into Dawson, a true one-horse town. That horse was in the pen behind the first house inside the city limits, munching on a round bale of hay. The main street had only a few businesses. A convenience store, a farm store where they sold a few groceries, farm supplies and grain, and at the corner of Main and Dairy Road was The Mad Cow Café. The name of the restaurant had been painted on the side of the building in big, black-and-white-spotted block letters.

Getting attached. He glanced in Jenna's direction as

he pulled into the parking lot of The Mad Cow. He could get attached to her.

She didn't beat around the bush, saying only what he wanted to hear. She was honest, blunt and sometimes shy. When she wanted something from him, this camp, she spelled it out and told him why.

He set the emergency brake and pulled the keys out of the ignition. Jenna was already opening her door, like nothing had happened, like getting attached wasn't an issue for her.

Maybe it wasn't.

Jenna noticed the crowd inside The Mad Cow, but she didn't mention it. Really, why should it matter? So what if people glanced out the window at them, or mouths moved as questions were asked behind hands.

He had more to worry about than she did. People knew him, knew his family, and knew what he'd accomplished since he'd left Oklahoma.

For years she'd kept this town fed with gossip, someone to talk about. Her antics had been reported in church prayer groups, at the quilting bee and right here at The Mad Cow on Monday mornings.

It didn't bother her at all that he was the "something to talk about" now. He had broad shoulders. He could handle it.

Broad shoulders and a hand that casually brushed hers as they walked across the parking lot. What would that feel like, to hold his hand? She shoved her hands into her pockets.

He pushed the door of the diner open and she walked in ahead of him. A few people turned to stare, to smile, to greet them.

"Jenna, how're the kids?" Opal, the hostess and waitress, hurried past with a coffeepot and a pen shoved through her thick, gray hair.

One of the regulars yelled at her to take his order.

"I'll give you an order," Opal bit back. "How about a full order of hush-it-up, with a side of bite-your-tongue?"

Opal turned her attention back to Jenna and Adam. "I tell you, this crowd gets more attitude in the summer. Must be the heat. Anyway, about the boys…"

"They're great. Clint has them for the day."

"Good, sweetie. He's a doll for giving you a break. You have a seat over there by the window. Take the booth that isn't in the sun or you'll be hotter than a flitter."

"Flitter?" Adam whispered in her ear.

She brushed him off and she didn't let herself smile.

"How're your horses, Jenna?" Gary Walker set his coffee cup down on the table. "Do you still have that gray?"

Jenna stopped at the table to talk to the farmer. "I still have him. Are you still interested?"

"I might be, let me do some figurin' on it."

A hand touched her arm. Adam's hand as he slid past her. He leaned, his mouth close to her ear. "What's a *flitter?*"

Laughter bounced around inside and she looked away, trying to ignore the look on his face, the ornery arch of his brows, the quirk of his mouth.

"Well?" He slid into the booth, sitting across the table from her. "Oh, it is okay if we sit together, right?"

"It's okay, and stop asking me what it is."

"You don't know?"

"Of course I don't. No one really knows what it is. It's just hotter than one, and sometimes someone is as ornery as one. Like you. You're as ornery as a flitter." She leaned toward him. "I think it might be a kind of pancake or something, but I've always been too embarrassed to ask. Do you want to ask someone?"

He leaned back in his seat and laughed. "No, I don't want to ask."

Opal was back with two ice waters and the coffee-pot. "What can I get the two of you?" She poured coffee.

"Pancakes for me." Jenna handed the menu back without looking at it.

"Pancakes for lunch?" Adam, still looking at his menu, glanced up.

"They serve breakfast all day."

"I think I'll have pancakes, too." He smiled up at Opal. "Make mine a double."

He was stirring sugar into his coffee when Vera walked through the door of the kitchen and saw them. Her eyes lit up, and he thought it had more to do with the fact that Jenna was with him than with her delight at having him in her restaurant.

Jenna had lived through more than he could imagine. And he'd used his childhood as a crutch for years. He could admit that. His dad had pushed him hard. Adam had been pushed in school, pushed in church and pushed into football. Or maybe he had started out as a kid wanting to play.

Too many years had passed to remember.

"How are you, kids?" Vera sat down next to Jenna, her hair in a net and perspiration beaded along her brow. "My goodness, it has been busy today. But that isn't why you're here. Do you have a list for food, Jenna?"

She dug around in her purse and pulled out a piece of paper. "I have a menu that I think might work. I'm not sure how much we'll need for fifty kids and staff."

"I'll give this a look-see and let you know what I think." She nodded as she read what Jenna had written down. A menu he hadn't even seen. "I know from experience working for the school that we need the right combination of foods. That food pyramid, you know. We want to make sure we're close to meeting it with the menu."

"I hadn't thought of that." Jenna turned a little pink. "I was just trying to think of stuff they'd like."

"This all looks good. Have the two of you ordered?"

"We have." Adam watched the two women, wondering what else they could cook up, and trying to calculate how much this would cost him. He'd transferred money to the camp account this morning, preparing himself for the inevitable.

"You do know that Jess is stirring up trouble, right?" Vera looked at Jenna, but the words were for Adam, and he knew it.

"He stopped by my house," Jenna answered for him.

"I was afraid he might. He's a mess, that man. He's just bored and lonely since Lucy passed."

"But he can't stop the camp, Vera." Jenna shook her head. "I'll talk him out of it."

Adam let them talk, let them plan, but a part of him thought about the relief it would be if Jess Lockhart managed to stop the camp from becoming a reality. He could sell the land and go back to Atlanta, without guilt, without anyone to blame him. He would have tried.

Unfortunately they were talking about ordering food, and that meant, for the time being, he wasn't going anywhere.

Adam was on the phone with Will when cars started rolling up the drive two days after he and Jenna had ordered food from the grocery store. He watched from the kitchen window, amazed by the people, and by the woman who had pulled this off. Her truck was the first in the line of vehicles pulling to a stop out front.

"What's up?" Will's voice reminded him that he was on the phone.

"The help we arranged on our trip to town has arrived. It's like someone called in the cavalry."

"Imagine that." Humor laced Will's tone, and a little of that I-told-you-so attitude was evident. "Adam, this is going to be a good thing, a gold star on your résumé."

Adam walked out the front door. It was already hot and the humidity in the air felt like it might be hitting a hundred and five percent.

"I'm a little old for gold stars, don't you think?"

"You have enough demerits. A gold star won't hurt when we go in for that job interview."

Demerits. Things he'd done that he regretted. Scuffles, too many late nights, too much hard living. For the last few years he'd stayed away from those places, things that could get him into trouble. People didn't remember the good Adam; they kept going back to the wild, twentysomething Adam.

"You got the appointment set up?" He brought it back to the job, not the past.

"It's set up. But let me tell you, it wasn't easy. These guys appreciate that your name will draw viewers to any program you're broadcasting, but they don't want bad publicity on their watch."

"Is that a warning?" He leaned against the rail of the porch and watched as Jenna got out of her truck. The boys weren't with her again. He felt a strange twist that could have been disappointment.

He hadn't expected to miss those two kids. He told himself he should be glad they weren't there, getting into trouble, finding snakes. Or eating bugs. He smiled.

"Not a warning," Will said, "just a word of caution to keep out of trouble."

"You know I'll stay out of trouble. What trouble can a guy get into in Dawson, Oklahoma?"

"I'm sure there's trouble to be found."

Trouble. Adam's gaze lingered on Jenna Cameron as she got out of her truck. He'd met trouble before and she looked like the real deal. She looked like a cowgirl that could get under a man's skin and make him think about promises, and forever. If a man was so inclined. He wasn't.

He had dated a lot. He hadn't treated the women badly. He hadn't hurt anyone. He'd just kept it simple and protected himself from entanglements and women who wanted to use him.

Or at least that's the life he'd lived for the last few years. Since Paula. He'd never admit she broke his heart. He could admit she'd temporarily broken his bank account. For a few months he'd really thought he'd found the woman who loved him, not his career, not the spotlight.

He'd been wrong.

Jenna walked up to the sedan that parked next to her truck. Adam slipped his phone back into his pocket, wondering if he'd ended his call with Will. Jenna nodded in his direction and smiled a faint smile. As he crossed the lawn, she headed toward him, halting once.

"Help has arrived." She waved her arm to include the cars and trucks that had lined up in the drive, some pulling off into the grass to park.

"Yes, this definitely looks like help." He turned at the sound of a tractor heading in their direction.

"That would be Clint with his Brush Hog. It'll get this place mowed in no time."

A tractor with a mower that would cut swaths a good five feet wide. He liked that idea. But the wheels in his mind were turning as he watched people get out of their cars.

"What was that look for?" Jenna's hand slipped through his arm and he didn't object. He looked away, pretending not to notice that she leaned against him, her grip on his arm tightening.

"What look?" he said, pasting a smile in place of the frown she must have noticed.

"The I'm-about-to-get-taken-to-the-cleaners look."

Had she really seen that in his expression? Had he gotten that cynical? He looked down, and he smiled because she was smiling at him. But he *had* gotten that cynical. He did expect to be used. The reality of that thought knotted in his stomach.

He didn't like seeing himself in a way he hadn't seen himself before. He didn't like looking at himself through Jenna Cameron's eyes.

"I had a budget for this place and the budget is pretty much used up, thanks to Billy," he admitted.

"Adam, this is a community and what you're doing will help kids here as well as outside the community. We're all here to be a part of that, no strings. Not for you, but for those kids."

"Ouch."

"Ah, did that bruise your ego?"

"Only a little."

"Do you really need for this to be all about you?"

"You are about the most scrappy female I've ever met. No, I don't need for this to be about me. I'm just…"

"It's okay. Now you know that we're just here to help, so let's get busy. Pastor Todd is going to be a big help. He was a youth minister for years and organized retreats and camps."

She nodded toward the pastor who had gotten out of his car. Jenna's hand slipped off his arm and she took a few steps, then waited for him to join her. Time to get started. Time to be involved in this camp and this community.

Six months ago, when he'd undertaken this venture, it had been Billy's camp and Adam's money. It had been about a tax write-off and something good on his résumé. He wouldn't have to show up, except once in a while for a photo opportunity.

And here he was, in charge.

No, not really in charge. He was the owner, but Jenna Cameron was definitely in charge.

Jenna couldn't stop smiling as she watched people getting out of their cars. The men had tool boxes, the women had cleaning supplies. She was so proud of her church, her community. She could think that now, with troubled years behind her and turbulent waters long under the bridge.

Ten-year-old Jenna had avoided these people like the plague. They were the people who had stopped by with casseroles when her mom died, or had pulled up in the drive and honked on Sunday mornings, wanting her to attend church and then driving away with Clint when she would no longer go, not in torn jeans and holey sneakers, tangled rats in her hair.

She had listened to her father talk about self-righteous people wanting to look down their noses at the Cameron family and turn them into a charity case. She had groomed resentment like a well-tended garden and fought hard against everyone, including God. She had fought against the cookies, hugs and stories of Jesus.

All the while, these people really were waiting to love her. And now they were here to help Adam, and to help kids they didn't even know.

"You okay?" Adam asked. The velvet and thunder tones in his voice sent a chill down her spine.

"I'm fine, why?"

"You stopped walking. You seem a little down today."

She looked up, meeting a deep look on his face that didn't tease. That look said he understood because maybe he'd felt this way himself. Of course he had; it was the look she'd noticed in his eyes when a game ended and reporters circled him, wanting to know how it felt to be him.

She had always thought that maybe it didn't feel as good as the world imagined. He was still waiting for an answer to his question.

"I'm fine, a little sore today." She rarely admitted that, because the words, once spoken, made it real.

Flashbacks happened, sometimes even in the bright sunlight of a summer day in Oklahoma. Sometimes she could smell the smoke, the blood, the dark mustiness of that closet where she'd been hidden.

Sometimes in the dark of night she wanted to scream for daylight.

Sometimes she wanted her life back, the hope and promise of marriage and love, a family. And then she fought it all back and she remembered faith and meeting God in that dark room, knowing He wouldn't let her down, believing He would get her home. Home to her family, to her boys.

He had. And she hadn't been let down. She could get through anything.

"You're fine." Adam's tone said he didn't believe her. "Pastor Todd, good to see you again."

He was good at pushing past pain, too. She knew a kindred spirit when she met one. He was smiling again, letting go of their conversation.

"Good to see you, too. I've got delivery dates for the food. The kitchen help is going to get the pans and dishes organized and we'll make out a work schedule." Pastor Todd fell in next to Adam and they, along with the group of church members, moved toward the kitchen.

Vera joined them, in jeans and a T-shirt today, not her customary smock apron. "I've got a schedule for the kitchen. I won't be able to be here to help, but I've got a sister, Louisa, who has helped me a lot in the restaurant. She's going to be in charge of cooking. Charm Jones is going to be in charge of servers and dishes. They'll make sure you have plenty of people on hand."

"Okay." Adam's tight smile didn't faze Vera. She had a list and she was ticking things off.

"And Gordon Flynn is bringing beef over from the packing plant. He's giving you a good deal on half a beef."

"Half a beef?" Adam's smile disappeared.

"Oh, honey, that's not all," Vera continued, as if she didn't notice his surprise. Or was it outrage? "We're also having chicken one night, and then there'll be sausage and eggs for breakfast."

A heavy sigh from Adam. Jenna felt a little bad for

him. He was probably envisioning his savings account dwindling, or maybe felt as if the community had hijacked him and his camp.

"Adam, a lot of the cost is being covered by the church."

That got his attention. He glanced from her to Pastor Todd.

"We want to help." Pastor Todd nodded in the direction of the chapel. "This camp is something the area needs. And the community should be a part of it. Our churches need to be a part of reaching out to the children who come here."

"That doesn't mean you get out of the work. We'll need your help hanging the mini blinds." Jenna nudged Adam with her elbow, hoping to ease the tightened lines around his mouth. "You probably won't even need a ladder."

Chapter Seven

Adam stood on the ladder, on the second floor of the dorm, attaching the first mini blind on the window. The older woman standing on the floor next to the ladder held the tools and the hardware for the blinds. She made a noise and he thought she might have said something.

"I'm sorry?" He looked down and the ladder shook a little. He held his breath and waited for it to stop weaving. Or maybe he was weaving, not the ladder. He started to close his eyes but knew from experience that would only make it worse.

Worse, being on the second floor, looking out the window at the ground. It seemed to be fifty feet down, and he knew it wasn't. He focused on the floor. On the woman helping him. She shrugged and her brows arched and drew in.

He was sure she'd said something.

"What?" She didn't smile.

He started to work again and again heard her mutter. "Did you say something?"

"No, of course not."

"Am I doing something wrong?"

She bit down on her lip and shook her head and that didn't convince him. "No, you're fine."

That tone. Of course he was doing something wrong. He wasn't a handyman. He didn't fix things. He played football. His home-repair skills were pretty limited.

"Mrs. Glenn, if I'm doing something wrong, please tell me." He counted to ten because he was about to lose his loose grip on what patience he had left. The lady watching him, gray hair permed into tight curls and T-shirt stating that everything she did was done for Jesus, was the woman pushing him to the end of his rope. And occasionally bumping the ladder he didn't really want to be standing on.

"Okay, I don't mean to be bossy, because this is your camp and your dorm, but it would be better if you put those blinds on the inside of the window frame, not on the outside. It'll just look a lot nicer."

"It isn't easier, though."

"Well, no, of course not." She frowned and shook her head. "Life isn't always about taking the easy way."

One, two, three, four, five... Counting wasn't helping. Adam closed his eyes and felt like he was swaying, about to fall. He grabbed the ladder and sucked in a deep breath.

"Are you afraid of heights?" The pleasant voice of Mrs. Glenn, sounding a little amused and tinkly. He got the impression that his fear made her day.

"No, of course not." He looked down and her eyes had widened and her smile beamed.

"I think you are." She pointed to the ground, and he knew she'd been waiting for an opportunity like this one. "Let me do that and you hold the tools."

"I really can do this." He unscrewed the bracket that he'd put on the outside of the window frame. He was a man. He could conquer a ladder. He could hang a mini blind.

He could grunt like Tim Allen, if need be.

"Of course you can." She backed away from the ladder.

Adam gave up. He climbed down the wobbly ladder and, when his feet touched the ground, he sighed, and he hadn't meant to sigh. Man, he hated ladders. And Mrs. Glenn loved that fact. She smiled as she handed him the tools she'd been holding.

"We'll have this done in no time. Now, you get the blinds out of that box while I get these brackets attached."

Screws went between her teeth, the tools slid into her pockets and she was up the ladder, happy as a lark. No more muttering. No more disapproving looks. If he'd known it was that easy to get her approval, he never would have gone up that ladder.

To prove he wasn't totally inept, he started taking blinds out of boxes and handing her what she asked for. They were on the fourth window when footsteps behind him caught his attention.

"Lunchtime." Jenna's soft drawl.

"Already?" He glanced over his shoulder, at the woman standing behind him, hair in a ponytail and clear gloss on her lips.

"Yep. Food is in the kitchen. Looks like you're getting the blinds up with no problem." Jenna smiled at Mrs. Glenn, who stood on the ladder, precarious and not caring.

"We have a system that works well." Mrs. Glenn pulled a screw out of her mouth and pushed it into the bracket.

Adam waited for her to mention the fact that she had

discovered his fear. Instead she finished the window and climbed down. She set the tools back in the box and dusted her hands off on her jeans.

"You're doing great." Jenna shot him a look that he ignored.

"We should probably head for the kitchen." Mrs. Glenn was ahead of them, nearly to the door. "I have sugar issues. I need to eat every three hours."

"Of course, I'd forgotten." Jenna smiled. "We're heading that way, too."

But slower than Mrs. Glenn, Adam realized. Mrs. Glenn obviously needed to eat soon. He watched as she hightailed it across the newly mowed lawn, in the direction of the metal building that housed the kitchen.

He liked the layout of the camp. There was a central yard. On the west side of the lawn was the barn and corral, east was the kitchen, south was the dorm. Behind the dorm an open-air chapel had been built.

Horses grazed in the fields, tails swishing to brush away the flies. He'd forgotten what it was like here, in Oklahoma. He'd forgotten the rolling fields, the smell of freshly mowed hay. He'd forgotten the way the setting sun touched the horizon and turned everything gold in the evenings.

It didn't matter, though, because he wasn't staying.

"The beds are being put together and the bathrooms are clean." Jenna offered the progress report as they crossed the lawn. He'd forgotten the sweetness of a country girl on a summer afternoon. "Willow brought the boys by. She has to take the baby to the pediatrician."

"Is the baby sick?"

"Not really, just a cough. But Willow's a first-time

parent and she's a little worried. She lost her hearing from meningitis."

"That happens?"

"Not often, but it can." She limped next to him, and he wasn't thinking about Willow, but about the woman at his side. And he knew she wouldn't want to discuss what was happening with her. He knew, because he thought they might be a lot alike.

He touched her hand, by accident, and her fingers brushed his, but then moved away, almost as if she had considered holding his hand and wouldn't. And she shouldn't, not if she wanted to protect her heart. He knew that as well as anyone.

The aroma wafting from the open windows of the kitchen were a welcome distraction. He opened the door and motioned Jenna inside.

"Where are the boys?" He glanced around the open room with the long tables and the open kitchen area with a counter full of warmers and steaming food. He had expected sandwiches today, not a buffet.

"They ate with Willow. She took them to town for pizza. But they also had half a peanut butter sandwich a little while ago. Now they're outside, playing."

"Oh, so are they okay outside?"

She pointed out the window. The boys were playing in the yard with trucks, obviously okay. "We can see them from here. If they leave that spot, we'll worry."

At that age, he wouldn't have stayed in one spot. He kind of figured the twins wouldn't be there for long. It wasn't his business, though. He grabbed a tray and followed the woman whose business it was.

"Stop looking out the window." She had her back to him, so how did she know? She turned and smiled. "I can almost feel you tensing up back there, wondering what they'll get into. They're almost six, they're old enough to play in the yard, especially since we're right here, watching them."

"I know that."

"You're going to be a nervous wreck by the time this camp is over."

"Which is why I should just sign it over to the church and be done with it." He plopped potatoes on his plate and drenched them with gravy.

"That would be the easy way out, wouldn't it?"

Of course it would. Watching her, he wondered if she had ever opted for the easy way.

"Yes, it would be," he admitted, and followed her to a table that was already crowded. He wanted a corner booth and no one staring. He wasn't going to get that, either. From across the table she smiled at him.

He glanced out the window, at the boys.

Jenna tapped his hand. "They're still there."

"Yes, they are." He cut his meat loaf and dipped it in gravy. "This is good."

"Vera's secret recipe. Don't ask what she puts in it. She doesn't mind sharing the packets of seasoning she makes up, but she won't tell you what's in it."

"No MSG, right?"

She looked up and shook her head. "You're a mess. Just eat."

He ate a few more bites, and then glanced out the window again. Jenna followed his look and her eyes widened.

"They're gone," he announced, standing as she stood. "I'll go check on them."

"I can do it." She headed for the door and he followed.

The boys were nowhere to be seen. They couldn't have

disappeared that fast. Adam left Jenna standing in the yard and hurried toward the stable and the horses. That's when he saw them.

"They're on the pony." Jenna had seen them at the same time and her anxious shout didn't help to calm his nerves. She was the one who didn't let things bother her.

But bothered was a good way to feel when he knew the boys were in serious trouble. They were on a spotted pony, bareback and with nothing but a rope around the animal's neck. How in the world had they managed to get in this much trouble, this quick?

And they didn't even seem to know the trouble they were in. They had sticks and were obviously fast on the trail of bad guys, the little horse obliging them by picking up his legs in a fast trot. The boys were bouncing and holding tight with sun-browned legs wrapped around the pony's round little belly.

"Timmy! David!" Jenna had caught up with him, her chest heaving a little with the exertion. "Stop that pony now!"

The boys waved.

"They're going to get thrown." Adam couldn't help but growl the words.

"They're not." But she didn't sound as positive as he would have liked. "Let's walk slowly and not scare the pony. The boys know how to ride, they'll be okay."

Walk slowly, don't run and grab the boys off the pony. He wanted to take her advice, but he couldn't. "I'm sorry, I've got to get them off her."

The boys were ripping across the lawn on the horse. Jenna grabbed his arm. "Okay, go get them, but be careful not to spook the pony."

The boys were bouncing along on the back of the pony.

The door to the kitchen had opened and Adam knew they had an audience. Pastor Todd and the church members who were still there had joined Jenna.

Adam walked fast, toward the pony and the boys. The little pony stopped and ducked her head to pull at a bite of red clover. As soon as she had it in her mouth, she took off again. Adam was starting to think she was in on the orneriness. She wasn't a victim of those boys, she was the coconspirator.

"Lady Bug, here, come here." He didn't shout, but the name got the attention of the spotted pony. She flicked her ears and looked at him, but then her ears went back. "Guys, pull back on your rope and stop her."

The twins nodded, but they didn't look convinced. They smiled at him as if they were having the time of their lives. And he had to wonder if he wouldn't have felt the same way. A smile and then a chuckle sneaked up on him. It was harder to be stern the next time he called out to them.

"Come on, when she stops again, you guys climb off. You're scaring your mom." And ten years off his life.

David glanced over his shoulder and made eye contact with Adam. The kid looked a little worried. Either he didn't want to get in trouble, or he was afraid of getting thrown. His blond hair was tousled and his little face was smudged with dirt and peanut butter. Adam was nearly close enough to grab the pony.

And then she lunged, Timmy encouraging her with a foot tap to her side. Adam ran, because this was no longer a game. He caught up with the little mare just short of a stand of cedars with low limbs that would brush the boys off if the pony decided to keep going. Rather than grabbing her, he grabbed the twins off her back.

They hugged his neck and he took a deep breath. Man, he was out of shape, or maybe it was fear. His lungs heaved for oxygen and his heart raced. He hugged the boys, one on each hip, and turned back in the direction they'd come. He could see Jenna standing with Pastor Todd, saw her hands come together and then cover her face.

One of the other men headed in the direction of the pony, a bucket of grain in his hand.

"You boys shouldn't do that to your mom. From now on, if you want to ride, you ask. You don't get on a horse without permission. You could get hurt doing that."

"I told you so," David muttered and glared, gray eyes narrowed at Timmy.

"You're always a chicken."

"Buddy, doing the right thing doesn't make a guy a chicken." Adam put the boys down and took them by the hand to finish the walk. Timmy tried to get loose. Adam kept hold of his little hand.

And Jenna was walking toward them, looking like he might be her favorite person in the world—for the moment. She didn't know him that well, and he planned on keeping it that way. Let her think he was a hero, not a jaded athlete who wouldn't stay long enough for her to really get to know him.

"I'm taking the two of you home. Adam, I hate to leave, but you have plenty of help and these guys are going to be spending time in their room, not playing."

"I understand. Do you need help getting them in the truck?"

She shook her head. "I can manage. Besides, I think that's Jess driving down the road. Probably with more complaints about the camp."

He thought she was probably right, but as she walked away, Jess wasn't on his mind. She was.

"Bologna sandwiches for supper tonight, guys." Jenna walked through the back door and the boys looked up. They were sitting at the kitchen table, looking at books, because she wouldn't let them play.

For the last two hours, since she'd left the camp with them, they'd been confined to the house and only allowed to do what she approved. While she'd gone out to feed her horses, the selected activity had been looking at books.

Her poor horses. Monday she really had to stay at home and do some work with them. She had a gelding that she needed to sell at the end of the month. He was nearly ready to be used in reining competitions.

"Bologna sandwiches?" Timmy wrinkled his nose at her dinner suggestion and brought her mind back to the kitchen and her dinner preparations. "Can I have cheese and crackers?"

"You can. And grapes." At least if they ate grapes she'd feel like they were eating something healthy.

David wrinkled his nose when she said grapes. She sighed.

"What is it, buddy?"

"Do I have to eat grapes?"

"Carrots?" she offered as she poured herself a glass of tea. "Or an apple."

He bit down on his bottom lip and stared at the floor. When he looked up, his eyes were watery. "There aren't any apples."

"I had a whole bag." She really needed to sit down. Pain was shooting up her leg, biting sharp, and her back ached.

"I kinda fed them to Charlie."

Jenna sat down. "Kinda? You fed them to your horse? All of them?"

He nodded. "He liked 'em a lot."

"Oh, David, honey, we need to check and make sure you didn't make him sick. You guys go clean up before we eat and I'll check on Charlie."

"Sorry, Mom." David kissed her cheek. "I can check on him."

She hugged him and she didn't sigh. "It's okay. I'll check on him."

He sounded so big, and she knew someday he would be a good man. She was raising good men. It meant everything to her. Protecting them meant everything. They had been left by too many people. They had almost lost her.

She tried to block the image of that moment earlier in the day when Adam had held both of her boys, and they had clung to him. He would leave them. After the camp was off the ground and running, he would go back to his life. The life that was so far removed from theirs, she couldn't imagine all of the differences. Once he returned, he would never think of them again.

Not that he needed to think of her. He was a blip on the radar screen of her life. She had two main priorities: Timmy and David. She had watched them cry when their dad left after his last visit, telling her he would send child support, but his life wasn't about her or the boys.

They hadn't seen him for three years. He was remarried, living in California. Someday she knew they'd want to know him. Maybe someday he'd want to see them again.

Six months ago she had seen the confusion on their

faces when they asked about Jeff, the man she'd planned to marry. She'd had to explain that he wasn't going to be seeing them anymore.

Her life, her recovery, was too much reality for a guy that wanted to stay young a little while longer. Sometimes she wished she could have stayed young longer. There were days that she felt twenty years older than her twenty-seven years. She felt like she'd lived a lifetime in the last seven of those years.

She remembered what it was like to feel pretty. She hadn't felt pretty in a long, long time. She couldn't remember getting dressed up for a date, or the way it felt to put on something other than flat-heeled cowboy boots or tennis shoes.

But she didn't have time to feel sorry for herself.

"Be right back, guys." She stopped at the door and looked back at them. They were on a stool at the sink, washing their hands. "Don't get into anything."

Wishful thinking on her part.

Chapter Eight

"Jenna, are you out here?" Adam walked into the barn, peering into the dark shadows. He'd been in the house for five minutes, waiting for her to come in, to feed the boys.

"Jen?"

"Jenna. No one calls me Jen but Clint." She was sitting outside a stall, looking inside the darkened cubicle. He peeked around the corner of the gate and saw the pony, bloated belly and head hanging.

"What's up?" He leaned against the post, looking at her, and then at the pony. They both—her and the pony—looked pretty miserable. He knew enough about women to know that the word *miserable* wasn't one that she wanted attached to her appearance.

"David fed his pony a bag of apples. I think Charlie is going to be okay, but I wanted to make sure. He's pretty uncomfortable, the little pig."

"How about you? You okay?"

She looked up, eyes dark, shadowy. Her nose was pink and her face was a little puffy. He wouldn't ask. He didn't want to go there. He had a rule about women, nothing personal. Go out to dinner, take a walk in the park, go to a show, but never ask personal questions.

Too late, he realized that his question was personal. He hadn't asked about her tears, but he'd gone far enough. Her eyes watered a little and she shrugged. But then she didn't answer.

"I'm fine, just a little tired."

"That's my fault." He reached for a bucket and turned it over to use it as a seat.

"Not really. I've just been pushing myself a little too much lately."

"The boys told me they're having bologna sandwiches for supper."

"Tattletales." She smiled.

"Yeah, I called from town." He took off his hat and ran a hand through his hair. It was getting shaggy. "I brought food from The Mad Cow."

"You didn't have to do that. Bologna sandwiches won't hurt them."

"Too late, it's done. So why don't we go inside and eat before the food gets cold. I can come back out before I leave."

"Okay." She stood, wobbling a little. She reached for the gate and held it a minute before pushing it closed.

Her first step was tentative, and he didn't know what to do, or how to offer help.

"You going to make it to the house?"

"Of course I am." She took another step, this one looking more painful than the last. A single tear trickled down her cheek but she looked up at him, smiling. "It might take a while."

"I'll be back in a minute."

"Where are you…"

"Right back."

He jogged to the house and found what he was looking for in a corner of the laundry room. When he returned, she was sitting on the stool. Charlie was still moping in a corner of the stall.

Adam opened the wheelchair and pointed. She glanced up, her cheeks pink.

"I assume this is yours?" He waited, holding the handles. "Come on, I'm a football player, I know how to drive one of these."

"I know." She sniffed a little as she stood up. "I want this in my past, not here, today."

"I could carry you." He winked, and she smiled a little, another tear trickling down her cheek. Tears were not his thing, especially soft tears that someone fought, trying to be strong. Hers weren't the wailing, I-want-my-way kind of tears. Hers were about being strong, but feeling weak.

And he didn't have a handkerchief.

"No, I think I can do without you carrying me." She moved to the seat and hunched forward a little. And he didn't want her to feel weak. "This isn't the past, is it? It's my life. One moment and everything changed forever."

He pushed her out of the barn. The sun was setting and the sky was pink. The trees were dark green silhouettes against the twilight sky. He maneuvered over rough ground, big rocks and clumps of grass.

"Moments do that to us." He pushed the chair over a rut. "Moments can change everything. That's life. A moment and my cousin was gone and I'm here. I know that isn't a moment on a dusty road in Iraq, but it's the moment that brought me home."

"With me," she whispered. "I'm sorry, that isn't what I meant. I'm just saying, this probably isn't where you expected to be, either. If you weren't here, where would you be tonight?"

"Saturday night in Atlanta?" He laughed because he didn't want to answer. "Probably not somewhere I'd be proud of."

"Life has taken you a long way from Oklahoma, hasn't it?"

"Life does that. This wasn't what I wanted—this land, the farms, the country. I worked my entire life to be where I am, doing what I've done, going where I'm going in my career."

"I'm not sure what I wanted before."

"What do you want now?"

She looked back, her hair brushing the back of the seat. "I want to raise my boys. I want to be a good mom. I want to survive this and be strong. That's about it."

"I think you're achieving your goals. You have great kids. You are strong." He was staring at the back of her head and he could see her hands clasped together in her lap.

The back door opened and Timmy pushed it wide, stepping out to hold it for them to enter. The kid didn't even look worried. Her boys had accepted their lives, too.

Adam respected that. He'd never been good at accepting. Sometimes it felt like he'd been fighting his entire life.

Today wasn't any different. Today he was fighting the urge to kiss a woman from Oklahoma. He was fighting the urge to promise her things would get better. Those weren't his promises to make. The best he could do was provide a meal.

He parked her at the table and left her to get the tea

he'd already poured for them. The boys raced out of the room, obviously relieved from their punishment.

Adam watched them go, shaking his head because they were all about life, playing and loving their mom. That probably wasn't hard for them to do, the loving Jenna part.

Jenna looked at her kitchen. The boys had already eaten. The takeout containers were open on the table, and mostly empty. The dog had run into the kitchen and was trying to nose his way onto the table, like he thought no one would notice.

"Dog, get." Jenna shooed him away, wheeling closer to the table and smelling fried chicken from The Mad Cow.

"Do you want tea?"

She turned. Adam had two glasses. One for him, one for her. Or that was her guess. He was staying? She felt weak inside, and he was staying.

"You know, I can take it from here. If you have some-where you need to go."

"Are you trying to get rid of me?" He set two glasses on the table and opened a container.

"No, I just know that you have a lot to get done in the next few days."

"The help I got today made a big dent in that."

"It's all coming together." She dug her fork into the chicken and took a bite. Adam was watching, his own meal in front of him.

"Yeah, it is." He leaned back in his chair, watching her, and she wasn't hungry. "But then what? Let it run its course for the summer, and then put it up for sale?"

"Or you could keep it going. You could be really good

for the camp and the kids. Even if you ran it from Atlanta."

"I don't think so. I'm not a role model or a camp director."

"You're not so bad."

His brows went up. "Yes, I am."

She smiled, shaking her head in disagreement with him, because she thought he had a kind heart that he'd been keeping tucked away, protected.

"Oh, what did Jess want?"

"Same as before. He wanted to give me a second chance to back out on this camp. Pastor Todd tried to talk to him, but he wouldn't listen. He said Pastor Todd has a history of bringing in strays, so why would Jess trust his judgment."

"I wouldn't worry. Jess will give it up."

"He's going to talk to the county planning and zoning committee."

"We'll have to pray."

"Right."

Jenna pushed her plate away, because she wasn't really hungry. "What happened to you?"

He looked up, no smile, just a look in his eyes that was soft, a little wounded. "What does that mean?"

"You know what I mean. What turned you against God?"

"I don't have anything against God. I attended church my entire childhood."

"And now?"

"I don't think anything happened. I left home." He shrugged and looked away. "I think I enjoyed the freedom of college a little too much. I was busy with football, busy with my social life."

"And no one to tell you to slow down."

"For the first time in my life. That kind of freedom can be a dangerous thing." He grinned a little. "I can't say that I'm proud of that, or how far I've gone from my roots."

"I guess I don't know your roots."

"Pastor's kid. And a dad who almost made the pros, but didn't."

She had missed that part of his bio.

But now she got it. She knew the secret to who he was, the look she'd seen in his eyes. "You thought you weren't good enough."

"I didn't say that."

"No, you didn't, but I'm right. You were a hero, from a good family, and you didn't feel any better about yourself than I did as a kid."

"Maybe. Why does it matter so much to you?"

Heat crawled up her neck and she looked down, at the napkin scrunched up in her hand. "I've watched you and I've wondered what your story was."

"Now you know." He stood, and after standing next to her for a minute, he leaned and kissed her cheek, his beard brushing her skin and his scent lingering with her as he moved away. "You're better than most people I know."

"You are, too."

He laughed and shook his head. "Jenna, you're not seeing things clearly. I'm going to run out and check on the pony. Do you think we should call a veterinarian?"

"I can do it." She stood and followed him to the door, fighting the urge to bite down on her lip, fighting past the pain that her own stubbornness had caused. She should have been more careful. The heat had caused her leg to sweat, irritating skin that was still tender. She knew better. Or at least she was learning.

"I can. You stay here with the boys. I'll come back and give you an update on his condition." He stood at the door. He was Oklahoma again, in jeans and a button-up shirt, the sleeves rolled to his elbows. His hat was pulled low over his eyes. The neatly trimmed goatee framed his smile, making it soft, tender.

"Thank you. Could you tell the boys to come inside?"

Jenna watched the boys run across the lawn with the dog. They had water guns and were shooting each other, soaking their clothes. Water dripped from their hair.

"Sure. You sit down and take it easy." He smiled down at her, and then he touched her hand, his fingers resting against hers.

Jenna nodded, because she couldn't talk, because he was near and she hadn't felt like someone who needed to be kissed in a long time. And he looked like a man about to kiss a woman, like he might be thinking about it, or even fighting it.

"Adam?"

He looked down, leaning a little with one hand on the door frame, and then he let out a sigh. His hand moved to the small of her back, holding her in a way that made her feel safe. He moved a little closer, his head dipping, closer to hers, closer, and then pausing. She thought he might move away. She wanted him to move away. She held her breath, waiting. And then their lips touched.

The kiss was tender, but strong. His hand on her back kept her close. She held on to his arms, needing to be steady, needing to be near him. She needed to feel like a woman a man might want to kiss, even if it only lasted a few seconds.

Thoughts played through her mind and she pushed them back, letting herself feel the moment in his arms, with his lips on hers and his hand on her back. And then she moved away, turning her head a little to break the connection.

Her boys were playing in the yard. Adam Mackenzie was passing through. He wouldn't stay in Dawson, or in her life. They were both temporary for him, this town and her. She made him feel strong. She knew that. And she didn't want to be his strength, not that way, as if she was the weak woman that needed him.

He had brought them dinner. She reminded herself of that fact and so she didn't say something she might regret. There was enough to regret without adding to it.

"I'll go check on the pony." And then he leaned again, kissing her one last time before he walked out the door.

She sat down, watching him go. He was checking on Charlie. And then he was walking back to the house, across the lawn where the boys were playing under one of the big trees that she had played under as a kid. He stopped to talk to them, to her boys. They stood up, showing him what they'd found.

Temporary. He was temporary in their lives. She had to make sure the boys knew, that they understood he wouldn't be in Dawson for long.

"I'm heading out." He stood outside the screen door.

Jenna nodded, but remained in the wheelchair. "I'll see you tomorrow."

"Tomorrow? We're not doing anything at the camp tomorrow."

"Church." She moved closer to the door, not standing up. Standing was suddenly overrated.

"Yes, okay. Do you need a ride?" He looked down.

She wished he wouldn't have done that. She wanted to remember the kiss, being held, and not that look.

"Of course I don't."

"Just asking."

"Thanks, but no. I'll be fine." The way she was always fine. She had said those same words to the father of her boys when he left. And she'd said them to Jeff when he left her in the hospital.

"I'll be fine," she repeated with a smile that wavered as he walked away.

At least Adam Mackenzie wasn't making promises that he would break. He wasn't making any promises at all, except one…that he would ultimately leave.

Chapter Nine

Church. Adam hadn't gone in years, not for real. He attended the dedication of Will's daughter. Kaitlin. Today he remembered her name. He pulled into a parking space and cut the engine of the truck. Jenna's truck was already here. He had thought about her last night, and this morning. He had considered calling Clint, because someone should know that she needed help.

He had a feeling she wouldn't thank him for interfering. And then he smiled, because hadn't she been interfering in his life since he showed up in Dawson? Hadn't she given him advice, prodded and pushed him?

She had made him smile more since his arrival than he'd smiled in years. Real smiles. That was the difference.

He got out of the truck, pausing for a minute before walking across the parking lot to the old church with the tall steeple and narrow stained-glass windows. It reminded him of the church he'd grown up in. He didn't want that reminder, of himself as a little boy in Sunday school, listening to Mrs. Pritchard tell him about Jesus. He didn't want to remember bowing his head and praying with her as she introduced him to salvation.

He didn't need a reminder of where he'd come from and how far he'd gone, away from that kid, those roots.

But he couldn't stop remembering. He'd been remembering since he came back here, the memories almost like an open photo album, drawing him back into the images of that childhood, and faith.

"Adam." Clint Cameron walked across the parking lot, no longer the teenager that wanted the same high school girl that Adam had given his class ring to. He smiled at that memory, of the two of them squaring off after a game, and Clint walking away.

Clint hadn't taken football or winning as seriously as Adam. A tinge of envy shot through him, because in the end, Clint had been the winner.

The tall blonde next to him, the baby in her arms. Those two meant more than a champion ring, more than trophies, more than anything he'd accumulated. His life had felt empty for a long time, now the emptiness burrowed deep inside him, pointing out the reasons why.

"Clint. Beautiful morning." But hot. The sun had eaten up the cool of early morning and June heat was already claiming the day. Adam locked his truck door and stepped closer to the couple walking toward him.

"It's supposed to rain later." Careful conversation about weather. "I think you met Willow the other day."

Adam made eye contact with Willow. "Yes, we met."

Adam walked with them up the steps of the church, its tall steeple reaching up. He motioned the couple through the doors of the church ahead of him.

No anonymity here. If he'd gone to church of his own volition, it would have been somewhere big, a place where he could walk in and hide in a back pew. Instead he was here, and people were smiling, waving. A few pointed.

Jenna was sitting on the stage, a guitar in her hands. A country girl in a floral top and jeans, her hair in a ponytail.

Cuter than a speckled pup. His grandfather had used that phrase. He doubted Jenna would appreciate it. But speckled pups were cute. They were easy to take home and keep.

That thought took him by surprise, forcing him to look her way again, to wonder what it was about her that made him think about her at the oddest moments. He'd even thought about her that morning as he drank his coffee and tried to think of reasons not to go to church.

He scooted into the pew next to Clint and he refused to look in the direction of Jenna, even when the music started and he could hear the guitar. She had a gift. She played classical guitar. It shouldn't have surprised him, but it did. She smiled when she caught him looking at her.

By the time Pastor Todd got behind the pulpit, Adam had never been so ready to be preached at. He relaxed a little. But Jenna was walking toward him, leaning a little on the cane. She slid into the pew, into the space next to him. Her arm brushed his.

He didn't think church was the place to remember a kiss, or to think about how good she smelled. It was a good place to think about his life, and leaving Dawson.

But the message was about leaving a person's own ideas and plans behind, and finding the path God has for them. Adam pretended the message wasn't for him. He tried not to think about what had brought him here, each incident or coincidence.

Coincidence. It was all a fluke—this camp, Billy, her boys in the road. Her. It wasn't about his life changing or a new direction. He was here to get a camp started. He had a job interview in a few weeks.

His life wasn't about Oklahoma.

Jenna felt as if she had held her breath through the entire service. Of course she hadn't, or she would have passed out. And then she thought about what a relief passing out would have been, if it had meant not being aware of Adam Mackenzie sitting next to her. He took up too much space.

With the closing prayer, she stood, ready to escape. Willow stopped her retreat.

"Lunch at our house?" Willow's tone was soft, the baby she held cooing against her shoulder, wrapping tiny fingers through blond hair.

Jenna had never been jealous of her brother and his wife, but at moments like this, she wanted what they had. She wanted to be a part of a couple that met their challenges together.

The man next to her moved, trying to slide past her. She stepped back, but Willow spoke again.

"Adam, why don't you join us? The Mad Cow is closed on Sunday, and Clint is grilling burgers."

"I am?" Clint gathered the diaper bag, his wife's purse, and Jenna thought she saw him gather his wits. "Of course I am."

"I shouldn't. I have…" Adam looked like he was searching for a good excuse. Jenna knew, because she was busy trying to think of something she needed to be doing. Scrubbing toilets seemed preferable to this.

"You should." Willow patted his arm. "Come on, we can use help. Clint always burns burgers on the grill."

Adam looked from Jenna to Willow and then he accepted, that easily. And Jenna wanted him to find his own excuse, his own reason that he couldn't go, because this should have been her safe time, in a safe place. She wanted to find a corner and hide.

Instead she met her brother's concerned gaze, his half smile, his wink. Clint understood. There were times when she wanted privacy, not curious stares and questions.

But she didn't have time to dwell on it. The boys would be waiting for her to check them out of children's church.

"I need to get Timmy and David." She walked away, leaving them to make their plans.

"Mom." Timmy ran out of the classroom to greet her as she walked down the hall to the room that was a dining area part of the time, and a classroom the rest of the time.

"Hey, sweetie. Get your brother, okay." She leaned against the door, taking weight off her left leg. If this kept up, she wouldn't be able to use her prosthesis until the sores healed. She had to give herself a break.

She didn't know how to take breaks. She didn't want to stop living her life, or stop being a mom. She had so much to do.

And now she had to face lunch with Adam invading her family.

She picked up the pen and signed the boys out. One of the workers gave her a sympathetic smile.

"Doing okay, Jenna?"

"I am, just tired."

"It's a good day for a nap," the woman encouraged. "Maybe the boys will take one, too."

"Look what we made!" David held up a scroll with the Ten Commandments written in his childish handwriting. He was bouncing and had a red juice drink mustache. She doubted the nap idea.

"Wow, that is pretty neat." She took it from him, and smiled. Thou Shalt Not Convict. She was sure he meant *covet.*

"Isn't it great? We learned the commandments." Timmy handed her his scroll.

"Very good, guys. Those are important rules to remember."

"We're not going to kill or steal, Mom." David took his scroll back. "But I don't even understand all those other ones."

"You'll understand them better as you get older. Some of them are about jealousy. Jealousy is when you want what someone else has. We're supposed to be content with the good things we already have."

The good things.

Hadn't she just battled her own jealous feelings? Clint and Willow deserved their happiness. And even happiness had its moments of regret, failure or trials. Clint and Willow had battled to get where they were. They still had some battles to face as Willow's hearing loss progressed.

She knew that it was easy to look in from the outside and think that someone else had a perfect life. She knew no one had a perfect life.

She followed along behind the boys. And at the door, Clint and Willow were waiting with Adam. He unbuttoned the top two buttons of the deep blue shirt he was wearing and pulled at his collar. She almost felt sorry for him. Almost.

Instead she smiled and laughed a little. "It wasn't so bad, was it?"

"What?"

"Church?" She pulled her keys out of her pocket. Carrying a purse was sometimes too much. She had her driver's license in her pocket, too.

"It was good. I didn't realize you played guitar."

"Classical lessons from a music teacher in school. She thought I had promise, but lacked direction." She shaded her eyes against the sun as she looked up at him.

"Really?"

She laughed. "Yes, really. I was a little on the wild side back then."

"I can't imagine."

"You don't need to. Just take my word for it. Come on, boys." She herded them across the parking lot toward her truck. "See you at Clint's."

As they drove, she noticed a car pull in behind Adam's truck. It followed them through town, turned when they turned and followed them to the drive that led to Clint's. Jenna kept her eyes on the road in front of her, but occasionally flicked her attention to the rearview mirror and that car. She could see Adam's face in her mirror, could see the way he watched his own mirror.

Jenna pulled into the drive next to the log home that had once been Janie's, but was now Clint's and Willow's. A baby swing sat on the front porch next to the swing and rocking chairs. Life had changed a lot in one year.

A year. The boys climbed out of the truck, exiting through the passenger's side door. They wanted to see Willow's dog and the llama that Clint had bought at an auction. Now the boys were begging her to get one of the silly creatures.

One year. She had left the boys here one year ago, with Clint, Willow and Janie. She had returned six months later, her entire life and her future completely changed. She had returned to be a single mom, without an engagement ring on her finger, and with new challenges to face. This challenge would never go away.

She had returned with something new. She had returned with faith. She knew she could make it through anything. She'd already been tested, and she'd survived.

She eased out of the truck, always a reminder of how things had changed. There were new ways of doing everything. The things she'd always taken for granted were now appreciated. Walking wasn't taken for granted.

There were days, like today, when she knew that she couldn't do what she wanted to do. She couldn't run after her boys. She couldn't climb a fence or get on a horse. Not today, but tomorrow, if she took care of herself.

She made it to the front porch and sat down on the swing. Adam had gotten out of his truck and he was walking up to the car that had followed him. A woman got out. The woman, a brunette, stared at Adam, wiping her eyes as she took a few steps toward him.

Jenna got up and went inside.

"Elizabeth." Adam approached his older sister. He hadn't seen her in a few years. Seeing her now, he realized what a mistake that had been.

"Creep." She had always called him that. Sometimes she had said it with a smile, and sometimes she had meant the word.

He smiled. "Good to see you, too."

She wiped at her eyes. "No, I mean it this time. You could visit your family."

"Yeah, I know."

Adam leaned back against her car and pulled sunglasses out of his pocket because he'd left his hat in the truck. He slipped them on and Elizabeth moved to stand next to him. She hadn't changed a lot. She still knew how to put him in his place. She had never been his biggest fan.

"You could have come to see us. Or invited us up to see you."

"I didn't think you'd be interested."

"Really? You thought that?" She let out an exasperated sigh. "You're my brother."

"Yes, I am." He wondered if she had forgotten the rift that had grown between them, and how it had happened. "You made this rule, Elizabeth. I just honored it."

"You took the easy way out."

"'I'm so sick of you being the star, Adam. I'm in this family, too, but when was the last time anyone noticed me?'" He repeated her words, because he'd never forgotten them, or the stark pain on her face when she said them.

Or how it had hurt him to hear that from her, to know how much she resented him. He had envied her, she had resented him. What a crazy way to grow up.

"I was eighteen, going away to college and Dad wasn't going to drive me to Oklahoma City because you had a game." She turned to look at him, and the pain was still there in her eyes.

"I know. But I didn't ask him to be that way. I didn't want it to be that way."

"We let this happen, didn't we?" She started walking toward the barn. Adam walked next to her, not sure what to say.

They crossed the road and she walked up to the metal pole fence that held Willow's bulls. She stood close, finding a shady spot beneath an oak tree. He stopped next to her.

"We're brother and sister. That should mean something. We should spend holidays together. You should call me when you're in town. Those are the things families normally do."

He had to agree because he knew from watching other people, from watching Clint and Jenna, that families should share their lives. They hadn't learned to do that in their family. His family had been about football. Elizabeth had stayed at home, reading.

"You're right." He really didn't know her. She sent pictures each year of the kids, and of their Christmas. They had an occasional holiday together. But he didn't know her, or her family.

"Of course I'm right." She touched his arm. "I'm also sorry. Really sorry."

"I'm sorry, too."

"Whose place is this?" Elizabeth looked from the barn to the house.

"Clint Cameron's." He glanced back at the house. Jenna had gone inside. "I was jealous of you, too."

"Why?"

"You had freedom." Adam felt childish making that statement. The thoughts of a teenager weren't easy on the lips of a man.

"I wasn't the star of the family."

"I would have given you that place. I didn't ask to be the star of the show."

She closed her eyes. "You know, I played the flute in band. Dad never came to a parade, a concert, not once did he acknowledge my achievements from the pulpit like he did yours. He was all about you."

"I guess I didn't see all of that." He slid an arm around her shoulder and pulled her close. "I didn't have time to really look at what was going on in our family. I slept, ate and played football. If I wasn't playing, I was practicing. Winning wasn't enough for him."

"He wanted to be you. He wanted to be the champion. You were the way for him to be that person."

"But I didn't want it as much as he wanted it. He could taste it."

"Why did you keep playing?"

"I didn't know how to stop. I didn't want to disappoint him."

Adam Mackenzie hated football. Not the game, but what it had been in his home, his life. There were times that he loved to play. He loved victory. He loved that it had gotten him out of Oklahoma.

And now he was back. His sister was standing next to him, and the past had become the present.

Adam stared out at the bulls grazing in the pen, trying to decide if he was happy with the change of events. His sister in his life, not wanting something, just wanting his niece and nephews to know him. She shouldn't have to ask him for that.

"It shouldn't be a difficult thing for you, having a family," she half teased, but the expression on her face questioned him.

"It isn't difficult, just new territory." He turned his back on the fence, and they started back toward the house, crossing the gravel drive and being greeted by a blue heeler. "You should bring your family to the camp while I'm here."

"This camp, is this what Billy was doing?"

"It is."

"Now you're doing it?" She walked next to him.

"Not really. I'm taking care of what was already started. This isn't my thing, or where I want to be."

They were almost at the house, a long, ranch-style home, the covered porch running its entire length. The front door opened and Jenna walked out. She had stars in her eyes, but she didn't know him. Not really.

He wondered if he even knew himself.

"Clint has burgers on the grill." Jenna focused on the woman standing next to Adam. She could see the resemblance between the two and knew that it was the sister she had spoken to. "You can eat with us, if you like."

"I should go."

"There's plenty." Jenna ignored the warning look in Adam's eyes, telling her to stay out of his business.

"No, really, I have a family waiting for me." She stood on tiptoe and kissed Adam's cheek. "Call me. I know you have my number in your phone."

"I do." He hugged her. "We'll talk soon."

"For real this time." Elizabeth walked away.

Jenna walked down the steps and stood next to Adam. He needed a friend. She could be that for him. She wondered if he even knew what it was, to have a real friend.

"The boys found a football in the garage. They want to know if you'll play with them."

"There are better things to do with their time." He turned and walked into the house, leaving her on the steps, watching his sister drive away.

"Okay, maybe we won't play football," she muttered to herself as she followed him into the house. He didn't even know where he was going.

He was waiting in the kitchen.

"Through the dining room and out the French doors." She pointed. "I'll be out in a minute."

"What are you doing?" He didn't leave.

She sat down at the kitchen table, not knowing what to say. And this was why she hadn't wanted him here. "I have to rest."

"You can't do that outside?"

Of course he wasn't making this easy for her. She looked down, avoiding his deep blue eyes.

"I have to take the prosthesis off. I'm still gaining strength in my muscles, but some days are difficult." She said it with as matter-of-fact a tone as she could master, keeping emotion out of it, making it easier to look up, meeting his steady gaze. And then she saw tenderness in his eyes.

She felt heat work its way up her neck into her cheeks. This was not the way to feel beautiful, like someone a man would want to hold. She wasn't whole. She would never be whole.

Adam was still standing in front of her.

"What can I do?" He kneeled in front of her, a big giant, suddenly at her level. She wanted to touch his cheek.

Worse, she wanted someone to hold her.

Man, she really thought she was past that. She had worked hard at convincing herself that she was good at being alone. She had the boys. She had her career. And now this guy had blown into her life to upset her plans about making it on her own.

It was something that would pass. Of course it would. At this point, any man probably would have caused this weak moment.

"Jenna?"

"Tell me what your sister wanted. You can take my mind off what must be pretty red cheeks and a lot of insecurity by sharing your family drama." It was easier to laugh than to cry. It gave her a moment to remind herself that she was a whole person. "I'm really nosy, if you hadn't noticed."

"She wants to fix our relationship." He shrugged. "It's probably about time."

"Oh." Jenna hadn't expected an answer, just a momentary distraction, maybe an argument or a "none of your business."

"And she told me to visit my dad."

"Why?"

"None of your business." That was more like it, and it made her smile. "Come on, let's get you back to the party, Cinderella."

"What?"

"Do what you need to do, and I'll carry you outside."

"You can't carry me around." The heat that had vanished returned to her cheeks. "I have crutches, in the hall closet."

"I really can carry you." He stood and flexed his biceps.

"So, you'll carry me outside and leave me?"

"No, I won't do that."

But he would. She knew that he wasn't even with her at that moment. She could see in his eyes that he'd detached. Maybe to deal with her, maybe to deal with his own pain.

She pulled up her pant leg and removed the prosthesis. Adam watched. She pointed to the hall, distracting him, taking his careful gaze off her. "Closet, crutches."

He nodded and obeyed. When he returned, he held

them out to her and reached for her hand. She pulled up, situating herself and getting her balance.

"This is embarrassing," she whispered as heat crawled up her neck into her cheeks.

"Don't. You really don't have to worry about me."

"I'm sure it isn't the relationship you thought we'd have when you crashed into my ditch."

"It isn't. I thought I'd drive into town, square the camp away and be gone." He brushed her cheek with the back of his hand and it rested there. "I hadn't expected to find a friend."

"We should go outside." She moved, turning to head out the back door. Adam whispered something about her being a chicken. She walked through the door pretending she hadn't heard. She knew what she was. She also knew how to protect herself.

Chapter Ten

 $Adam$ watched as she settled herself in a lawn chair under an umbrella. Jenna Cameron, Clint's little sister. He was glad when she seemed ready to be on her own, meaning conversation with him wasn't necessary. That was fine, he would rather it be that way. He didn't want to be the person that hurt Clint's little sister.

Adam walked to the grill and Clint. Willow was watching the grill, a spray bottle of water in hand.

"Is that in case he starts a fire?" Adam smiled as he said the words and Willow nodded.

"He's not a good grill man."

"Could I help?"

Willow glanced past him. "No, that's okay. You can relax. We've got it handled. Lunch will be ready in five minutes."

"Are we going to eat out here?"

"We'll eat on the deck. The fan keeps it a little cooler." Clint turned, nodding to a covered area with a table.

Willow touched his arm when he glanced Jenna's way again. "She's fine."

"Oh, I know she is." But he wasn't convinced.

"Adam, play with us." Timmy ran across the yard, a football in his little hands.

Adam shook his head. "Let's play something else, guys. How about tag? I'll be it."

"No, football." David had joined them. David, who never pushed.

"What if…"

"Guys, leave Adam alone. He's on vacation from football." Jenna gave the twins a warning look. They nodded and ran off, still carrying the football.

And dreaming of being him. He knew that's what boys did. They wanted to be in the big leagues. He hadn't known what else to be. He hadn't been allowed to dream of anything else.

The boys tossed the football to one another, fumbling it, not getting it across the lawn. They didn't have a dad to teach them the right way to pass. He looked back at Clint.

They had an uncle who could do that for them.

A scream stopped Adam from walking away. He turned and David was standing in the middle of the lawn, a hand on his cheek and the football bouncing across the ground in front of him.

Jenna scrambled to get up. "What happened?"

"Timmy threw it hard." David rubbed at his face, the way a boy did when it hurt and he didn't want to cry. Adam knew that trick.

He also knew that sinking feeling of needing to do something. Jenna started to get up. He raised his hand to stop her. And this wasn't what he had planned, this much involvement in their lives.

"Here, buddy, let me see." Adam crossed the yard and David met him halfway. Adam kneeled down, putting himself at the child's level. "Take your hand down."

David rubbed again and then moved his hand. He shot a gaze past Adam, to Jenna. He wanted his mom. Adam could imagine that he was a poor second to Jenna. Out of the corner of his eye he could see her perched on the edge of the chair.

"You're going to have a shiner. That makes you a man. A real football player." Adam touched the skin that was already starting to bruise. "You sit by your mom and I'll get something to put on this."

"Steak?" Timmy was standing behind Adam, looking over his shoulder at the brother he'd injured. And he was jealous, Adam could hear it in his tone, as if steak on a black eye was the best thing in the world.

"No, not steak." Adam put a hand on David's slim shoulder. "A bag of frozen peas."

"They use steak in the movies," Timmy offered.

"I know, but frozen peas work and they're less messy." Adam stood. "Come on, let's go see your mom and I'll see if Willow has a bag of frozen peas."

David stuck a hand in his. The gesture shouldn't have been more than a guy could take, like that hand in his meant something. He'd never felt stronger in his life.

Jenna looked at them, at their hands joined, and then her face tilted, and her eyes met his, questioning him. Or maybe warning him. Yes, definitely a warning. Because he would be leaving soon, and the boys wouldn't understand. He led David to her and when her arms opened, the child flew into them, no longer the tough guy that rubbed away his tears.

Toughen up, be a man. Adam remembered his dad's words when he'd gotten hurt on the football field. His mom had never been the soft touch. She had wanted the dream almost as much as his dad. She had cheered from the sidelines, yelling when she thought the ref was wrong about a play, yelling at him to do better.

His success had taken them places.

Toughen up. He shook off pain that hadn't left a scar or a bruise on his body.

"Adam?"

He shook it off and smiled at the woman waiting for him to respond.

"I'll get that bag of peas." He touched David's head, and the little boy looked up, his eye squinting. A little hand quickly rubbed away the tears. "Let me take a closer look. You know, David, it's okay to cry."

David nodded and a tear slid down his cheek. He brushed it away. "I know."

"I'll be right back."

Or maybe he should get in his truck and start driving, as far from this family as he could get. It might be safer to be with his parents than to be here with Jenna and her boys.

It would feel a lot safer back in Atlanta, in his world, his life. He knew what to expect from the people in that life and what to expect from himself when he was around them.

Jenna held David against her, his tiny arms wrapped around her neck. "You stink," she whispered.

She snuggled against him and he snuggled back, a sweaty little boy who needed a bath. He climbed onto her lap, keeping his arms around her. Timmy climbed up next to her, not wanting to be left out, and biting his lip the way he did when he felt guilty.

"Be more careful next time, guys." She slipped an arm around Timmy and pulled him to her side.

"Are you okay, David?" Willow squatted in front of them. She had the bag of peas that Adam had recommended and she placed them on David's eye and cheek. "That's quite a bruise."

He smiled big. "I know. That's pretty neat, huh?"

"Yeah, pretty neat." Willow kissed the top of his head. "And you are really sweaty. Do you want them to wash their hands before we eat lunch?"

Jenna nodded. "And I need to get up and help you get the table set."

"No, you don't. Come on, Jenna, take a break. It really is okay. I bet Timmy can help me." Willow stood and reached a hand for Timmy to take.

"I like to help," Timmy assured Jenna, kissing her on the cheek. "Adam can take care of you and David. He's pretty good at that."

Jenna felt that heat again, and she realized it was becoming a pretty common event. And then another thought hit her, dispelling the warmth in her cheeks and leaving her cold. Was Timmy feeling the burden of taking care of his mom? The thought sunk to the pit of her stomach and rested there.

She watched Timmy and Willow walk away and then a shadow loomed, blocking the sun. She glanced up, into the darkened profile of Adam Mackenzie. She didn't want to face him, especially if he'd heard her son's proclamation that Adam was good at taking care of her.

Poor guy, he'd gotten more than he'd bargained for when he showed up in Dawson.

"Ready to eat?"

"I'm ready." She pushed herself up and maneuvered across the yard to the table. One hop up and then she could sit. Adam stood nearby, watching. "You can relax, I'm not going to fall or break."

"I know that."

She sat down and David took the seat next to hers. The fan pushed the air, cooling it to bearable. At least there were clouds floating over, sometimes blocking the sun. And maybe later there would be rain. At times she thought she could smell it in the air, a promise of moisture and cooler air.

Clint walked across the yard with the plate of burgers and set them on the table. They were barely burned. She smiled up at him and his eyes narrowed.

"Don't even say it." He handed her two plates.

"I only wanted to say thank you, nothing else. Don't be so touchy."

He laughed, her cowboy brother, dressed for church. Willow had taught him how to match his clothes. "Right, you were going to say thank you."

"I was." She smiled up at him, loving him. He had always been there for her. "And I was going to follow that by saying you're doing so much better. Remember when you asked me if cookies were a breakfast food?"

"I do remember, and for some reason you didn't approve."

"I thought there were better things for the boys. But you were there for them."

"See, I did something right."

She reached for his hand. "You did a lot of things right."

The door slid open. Adam walked out carrying the salad bowl. Jenna released her brother's hand and took the bowl from Adam. He didn't look at her, didn't seem to notice that their fingers touched, and the connection made breathing difficult. For her, not him. Okay, that was fine, she could play that game. When he walked back into the house, Clint sat down in the seat at the end of the table.

"Don't take it personally." He shrugged. "I don't think he's good at relationships."

"Stop reading tabloids." Jenna poured tea in her glass. "And his ability to handle relationships isn't any of my business. But I do like it when people make eye contact with me, rather than acting like avoiding me will make it easier to avoid what happened."

"Okay, you win." Clint stood up. "I'm going to see if Willow needs anything, and then I'm going to get my baby girl."

"She's beautiful."

"Yeah, she is."

The door opened again. Willow handed Clint the ketchup and mustard. He took them. "Do you want me to get Lindsey?"

She shook her head. "She's still sleeping. I have the monitor on."

Disappointment flashed across Clint's features and Willow smiled. "Clint, she needs to sleep. You can't keep waking her up."

"Yeah, yeah." He signed something and Willow turned pink.

"Not fair." Jenna laughed, because she had started learning sign language, but Clint and Willow were speed talkers compared to Jenna's weak attempts.

"Private conversation." Clint winked and kissed his wife before walking back into the house, making room at the door for Adam.

"Adam, sit down." Willow pointed to the seat that Clint had vacated. The one next to Jenna. He sat down and then he looked at Jenna.

"Do you need anything?" he asked, his attention focused past her, to David. Still no eye contact.

I need for you to look at me. She didn't say it. She

wouldn't. He was being kind. He wanted to be helpful. "No, I don't need anything. Do you?"

He grinned, that half smile touched with a boyish charm, and this time their eyes connected. "No, I think I'm fine."

"Good, because you were starting to get on my nerves."

"What?"

"Acting all sorry, and like I'm something breakable that needs to be kept on a shelf. Adam, I train horses for a living. I live on a farm. I'm having a rough couple of days, a setback, but I'm not broken."

"I know." His eyes met hers and held her gaze. "I do know that you're strong. I'm sorry."

"Good, as long as we have that settled, let's get the two love birds out here so we can eat. I'm starving."

The door opened and Timmy walked out of the house, shaking his head. He grinned. "Uncle Clint is kissing Aunt Willow. That's gross."

Jenna gave a fake shudder. "Ewww, gross."

But she remembered what it felt like to be held in Adam Mackenzie's arms. She remembered what it felt like to want to linger there, in a kiss.

She remembered feeling beautiful.

Adam left after lunch. He'd offered Jenna a ride home, but she had insisted that the afternoon rest would have her back on her feet by tomorrow and he didn't have to stay. Willow had even refused his help with the dishes.

So he got into his truck and drove away, away from the farm, away from a ton of conflicting emotions. Because he hadn't been ready to leave a Sunday afternoon with people he liked, and he had known it was time to go.

He drove past the entrance to Camp Hope, the sign

now up and the driveway widened and the weeds mowed so it could be seen. Camp would start tomorrow. And then what?

He didn't know, because this hadn't been a part of his plan. He hadn't expected to stay here. He sure couldn't have guessed that Will would discover that the accounts had been cleaned out.

If he left, what would people say? Probably not much. Staying was more of a surprise to people than his leaving would be. The world probably expected him to bail on the camp, on the kids. He was Adam Mackenzie, he didn't think about other people.

Wouldn't they be surprised if they knew that he couldn't stop thinking about Jenna Cameron? The reality of that surprised him more than a little.

He replaced thoughts of her with thoughts of his dad, and the home he'd grown up in. He kept driving. Thirty minutes later he was slowing down in front of that house, a white stucco, set back from the road and flanked by a barn. He drove past it, going the few miles to the church where his father had been the pastor.

Those people had loved his dad, really loved him.

What had Adam been missing? Or maybe it wasn't what he was missing, but what he knew. His dad wasn't perfect. His dad had pushed Adam, and then pushed him more, insisting that he be the best. Even at church Adam had been set apart, by his dad, by teachers. The pastor's son, the football star, the charming kid who had gotten away with too much.

He slowed in front of the church and pulled in the driveway. His dad was still pastor here. Twenty-five years of being the pastor of the same church, the same group of people. Twenty-five years of preaching a message that

Adam had accepted as a child, and then he'd walked away. Because he'd gotten tired of trying to be perfect.

And now, when he didn't know what to do next, he was here, trying to find direction for his life. He parked his truck and got out, remembering a childhood in this building, being taught by ladies who had hugged him tight and fed him cookies.

Memories he shouldn't have forgotten had returned. He remembered playing baseball in the field behind the church and his dad cheering him on.

A car pulled in the driveway. The automobile was familiar; Adam had seen pictures after he'd sent the check that purchased it from a dealer in Tulsa. He watched his dad pull into the designated parking space and get out, a little older, a little less hair.

"Son."

Adam took a few steps to separate the distance between them.

"Dad, I didn't expect to see you here."

"No, I guess you didn't. I came down to make sure the air conditioner is on for this evening's service. You going to stay?"

"No, I have to get back to Dawson."

"Yes, I heard you've been there." The older Mackenzie rubbed the bald area of his forehead. He pulled off wire-framed glasses and cleaned them with the tail of his shirt. "We thought you might come by the house."

"I've been planning on it." Which wasn't a lie. He had planned on seeing them at least once before he left.

"Adam, life is too short to go on this way." His dad looked away. "I've done funerals lately, burying people that were my friends. It makes a man think about what he's missed out on."

"Yeah, that does make a guy think."

Adam pushed his hat back on his head and made eye contact with an older version of himself. Except the hair. His dad had started balding in his twenties. It was genetic, just like the two of them always believing they were right was genetic. That was the trait they shared.

They'd been butting heads since Adam learned to walk, his mom said. Adam had been the kid that if his dad said it was snowing, Adam would insist it was rain. And when it came to football, sometimes the teenaged Adam had stopped trying because he knew that no matter what, his dad would push him when they got home, push him to rethink, to replay, and to do better.

"Boy, it's hot out here."

"Yeah, it is." Adam walked up the sidewalk and sat down on the steps that led to the front entrance of the church. His dad followed. The church sat on the edge of town, surrounded by farmland.

"How's the camp going?" His dad sat down next to him.

"I hope it's good. The first group of campers shows up tomorrow."

"Are you going to stay and run this thing?"

"No, you know I'm not qualified for that. I'm just the lucky guy that inherited this mess."

"It isn't such a mess. Billy meant well."

"I know he did." A normal conversation. Adam sighed and tipped his hat a little lower. "It really is hot out here."

"Yeah, you're just not as tough as you used to be. You used to practice for hours in weather like this."

"Not my best memories, Dad."

"I know. Adam, I'm sorry if I pushed you too hard. Your sister and I have talked about this. I don't know why I didn't see. She said we never took a family vacation. I guess I thought football was what our family did together."

"Yeah, I know." Adam glanced sideways, shrugging a little, trying to brush it off.

He had meant to come home, put the camp up for sale and leave. Instead it was turning into a bad episode of *Dr. Phil,* and everyone was feeling better but him.

Because he wondered how it would feel to leave, and at one time he could think of nothing but leaving.

"It wasn't such a bad life, was it?" His dad stared out the parking lot, but he shot Adam a quick look. "I mean, look at where you got."

"It got me where I am. But sometimes I wonder where I'd be if it had been my choice. If you hadn't pushed, where would I have gone and what would I have been?"

"I pushed you because I knew you wouldn't push yourself."

"So what? What if I hadn't pushed myself? What if I hadn't succeeded in football? Maybe I could have made decisions about my life, my future." Maybe he wouldn't resent his father, if it had been about something more than success.

"What would you have picked, Adam?"

"I don't know, Dad. Maybe I would have been…" A fireman? He smiled, because every boy probably wanted to be a fireman. "I don't know what I would have done. But I don't think I would have been a failure."

"You can still make decisions for yourself. I pushed you and now you have opportunities you wouldn't have had."

"Yeah, I guess." But he could only remember nights

with floodlights on in the backyard, running drills as his dad yelled, coaching him to do better, to not give up.

And he remembered two little boys playing football in the backyard, thinking it was the greatest thing in the world. And he hadn't tossed the football for them, hadn't shown them a better way, because he didn't want to take away the fun of just playing, of being boys.

He should have played with them. Next time—if there was a next time—he would.

"I need to go." He stood and his dad pushed himself up, nearly Adam's height, not quite. A long time ago Adam had thought his dad was a giant. "Tell Mom I'll stop by the house in a few days."

"She'd like to see you. We both would."

"Maybe we can have a family dinner, with Elizabeth and her family."

"That would be good." His dad crossed the parking lot at his side. "Adam, I hope someday you'll forgive me."

Adam stopped walking. "It isn't about forgiving you, Dad. I think it's about trying to understand you. I'd like for us—would have liked for us—to have a relationship that included something other than football." He pulled his keys out of his pocket. "I would have liked to have gone fishing, or camping."

"I get that." His dad stepped back as Adam opened his truck door. "I'll see you soon. Maybe I'll come down and take a look at that camp."

Adam nodded and shifted into Reverse. "That would be good."

Chapter Eleven

Adam drove for hours after leaving his dad. The sun was setting when he drove back to Dawson and turned on the road that led to his temporary home. He slowed as he passed Jenna's drive on the way back to Camp Hope. The little farmhouse, white siding and covered front porch, was aglow with lights. He could see the dog on the front porch and a shadow as one of the boys walked in front of the window.

He stopped and backed up to turn into her drive, rather than going on up the road to the drive that led to his new home, a single-wide trailer at the edge of a field. What would his friends think of this new life, of Jenna?

When he stopped in the driveway next to her house, the dog got up and barked, but then his tail wagged and he ran down to greet Adam.

He hadn't had a pet in years. Morgan's son, Rob, had had a kitten that they picked up in a parking lot, a stray with greasy gray fur and big ears. Rob had loved that kitten. Adam had really cared about Rob. Too bad Morgan had only wanted invitations to certain parties, and then she'd dumped him.

He didn't get out of his truck, because a single mom was inside that house and she had two boys who needed a dad. That was the talk around town. He'd overheard it in the grocery store, what a pair the two of them would be. How Jenna needed someone like him.

He'd had a lifetime of being used.

The front door opened and Jenna stepped out, still on crutches, looking smaller than ever, and fragile. But she wasn't.

She moved to the edge of the porch but didn't come down the ramp. He lowered his window. "I was driving by."

"It looks to me like you stopped driving. Driving by would mean going on down the road, not stopping."

He smiled. "Yeah, you got me there. Do you have iced tea?"

"I'm from Oklahoma, of course I have iced tea. The boys are getting into the tub. Do you want to come in, or are you going to stay in your truck?"

"I'll get out." The dog met him, tail wagging. He reached down to ruffle the thick fur around his neck and then the dog followed him to the house.

"Come in. Let me check on their bathwater, and you put ice in the glasses."

As if he'd always been here, always been in her world.

He walked through the living room, aware of his boots on the hardwood floor that glowed like warm honey. The house was small but, man, it made him feel at home. It was the kind of place a guy didn't want to leave.

This house had overstuffed furniture with throw pillows embroidered by hand, curtains that lifted in the early-evening breeze, and candles that scented the air with the aroma of baked apples. It also had two boys who needed a dad. And he wasn't the best candidate for that job.

He opened the freezer and pulled out ice cube trays, listening as Jenna talked to the boys about how to wash, and then told them that if they made a mess, they had to clean it up. Her voice was soft with laughter and the twins jabbered nonstop.

The sounds were as foreign to him as Atlanta had once been, and yet, somehow it was all familiar, as if it had always been a part of his life.

Warning signs were going off, telling him to retreat, to get out of her world before he got pulled into something that hurt them all. But he couldn't walk away.

Jenna walked into the kitchen as he was filling up two glasses and she pulled a container out of the cabinet. "Willow made chocolate chip cookies. Want one?"

"Can I have two?"

"Have as many as you want." She took two and nodded to the table. "We can sit in here. Or on the porch."

"The porch would be great." Without asking, he grabbed her tea. She smiled and didn't protest.

He followed her out the door onto the small porch with the two metal chairs and a swing. Lamplight glowed from the living room and he could hear the boys playing in the bathroom, just off the living room.

"I love nights like this." Jenna sat down and reached for her glass. "I love it here."

"It is a good place," he admitted. He looked out at the lawn, at the sky that had turned deep twilight-blue. The stars were amazing, maybe because he hadn't seen them like this in so many years. In Atlanta, he never looked up.

"Where'd you go today?" She sighed. "Sorry, that's none of my business."

He smiled at her. "I went home. I saw my dad."

"Good. A guy should always be able to go home." She made it sound so easy.

He wished it was. Maybe it was, for other people. He had come to the conclusion that the water under the bridge had washed him downstream a little too far, taking him too far from his family, too far from where he'd grown up. And too far from faith.

Now none of it felt as far away as he'd once thought.

"Are you always such an optimist?" he asked, but he already knew the answer.

"Not always. I know what it's like to have to forgive someone. I had to forgive my dad for hurting me, for hurting us, and for spending so much of my childhood drunk."

"I'm sorry, Jenna."

"I've worked through it. He's in the nursing home now, suffering from dementia. Sometimes he doesn't even know who I am. The past doesn't seem as important as it used to."

"Yeah, my dad told me that he's had to do the funerals of friends his age. It does make you stop and think. I also realize I've spent too many years angry with him for pushing me the way he did."

"You would have played anyway." She smiled in the dim light on the porch, and her hand moved, like she meant to reach for his, but she didn't. "You could have walked away. You went to college. If you hadn't wanted this…"

"I could have done something else." He laughed a little, because she never gave him any slack. "You're right, I guess I could have. And now I *am* going to do something else. The job with the sports network."

"See, doors opened because your dad pushed you."

"Yes, he pushed." Adam leaned back, thinking about those ladies and their whispered comments about the two of them. "Jenna, I'm not a good person."

"Have you been reading too many stories about yourself and believing what other people say?" She winked, teasing with her smile.

"Don't you believe those stories?"

"No, I don't believe them. I think you've done things you regret. But I don't believe that's who you are." She cocked her head to the side and he didn't talk. He knew she was listening to her boys. They were still chattering, still splashing in the tub.

"The kids show up tomorrow for the first day of Camp Hope."

"I know." She shifted in the chair. "I might not be around for a day or two. I need to take some time with my horses."

"You don't have to explain that to me. I know you have a life."

"I'm not explaining." She laughed a little. "Okay, maybe I am. But the horses are important to me. When I was little, this is what I dreamed of."

"Didn't you have other dreams?" He turned in his chair, watching her in the soft light that glowed from the living room window.

She sighed a little. "I wanted to run away from home. I wanted to show horses on the national circuit and never come back to Dawson. Kind of like you. But my dream changed. Now it's about this farm and raising my boys. What was your dream?"

His dream? The likely answer, the one he'd always given to reporters, was that he'd always wanted to play pro football. But there had to be other dreams, other things he wanted in life. He smiled, not looking at her, because he knew what she'd think.

"I wanted to be a fireman."

Her laughter filled the night air. "Of course you did. Every little boy wants to be a fireman. But what else? What did you really want to be?"

"I'm serious. I wanted to be a fireman."

"So, volunteer for the Dawson Rural Fire District. They can always use help."

"I won't be here long enough." The words plunked into the night, having the opposite effect of her laughter. He wouldn't be here long at all.

"No, I guess you won't."

He glanced at his watch, and then out at the dark sky. No streetlights, no traffic, no sirens. He had forgotten that this type of silence existed. He had forgotten, or maybe never known, what it was like to sit and talk to a woman like Jenna Cameron.

"I should go home."

She stood when he stood. "Yes, it is getting late."

And her smile was gone, and he knew that it was because he was leaving. Did she wonder if he would sell the camp? He wished he had an answer for her.

He picked up both their glasses. "I'll take these in first."

"Thank you."

Jenna didn't follow Adam into the house. She could hear the boys playing in the bath, fighting with toy men and splashing water, probably all over the floor. Adam came back, his face in shadows with the living room light behind him. She waited on the porch to tell him goodbye.

He stepped onto the porch and the dog came up, rolling over in front of Adam so he could scratch its belly. Adam gave the dog the attention it wanted and then straightened, reaching for his hat that he'd left on the table.

Jenna knew that he should go. For her sake and for the boys'. They didn't need to get attached to him, or get used to him in their lives.

Adam still stood on her porch, though. He smelled like mountains and cedar. And when he was this close, she could hardly breathe.

She needed to breathe.

She took a step back, taking in a deep breath of humid June air. Adam backed up a step in the other direction. He had to know as well as she did that this—whatever *this* was—couldn't be real. It was moonlight and missing something they'd never had, would never have. She had two kids. He had career plans that included Atlanta, not Dawson.

"Adam, you should go now."

She had a list of reasons why he should go. She had a five-year plan that didn't include dating. Her boys were in the bathroom splashing, playing and needing for her to be there for them.

If she closed her eyes she could remember how it felt when Jeff looked at her that day that he said goodbye. She could remember how his gaze had lingered on her leg. She would never open herself up that way again, to feel that way, with a man looking at her as if she was less than beautiful.

She was past the anger, past the hurt. She had worked through so many stages of grief. She couldn't remember them all, but she knew that it had left something raw and painful inside her, an unwillingness to ever be hurt that way again.

"I'll see you tomorrow. Or in a few days." Adam's voice, reminding her of this night, and her life here.

She opened her eyes and nodded. "I'll be around."

"Okay then." He didn't walk away. "Jenna, people are talking about us."

"Oh?" What was she supposed to say? "I haven't heard, but I can imagine."

"It's just that I know how you feel, about the boys."

"Don't worry, I know you're going back to Atlanta. The boys know it, too."

The boys yelled that they were finished, saving her from saying more, or doing something stupid, something she would regret.

"See you later." He tipped his hat, pivoted and walked off the porch, a dark figure in the night. Her dog followed him.

Jenna walked back into the house, knowing that Adam wasn't a superstar, or a man who'd dated more women than Dawson had people. He was really just a cowboy who had dreamed of being a fireman.

And before long, he would be a memory.

Jenna had always dreamed of training horses. But the morning after Adam's visit, with the sun barely up, she was trying to remember why that dream had been important—especially on a morning when she would have liked to sleep late, a morning after a sleepless night.

She cinched the saddle on the gray gelding she was hoping to sell, talking to him, distracting him because he had a tendency to hold his breath and once she got the girth strap tight, he'd let his air out and the strap would be loose, causing the saddle to slide.

But she knew a few tricks, too. She moved him forward, slapped his belly and gave the strap a yank. The horse sidestepped and nodded his head a few times, his ears back to let her know that he didn't like losing.

"Oh, you poor baby." She led him to the mounting block Clint had made for her, to help her mount without the stirrups. There were challenges. Each day she faced something new, but horses she knew how to handle. She felt free when she rode, as if nothing could stop her, not even her injury.

Amputation. She could say it. Her life didn't need a man to be complete. It was complete because she was alive and she was content.

As she settled into the saddle, Jack moved a little, adjusting to the weight in the saddle. He reached back, nipping at her booted foot. She nudged his head away and urged him forward.

She rode him into the arena and from the saddle she pulled the gate closed. Jack skittered a little to the side, but she held him tight, talking to him as she edged him forward, not letting him take control.

After a few laps walking around the arena, she loosened the reins and leaned slightly. With that sign of permission, he broke into an easy lope around the arena, taking the lead with his inside front leg.

"Jack, maybe I shouldn't sell you. You really are a pretty decent guy. And decent guys are hard to find." She laughed softly because his ears twitched and went back, as if he wasn't sure if her words were an insult or compliment.

She slowed him to a walk and then stopped him with

barely a flick of her wrist and the tightening of her legs. A touch of her left foot and he turned away from the pressure. She could feel his giant body rippling beneath her, beneath the saddle. He was more than a half ton of power, and yet he submitted to her control.

A truck rumbled up the drive. Jenna flicked a glance over her shoulder, expecting her brother.

It wasn't Clint.

Jack shifted, stepping a little to the right and then backing up against the pressure of the reins. She took him around the arena again.

Adam stepped out of the truck and walked across the lawn. He looked like every other Oklahoma cowboy that she knew—faded jeans and a short-sleeved shirt buttoned up, but not tucked in. The deep red of the shirt worked with his golden tan and sandy-brown hair. This morning he wore a baseball cap, not the white cowboy hat he normally wore.

Memories of last night, of a moment when she had wanted to be held, rushed back, and so did the realization that those feelings had been hers, not his. She might not give credence to tabloids, but single at thirty-three and the number of relationships in his past did point to a possible commitment phobia on his part.

She reminded herself that she had the same phobia, because she was tired of getting left behind. And he would definitely leave her behind. He'd made that clear last night.

He stopped at the arena, leaning against the top rail of the enclosure.

"What are you doing up and around this early?" She rode Jack up to the fence. Adam ran a hand over the horse's jaw and down his neck. She glanced away, toward the house, where there was still no sign of the boys, and back to Adam. He leaned against the fence, tall and confidant.

"I thought I'd return the favor you've done me and help you out a little."

She pulled the horse back so he could step inside the enclosure. "Help me?"

"With the horses. I know you have a lot to get done this week."

"Don't you have kids showing up at your camp?"

"I do, but not until noon. Pastor Todd is going to be there in an hour. He's bringing kitchen staff to start lunch. I'll stay here a couple of hours and head that way."

"If you insist. But you won't like the job."

"I bet I won't mind."

"Could you clean the stalls? I need to work him for another fifteen minutes or so, and those stalls really need to be cleaned."

"I can clean stalls, if you have coffee."

"I keep a pot of coffee inside the tack room. I know, bad habit, but I can't help myself."

"Works for me. Pitchfork?"

Jenna smiled, because he was really going to do this. "Adam, you really don't have to do this."

"I want to."

"Fine. Pitchfork and wheelbarrow in the first stall."

He tipped his hat and nodded. "Where are the boys?"

"They'll sleep late. We stayed up and watched a movie last night."

"They're great kids. Not that I'm an expert." He didn't move away from the fence.

And Jenna couldn't untangle her thoughts from the

memory of being away from the boys, worrying about them when she couldn't hold them.

"They are great. It wouldn't seem like a mom would miss much in an eight- or nine-month time period, but I missed a lot."

"You were in Iraq all that time?"

Of course he didn't know. "No, I was in rehab for nearly five months. I've only been home for five months. They were with Willow and Clint."

"I used to think I was strong." He winked and walked away, and she didn't know what to do with his statement or the way it made her feel. But he was walking away and she couldn't tell him, couldn't tell him how it felt to be so afraid, and to not feel strong at all.

The barn was stifling hot, even that early in the morning. There wasn't any breeze at all, and all of the heat got trapped inside that building beneath the metal roof. Adam pushed the wheelbarrow toward the open double doors at the end of the barn, feeling a little breeze as he got closer to the opening. He brushed his arm across his forehead and paused to watch the woman outside, pulling the saddle off the big gray horse. It was heavy and she backed up, not steady on her feet, but strong.

He knew she wouldn't want his help. He pushed the wheelbarrow out to the heap a short distance from the barn. It didn't take a genius to know that he needed to dump the old straw in that pile. He lifted the handles of the wheelbarrow and lifted, giving it a good shake and then turning it to the side to get the rest out.

Jenna walked up behind him. "You look like you could use something a little colder than coffee."

He turned, and she wrinkled her nose and smiled. "Ice water would be good. I just finished the last stall."

"You're good help. I might keep..." She laughed. "Forget that I said that."

"Yeah, I know, good help is hard to find. The boys are on the front porch."

"I saw them. They know not to come running down here when I'm working a horse. I nearly got dumped a month or so back."

"You've done all of this in a matter of months? That's pretty impressive."

"I didn't want to waste a single day getting back to life and making my dreams come true. Come on, let's get something to drink. And I have boiled eggs in the fridge if you're hungry."

"I had breakfast at The Mad Cow. Vera wanted to give me the latest on Jess and his attempts at stopping the camp. He has a lawyer, some second cousin twice removed, who is willing to help him."

"Great, that would be Kevin, and he's only doing it to help his career, which is nonexistent. But I guess this would get a guy some good publicity, trying to take down a camp owned by Adam Mackenzie."

"I guess this is one more reason for me to sell or sign the camp over to the church."

"If you think so," she said, as if she wanted to say more.

She wanted to tell him he was a quitter. She didn't need to say it, because he knew that's what she would say if she thought she could get away with it.

"Jenna, I'm not staying. And if Jess gets his way, this camp won't last. If he's doing this to get money from me, signing the camp over to the church will end that."

"I know that." She stopped and smiled up at him. "I'll miss you, that's all. And don't get that trapped look. I'm not after anything. It's just that you feel like a friend. One that I won't see again after you leave here."

"Yeah, I know." He reached for her hand. "Jenna, thank you for being the first person in a long time who doesn't want something from me."

She squeezed his hand once and let go. "You're welcome."

The boys were off the porch and running toward them, blond hair sticking up, feet bare. They wrapped their arms around Jenna and started to tell her about the mouse they'd seen the cat catch. He didn't even know that she had a cat.

"I'm going to get back to the camp. Todd will be there, and…"

She nodded. "Go ahead, I understand."

He was escaping, and she knew it. He walked away, not even understanding what he needed to escape from, or how she knew him so well, sometimes better than he seemed to know himself.

That scared him. When had anyone known him that well?

Chapter Twelve

Kids poured off the church bus as Adam parked his truck next to his trailer. They stood in groups, gangly and awkward, kids in jeans, shorts, T-shirts, with acne on their faces. The girls had short hair, the boys had long hair, they had guitars and backpacks, a few had their clothes in garbage bags.

"This is amazing." Pastor Todd walked up and stood next to him as he got out of his truck. "Wow, you could use a shower."

"I was cleaning stalls." Easy answer, but he didn't know what to say about this, about what it meant. This camp was someone else's dream. Now it was Todd's dream.

Football had been his dad's dream.

And Adam wanted to be a fireman. He smiled a little and Todd pounded him on the back, like the smile was an acknowledgment of the dream.

Adam stood back and watched, because he didn't know what to do with kids, not really. He couldn't stop his gaze from traveling down the driveway, in the direction of Jenna's. He could see the top of her blue roof from here. She knew what to do with kids.

A younger man, probably in his twenties, left the group of kids and crossed to where Adam was standing, watching.

"Adam, I'm John, the youth minister at Christian Mission. We really appreciate what you've done here, getting this together in such a short amount of time. The kids are really excited."

"I'm glad it came together for you." Adam pointed to Pastor Todd. "This is the guy who will be keeping us all on the right path. Pastor Todd from the Community Church of Dawson."

A car eased up the drive. Not just a car, it was Jess's sedan. He parked and got out. A man in a suit got out on the other side.

"Great, we don't need this."

Todd shot a glance in the direction Adam was pointing and his eyes widened. "He doesn't give up."

"No, he doesn't. He's one annoying burr under my saddle."

"He shouldn't be." Todd started in the direction of the older man. "Jess, how are you today?"

"I'd be a lot better, Pastor, if you'd give up on this crazy idea. I have my nephew here and we'd like to work out a deal with you."

"So it's all about money?" Adam joined the three men. "You know, I'm not much of a kid person, either, Mr. Lockhart, but it's just a camp. It isn't going to interfere with your life at all."

"It's a nuisance, and I have information here from county records. You didn't go through the Planning and

Zoning Committee to get this place done. There are fines, laws, and permits are required."

"So you want us to send these kids home, Jess?" Pastor Todd swept a hand, indicating the kids that were being led to their dorms by workers that came with the church group. "You would really want us to do that?"

"Well, I…" Jess looked up, at the man Adam supposed was the nephew lawyer.

"We want you to go through the proper channels and get the camp approved. Which we don't think you can do. We think that it isn't in the best interest of the community, of farmers who use their land for farming, to have this camp here."

"One man with a burr under his saddle." Adam shook his head. "I'll write you a check. Tell me how much."

"Planning and Zoning, Mr. Mackenzie." The lawyer bristled.

"Right, Planning and Zoning. I need a shower, so you let me know when you decide how much you want."

Adam walked away, leaving the other men to work things out. As he walked up the steps to the trailer, he pulled out his cell phone and dialed Will.

"Adam?"

"We're going to need a lawyer."

Silence.

"What have you done?" Will's voice, a little tense. Adam smiled.

"I haven't done anything. This neighbor situation is getting crazy. He says the camp doesn't have the proper permits from Planning and Zoning. I didn't know little counties like this had Planning and Zoning." What was he thinking? This could be his way out. The county would shut the camp down. The kids would all go away. He would contact a Realtor.

"You want to save the camp?" Will's voice held a hint of laughter Adam didn't appreciate.

"I don't care about the camp." He looked out the window at kids running around the dorm, and two boys playing catch. "The people around here want the camp."

"Right. Okay, you're the hard-hearted football player who doesn't care. The community cares. Gotcha. I'll make sure no one ever knows your secret."

"Thanks, I'm sure you'll do that. So, contact a lawyer, see what we need to do with this county situation, and with Jess Lockhart. He says it is about zoning, but I have a feeling it's about a check. I think if I'd paid him off to start, it never would have gone to the county officials."

"So you called his bluff and now he's stuck being the bad guy taking down Camp Hope."

"Yeah, he's the bad guy." Adam stood at the door and watched the old guy in bib overalls get in his car. Not exactly the picture of the villain.

"I'll get on this. But I really think Billy got the permit."

"Then we need to get that information. Or find out who he talked to on that committee."

"I'll take care of it." Will sounded confidant. Adam was glad, because he felt more like someone about to write another big check.

Adam slipped the phone back into his pocket and closed his eyes. For a long time he'd been too busy for God. And then he'd thought he was too strong to need God.

And now, he wasn't busy or strong. He was wandering in a desert, wondering if there was a clear way out, or any real answers.

* * *

Jenna pulled up to the camp as kids filed out of the dorms and down to the chapel. Next to her, Timmy and David unbuckled their seat belts.

"Stay with me, guys. I know they have activities for you, but until we know what and with whom, you're not going to take off. Understood?"

Twin looks of wide-eyed surprise and disappointment. "Okay."

She got out of her truck and the boys each grabbed a hand. Sometimes they swung too hard, knocking her off balance. But she didn't want their lives to be about the words *Be careful with Mom*.

As she walked up the steps to the cafeteria, she heard the door of the trailer close. Glancing back, she watched as Adam took the steps two at a time, and she knew that he was in his own world, not aware of what was going on around him.

She stepped through the doors of the kitchen and the boys let go of her hands and ran to Pastor Todd's wife, Lori.

"Jenna, I can take them with me. We're going to eat lunch and then I have little projects for the children of the camp workers." Lori had hold of the boys.

Jenna eyed her offspring. "You boys go with Miss Lori, and make sure you do what she says."

And then they were gone. She walked behind the stainless-steel serving counter where Louisa and several others were fixing the last pile of sandwiches.

"I'm here to work."

"That's great, honey. Why don't you help us serve sandwiches." Louisa handed her a pair of gloves. "How you feelin' today, Jenna?"

"Good." She slipped the gloves on as the door opened. It wasn't the campers. Adam paused in the doorway and then closed the door behind him.

She had been right; he looked like it had been a long day. Maybe cleaning stalls was too much for him. She smiled at the thought. She'd like for something to get the better of him.

"Jenna." He walked back to the sink to wash his hands. "Get all of your work finished?"

"Yes, thanks to you." And she shouldn't have said that, because a half-dozen pairs of eyes turned in their direction.

He stepped into place next to her behind the serving counter and pulled on the latex gloves that Louisa handed him. Jenna tried to ignore him, but he was grinning as he leaned closer.

"Bet you wish you wouldn't have said that out loud."

"I kind of do wish that," she whispered back, keeping her focus on the door that the teens were about to plow through.

"You're cute when you're beet-red. But don't worry, I don't think anyone else has noticed."

She glanced up at him. "Thanks, cowboy, you're such an encourager."

"I do my best." He nudged her a little with his shoulder. But then the door opened and the moment ended as a line of hungry teenagers swarmed the kitchen like ants on a honey trail. Or so Louisa said.

Jenna dropped a sandwich on the tray that one of the teens slid in front of her. She smiled at the girl, thinking about those years, how it had felt to be that young, that worried about the future and what people thought about her.

And now, she had other worries, but she knew who her friends were. She knew not to worry about things like being a part of a crowd that didn't really care about her.

She knew now that real friends mattered, and if she had to work at earning a friendship, acting like someone she wasn't to impress somebody, it wasn't friendship.

"How you feeling?" Adam's voice took her from that moment of looking back.

"I'm good. Why do you ask?"

His hand slid behind her back. "I'm asking because I really don't want you to wear yourself out. I've been doing research and..."

"Oh, no. You have?" She cycled through a flash of emotions and landed on the one overwhelming truth—it was really very sweet. The shy expression on his face made her want to cup his cheeks in her hands and kiss him. What a mess. "You're a good man, Adam Mackenzie."

"Well, I can't say that anyone has ever called me that."

"Then they should have. I'm going to finish up here and then help with crafts. What about you?"

He dropped chips on the tray of the young man who had just come through the door. There were more outside, still being herded in by camp counselors.

"What do you mean, what about me?"

"Are you going to help with anything this afternoon?"

"I hadn't planned on it." He kept a steady action of placing bags of chips on the trays of the young people walking through the line. "I don't even know if I'm qualified to serve meals let alone do other things."

"You're doing a great job."

A break in kids gave them privacy. He turned to face

her, pulling on the latex gloves that were tighter on his hand than on hers.

"I'm pretending. Jenna, I'm not the guy who works with teens or runs a camp. When I look in your eyes, I can see that you want me to be that person. I'm not."

More kids filed through the line.

"I'm not trying to push you." She put the last sandwich on the tray of the last kid.

He pulled off his gloves and tossed them into the trash. "Yes, you are. Since I showed up in Dawson, people have had plans for me. I could really do without that for a while."

"What does that mean?" She followed him out the door of the kitchen. He had been walking fast, but he slowed for her, holding his hand out as she approached the steps.

She took his hand and eased down the steps, easing because of the pain, and feeling less than confident. "So?"

He kept hold of her hand. "Jenna, I played football because it's what I'm good at, and because I didn't have time growing up to think about anything else. My dad, coaches, agents, they've always been there to tell me my next move. And now this camp, also not my idea, my plan."

She wanted to tell him he had everything, but maybe he didn't.

"What do you want to do? I mean, you don't have to help. There are plenty of people here. I just thought…"

"That I'd like to string some beads?"

"Help. I thought you'd like to help. There's nothing like helping a child, watching them smile and grow, to make you think…"

"About something other than myself."

She smiled up at him. "I can't tell you what to do,

Adam, but at your age, maybe it is time to think about what *you* want, and where you want to be."

"Maybe it is."

Jenna let go of his hand. "I'm going to string beads, and I understand that this camp isn't what you do."

"Thank you."

Jenna walked away, and she knew that he was still standing behind her, still watching. And then she heard him running to catch up with her, and something new and unexpected sparked inside her heart.

"I thought you had other things to do?" She glanced sideways at the giant of a man walking next to her.

"I thought I did, but I checked my schedule and I'm open for the rest of the afternoon."

She touched the tips of her fingers to his. "I'm glad to hear that."

"Jenna and Adam, it's great to see the two of you. You're going to help with crafts?" Marcie Watkins handed them each a long apron. "Put this on. It'll keep you a little bit clean. Notice, I said *a little*."

"I thought we were stringing beads?" Adam leaned and whispered in her ear.

Jenna shrugged. "Me, too. Marcie, aren't we stringing beads?"

"I have choices." Marcie pulled out macaroni from a box and started setting up paint. "They can make a cross necklace with beads, or paint macaroni and string it."

"Paint macaroni?" Adam shook his head. "Sounds like fun."

"It will be fun. Stop being a scrooge."

Jenna slipped the apron over her head and then pulled it to tie behind her back. As she pulled the ends tight, she watched Adam trying to get his straight, fussing with the tie behind his back. Awkward didn't begin to describe it.

"Can I help?"

"Probably." He turned so she could tie the apron.

When he turned around she laughed. He was a giant in a paper bib and a cowboy hat.

"Okay, this is funny, but here come the kids." Marcie was in the middle of her little group of helpers, four of them in aprons. "Today they can either make a cross with beads—Julie will help with that—or they can paint the macaroni. We'll let the kids string the macaroni tomorrow. We'll have a station for painting red, green, white, black. Got it, everyone?"

"What if a kid wants blue?" Adam mumbled as Marcie stationed him in front of the red paint. A tub of paint, four plates, four brushes and wipes to clean their hands. "What teenager is going to want to do this?"

"You'd be surprised. Kids like simple things. Adults always believe that only complicated things can make a kid happy." Jenna poured paint into the pan on the table in front of her. "Besides, there are kids as young as ten in this group."

"Oh." He looked around them, distracted. "You need to sit down."

"I don't." But she really did.

He was already moving away from her, toward chairs stacked in the chapel. He grabbed one off the pile and walked back with it, putting it behind her.

"There, does that work?"

She sat down, nodding. "It works. Thank you."

"Okay, now, why can't the kids have blue?"

She laughed. "You really do have a one-track mind. Black for sin, red for the shed blood of Jesus, white for sins washed away, green for peace or love, I always get that one confused."

"Got it. No blue."

"No blue." She reached up, letting her fingers slide through his for a moment, not wanting to think about how it felt to have this giant of a man caring about her, and caring about these kids.

Marcie slid past them, her glance on their intertwined fingers, and she looked away, because Marcie didn't gossip. Jenna loved that about the older woman.

"Mr. Mackenzie, the kids will be at your station first." But there was an edge to her voice. A protective, mother-hen edge.

Adam moved, breaking the connection between their hands. And Jenna didn't blame him. It had been a silly high school thing to do, reaching for his hand that way. She thought about her heart, broken one too many times, and the boys, because they thought he was a hero.

None of them needed to go through this, through moving forward, getting over a silly summer fling.

Chapter Thirteen

The group of kids lined up in front of the macaroni-painting station, and Adam thought it looked like a lot more than ten. But after counting, he realized it really was just ten.

"Can we eat this?" one boy asked, his smile crooked and his eyes full of humor. His T-shirt was too big and his jeans a little too short.

"No, this shouldn't be eaten. It isn't cooked. We're just painting it." Adam handed the boy a brush.

"I was joking, man. Don't get so uptight."

Uptight? Was he really? He shrugged a few times, thinking that might loosen him up. Nope, still uptight. The boy shook his head and laughed. "Dude, you gotta lighten up."

"Young man, that is not a dude. That is Mr. Mackenzie and you need to learn some manners." Marcie slipped in between them, a powerhouse of a woman with gray hair and glasses. She stared the boy down, and still managed to look loving. "While we're here, we won't say *dude*. Understood?"

"Yes, ma'am." The boy lost his mirth, lost his swagger. Marcie could put a pro coach to shame.

"Hey, partner, it's okay." Adam smiled because he'd almost said *dude*.

"Mr. Mackenzie, do you think we could shoot some hoops?" The boy nodded to the basketball court fifty feet away and the ball, still lying in the grass.

"We might manage to do that, if it fits into the schedule."

"You'd play with us?" the boy continued.

"Sure I would." Adam swallowed against the painful tightening in his throat. "What's your name?"

"Chuck." The boy painted his macaroni. "This is cool. I like the red the best. I'm going to be a preacher someday."

"That's great, Chuck." Adam loosened up, and it was easy with a kid like that smiling at him. It wasn't about his autograph or football; it was about this camp. And the kid was the hero.

He wasn't a kid person, had never been the guy on the team that signed up for children's charity events. Now he wondered why.

"Come on, move on over to Jenna's station, kids. We need to get this moving along." Marcie clapped, but her smile was big and Adam knew she loved the kids, every single one of them.

He watched as they painted and she walked behind them, talking to them, hugging them, sharing stories about herself and the days when she'd been young enough to paint macaroni necklaces. One boy asked her if he had to wear it. She told him that he didn't have to, but he could give it to someone, to a younger child and tell them what he'd learned. She hoped they would all go home and tell what they'd learned to younger children who couldn't attend.

"Why aren't there younger kids here?" Adam whispered to Jenna.

She stood and poured more paint into her container. "They don't want to get kids too young in here with the teens. I think this group ranges in ages from ten to fourteen. They have a senior high class they'd like to bring later."

"Oh." Adam handed a younger girl a few wipes to clean her messy hands. "Wipe them up good, so you don't ruin your clothes."

She looked down at her knee-length shorts and T-shirt and then smiled up at him. "It's okay. I don't think I can hurt these."

The hole in his heart grew. He'd never gone without, not once in his life. He wondered how many of these kids went without decent meals, or woke up cold in the winter. He knew that it happened, but facing it, seeing it for himself, was shifting the part of his life that had been all about him.

This had changed Billy. He had seen kids like these and wanted to do something about it. He had just gotten sidetracked along the way. Billy had had a good heart.

"More paint." Jenna sat back down, but she nodded toward his paint. It was nearly empty and three children remained. A girl with a thin face and long brown hair moved up to the table. Her clothes were threadbare and her smile was weak. Her hands shook when she reached for the brush.

"Are you okay?" Adam lowered his voice, so it didn't boom and scare her to death.

She looked up, big gray eyes averted, not looking at

him. She nodded but he didn't believe a kid could look like that, with a face that pale, and be okay. He glanced down at Jenna. She was already on her feet.

"Honey, can I do something for you?"

The child shook her head. The paintbrush was in her hand and she swiped red over her macaroni. She sniffled and wiped at her nose and eyes with her arm.

Where was Marcie? Adam looked behind him. She had just been there, but she mentioned cleaning supplies for when they finished. Jenna stood and started around the table.

"Let me help. Are you hungry?"

The girl nodded.

"Didn't you get lunch?" Jenna asked, her voice tender, gentle.

The girl shook her head. Chuck, at the end of the painting table, came back to them, his freckled little face a mask of seriousness. Adam really liked that kid.

"She didn't get any lunch 'cause that bully, Danny, took her sandwich and chips. She just got milk."

"Well, now, that isn't going to work." Adam knew his voice probably rattled the poles that held up the tent. The girl cowered against Jenna, her gray eyes wide.

"Calm down, Goliath." Jenna's lips pursed and she scrunched her nose at him.

The girl giggled a little. "He does kind of look like Goliath."

"Yeah, well, we can take him down with a single stone and a little faith, so we won't worry about him. He's just loud and doesn't know any better."

"We need to get her some lunch and have a talk with Danny." Adam kept his voice a little quieter, and he hoped a little less frightening.

"We'll do that. But how about if we let Pastor Todd or John talk to Danny." Jenna winked at the girl and then smiled a silly smile at him. With her arm around the girl, she moved away from the tent. "We'll go see if we can get her something to eat."

"Okay." And leave him with the kids? He did have another helper or two, but they'd kept pretty quiet at their end of the table, casting curious glances his way, but not speaking.

"Can we still play basketball?" Chuck, not about to give up.

"Yeah, we can play."

"Cool. I'm going to play basketball with Adam Mackenzie."

Adam laughed, because he couldn't believe that was all it took for this kid. He glanced behind him, watching as Jenna walked across the lawn with the little girl. And he wondered who Danny was that he'd take food from another child.

Jenna watched the little girl Cara eat the sandwich and chips that they'd found with the leftovers in the fridge. The child barely chewed the food and then she licked her fingers, not caring that she was being watched. When she finished she wiped her hands and looked up.

"That was good." Cara smiled again, the gesture transforming her pixie face. "Can I go play now?"

"You can. I think it's free time for an hour or so." Jenna nearly fell over with the force of Cara's hug. And then the girl was out the door and running across the lawn.

Slower than earlier in the day, Jenna walked out the door and watched as Adam shot the basketball, mak-

ing it into the basket and then catching it, tossing it to
Chuck. The boy aimed, but the ball hit the rim of the net
and bounced away. He ran after it and when he returned,
Adam stood next to him, showing him how to throw, how
to make the shot.

He was a hero. Her boys had seen that in him from the
beginning. He knew how to stop, how to just give what
the kids needed. And he didn't even know that about
himself. He didn't know that part of Adam Mackenzie
that made people feel good.

Jenna sat down on the bench a short distance from the
court. Timmy and David ran out of the back part of the
kitchen where there were classrooms. They were carrying crosses made from sticks and yarn.

"You guys ready to go?"

"Do we have to?" Timmy hugged her tight and she
leaned back, sitting hard on the bench that she'd vacated.
He plopped down next to her. "We like the camp."

"I know you do, but the camp is for older kids. You got
to come today because I was working. And now we need
to go home, clean house and feed the horses."

"Couldn't Uncle Clint feed?" David sat down next
to her, his curious gaze lingering on her face, because
he was always the one who noticed. "We could watch a
movie together."

"No, Uncle Clint can't feed. He took a load of bulls
to Tulsa today. We'll be fine together. Come on, guys,
cheer up."

"We'll get to come back?" Timmy asked as he stood
and reached for her hand, thinking he was big enough to
pull her to her feet. He did a pretty good job of it.

"Yeah, we'll come back." She followed them across
the lawn, past the trailer that Adam lived in, and past the

row of cars the workers had parked next to it. Her truck was at the end of that line of cars.

Today it was a really long walk.

"Hey, where are you going?" Adam's voice, and she could hear his feet pounding the ground. She turned and he was running after them, his long legs in shorts, no jeans this time.

"I'm taking the boys home. They're exhausted." She was exhausted. "And I need to get things caught up at home."

"Do you need help?"

"Of course I don't." Her eyes stung with tears she wouldn't let fall, because maybe she was the only person that got it, that he was this kind. The boys ran on to the truck and she let them go.

Adam stood next to her. "Jenna, I can feed the horses. Let me change and I'll even drive you home. I can walk back."

"Adam, really…"

"You can stop arguing."

She closed her eyes and nodded. "I can stop arguing. But it isn't time for them to be fed."

He smiled. "Okay, then I'll come over later?"

"We'll see. You know, I really can do this myself. I'm used to it. I'll go home, rest a little, and be back at it."

A car door slammed. She glanced behind her, and Adam groaned a little. "My dad."

"Really?" She watched the older gentleman as he walked toward them, his smile a little hesitant.

"Dad." Adam held out a hand to his father, and Pastor Mackenzie took it, holding it tight for a minute.

"I came here to help you work. I'd like to see this camp

that Billy couldn't stop talking about. You never know, our church might want to help out."

"I'll give you a tour." Adam looked trapped, and Jenna backed away, giving what she hoped was a clear signal that she didn't need him and he should spend time with his dad.

"I'll see you tomorrow." Jenna touched Adam's arm briefly. "Mr. Mackenzie, it was good meeting you."

Adam rubbed his forehead. "I'm sorry. Jenna Cameron, this is my dad, Jerry Mackenzie."

"Good to meet you, Jenna."

"The boys." Jenna nodded in the direction of the truck. "I need to go before they start it and drive themselves home."

"I'll talk to you later." Adam winked. "Not tomorrow."

"Well, she seems like a nice girl." Adam's dad stood next to him, watching the truck pull down the drive.

"She's a mom, not a girl." Adam let out a deep breath and relaxed. "I didn't expect to see you here today."

"I know you didn't, but I told your mother that I'd like to see what's kept you here."

Adam bristled a little under that comment. "You didn't expect me to stay?"

"Did you expect to stay?"

Adam stopped walking. He stared out over the camp, quiet in the late-afternoon heat. The kids were in the chapel behind the door, doing skits. Everything was neat and clean. It looked like a camp—not a summer camp like the ones attended by the children of his friends, with pools, tennis and gymnasiums, but a good camp where kids could have fun for a week.

And he hadn't planned to stay. He had wanted to sell

it as soon as possible. Until just a few days ago he had wanted Jess Lockhart to get his way and shut it down.

A couple of weeks and his life had changed.

"No, Dad, you're right. I hadn't planned on staying. At least not staying for this reason, to get it up and running."

"Maybe this is your fire?"

Adam shook his head, not getting it. "My fire."

"You wanted to be a fireman. Remember, even when you were little, you begged me to take you to town so you could ride on the fire truck."

"Yeah, I remember." He had forgotten, but now it came back to him, that moment on the front seat of that truck, flipping switches that sounded sirens. He had always wanted to be a fireman.

But this wasn't his fire. Unless a fire was just an emergency that needed to be put out. He could admit that the place meant something to him, something more than he had planned. But it would feel good to turn it over to Pastor Todd, knowing it would continue.

"Are you still planning the job in Atlanta, then?" Jerry Mackenzie stopped a short distance from the chapel. It was a big building with screened sides, a roof and a tall steeple. Ceiling fans circulated the air, adding a little breeze to cool the kids sitting on the wooden pews.

Adam watched as four kids on the stage worked together to create a skit. He smiled at their seriousness. And he remembered church camp when he was ten, and how he had felt about his faith.

"Yeah, I'm still leaving." And it wouldn't be as easy as he had once thought. He had found a group of people that were as willing to be used as he was unwilling to be used. Two weeks had changed his life.

"Let's look at what else you have here. I don't want to interrupt the kids."

But for a minute they stood watching the kids who were talking now, saying the words to "Amazing Grace," and acting it out. Adam smiled as one child wandered around on the stage and another went to help him find his way to a child who was playing Jesus: "was lost, but now he's found."

"Let's go." Adam walked away, hurting on the inside, because he felt like he'd been lost for a long time and now that he was found, he was going to leave again.

After dinner, Adam watched his dad drive away, and then he started down the drive on foot, in the direction of Jenna's. He wanted to check on her. He also wanted to walk and think. Maybe even pray.

As he walked up her drive, the dog ran to greet him.

"Dog, you really need a name. I can't believe that someone as emotional as Jenna Cameron left you with a moniker like that."

He walked past the house to the barn. He could see her inside, sitting at the table with the boys. They had their heads bowed. His heart did a strange clench. He'd have to tell them goodbye.

And it wasn't going to be easy.

Now he understood why Jenna hadn't wanted the boys to get attached. But at least they were prepared. He hadn't been prepared for the thoughts of missing her, missing them, that assailed him. He had never expected it to be hard to leave.

The dog nudged his leg. He looked down and the animal pushed him again with the stick it had picked up. Adam took the stick and tossed it and then he walked through the double doors of the barn, taking a second to adjust to the dark, and to the smell of animals, hay and dust.

From outside in the corral, horses whinnied to him, not caring that it wasn't Jenna. They just wanted their evening meal. He opened the door to the feed room and flipped on the light. A bare bulb hanging from the ceiling flashed on, bright in the dark, windowless interior. A mouse ran behind the covered barrel that held the grain and something rustled in the empty feed sacks.

He grabbed a bucket, pulled off the lid of the barrel and scooped out grain. Three scoops for the two horses in the corral. She had fed the horses in the field that morning. So the two in the corral needed grain and hay. He couldn't forget water. In the late-June heat, that was easy to remember.

He walked outside, back into bright sunlight. The horses trotted over and he poured the feed in the trough, half on one end, half on the other. Not that it mattered, because the two animals went back and forth, ears back, the dominant horse, a big bay, eating at one pile and then chasing the black-and-white paint away from the other pile.

The dog barked, like he knew and wanted to do something about it. "Buddy, you're going to have to let them work it out."

The dog wagged his tail. "Yeah, Buddy. That's your name."

The dog wasn't his.

The dog looked up at him, sitting back and wagging his tail. "Yeah, you did good. Come on, let's drag the hose out here and fill up the water."

A car rolled up the drive, drawing the dog's attention

away from farm work. The animal sat at the gate and barked. Adam turned on the hose and stuck it in the tank and then he walked out the gate to greet Pastor Todd.

"Jenna's in the house," Adam explained as he met the other man at the front of the barn.

"I know, but I'm here to see you. Jess called me."

"Great. What now?"

"He finally came clean."

Adam lifted his hat, ran a hand through his hair and settled the hat back in place, pushing it down a little tighter.

"He has demands? What is up with this guy?"

"He wants to sell you the twenty-acre field that sits between your place and his."

"I don't want his twenty acres." Adam turned and walked back to the barn. "You can come with me. I have another water tank to fill."

"I know you don't want the land, but I told him I'd talk to you. He gave me a fairly good price."

"I don't want his land." Adam turned, shaking his head. He grabbed the hose and walked the short distance to the tank that watered the horses in the field. "I'm not going to have this old guy extort money from me. If I buy this land then he'll have another problem, something else he wants from me."

"I don't think so. I think he's looking for a way out of town. This was his wife's hometown and he wants to go back to Nebraska."

"Let him go." Adam reached to scratch the jaw of the gray gelding that came up to the fence to drink. The horse pushed against his hand and then moved away, sticking his nose into the fresh water and swishing it before taking a long drink.

"Adam, he's going to a meeting tomorrow, taking his lawyer. They're going to try and find a loophole that takes away your right to have this camp."

Adam rubbed his brow and thought about it, about the camp, about the church and the kids. It was all on him.

The one guy who didn't even want to be here had to make the tough decisions for this camp that he'd never planned to have anything to do with. A short month ago he'd been living his life in Atlanta, clubbing on weekends, dating a model who had only one name, and never knowing who he could trust.

That part of the equation had been left out of the biography of his life. When magazines wrote about him, it was about the nightlife, the women, the money and the rumors.

It was never about loneliness.

"Give me time." Adam sighed, because maybe they didn't have time. They had another group of kids coming in two weeks. The camp had, not him. "I have lawyers working on this."

"I'm sorry, I don't want to push you into something you don't want to do. I wanted to present the facts, and then the decision is up to you."

"I'll take that into consideration." He smiled at Todd. "I'll even pray. But let me see what my lawyer comes up with. You know, this is something Billy should have taken care of, this zoning problem. And there's a chance he did take care of it."

"Or he saw something he could do and he went forward, not realizing how much trouble it could cause."

"Yeah, he had a habit of doing that." Good-hearted or not.

"Well, I'm going to head out. They're having a song service at the camp and then roasting marshmallows."

"Sounds like a good time." Adam liked the idea of roasting marshmallows. He hadn't done that in years. "I'll be over to join them after I check on Jenna and the boys."

"I think the kids at the camp would love it if you joined them."

Adam nodded and watched as a guy that felt a lot like a friend walked away. When he walked back to the corral, the water was running over. Adam pulled the hose out and walked back to the barn to turn off the spigot. When he walked out of the barn, the boys were waiting for him.

"We had pizza for supper," Timmy said. "It's the frozen kind, but it's good. We have leftovers if you want some."

"That's great, guys." Adam walked toward the house, the boys at his side.

"Mom said you can have ice cream, too."

"Did she?" He grinned down at them. They were running around him, full of energy, the dog chasing, barking. He couldn't help but think about the quiet days, when he'd only had himself and his team to think about.

"Yep, she did. She said, 'If he wants to eat, he can, Timmy, but you can't make him.' And I said we could, probably."

Adam laughed at the little mimic and reached down to rub the kid's blond head. "Timmy, you crack me up."

"Yeah, my mom said that, too."

"I thought you might like the kind of pizza with everything." David grinned up at him. "That's the kind that grown-ups who eat onions like."

"Yep, I must be a grown-up."

"Do you know that my mom's leg has a sore on it?"

David looked down, kicking at a rock and then walking on. "She might need a doctor if that keeps up."

David, repeating Jenna, the way Timmy usually did. "I'll check on her, okay?"

"That would be good, because she doesn't want Uncle Clint to worry." David ran on ahead of him, into the house. Timmy looked up, like the little man of the house, taking things more seriously than people thought, Adam guessed.

"We think she needs to rest."

"I think she probably does, too," Adam agreed. He reached and Timmy took his hand. And possibly his heart, if that's what it felt like to lose a guy's heart to a kid, to a family. Like a squeeze, netting his emotions, making him rethink everything.

It took him a minute to shake himself loose from that feeling, to remind himself that he wasn't what Jenna or these kids needed. But for that minute he wanted to be the one who took care of them.

Jenna and the boys needed someone who didn't have doubts, a guy that knew how to keep his life together, a man who knew how to be from Oklahoma.

Not him.

Chapter Fourteen

Jenna opened the front door, offering a smile to a guy that looked pretty cornered. The boys had done that to him, the way she knew they would. Because they thought he was it. And she didn't know how to explain that he was a friend who would only be a friend for a season. Life brought people who stayed forever and people who stayed for a short time.

She knew that. Her boys had other plans. They wanted him to coach their little league, teach them to play football and go with them to the lake because they thought he lived at the camp. Jenna wanted to cry because she hurt all the way to her heart.

"I heard that you have pizza." He walked up the steps.

She nodded and motioned him inside. "I do."

"The boys invited me."

"I told them they could." She started toward the kitchen, knowing he'd follow. "I had a salad. You go ahead and help yourself. I need to take care of something while you guys eat."

He looked down, blue eyes studying her face, and then he nodded. "Let me know if you need anything."

"I'm good."

But she wasn't. She walked into her room and sat down on the edge of her bed, wanting to cry. She buried her face in her hands, fighting back the tears, fighting to be strong.

For a long time she didn't move, just enjoyed not having to stand up. Finally she did what she needed to do—took off the prosthesis and then the socks that kept it in place.

Outside her room she could hear David and Timmy telling Adam why they liked the cartoon on TV, and he agreed, laughing when they said he was as strong as that hero, and probably faster. She used to be their hero, the person who was able to climb trees to save kittens, show them how to jump rope and run around bases.

Now she felt weak, and not at all like the woman who should have Adam Mackenzie sitting in her living room. She smiled a little at that, because she knew that her life would be a story for the media that liked to report on his life. And her life wasn't a story at all. She was a mom making the best of the hand that she'd been dealt. And she was more than a survivor. Surviving sounded more like someone getting by, hanging on, and she planned on doing more than that.

She wasn't going to sit in a dark bedroom, hiding in shame. She had nothing to be ashamed of.

She grabbed the crutches and stood. When she walked into the living room, the three guys turned and smiled at her, but then went back to their cartoon. As if this was a normal night and she hadn't just tripped over the rug. She loved them for that. Loved her boys.

Her gaze shifted from the two tiny faces of her twins to the other face, now familiar to her. He was a friend. Nothing more.

"Did you have ice cream?"

Adam nodded, but kept watching the cartoon.

"Okay, I'm going to have some. You guys have fun."

"I am." He hugged the boys close and stood to follow her. She knew without looking because the boys groaned and then told Adam she really didn't need his help. He told them he knew that, but he thought he'd keep her company.

She was scooping out butter pecan when he walked through the door. "I really don't need help, you know."

"I know. But you do look exhausted."

"Thank you, that's what every woman wants to hear." She set the timer for thirty seconds before turning to face him, leaning a little against the counter. "Truth is I am exhausted. Walking with a prosthesis takes more energy per step than walking with two good legs. Some days it wears me out. But I am better. In the beginning I could make it for a few hours and had to give up. Now I can get through a good day, sometimes a long day. I'm not up to long trips to the mall or five-mile hikes, but I'll get there."

"I think you will, too. I think you'll climb mountains."

He watched as she poured tea into a thermal cup and snapped the lid into place. She could eat standing up, and then carry the mug without spilling it. Adam reached for the bowl of ice cream.

"I can carry this for you."

"Thank you." Heat started up her neck into her cheeks. "I'm going to sit at the table."

He set the bowl down.

"Todd says that Jess wants to sell me some land."

Jenna nodded and sat down. He sat across from her. "That sounds about right. I think he had a lot of medical bills when he lost his wife."

"So the camp is bad, a blight on the community, unless I give him money."

She smiled. "Adam, he's hurting."

"You think I should give him the money?"

"I can't tell you how to handle this."

"I don't know. I'll see what my lawyer comes back with."

"It'll work out." She looked up. "When are you leaving?"

That night her boys had prayed for him when they blessed the food, asking God to keep him at the camp. Afterward she'd explained that Adam had to do what he was supposed to do and they had to accept the fact that he was leaving.

"Soon, I guess. I promised my family I would come over for lunch this Sunday. I'm still waiting for Will to finalize the date for my interview." He twiddled his thumbs and didn't look at her. "The church that's here now, they want to bring older teens in two weeks, if we can pull it off. Todd thinks it can be done."

"I think it can. And about that job, they're going to want you to work for them. I know you'll get it."

"I don't know. They had a problem a year or so back with one of their guys having some personal issues. They're a little more cautious these days."

"And their issue with you is what?" She should have stopped herself from asking that question, but curiosity got to her.

"My partying ways. My so-called rough edges. I have a lot of them, you know? I've been fined for fighting with refs—back in the old days, of course. I've fought with reporters." He smiled but it didn't quite reach his eyes. "A few years ago I had some problems with a woman. She tried to claim we were married. We weren't. She claimed that one of her boys was mine. He wasn't. She put him through—" He looked up. "She put him through a lot. He was eight. I had only known her for three months."

"What did she want from you?"

"Money and a dad for her kid."

Jenna stood up, not sure what to say or if she should defend herself. She didn't need a father for her boys. She wasn't looking for someone to fill that role in her life. Definitely not an unwilling someone. More important, she didn't want her boys to think of him like that, because she didn't want them to be hurt.

All of those thoughts rolled through her mind, but she didn't say any of it. She walked out and into the living room, where the boys were dozing off on the sofa. They'd had a long day. The room was dark and the air conditioner was working hard to keep the heat out of the room.

To keep from waking them, she walked outside. Adam followed her, closing the door behind them. He stood behind her at the edge of the porch.

"I don't think that you're like Morgan." He spoke softly. "I know that you aren't. You're strong and independent. Maybe a little too independent. Your boys have you. They have Clint and Willow. They have this community."

She nodded. Yes, the boys had all of those people. And so did she. So why did she feel so lonely with Adam standing behind her, not touching her? Why in the world did her heart feel as if it was yearning for something she had marked out of her life, out of her future, left off her list? She didn't need more rejection, more goodbyes. Or worse, someone walking away without looking back.

And her heart ached because she wanted him to touch

her, to reach out and hold her, even as her smart self was telling her to say goodbye and walk away before he did.

Her smart self was so not in control of this situation.

She turned, and when she did, he wrapped an arm around her and took the crutches. He leaned them against the wall of the house. "You don't need those. I'm here."

His words were soft, whispered against her cheek. His arms were around her, holding her close, and she held on to his upper arms, solid muscle, strong. Strong enough for both of them.

When his lips touched hers, she heard him sigh, felt his chest heave, and she reciprocated, because there was something so sweet, so gentle in his touch, in that moment when their lips met. Her heart felt like it had finally grabbed hold of what it had been seeking.

She held on to him, leaning into his strength, and his lips grazed her cheek, rubbing lightly. His hands remained on her back, holding her tight.

"You're beautiful." His whispered words brought her back to reality.

"Stop." She moved away, but his lips followed, claiming hers again.

"You're beautiful." He whispered it again, near her ear, his cheek brushing hers.

She hopped to her crutches and leaned against the side of the house. "You can say that because this is easy for you. You're going back to Atlanta. I'm staying here in Oklahoma. This will be a memory for you. But this is my reality. This is my life."

"Jenna, I'm sorry. I thought we both…"

"Wanted to be kissed, to be held. Yes, we did. But don't complicate this. Don't make it about us. I'm a mom, Adam. This is about more than me and you, and a sweet moment on a summer night. It's about two little boys. It's about what happens tomorrow."

"I know." He closed the distance between them and his arms slipped around her waist, holding her close. "I know, and I think I've just taken advantage of what felt like a great friendship."

"I think we've both messed up." She didn't move from his embrace, because it felt good in his arms. But she was coming to her senses, remembering why romance wasn't a part of her five-year plan. "I had my convictions, to keep you at the edge of my life so we wouldn't get hurt. The boys love you so much. And they've been walked out on too many times."

He brushed his cheek against hers and paused there. "*You've* been walked out on. Let's be honest, honey, this is about you, *your* heart, not just the boys. You need to know you really are beautiful."

She wiped away tears that rolled down her cheeks, turning away when he tried to help. "This is too much. You're too much."

"Yeah, maybe it is." He kissed her cheek. "See you tomorrow?"

Jenna shook her head. "I've made an appointment to get my prosthesis checked, or refitted. I might be out of the loop for a day or two."

"Okay. Why don't you let me stop by and feed in the morning?"

"I can do it. But thank you." She had Clint and Willow. It wouldn't be good to start relying on him, on someone who was leaving town as soon as possible.

"Jenna, you're stubborn."

"I know I am." She smiled then, and he winked as he

turned and walked away, another guy who wasn't looking for reality, just a summer in Oklahoma.

Adam was sitting on his front porch the next morning, a clear view of the road, when Jenna's truck lumbered past. She was on her way to Tulsa. And he was here, with a camp full of kids. Fortunately there were people who knew what to do with those kids. He barely knew what to do with himself.

He sipped his coffee, glad for a few minutes of peace, and groaning when his cell phone rang. He picked it up, glancing at the caller ID before answering. "Hey, Will."

"Adam, I have an appointment for you. And bad news on the camp situation. I can't find anywhere at all that Billy went to Planning and Zoning. I looked at the county regulations with your lawyer, and he really feels like you did need to have a permit, some special zoning. I can get a lawyer there and have that taken care of."

"Yeah, okay, get it taken care of, and then draw up the paperwork to give this place and any funds raised on its behalf to the Dawson Community Church. Also, contact that little lawyer person that represents Jess Lockhart. Buy his twenty acres and put it in the name of Dawson Community Church."

"Got it. Here's the date of the appointment."

Adam wrote it down as Todd came up the steps. "Talk to you later, Will. And I guess I'll see you soon."

"Job interview?" Todd sat down and reached for the thermal coffeepot. "Do you have another cup?"

"Yeah, inside on the wall hook. Bring out the muffins from the bakery."

"Anything else?" Todd laughed as he walked through the door.

Adam couldn't laugh. He could only think about last night, and about packing his bags. He glanced out over the wide, open field that was his front yard, a place where he'd watched deer grazing as he drank his morning coffee two days ago.

He'd gotten used to the mobile home, to this deck, to Dawson. And now he was leaving.

"What's up?" Todd poured himself a cup of coffee and sat down. "Bad news?"

"No, good news. I have a job interview. And I'm having papers drawn up to sign this place over to you. As well as the twenty acres. I'll hire a lawyer to get the proper zoning taken care of, and we'll pay whatever fines they toss at us."

"Adam…"

"Todd, I think we're friends. This is what I want to do."

"I know, but it feels like you're cutting it loose. And I think that would have worked a week or two ago, when the camp didn't mean anything to you. But do you really want to walk away from it now?"

"I'm not walking away. I'm turning it over to someone more fit to take care of it. I'm not a camp director. I'm a football player, maybe a sports reporter or an anchorman for a network. This is your dream, and I know you're the best guy for it."

He tried to push Jenna and the boys from his mind, but it wasn't easy, especially when he saw that turtle of theirs scooting along in the weeds a short distance away.

"What about Jenna?"

Todd sipped his coffee and looked out over the camp, in the direction of the cafeteria where kids were starting to line up for breakfast.

"Jenna is great. She's been a big help."

"That's it?"

"She's a friend." Adam didn't know what else to say. He'd known her just a few weeks and she'd taught him to trust someone, and maybe to trust himself.

"Okay, she's a good person to call a friend."

"I think so."

Adam emptied the cup of coffee. "I'm going to spend the morning mowing. The grass is getting a little long."

Todd laughed. "No, it isn't, but you had that new mower delivered yesterday and like any guy, you're dying to get on it."

Adam nodded. But the truth was, he was dying to be alone and think about the fact that he was going to be leaving. And Jenna wasn't home to share that news with her. He'd watched her truck leave earlier, barely after sunrise.

And he'd be gone by sunset.

Jenna answered her phone on Wednesday afternoon, the day after her doctor's appointment, expecting it to be Clint. He'd been out of town and Willow had helped with chores.

The doctor's appointment hadn't gone the way Jenna wanted. She'd been given strict orders to rest for a few days while her prosthesis was adjusted. And she had explained that she didn't have time to rest. The doctor had asked if she had time to be hospitalized. That had seemed like the worst option, so she'd taken option B: rest.

"Hello." She stretched on the couch and reached to turn down the TV. She couldn't turn down the volume of the two boys playing upstairs. "Hey, guys, calm down."

"Jenna?"

"Adam." Missing in action. She hadn't heard from him all day yesterday.

"I'm in Atlanta."

"Oh." Her heart thudded hard against her chest. Atlanta.

"I—" he cleared his throat "—got a call that they wanted to interview me. I left yesterday. I didn't want to leave that message on your answering machine."

"Oh, okay. When are you coming back?" But her heart already knew the answer.

"I got the job, Jenna. I'm signing the camp over to the church and buying the land from Jess."

"That's good. I'll let the boys know that you had to leave." Her heart was pounding and wounded. She was so angry, so hurt. It shouldn't feel that way to say goodbye to him.

"Tell them I'm sorry I didn't get to say goodbye." He paused. "Jenna, I am sorry."

"I know, and I'll tell them." *Stoic,* she knew the word, knew how to be that person. "Adam, we knew this day would come. The boys knew you weren't staying here. But they will miss you."

"I'll miss them, too." He sighed, and she remembered too much about being in his arms. "Jenna, are you okay?"

"Of course I am."

"The doctor's appointment."

"Oh, that. Yes, well, I'm off my feet until tomorrow. Oh, someone is here. I'm glad you called."

She watched Clint's truck pull up her drive as she hung up the phone, pretending it was her idea to let Adam Mackenzie go. It felt better that way.

Clint knocked on the door. She waved them in and held her arms out for the baby. Willow handed her over and Jenna cuddled the infant close, enjoying the feel of her, and the way she smelled, like soap and lotion.

"You've been crying." Clint leaned to hug her.

"I haven't."

Willow nodded and pointed to her own eyes. "Mascara, puffy lids. I don't think it's a virus."

Jenna bit down on her bottom lip and swallowed the sob that welled up from inside.

"He's gone." Jenna sighed and said the words. "Did you know that he was gone?"

Willow nodded. "I'm sorry. We found out yesterday evening when we went to the camp chapel service."

"Jenna, you knew he'd have to go." Clint, pragmatic, brows scrunched together. "Why in the world does that bother you so much? He didn't walk out on the camp, and that's what you were worried about."

Willow punched his arm and he yelped. "You idiot, she's in love."

"I'm not in love. I'm mad because he didn't say goodbye to the boys."

"Who didn't say goodbye to us?" Timmy was standing in the door of the kitchen. "Who's gone?"

"Honey, Adam had to leave. He had a job interview and we weren't here." Jenna said it like it was expected, like it shouldn't hurt.

Timmy was shadowed by David, and both boys stared, eyes wide and welling up with tears. "He was gonna play football with us."

"Hey, guys, you still have me. I know how to play football."

The boys stared at Clint like he'd lost it. "You're not pro."

He laughed but Jenna thought he looked a little hurt. "No, I'm not pro, but I can throw a football as good as

Adam Mackenzie. Why don't you guys help me with chores, okay?"

The one thing Jenna knew about Clint. He would always be there for them.

She watched as her brother took the boys out the back door, listening as they talked about their pony and the dog being called Buddy now. But Adam was gone, and he was the one that told them the dog liked that name.

Willow sat down in the chair next to the couch and she didn't say anything. Maybe because Willow knew what it was like to have that moment when a guy broke her heart. And Willow knew that a heart couldn't be glued back together with nice words.

Jenna rubbed her hands over her face and told herself she really wasn't going to cry. But tears burned her eyes and she felt the pain like a lump rising from her heart to her throat, tightening in her chest.

"I don't care about him." She took the tissue that Willow handed her. "Oh, this is ridiculous. He was a nuisance. He was never planning on staying and I knew that. And what did I do?"

"You fell in love?"

Jenna nodded. "I fell in love. And I knew that I was falling in love."

"Love. Who would have thought." Willow smiled.

"But three weeks doesn't a relationship make." Jenna uncovered her face so Willow could hear her, because Willow had reminded her by touching her arm. She needed to read lips.

"Three weeks isn't long enough to call this love," she repeated.

Willow laughed. "Right, tell that to your heart."

"My heart is obviously defective. It always picks

the guys that aren't going to stay around." She gasped. "That's it. I am defective. I purposely form relationships with men who aren't dependable. That means I'm not really looking for a relationship. I'm sabotaging myself, which means…"

Willow shook her head. "Give it up. You love him. He was dependable. He was kind to you and the boys. He was gentle. Of course you fell in love with him."

"Three weeks. He'll be easy to get over." Jenna looked at her sister-in-law and sighed words she knew. "I need chocolate."

"Right. But I don't think they make enough chocolate to fix this."

And her boys. They would miss him. And she wasn't going to do this again. Next time she really would know better than to let her heart get involved.

Adam started his new job on Monday. He sat behind his new desk, in his new office, and he took phone calls. He made phone calls. He answered questions. He planned travel for the games he'd be announcing.

And he hated it.

A fist rapped on the door, short knocks, and it opened. A familiar face, blond-headed and a cheery smile. Adam leaned back and groaned. He didn't need cheering up. He didn't need optimism.

"How does it feel?" Will closed the door behind him. He stood in the center of the room, surveying the office with the dream view of Atlanta.

"It feels…" Adam leaned back in the chair and shrugged. "It feels like torture. It feels like a cage."

"Buddy, don't do this to me. This is your dream, right? This is still what you want, isn't it? Because we're still negotiating a few details on your contract and if you're going to flake out, I need to know."

"I'm not flaking."

Will sat down in the seat on the opposite side of the desk. He lifted his left leg, situating it over his right and leaning back, his arms folded behind his head. "Tell me who she is. Do we need to pay her off?"

Adam sat up, no longer amused. "That isn't funny."

Will put his foot down and leaned forward. "I know. But sometimes it's the only way to get your attention. It's the girl from the camp."

"Woman."

"Fine, woman with two kids." Will shook his head. "As much as I wanted this for you, I really wanted it to happen here, in Atlanta. Settle down, I told you. Find some nice woman."

"I'm not thinking about settling down. We were talking about this job."

"*Torture.* I think that was the word you used."

Adam turned his chair to look out the window. He'd been doing that all morning, and comparing it to his view from the front deck of the mobile home in Dawson. He'd been thinking about Jenna driving up the road in her old truck, the two boys buckled in behind her.

Jenna Cameron was five feet of temptation that he couldn't get off his mind, because she'd taken his leaving and acted as if it didn't matter. Maybe it didn't matter.

His life was going in the direction he had planned. "This is what I want, Will. I planned this. It's one of the few things in my life that I planned for myself. I own this decision."

"Alrighty then." Will smiled big. "And you're not defensive. You've made other decisions for yourself. The camp. You made a decision to keep it going."

"Yeah, well, God might have had something to do with that."

Jenna was a distraction. He knew when he met her that she wasn't a summer romance. She was the type of woman a man married, the type he took home to meet his family. And he wasn't the type of man who married a woman like that.

She wasn't a Friday night and unreturned phone calls when things got too confining.

But man, she'd made him a better person.

"She made me feel like the kind of guy who could love a woman like her forever."

"Whoa!" Will coughed. "That's not what I thought I'd hear. I was just razzing you."

"Yeah, well, I've had nearly a week to think about the fact that I miss her more than I've ever missed anyone. I miss her boys."

"Kids. You miss kids? If you tell me you remember my daughter's name, I'm going to know that something happened to you in Oklahoma."

"Kaitlin."

Will stood up. "I'll hold off on the contract until you decide if you are positive about this job."

Positive about the job. Adam looked out the window. And he had to be positive about what he was feeling for Jenna and her kids. He couldn't go back if he didn't know for sure.

Chapter Fifteen

Jenna watched the boys play in the water hose. It was the second week of July and hotter than ever. Hotter than a flitter—whatever a flitter was. But Adam wasn't there to laugh at the joke, so it wasn't as funny.

She hadn't heard from him since he left.

The toughest part of that was that she hadn't expected to miss him so much. Two weeks of missing him shouldn't feel like two weeks separated from oxygen. The boys were laughing, spraying each other, and it wasn't about them, because they believed Adam would come back to see them.

Or maybe they were waiting for God to answer their prayers, the ones they prayed each night when they thought she wasn't listening. That Adam would be their dad. The first time she'd heard them, she'd tried to explain that for them to have a dad, she would need a husband. And she didn't want a husband. So then they'd started praying that she'd want a husband.

As much as it hurt, she smiled, because they were so sweet and she loved them so much.

"Guys, I have to feed the horses. Stay here, okay?" She

walked past them and they laughed, spraying at her, but not getting close enough to hit her with the spray of water.

A car pulled up the drive. Jenna held her breath the way she always did when she heard a car, thinking it might be Adam. And it never was, and she couldn't believe she missed him this way.

It was Pastor Todd. He stopped and got out. She waited for him. He made a wide path around the boys and met her at the front of the red-painted barn. His wife had gotten out of the passenger side. She wasn't afraid of the boys and the water hose.

"What brings you out here?" She walked into the barn, enjoying that it smelled like horses, hay and grain. She had always loved this barn. Even as a child this had been her hiding place.

"I came out to tell you that we're going to do a ladies' retreat at the camp, maybe in September."

He didn't drive all the way out to her house to tell her that. She turned, giving him a look, and he blushed a little. "Really?"

"I came out to check on you." He looked into the stalls as they walked through the barn. "And to tell you that Adam called. He asked about you."

"Did he?" She pretended not to care, shrugging it off as she opened the door to the feed room. "And you told him that we're fine, right?"

She filled the bucket and walked out into the sunshine. The three horses in the corral nosed in, doing their typical chasing dance until they each settled on one of the tubs of feed.

"I told him we all miss him." He smiled as he answered.

"I guess we probably do." She stood next to Pastor

Todd, watching the tank as the water level rose. The horses came up, sucking up the cool water and then playing in it, splashing with their faces in the water.

"Would you mind playing this Sunday at church?" Todd reached out and rubbed the face of the bay mare she'd bought the previous week. The horse left the water and walked up to the fence, wanting more attention.

That personality was why Jenna had bought her. She had seen the mare on the Internet and liked her eyes. It was always in the eyes—kindness or shiftiness. Even in people. She closed her eyes, remembering Adam's face, his eyes.

He had good eyes, full of light and laughter. That's what she'd seen in his interviews, that hidden part of him—maybe hidden from himself, not just from the cameras.

"Is there anything else I can do around here before I leave?" Todd pulled the water hose back and dragged it to the barn to turn it off.

"No, I'm good. Do you know the songs for Sunday?"

"Kate can give you a list. Jenna, do you love Adam Mackenzie?"

She turned, not sure how to answer, surprised that he'd ask the question. "I didn't know him long enough to love him."

"Oh, I don't know. Maybe love at first sight is really attraction or chemistry at first sight. But love, that grows from knowing someone, from the way they make us feel about ourselves—how we feel when we're with them."

Love. She blinked a few times, because her heart breaking wasn't about attraction. It was about losing someone who had changed how she felt about herself.

He had called her beautiful and she had wanted to believe that he really thought she was.

They finished feeding, turned out the lights in the barn and walked back into the bright sunlight, where the boys were playing with their trucks in the mud they'd created with the hose and Pastor Todd's wife was talking to them, complimenting their trails and hills.

"Mom, can we go see our turtle?" David pushed his truck over a pile of rocks.

"Turtle?" She stayed a safe distance from the mud puddle.

"The one at Adam's trailer. Could we go tonight and make sure he has food?"

"Not tonight, David. And he does have food. He's a turtle, and God gave them instincts so that they would know how to feed themselves."

"God gave them insects?" Timmy's nose scrunched.

"Instincts, Timmy. They know, without being told, how to eat, how to keep safe, where to go in storms."

"Sounds like a Bible lesson, doesn't it?" Pastor Todd patted her shoulder. "Turtles know when to duck into their shell, they know where to go for shelter."

Jenna groaned. "I bet we'll hear that on Sunday morning."

"You'd better believe it." He bent down and picked up a toy truck. The boys smiled up at him when he rolled it through the dirt and then parked it back on the pile of rocks. "You guys take care of your mom."

They looked up, nodding at him. They always took care of her. Even their prayers were about taking care of her. And hers were all about taking care of them.

And that's the way it should be, a mom taking care of her boys. No one was going to hurt them again. It seemed as if she'd learned that lesson more than once, but her heart kept taking chances, trying again.

She smiled at the boys. Pastor Todd was getting into the car with his wife. The dog was nipping at their tires. Timmy and David were looking up at her, as if they were waiting for an answer to a question she didn't know.

That meant they weren't giving up on the camp idea. They wanted to see the turtle. She knew what they were thinking. They probably thought Adam would be there. He wasn't. Adam was somewhere in Atlanta. He had called to check on them. But that wasn't enough. That would never feel like enough.

"Guys, we'll go see the turtle tomorrow. Tonight we're going to take it easy. We're going to have a big dinner with food from the garden and watch a movie together."

The boys didn't look as if they thought that was the best plan. She hugged them close and walked toward the house, one on each side of her. But her gaze drifted, across the road, and down. No lights shined from Camp Hope, because he was gone. He had found his dream in Atlanta.

And she was still dreaming in Oklahoma, no longer dreams of the darkness and pain, but dreams of what it had felt like in his arms. These dreams were just as painful as the nightmares they'd replaced.

Adam had driven all night, but he wasn't tired. He was wide awake, watching the sun come up over the Oklahoma horizon, turning the fields pink and gold. The horses were grazing in the field and as he poured a cup of coffee, a deer ran through the yard, right outside his kitchen window. Adam stretched and pulled his shirt down.

It was good to be home. He smiled at that thought, at

how this place had become his home. This was his place. He picked up his coffee and walked outside, wondering how long it would take Jenna to find out that he was back, and what she'd say.

Maybe she'd tell him to take a hike. Or maybe she would say they could still be friends. He had a list of things he wanted to tell her about his job, about dreams and about Atlanta.

In the quiet of the morning he heard the distant roar of a truck engine coming to life. He sat down at the patio table and watched the field, the road, looking for the deer.

And then her truck came up the road, totally unexpected in the gray of early morning. He didn't stand, just waited, wondering what she was up to. She couldn't know he was here, not yet. Her truck idled up his driveway and came to a stop a short distance from the deck. She didn't get out. She sat in the truck, staring through the windshield, her eyes wide, surprised. Or maybe he imagined that look, like maybe she was glad to see him.

He stood and walked to the edge of the porch. The back door on the truck opened and the boys tumbled out, messy hair and still in their pajamas, with flip-flops on their feet. Jenna was slower getting out. She walked around the front of the truck and paused, but not the boys. They rushed him, running up the steps and tackling his legs.

"We knew you'd come back." Timmy hugged tightest. "But Mom said God didn't answer prayers that were wishes. But it was really a prayer, not a wish."

"Okay, guys, let him breathe. He's here to check on the camp and we surprised him." She looked up, a cowgirl in denim shorts, a T-shirt and canvas sneakers, her hair in a loose bun. "We came to check on the turtle. They didn't believe me that it could take care of itself. And that we probably can't find it."

She looked down, and then away from him. Her cheeks were pink and he knew that she was embarrassed.

"I haven't seen the turtle." He continued to watch her, wondering if she knew how beautiful she was, and if he told her, would she believe him.

He'd never really believed in the whole heart-in-the-throat condition, but at that moment, he knew that it existed. It was a lump that worked its way up, cutting off his air, making him want to say things that he'd never thought he'd say to anyone.

"How long are you here for?" She walked with the boys to the longer grass and he followed.

"I don't know." And he didn't. He had taken a leave of absence from a job he'd barely had a chance to start. Not a good way to start a career. "I have to be in Miami next week. But my dad's having some medical tests done and I wanted to be here."

"That's good—that you can be here." She looked away, her face in shadows. She walked a few steps, looking for the turtle. He followed her.

The boys ran ahead of them, positive the turtle wouldn't have gone far, because this was his home. As they searched, their dog came running up the road. He joined in the search, sniffing in the weeds, circling trees. The boys urged him on, like he was the greatest tracking dog in the world.

"Jenna, I'm sorry for what happened. I think we started out trying to be careful for the sake of the boys. Neither of us wanted them to be hurt, to think that there might be something…"

"Don't." She stopped and turned, her face set, not

moving, not smiling. "We're grown-ups. I knew better. I knew not to let myself get involved in something that would only last a month or two. We're both too old for summer romances. Stop blaming yourself. I'm a grown woman and I made a choice. I let you into my life. I walked into yours."

"Yes, you walked into mine." He walked next to her. "And I crashed into yours."

Her mouth twitched and he knew she was fighting a smile.

"Adam, I should take the boys and go. They've been praying for you to come home. This will just confuse them."

"Confuse them?"

"They saw us kiss, and they think that means a man and woman are supposed to get married."

"Sometimes it does."

Jenna didn't know what to say. She waited, not sure of what he meant. He smiled, that soft, tender smile with a little bit of naughtiness that made him so charming.

"Yes, sometimes it does." She continued walking, away from him, from the power of his presence.

"Sometimes a kiss means I love you. Sometimes we just don't know it, not right away." He kept talking. She wanted him to stop. She wanted to tell him he couldn't walk in and out of their lives this way, with his charming wit, his cute smile, his way of making her feel like she belonged to someone.

"We have to find the turtle." She stepped through some weeds, stumbling a little when the wrong foot hit a rock. A strong hand caught her arm and held her tight.

"Careful."

"I know." She didn't mind that he didn't move his hand. They walked together in silence, not really looking for the turtle. The boys were scouring the area, talking about breakfast and bugs, and how long Adam would be in town.

"So, how long?" she asked.

"Maybe awhile."

She looked up. He paused, pulling her to a stop next to them. He pointed and she saw the turtle. Maybe their turtle, it was hard to tell.

"Guys, here it is." Adam pointed.

The twins hurried toward them, all smiles—over a turtle. She wondered if she had worn the same silly smile when she'd seen Adam on his front porch.

Timmy picked up the turtle and turned it over. "We have to see if he's ours."

Black marker on the bottom of the shell proved it was. Timmy held it up for her to look at. He'd be six in a week and reading wasn't his strongest skill, not yet. "It has more names."

"I found him before I left." Adam turned a little red, and Jenna liked that. She'd never seen him embarrassed before.

She took the turtle from Timmy. "Adam wrote his name on there with yours."

David stood on tiptoes and peeked at the shell. He smiled up at Adam. "Mom's name is on there, too."

"Yeah, I thought all of our names should be on there, because he's kind of like all of ours." Adam rested his hand on David's shoulder. "I really missed you guys."

"We missed you, but we knew you'd be back." David took the turtle. "We're going to find him some bugs to eat."

They were off and running toward the trailer. Jenna turned in that direction, taking it easy over the rough ground. Adam walked next to her, matching his pace to hers.

"Jenna, I'm not leaving." He kept walking, but she couldn't, not with an announcement like that.

"What about your job? I thought it was your dream?"

"It's still my job, but I'm going to work from here, and I only signed for six months. It'll mean traveling quite a bit." He took her hand and they kept walking. "Somewhere along the way I realized something about myself. I kept thinking about what my dreams were, and it hit me that this camp is my dream. Funny that something that started out as a thorn in my side has become the thing I dream of doing."

"You're going to run the camp?"

"And be a fireman."

She laughed and, for the first time in weeks, she felt like laughing was okay, like life was okay. "I'm glad. We need more firemen."

"I'm also going to do some dating." His fingers laced through hers. "I realized something else while I was gone—how much I missed you and the boys. I've never missed anyone before, not like this."

They walked out of the woods into the clearing next to the trailer. The boys were sitting in the grass, talking and feeding the turtle. Jenna looked up and Adam was smiling at them, the way a man smiled at people he loved.

And then he looked at her, and that look was still in his eyes, for her. He touched her cheek and then brushed his fingers through her hair, smoothing it back and then pulling it free from the bun that had kept it off her neck.

Her heart froze and then caught up with an extra few

beats. He leaned and his lips touched hers, tender, strong, capturing hers in the moment, a moment she wanted to hold on to—forever.

When he moved away, she could still feel the imprint of that kiss, and his hand on her back. She kept her hands on his arms, afraid her legs weren't steady, afraid she'd already fallen further than she'd ever fallen before.

"Jenna, you're my dream, you and the boys. You're the best thing that has happened to me. You changed everything. I thought I could go back to Atlanta, carry on with my life and be fine, but I couldn't. I missed you every single day."

"I missed you, too," she whispered, because the words felt trapped somewhere near her heart. "I wanted God to hear their prayers to bring you back, because they were my prayers, too."

"He brought me back. I couldn't settle in Atlanta, not with the three of you here." He leaned, kissing her again. "I want all of our dreams to come true."

"Okay."

"So if I stay this year, we can go steady." He smiled and kissed her cheek, holding her close, his cheek brushing hers.

"And get married." She leaned into him, finally free to fall in love, because he thought she was beautiful the way she was.

And he loved her boys.

He was holding her, smiling. "Jenna, did you just propose?"

She blinked a few times, and laughed. "Yes, I guess I did. I think maybe I'm not supposed to do that."

"Then why don't you let me." He turned to find the boys. "Timmy, David, come here."

The boys scurried over, still holding their turtle. "We fed him a little bug."

"That's great. But could you guys do me a favor?"

Both boys nodded their heads and Jenna wondered what he would do. He placed the boys in front of her, and then he went down on one knee.

"You know I've had knee surgery, right?" He winked at Timmy and David. "I might not be able to get up, but that's okay. I think I'm supposed to do this from down here.

"Jenna, Timmy and David, I'd really love it if the three of you would marry me."

And the boys flew at him, knocking him back and then they were in his arms and Jenna waited, because she knew he would be holding her forever.

* * * * *

Dear Reader,

I hope you loved *Jenna's Cowboy Hero*. If you read *A Cowboy's Heart*, you'll remember Jenna as the sister of bull rider Clint Cameron and the mom of those two rambunctious boys, Timmy and David. She's a strong young woman who has had to overcome some difficult situations, and along the way she found faith. The one thing she has a hard time believing is that a man can love her. She no longer feels beautiful, and it takes a special man to change all of that for her.

It takes a man as strong as she is. I think there is a special lesson in this book: don't sell God short. Don't use the word *never*. We don't know what is around the corner, and we might find that it is exactly what we thought couldn't or wouldn't happen.

Blessings,

Brenda Minton

We hope you enjoyed reading
this special collection.

If you liked reading these stories,
then you will love **Love Inspired®** books!

You believe hearts can heal. **Love Inspired**
stories show that faith, forgiveness and hope
have the power to lift spirits and change
lives—always.

Enjoy six new stories from
Love Inspired every month!

Available wherever books and
ebooks are sold.

LoveInspired

**Uplifting romances of faith,
forgiveness and hope.**

Use this coupon to save

$1.00

on the purchase of any
Love Inspired® book.

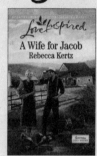

Available wherever books are sold, including
most bookstores, supermarkets, drugstores
and discount stores.

Save $1.00

on the purchase of any Love Inspired® book.

Coupon valid until July 20, 2015. Redeemable at participating retail outlets
in the U.S. and Canada only. Limit one coupon per customer.

52612262

Canadian Retailers: Harlequin Enterprises Limited will pay the face value of this coupon plus 10.25¢ if submitted by customer for this product only. Any other use constitutes fraud. Coupon is nonassignable. Void if taxed, prohibited or restricted by law. Consumer must pay any government taxes. Void if copied. Millennium1 Promotional Services ("M1P") customers submit coupons and proof of sales to Harlequin Enterprises Limited, P.O. Box 3000, Saint John, NB E2L 4L3, Canada. Non-M1P retailer—for reimbursement submit coupons and proof of sales directly to Harlequin Enterprises Limited, Retail Marketing Department, 225 Duncan Mill Rd., Don Mills, Ontario M3B 3K9, Canada.

U.S. Retailers: Harlequin Enterprises Limited will pay the face value of this coupon plus 8¢ if submitted by customer for this product only. Any other use constitutes fraud. Coupon is nonassignable. Void if taxed, prohibited or restricted by law. Consumer must pay any government taxes. Void if copied. For reimbursement submit coupons and proof of sales directly to Harlequin Enterprises Limited, P.O. Box 880478, El Paso, TX 88588-0478, U.S.A. Cash value 1/100 cents.

5 65373 00076 2   (8100)0 12011

® and TM are trademarks owned and used by the trademark owner and/or its licensee.
© 2015 Harlequin Enterprises Limited

LICOUP021 5